THE SILENT ~~D~~

It is through first contact with an alien species that humanity learns of the Dream. It is a plane of mental existence where people are able to communicate with one another by their thoughts alone— over distances of thousands of light-years. To ensure that future generations will have this ability, human genetic engineering produces newborns capable of finding and navigating the Dream.

They become known as the Silent.

NIGHTMARE

Her eyes snapped opened. "You don't care for poetry?" The man was right in front of her. She could smell his sour breath. "But I love you."

The glen changed. Grass and flowers withered and died. Night-black clouds blew across the sun. A chorus of voices wailed on the wind. Terror suffused Prinna Meg. She couldn't think, couldn't breathe, couldn't . . .

continued . . .

NIGHTMARE

A NOVEL OF THE SILENT EMPIRE

STEVEN HARPER

A ROC BOOK

ROC
Published by New American Library, a division of
Penguin Putnam Inc., 375 Hudson Street,
New York, New York 10014, U.S.A.
Penguin Books Ltd, 80 Strand,
London WC2R 0RL, England
Penguin Books Australia Ltd, Ringwood,
Victoria, Australia
Penguin Books Canada Ltd, 10 Alcorn Avenue,
Toronto, Ontario, Canada M4V 3B2
Penguin Books (N.Z.) Ltd, 182–190 Wairau Road,
Auckland 10, New Zealand

Penguin Books Ltd, Registered Offices:
Harmondsworth, Middlesex, England

First published by Roc, an imprint of New American Library,
a division of Penguin Putnam Inc.

First Printing, October 2002
10 9 8 7 6 5 4 3 2 1

Cover art by Royo
Cover design by Ray Lundgren

ROC REGISTERED TRADEMARK—MARCA REGISTRADA

Printed in the United States of America

PUBLISHER'S NOTE
This is a work of fiction. Names, characters, places, and incidents either are
the product of the author's imagination or are used fictitiously, and any resemblance to actual persons, living or dead, business establishments, events, or
locales is entirely coincidental.

To Kala

(They're always for her, though
it doesn't always say that in print.)

ACKNOWLEDGMENTS

I would like to acknowledge the ever-helpful members of the Untitled Writers Group (Karen Everson, Anne Harris, Jonathan Jarrard, Lisa Leutheuser, Erica Schippers, Shannon White, and Sarah Zettel), and my editor Laura Anne Gilman for support, snacks, and an endless supply of editorial comments. Thanks also to my agent Lucienne Diver, who does her best to keep me out of trouble.

PROLOGUE

Sometimes bad things happen to good people.
—Yeoman Daniel Vik,
First Bellerophon Landing Party

Sister Prinna Meg stretched her Dream body and yawned beneath her rowan tree. It had been a long shift. Time to go. Her drugs were wearing off in any case, and if she didn't leave the Dream soon, she would be yanked out of it instead, an uncomfortable experience at best.

Prinna's Dream landscape was a sun-dappled glen with green grass, yellow flowers, and a pair of rowan trees. The breeze was sweet and light, as in late spring. Prinna inhaled appreciatively of her own creation. Bellerophon was currently undergoing a rainy stretch, and the overhead sun, Dream or not, felt wonderful. Perhaps she could eke out her stay for a few more—

A heavy footfall jarred her to the core. Startled, Prinna looked around. Someone was encroaching on her Dream territory without asking permission first. It was an unpleasant presence. When Silent like Prinna wished to confer with another Silent in the Dream, they had to decide between them who would shape the landscape of their meeting place. Treading on someone else's turf without permission was like someone running an uninvited hand over that person's face.

More jarring footfalls. The intruder—Prinna sensed it was a man, a human like herself—was stomping toward her without regard to her landscape, forcing bits of his own impressions on this part of the Dream. This went beyond rude.

Prinna drew herself up, gathering her brown robes around her beneath the rowan tree. She was a brown-haired, blue-eyed woman in her third decade, not really pretty, but not unattractive either. A silver ring with an amber stone graced her right hand, indicating her rank as a Sister among the Children of Irfan. Prinna put her hand on the front of her robe to ensure ring and rank were visible. Overhead, a small flock of birds wheeled and twittered in the blue sky.

"Who is that?" she demanded.

Silence. Then another footfall. Maybe she should just let go of the Dream, go back to her body. Her work was done. What did it matter if a rude lout was stomping around? The glen would disappear when she did. Then the teacher in her, the part of her that had tutored half a dozen Silent students, came to the fore. If no one told him what he was doing was wrong, he would keep on doing it. It was her duty to let him know he was breaking with etiquette.

"Who is that?" Prinna said. "Show yourself! Stop stomping around like a half-grown bull."

A figure emerged from behind the other rowan tree and took several steps toward her. Prinna had been right—a human man. He was quite a lot bigger than she was and she found herself wanting to take a step backward. Then she realized she was being ridiculous. In the Dream, the only thing that mattered was will-power and mental strength. Physical size meant nothing at all. She held her ground. A small part of her noticed that his feet had left empty earth where they touched down on her grass and flowers.

"You're pretty," the man said. "Did you like the poems?"

Prinna blinked, confused. What was he talking about? Uncertainty tinged her again. "I don't read poetry," she said, clutching the front of her robe. "I don't care for—"

The man raised his head to the sky and howled like a dog. Fear tanged Prinna's stomach. Her cue to leave, thank you. Someone else would have to teach this weirdo some manners. She closed her eyes to gather her concentration so she could let go of the Dream. But before she could finish, something cold wrapped itself around her waist. Her eyes snapped open, her concentration destroyed. A rowan branch was holding her prisoner, squeezing hard enough to choke the air from her lungs.

"You don't care for poetry?" The man was right in front of her. She could smell his sour breath. "But I love you."

The glen changed. Grass and flowers withered and died. Night-black clouds blew across the sun. The ground rumbled, and blackened, evil trees without leaf or blossom twisted out of the ground and formed a tormented forest. A chorus of voices wailed on the wind. Terror suffused Prinna Meg. She couldn't think, couldn't breathe, couldn't . . .

"I love you, you stupid bitch," the man said.

Prinna Meg's pain began.

ONE

You can sell a body without consent, but never the soul.

—Captain Irfan Qasad,
First Bellerophon Landing Party

The slave auction took place in a room big as a school gymnasium. Evan Weaver, hands shaking, shuffled ahead with the rest of the colonists as the slavers herded them forward. A silvery metal band encircled his left wrist, and a similar one bound his left ankle. The auction-room floor was gridded with green squares, each a meter on a side, with yellow pathways painted between them. The air smelled stale, as if poorly recycled.

"Pick a square and sit!" ordered a slaver in blue coveralls. "Move!"

The colonists slowly scattered themselves across the floor. Mystified, Evan picked a square and sat. His mother, father, older brother, and younger sister did the same. The moment Evan sat down on the floor, his square turned red. The plain white tunic he had been given to wear did little to blunt the chill of the hard floor. More and more white-clad people from the colony ship arrived and were told to take up squares. Green squares steadily changed color until nearly all of them were red. Voices rumbled and echoed around the huge room until a computer tone announced the PA system was active. The colonists instantly fell silent, already knowing from experience that talking during the PA announcements resulted in instant pain.

"The auction will be starting soon," announced a harsh voice. "When the buyers come in to look at you, do what they say, but don't leave your square. Any question the buyers ask, you answer, and say 'Master' when you do. Otherwise, keep your mouth shut. It's a silent auction, so you won't see who's bidding."

The PA snapped off. Evan's heart was pounding again. Martina, his ten-year-old sister, whimpered and reached for their mother. When her hand crossed the boundary of her square, her silver bands snapped blue. Martina screamed and snatched her hand back. Rebecca Weaver started to reach for her daughter, but stopped herself barely in time. Rhys Weaver's jaw worked back and forth, his dark skin mottled with helpless anger. Evan's brother Keith, who at fifteen was three years older than Evan, stared at the floor. Around them, the other colonists also looked at the floor or whispered to each other in frightened voices. Evan's mouth was dry.

Then the floor shifted. Evan tensed as all the squares, including his, rose slowly upward until they were about a meter above floor level. They locked into place with a bone-jarring *thump*, creating dozens of platforms all around the auction hall. A moment later, a set of doors opened and more people strolled into the room. Evan blinked, then stared. His mother gasped and the buzzing among the slaves rose in volume. Not all the "people" were human. A tall, willowy being with a shock of white hair like a dandelion clock glided across the floor, followed by what looked like a giant caterpillar. Two humanoid lizards came in, tongues flicking in and out, and a short, shaggy thing with three legs skittered by. It carried a smell of wet leaves. Evan almost missed the twenty or so humans who were with them.

"Aliens," Rebecca said in awe. "All life!"

Similar murmurs rose around them. Evan continued to stare. He had overheard the slavers talking about aliens and alien buyers, but hadn't actually thought about what they meant. Aliens were the stuff of the entertainment industry, something you only saw on a screen or in a VR game. Now they were here, real and breathing. The caterpillar pittered by, its legs moving in a dazzling pattern.

Evan swallowed hard. From his perspective, he had boarded the colony ship only four days ago, along with his family, various other members of the Real People Reconstructionists of Aboriginal Australia, and other groups. They were all bound for a planet named Pelagosa. Evan's last memory was the lid of the cryo-chamber clanging shut above him. There was a slight hiss, a heavy feeling, and blackness.

The next thing Evan knew, he was being yanked shivering out of the chamber and fitted with a silvery wristband and ankleband before his half-frozen mind could comprehend what was going on. His family and the thousand-odd other colonists had been fitted with similar shackles. The slavers had unceremoniously hauled them on board their ship and stuffed them into cell-like rooms. The colony vessel was taken for salvage. Anyone who fought back or even protested received a debilitating shock from the bands. Even saying the word "escape" or "revolt" earned a shock. No amount of banging, picking, or clawing would get the bands off, though Evan's wrist and ankle became red and raw from the attempt.

During four days of captivity, they had picked up tiny bits of information here and there, mostly from what the slavers told them. The colonists had been sleeping for either nine hundred years (real time) or fifty years (ship time), take your pick. While the colonists lay in cryo-sleep, someone had discovered something called slipspace, which allowed faster-than-light travel between solar systems. Pelagosa and hundreds of other inhabitable planets had quickly been colonized. Slower-than-light ships vanished into history and the vastness of space, their slumbering inhabitants forgotten.

But the slavers remembered.

It didn't matter that the colonists and crew of the ship were not legally slaves. All records of their existence had long ago been lost or purged, and in any case, Earth was trillions of kilometers away under a different government.

"Who are you going to complain to?" laughed a slaver named Feder when Evan's parents Rhys and Rebecca Weaver had expressed outrage and disbelief. "You're slaves because we say you are and no one who counts will say different."

Feder. Evan shot Keith a quick look. He still hadn't taken his eyes off the floor of his platform. Maybe he was trying to hide his startling eyes. Blue was an extremely uncommon eye color among Australian Aborigines, and Keith's eyes made an arresting contrast with his dark skin and curly black hair. Evan quietly believed that it was Keith's eyes that had grabbed Feder's attention in the first place. Although Keith steadfastly refused to talk about any of it, Evan knew that Feder's attention, given in the privacy of the slaver's own quarters, had not been kind.

A thin woman with white hair approached Keith's platform. "Stand up, you," she said. "What's your name?"

Keith slowly got up. "Utang, Mistress," he said, giving the Real People name he had chosen for himself only a few months before the People decided to board the colony ship. The word meant "strength," though Evan, playing the part of annoying kid brother, hadn't been able to find it in any language database for the Aboriginal tribes. Keith had airily claimed the name had come to him in a dream. Evan rarely thought of Keith as Utang, even though Keith—Utang—used it regularly.

"Stand, boy."

Evan tensed. An older man with brown eyes and a fringe of gray hair was standing next to Evan's platform, looking up at him. Evan got to his feet, feeling naked and exposed. The man made a spiral motion with one hand.

"Turn around."

Evan's stomach tightened as he obeyed. It seemed as though he could feel the man staring at him and he found his face growing warm. It was like being a dog in a kennel. The white-haired woman moved away from Keith's platform.

The man consulted a computer pad. "You're twelve years old, is that right?"

Evan nodded. Suddenly he wanted his mother's arms around him, hiding him from this. His chin quivered and tears welled up.

"You ever work a farm, boy?" the man asked. He had a hoarse voice.

Evan shook his head. "I grew up in Sydney. It's a city in Australia. Master," he added quickly, and hated himself for it.

The man tapped the pad and moved on. Evan wondered if that was good or bad.

"Turn around, child, and let me see you," said another voice. Evan turned and saw a woman, also older. Blond, with gray eyes, perhaps ten years older than his mother. She wore a green robe with a gold frog embroidered on the shoulder.

"Walk around your platform," she ordered.

Evan did so. Out of the corner of his eye, he saw the white-haired alien talking to his father. The frog woman made a note on her pad and turned to Rebecca.

"You're the boy's dam?" she asked.

"Yes," Rebecca said. Her voice was quiet. "Mistress."

"Can you follow a recipe and cook?"

"Yes, Mistress."

The embroidered frog rippled as the woman made another note. Then without a word, she walked away.

Over the next two hours, several more humans and two different aliens examined Evan. They asked him questions and made him stand and walk. One pair of humans, a man and a woman, entered and reached up to prod and poke him.

"This lot has been in cryo-sleep for nine hundred years," said the man as if Evan weren't there. He was fat and balding, with fleshy lips and a tiny nose.

"They won't have very many useful skills then," observed the woman. She was equally heavy and wore a heavy string of glittering gems around her neck. "I suppose this one might be able to do housework and we could teach him to drive when he's old enough, but he isn't really attractive enough to put out in front of guests. What do you think of that one over there?"

Evan didn't know how to react to all this, so he didn't react at all. He merely sat in his tiny square platform. Occasionally Evan glanced at his mother. She looked frightened, though whenever she noticed him looking at her, her expression changed into something Evan supposed was meant to be reassuring. That frightened him even more. On some level, he had expected his parents to figure out what to do, how to solve their problem and get them ultimately to Pelagosa or back home to Sydney. His mother's face, however, made it clear that she didn't know what to do any more than he did.

The day wore on. In the background he heard someone shouting, "Fifteen! Do I hear fifteen? Fifteen, thank you! Twenty! Do I hear twenty?" and Evan assumed a non-silent auction had started up some-

where. Later, a woman came around with food that
Evan ate without really tasting. Humans and aliens
looked, prodded, asked the same questions. Eventually, Evan fell into a sort of stupor. The bidders became a blur of noise and faces.

"All right, you," said a voice. "Come with me. Both
of you."

Evan roused himself. The woman with the gold frog
embroidered on her green robe was standing in front
of him. Scattered around the echoing room, Evan saw
other buyers standing in front of different slaves. One
woman's platform faded from red to green and sank
to floor level. She crossed the boundary and fell into
step behind the giant caterpillar. A coveralled slaver—
not Feder—stood in front of Keith's platform, and it
sank to the floor as well. The slaver hauled an unre-
sisting Keith to his feet. Rhys leaped up, halting a
thumb length from the edge of his own red platform.

"Where are you taking him?" Rhys demanded.

"Special delivery," was all the slaver said as he led
Keith away.

Rhys made as if to jump off his platform, then
halted. Rebecca was on her feet as well. Martina
started to cry. Evan's stomach clenched and he balled
up his fists. The helpless feeling dropped over him.
Keith needed his help, needed his family's help, but
they couldn't do anything. Keith shot one last blue-
eyed look over his shoulder as the slaver took him
away. Platforms sank to the floor all around the room.
More shouts and cries started up as other families realized they were being split up.

"We'll find you, Utang!" Rhys shouted over the din.
"We'll find you!"

"Come on, you," said the frog woman, her face im-
patient. "I don't have the entire day."

Evan's platform sank, as did his mother's. So much

was happening so fast, he couldn't keep track of everything. He wanted to run after Keith, but didn't know what he'd do if he caught up to him.

"Well?" the woman demanded. "I dislike using pain to motivate my slaves, but if you two won't move, I'll have no choice."

Evan snapped his attention around to her. "Are you my— Did you—" Evan found he couldn't say the words *owner* or *buy me.*

"I am Giselle Blanc," she said, talking both to him and his mother. "I own you both. You will address me as *Mistress Blanc* or *Mistress.*"

"Did you— What about my husband?" Rebecca said softly. "And my daughter? Please, Mistress—did you . . . buy them as well?"

Evan wanted to cry. He had never seen his mother act like this. Her proud face was abject and full of pleading.

Blanc shrugged. "I bid on both of them, but lost. Come along, now. Control of your bands has been passed over to me. If you stray more than four meters from me, it will be unpleasant, and if you approach closer than one meter, it will be unpleasant." She turned and began to walk away.

Horror crashed over Evan and he froze where he was. His family was being split up even further and he felt helpless to stop it. A warning tingle passed through him, and he leaped forward to stay within range of Giselle Blanc. His mother walked ahead of him, white tunic fluttering like a ghost. Rhys and Martina were standing at the edge of their red platforms, tears running down both their faces. Evan realized his own face was wet, his throat thick. Blanc continued to walk ahead of them.

Rhys reached down and snatched Rebecca's hand as she passed. His face contorted with pain as his shackles glowed and delivered a punishing shock.

"Find us!" he gasped. "If we all keep looking, we'll find each other. Don't give up!"

Evan reached up to touch his father's hand. Rebecca had time to kiss Rhys's fingers above the glowing blue band before he fell backward with a moan. His hand slid away. "Find us!" he cried again. "I love you both."

Another warning tingle forced Evan to move forward. He caught a glimpse of Martina, tears flowing down her face. "Don't worry, Martina," he said to her, forcing a brave note into his cracking voice. "We'll find you. Don't worry. Be brave, okay?"

But Martina continued to cry silent tears.

Another warning tingle forced Evan to turn around and pay attention to where he was walking. Blanc wove her way up and down the yellow pathways between red platforms and green squares. She picked up half a dozen other humans—none of them were Real People—and finally headed for the double doors that lead out of the bidding room. Evan looked over his shoulder one more time but didn't see Martina or Rhys.

The little group of humans walked quietly down the wide white corridor of the station. Large windows showed a spectacular view of an unfamiliar planet as it turned slowly toward darkness, and the stars behind it gleamed like grains of purest white desert sand scattered over a black mirror. Aliens in surprising shapes and colors walked, slithered, or scuttled past. Evan barely noticed any of it. Crushing sorrow rode his shoulders. He found he was holding his mother's hand, though he didn't remember taking it. Blanc walked ahead of them. Somewhere along the line, she had been joined by a man with whom she conversed in a low voice. Her husband? Another slave? Evan didn't know, just as he didn't know who had bought Keith and who had bought his father and sister—or if they had been bought at all. What happened to slaves who weren't bid on? Were they killed? Imprisoned? Sold later? He had no idea. Not knowing, he thought, was the worst feeling of all.

The other slaves in the group, all dressed in white tunics and silvery wrist-and-anklebands, walked obediently behind Blanc. Some of them wept silently, others remained stoic.

Several corridors later, they came to a series of airlocks. Blanc's male companion chose one and cycled it open. The entry bay of a ship lay on the other side. All of a sudden it hit Evan hard. He had been sold, and his father, sister, and brother were gone. Once he left this station, he would never see them again. Panic suffused his chest and limbs. He turned and ran back up the corridor.

"Dad!" he shouted. "Martina!"

He got only a few meters before the pain knocked him flat. Evan struggled to his feet, ignoring the hands that grabbed at him. His bands glowed electric blue, but Evan's feet carried him farther along. The pain got worse. He was running over hot coals, through molten lava.

"Dad!"

The hands were on him again, and his bands glowed so brightly, they hurt his eyes. Raw, undiluted agony ripped his body to pieces. Evan fell, and blackness came before his body touched the floor.

The sun burned low in the cloudless sky, and the sandy soil was hot beneath Evan's bare feet. His soles hurt, pierced countless times by spiny spinifex and slashed by sharp rocks. His skin was dry, and it felt stretched over his body like a heated drum skin. Rhys and another man had started a fire of wood and dried animal dung. Keith—Utang—was skinning a big snake, clumsily but effectively, and Rebecca worked with another woman piling white grubs into big green leaves. They would roast in the fire, Evan knew, and his stomach twisted at the idea of eating them. Still, he knew he would. The grubs would contain moisture even after cooking, and they were worth eating for the water content alone. Rebecca rolled the first leaf shut, pushed it into the fire, and reached for another. The smell of roasting grubs wafted over the dry air, and the rocky Outback stretched empty in all directions.

Evan hated these trips. The hot sun, the constant thirst, eating things he would have only stepped on back home, stupid meditative exercises that were supposed to get them in tune with each other enough to use "head talk" instead of words to communicate, evenings spent listening to boring stories around a smelly fire, all in an attempt to rediscover "tribal ways." It was all stupid and pointless. The vast majority of Real People culture had long disappeared with the People themselves, either dead or swallowed up by mutant—white—society.

A curl of manure-scented smoke drifted into Evan's eyes and he shifted position, trying to get out of the way without standing on his aching feet.

"Your feet will harden in time," said Neluukatelardin. "In the meantime, pay the pain no attention."

Evan glared at him. Neluukatelardin was a sort-of leader to the Real People Reconstructionists movement, and he was currently lobbying for a tribal place on a colony ship that would soon leave for a planet named Pelagosa. The plan was to reestablish the Real People's way of life in a place untouched by mutant society. Evan was far from thrilled with the idea, but his parents were seriously considering it.

Rebecca pulled the leaf from the fire with a pair of sticks and opened it. The grubs inside had turned into a sort of mush that looked almost like oatmeal. Keith,

meanwhile, sliced the snake meat into chunks and
skewered them on sticks, which he passed around to
the dozen-odd people surrounding the fire. Martina
poked a hesitant finger into the grub mush, then
scooped some up and ate it. Evan grimaced, but thirst
forced him to reach for it.

Cold droplets landed on his head. Startled, Evan
looked up. The Outback hadn't seen rain in months,
and the sky was cloudless. More droplets spattered
him and dripped icily down the sides of his head. The
sun set, and suddenly everything was dark. Even the
campfire had vanished. After a moment, Evan realized
his eyes were shut. Puzzled, he opened them.

The room was dim and gloomy. Evan lay on a pallet
on the floor with a scratchy blanket drawn over him. A
ceiling slanted high overhead, with dark beams rising
into the shadows. The inside of Evan's head felt fuzzy,
and his mouth was dry. The Outback had been a
dream? It had felt so real. Maybe this was the dream.

He put a hand to his forehead and found a dripping
wet cloth. The cold felt good and helped clear his
head. An odd sound came to his ears. He couldn't
place it. It reminded him of a lot of birds twittering,
but that wasn't quite it.

"How do you feel?"

Evan turned his head without sitting up. A boy with
white-blond hair, pale blue eyes, and a deep suntan sat
cross-legged next to the pallet. He looked to be Evan's
age, about twelve. His feet were bare, and he wore a
brown shirt and shorts. A silver band encircled his left
wrist and left ankle. Automatically, Evan touched his
own wrist. The metal shackle was still there.

"I'm . . . okay," Evan said slowly. "What's going
on? Where am I?"

"This is Mistress Blanc's farm," the boy said. "You
got here some hours ago, and they bad me keep an
eye on you until you woke up. Nater—him that's the

headservant—Nater said they had to sedate you on the ship or you would have killed yourself."

Evan pushed himself gingerly upright, expecting dizziness or nausea, but feeling neither. The cloth slid from his head and landed with a wet *plop* on the pallet. "Where's my mom?"

"At house, I think." The boy dropped the cloth into a bucket. "She's going to be working kitchen. You're supposed to be working ponds with me. Come on. I'll show you."

He unfolded long, skinny legs and got up. Evan didn't move. "I want to see my mom."

The boy hesitated. "We're pond hands. Muckers. We don't go into house much. Mistress Blanc said you'll be starting at ponds."

"I want to see my mom," Evan repeated stubbornly. What if they were lying and Rebecca was dead or sold to someone else? And she had to be worried about him. The boy gave him a reluctant look.

"I'll bring you up to house," he said dubiously. "But I'm not promising nothin'. Come on."

Evan got up off the pallet and followed the boy to a chunky wooden ladder that led down to a large main floor. It turned out they were in the loft of a barnlike structure. The place smelled of dust and straw. Several pallets were scattered across the floor, along with a few personal items and open wooden crates that stored clothes. Evan's white tunic had been replaced with the same brown shorts and shirt the boy wore, and he wondered who had dressed him.

"I'm Pup," the boy said, starting down the ladder. Evan followed.

"I'm Evan," he said. A small shock hit him and he almost lost his grip on the ladder. "Ow!"

Pup looked up at him. "Mistress said your name's Lizard on account of you being so small and quick."

What? They were going to change his name? "My

name is Evan," Evan repeated, and got another shock, stronger this time. "Hey!"

Pup shrugged, continued on down the ladder. "Mistress says your name is Lizard."

The main floor was piled with bales of golden straw. A pair of giant double doors that stretched up to the ceiling three stories above them gaped open just wide enough to let a person slip in or out. Sunshine poured through the gap, illuminating dust motes that hovered on the still air. The odd twittering noise was louder down here. Another wooden ladder led up a loft opposite the one Evan and Pup had descended from.

"That's the girls' loft," Pup told him. "Boys aren't allowed up there, and you'll get a shock if you get too close."

He slipped through the gap in the doors. Evan followed him. The sunshine hit his eyes like a hammer, and the twittering noise burst into full volume around him. It was nearly deafening. He squinted and put a hand up to shield his face until his eyes adjusted. Evan caught his breath. Stretching into the distance before him was a field dotted with a series of ponds that made green and blue circles under a dazzling azure sky. Odd trees of a kind Evan had never seen before lined some of the ponds. Tall grass surrounded others, and a few had sandy shores. It was amazing. Australia had been battling constant drought when Evan had left, and he had never seen so much freestanding water in his life, except for the ocean.

A wide strip of green grass, bisected by a dirt path, separated the pond area from the barn, and Evan saw people moving along other pathways between the little pools, though he couldn't make out what they were doing. The sun was hot overhead.

"What is it?" Evan asked, still awed by the water.

"Frog farm," Pup said. "We take care of the frogs. Come on—the house is this way."

Pup lead Evan around behind the barn and across another wide green field. The grass was soft and green under Evan's soles. It felt soothing and pleasant. Plants in the Outback were scrubby, tough, and usually prickly, certainly no pleasure to walk on. Sydney was a place of concrete and broken glass. Walking barefoot on something soft was a new sensation.

Ahead of them lay a wide, white house, three stories tall, with a gently sloping red roof. Several outbuildings dotted the grass around it like chicks around a hen, and people moved slowly among them. Bright sunlight glittered off silver bands.

The slaves working around the house wore white, and Pup and Evan's brown clothing drew baleful stares. Pup clearly felt uncomfortable but lead Evan around to a back door. The smells of yeast and onions floated on the air. Pup knocked shyly and a moment later, Rebecca stuck her head out. She wore a white blouse, white trousers, and a blue apron dusted with flour. Her silver wristband was coated with it.

"Mom," Evan said, and she gathered him into her arms, even though he was as tall as she was. He stayed like that for a moment, pretending everything was safe and all right.

"Are you all right?" she asked. "They wouldn't let me see you."

"I'm fine." He reluctantly backed up a step, ending the embrace. "This is Pup. He took care of me. He said my name is 'Lizard' now." He said the last with distaste.

"They call me 'Bell,' " Rebecca said. "Blanc"—she winced and clutched her wrist—"*Mistress* Blanc always renames her slaves. I guess everyone does. We'll just have to live with it until we can figure out what else to do."

Evan gave a grim nod. A voice from inside the kitchen said, "Bell! We need that pastry rolled out!"

"I have to go," Rebecca said. "Here, hold on."

She vanished into the kitchen and came back with a pair of large rolls, which she handed to Evan and Pup. The latter snatched it eagerly. Evan realized he was hungry, too.

"I don't know if they fed you or not," Rebecca said. "If you get short of food, come round and see me. I'll see what I can do."

"Where are they keeping you?" Evan asked. "Where do you sleep?"

"In the garret with the others," she replied.

"Bell!"

"I'll see you later." Rebecca stood on tiptoe to kiss the top of Evan's head and vanished back into the house.

TWO

Every so often, life just sucks.
—Yeoman Daniel Vik

"Come on," Pup said, his mouth full of bread. "I'm supposed to show you around."

He took Evan back around the house toward the pond area, and they ate as they walked. The rolls had a spicy meat filling that tasted unfamiliar to Evan, but he was hungry enough not to care.

The heat lay hard on the boys as they walked. The very air itself was heavy with moisture, and Evan's shirt began to stick to his back. He felt as if he were pushing his way through the muggy air. He had never felt anything like it in arid Australia, and he found it a little hard to breathe as they reached the first pond, which was partly shaded by a large tree. The shore of the pond had been landscaped so that several strips of raised earth extended like curving fingers into the water. The twittering noises continued, punctuated by odd *glumps*, and Evan realized it was the sound of frogs. When Evan and Pup reached the pond shore, alarmed plopping sounds greeted them, and a host of ripples scampered across the water. A moment later, several dozen bulbous eyes goggled suspiciously at the boys from the pond's surface.

"These're American bullfrogs," Pup said. "We have sixteen ponds of them. That's the most. They're used in laboratories and for eating." He squatted and held out a bit of bread from his roll. A blur of movement launched itself out of the water with a great splash.

Evan jumped and Pup snatched his hand back. The bread was gone.

"They eat bread?" Evan said.

"They eat just about anything," Pup replied, wiping his hand on his shirt. "Crickets, worms, fish, mice—"

"*Mice?*"

Pup nodded. "They eat anything that fits in their mouths, so don't hold out anything they shouldn't have. They got no teeth, though, so you don't need to worry about getting bit."

"Why is the pond shaped funny?" Evan asked.

"They all want their own bit of land," Pup said. "There ain't enough shore for all of them, so we make more. Otherwise they'd fight all day." He gestured toward another set of ponds. "Over there are the bubble frogs. They're valuable because they ooze this stuff that can be made into a couple of different drugs. The tree dumpies in that pond cure cancer. The winslows over that way are mostly pets, but there's some alien race that thinks they're sacred and they buy 'em by the hundreds. They live a long time."

The boys walked among the ponds as Pup talked on and on about frogs, and Evan's head swam with information. Warm mud squished between his toes, and the hot sun alternated with cool shade as they made their way between trees of varying sizes. Pup explained that some frogs needed sun, others needed shade, and still others needed both, and every tree was carefully placed with the frogs' needs in mind. Some places were more like small swamps than ponds because breeds like tomato frogs needed to burrow more than they needed to swim. The ponds themselves were sometimes clear, sometimes muddy, sometimes covered with floating plant life. Twitters, mutters, *glumps,* cheeps, and splashes followed them everywhere, though Evan saw very few actual frogs. The ones Evan did see, however, came in a surprising variety of sizes and colors, ranging from plain green to milky white to blaze orange. They crouched on banks or hid among weeds or floated serenely on water.

Evan and Pup also encountered several brown-clad slaves, all human, ranging in age from a bit younger than Pup to gray, wrinkled oldsters. They variously worked with shovels, knelt among greenery, stood knee deep in water, thrashed the air with nets, or popped squirming frogs into covered baskets. Pup waved to most of them, and they waved back or called greetings. He paused by one woman who stood next to a pond with a large mesh cage, her hand on the clasp.

"Feedin' time, Grace?" Pup said.

"Sure is," she replied. "Want to watch?"

"Yeah." Pup cocked a thumb in Evan's direction. "This is Lizard. He came in with that other lot."

"Actually," Evan put in, "my name's Evan, not—" A shooting pain drove up his arm, interrupting him. Evan grunted and grabbed his wrist.

"Your name's Lizard," Pup said a bit sharply. "That shock was in case you forget. There's a computer in your bands. It listens to what you say, so you better learn quick."

Evan bristled but didn't reply. His name was Evan, not Lizard. Maybe he couldn't say it aloud, but that didn't mean he'd lost it or accepted the change. Grace, meanwhile, nodded at him. She was a short, sturdy woman, deeply tanned, with short black hair that curled tightly across her scalp. A black mass seethed inside the mesh cage with a slight hissing noise. Evan looked at it intently, changing the subject without actually saying anything.

"Crickets," Grace explained. "Don't try this at home."

In one smooth motion she opened the cage and swept it in an arc. A small cloud of insects scattered over the pond, dropping into the water with a drawn-out splash. The pond instantly erupted in bubbles. The water thrashed and frothed. A few moments later, it calmed again. More peeps and croaks peppered the air. Evan didn't see a single remaining cricket.

"Piranha frogs," Grace said. "They got no teeth—no frog has—but they're so aggressive you'd hardly notice."

Evan was impressed despite his anger. "Do they attack the other frogs?"

"They would if we let 'em," Grace said. "But we got a whole bunch of sensors in the ground and in the trees. They notice a frog leaving its habitat, and it gets zapped with ultrasonics. We can't hear it, but they can, and it sends 'em straight back. Otherwise, we'd have to use wire fences." She closed the cage. "What are you two on for today?"

Pup shrugged. "I'm showing Lizard"—Evan bristled again—"around a bit. Easy day for me."

"Then you can help me for a minute," Grace said. "Here. Take this back to the bug barn and bring back a full one. Make sure they're dusted."

Grumbling, Pup accepted the cage and left. A bit nonplussed, Evan followed.

"How do we know what to do?" Evan asked.

"You and me? We do pretty much what everyone else tells us. Don't matter who—if they're older, we do what they say. 'Course you pay special attention to the managers. They tell you to jump, you act like a frog and jump."

"Managers?"

"There's five of 'em—Master Ting, Master Varl, Mistress Quick, Mistress Yee, and Master Greenleaf. They ain't slaves. They work for Mistress Blanc. She's the owner."

"I know that," Evan said, trying to show he knew *something*.

They approached a great white building shaped like

a giant log half-buried in the ground. On one end was a set of sliding double doors large enough to drive a brace of tractors through. Pup chose a smaller door off to one side and Evan, who was starting to feel like a stray puppy, followed.

The inside was dimly lit and cooler, with a clean concrete floor. Rows of mesh cages and huge glass terrariums stretched the full length of the building, interspersed with sinks, gleaming worktables, and racks of equipment Evan didn't recognize. In several places he saw what looked like bathtubs. Insects crawled, flapped, and fluttered inside various cages and containers. The air was alive with clicks, chirps, and whirrs that were very different from the frog noises outside. More people, recognizable as slaves by their silver bands, moved among the rows, though they were dressed in blue and wore shoes. One man noticed Evan and Pup and hurried over.

"Don't get your muddy feet on my clean floor," he said. "What do you want?"

Pup held up the cage. "Grace sent us for more crickets. She wants 'em vitamin dusted, too."

The man snatched the cage and stalked away, muttering about filthy muckers.

"What's his problem?" Evan whispered.

Pup shrugged. "He's above us. Buggers—don't let 'em hear you say that word—are higher up than us. Most of them sold themselves into slavery by choice to pay debts, so they get better treatment and the easier work. They got family what's free, too."

The man returned and all but shoved the cage— now full of crickets—at Pup. They delivered them to Grace at another pond, but before Evan got a chance to see another piranha frog feeding, Pup took him by the arm and lead him away. His hand was rough and callused.

"Got to make a break for it before she gives us

something else to do," Pup muttered. "I can stretch out showin' you around for the rest of the day, and I mean to enjoy it."

Pup kept his promise. Evan got a careful tour of the Blanc frog farm, including a detailed demonstration of how to scramble up a tree in time to avoid Master Ting, a short man dressed in yellow, who came up the path with a purposeful stride. The slaves bent more closely over their work, and even the frog song seemed to diminish as he passed. Evan's heart pounded as he noticed the small control on the man's belt and wondered how much pain it would cost them if they were caught, but the manager took no notice of them. Once Pup decreed it safe, they climbed down and resumed the tour.

By the end of the day, Evan's head was swimming with facts about frogs, and his ears longed for silence instead of the incessant croaks and peeps. His feet were wrinkled and waterlogged from the mud and his stomach rumbled. Rebecca's meat roll seemed long ago and far away. The sun had made considerable progress toward the horizon, but it wasn't anywhere near sunset yet. Just as he was about to ask Pup about food, a chime sounded from their wristbands.

"Suppertime," Pup announced. "Come on."

He took Evan's arm and pulled him toward the barnlike structure in which Evan had awoken. Other slaves were moving in from the ponds and swamps, tools and baskets in hand. One outer wall of the barn was lined with a series of faucets set at knee level. Pup rinsed feet and hands and splashed water on his face. Evan did the same. The cool water felt wonderful on his sweaty, mud-streaked face, and it felt fine to have clean feet again.

A series of long trestle tables and benches were lined up across the grass beneath a series of tall shady trees. At the end of each table was a kettle, several

large serving bowls, and stacks of deep-dish plates. A
slave armed with a ladle stood at each kettle. Pup and
Evan, who had a head start, arrived at one of the
tables before any of the other muckers did. Evan took
up a plate, and the kettle slave filled it with what
looked like a soupy stew. Pup also caught up several
pieces of flat bread, and Evan did the same. They took
up places farther down the table and ate in silence,
using the flat bread to scoop up the stew. It was bland
and filling. Evan wondered if the meat was frog, but
didn't ask. Instead, he scanned the kettle slaves, looking for his mother. He didn't see her.

"Mistress Blanc must have been hard up for kitchen
help," Pup said, as if reading Evan's mind. "Your ma
got put in the house kitchen straightaway, instead of
cooking for the slaves first."

"Mom's a good cook," Evan said. "My dad, though,
can't even . . . even . . ." He trailed off. The mention
of his family brought an unexpected lump to his
throat. Tears welled up and he looked away so Pup
wouldn't see them.

"Sucks," Pup said.

"What?" Evan continued to stare at the ground.
Bowls thumped on the table around them, competing
with the noise of conversation. Sweaty brown shirts
and tired, tanned bodies streamed steadily toward the
food and tables. The air was a bit cooler under the
trees, though it was still humid.

"Sucks getting sold away from your family. 'Least
you got your ma here."

"You have any family?" Evan surreptitiously wiped
at his eyes as if there were something in them.

"Older sister. She's a house slave, so I don't see her
much. My ma and dad are gone."

"Hi, Pup! Where you been all day?"

Evan looked up and was abruptly surrounded by
eight or nine boys and girls his age, all dressed in

brown. They took up places on the benches, bowls and bread in newly washed hands. The question came from a dark-haired boy with the biggest brown eyes Evan had ever seen.

"Got an easy duty today showin' round a newbie," Pup said, flashing a grin. "Everybody, this is Lizard. Lizard, this is Flint and Jackie and Vera and Leaf and Keri and Zell and Cat and Bird and Jess. They're all muckers, too."

Evan, who had been braced for remarks about his new name, found himself the center of a flurry of friendly greetings instead. Evan gave a small smile, feeling suddenly shy. He made short, quiet answers to the questions that came his way, but initiated no conversation himself. Everything was completely foreign here. The food tasted strange, there were strange noises, strange animals, strange customs. Even the weather was strange. Suddenly, he found himself longing for the quiet, dry Outback. His throat tightened. How long was he going to live here in this strange place with these strange people? He wanted to go home, home with his father and mother and brother and sister. But home was trillions of kilometers and nine hundred years away.

Another chime sounded from everyone's wristbands. With a groan, the slaves slowly got to their feet.

"Now what?" Evan asked hoarsely.

"There's another hour of work after supper," Pup said. "But we can probably—"

"Pup! Lizard!" called Grace. "Don't you think of going anywhere. You've had enough of a slack day. We're adding another bullfrog pond, and you two can help with the landscaping."

Pup sighed and picked up his bowl. "So much for that, then. Come on."

Grace was as good as her word. She set the boys to work with trowels, making the extended fingers of shoreline required by the massive, territorial bullfrogs. The dark earth was wet and heavy, not quite mud, and Evan, who was forced to kneel in it, was soon covered with the stuff. His back and legs quickly became sore, and sweat ran steadily down his back and sides as he piled up long mounds of earth. Even his silvery bands turned black with dirt. Pup and three of the other younger slaves worked in silence next to him. The ever-present frog noises continued.

"You're one of the new ones, is that right?"

Evan looked up. An older man, perhaps in his late forties, with silvering hair and a fleshy face, stood next to the mud pit.

"Master Varl," Pup murmured.

"Stand up when a manager addresses you," Varl snapped.

Evan got to his feet. The other children continued to work diligently.

"What's your name, kid?" Varl demanded. Like Ting, Varl wore yellow. His clothes were clean, though his feet were as bare and mud covered as everyone else's.

"Ev— Lizard," Evan said, keeping his face stoic.

A shock traveled up Evan's arm and he dropped his trowel with a cry.

"Lizard what?" Varl said.

"Call him *Master*," Pup hissed.

"Lizard, Master Varl," Evan said, hating the word.

"You had an easy day today, Lizard," Varl said. "Hope you enjoyed it. Tomorrow you're working your ass off." And he strode away. Evan watched him go. Then, not knowing what else to do, he returned to work.

A long time later, the wristband chime sounded again. Everyone immediately stopped digging and trooped back to the barn area, where they rinsed their feet and hands. By now, the sun was coasting toward the horizon. Pup took Evan into the barn to a tiled room full of showers. Water hissed, and several tired-looking men were already washing off their daily quota of dirt and sweat. A changing area was lined with shelves of clothes and rough-looking towels.

"Throw your dirty clothes in that basket," Pup instructed. "Take a shower and get another set of clothes from the shelves. They're sorted by size. This is the men's shower, so you don't have to worry about the girls coming in."

After showering and dressing—Evan still went bare-foot—Pup led Evan back outside toward the ponds. They sat down under one of the trees amid gathering darkness.

"You'll want to see this," was all Pup said.

They sat in companionable silence for a while. The darkness continued in its intensity, completely unlike the streets of light-polluted Sydney. Unfamiliar stars came out, dazzling in their brightness, and again Evan felt homesick for the Outback he had so hated. On Outback walkabout, his family had been with him. He wondered what his mother was doing and if he would be allowed to see her again.

Frogs croaked everywhere. The pair of boys leaned back against the scratchy tree trunk, enjoying the feeling of sitting on something that didn't squish, and suddenly Evan was very glad for Pup's presence. Pup might be one step above a stranger, but he had been friendly and kind all day. Evan felt an odd urge to reach over and take the other boy's hand. Disconcerted, he cleared his throat.

"What are we looking at?" he asked.

"Wait a second," Pup replied. "It should be—there!"

Out of nowhere, a crowd of round white lights swooped down over the ponds. They circled and dipped and soared, their movements duplicated by their reflections in the water like tiny moons dancing above a roomful of mirrors. After a moment, each one moved to a position about a meter above each pond or swamp, shedding cool silvery light over every leaf and blade of grass.

"What are they?" Evan asked, awed.

"Bug bait," Pup said, clearly pleased at Evan's reaction. "The buggers can't come up with enough food for all the frogs on their own, so they release the nightlights to lure in more." He laughed, and Evan found he liked the sound. "The lights are here for a practical reason, but I think they look nice in the dark. I like to come out and have a look."

A mosquito whined in Evan's ear and he slapped at it. Then another one landed on his neck. Pup smacked a shoulder.

"Problem is," he continued, "you can't watch for very long without being eaten alive. Come on."

They went back to the barn, which Pup said was the slave quarters for unmarried adults and children over eleven, and climbed the ladder up to the men's loft. Large screened windows kept the insects out and let a cooling breeze flow through the building. A warm yellow light leaked over the edge of the loft and Evan heard voices talking. The frog noises grew even louder, and Evan wondered if it was because it was night or because the frogs were feeding off the bugs lured in by the floating lights.

Evan reached the loft. Thirty or so men and boys were there, some talking, some lying on their pallets. A small group was engaged in some kind of card game in one corner of the loft. Small yellow lamps provided illumination. It felt a little like a camp-out to Evan, for although they were technically indoors, the wide windows, high ceiling, and smell of straw made it seem like they were outdoors.

"What's this place like in winter?" he asked Pup. "Doesn't it get cold?"

"Nah." Pup dropped down on his pallet, which was next to the one Evan had woken up on. "It gets a little chilly sometimes, but not bad. Why? Do you come from someplace where it snows?" This last was said with a trace of wonder.

Evan sat on his own pallet. "Not where I lived, but it does get kind of cold."

"I've always wanted to see snow," Pup said wistfully.

Something occurred to Evan. "What's the name of this planet? It can't be Earth."

"Nope. It's called July IV. I hear it's some kind of joke, but nobody I know can explain it to me."

"How long have you lived here?"

"For my whole memory. Mistress Blanc sold my dad away when I was eight and Ma accidentally drowned in one of the ponds the year after that. She tripped and hit her head and no one saw until it was too late."

"Sucks," Evan said, and Pup grinned at him. Evan moved closer to him and lowered his voice. "Does anyone ever try to escape?"

Pain flashed down Evan's arm and leg. He started to cry out, but Pup clapped a quick hand over Evan's mouth. Evan thrashed for a moment as agony ripped at muscle and bone. Then it ended. Evan went limp.

"Don't scream if you get shocked," Pup said quietly. "Some of the slaves—the ones who toady up—get mad at you."

"So we still can't say . . . certain words," he muttered.

"Nope. And if you just mouth them, the computer catches that, too. And it learns code words after about twice. And if you go past the boundaries of the farm without permission, you get zapped." Pup picked at the rough padding on his pallet. "It ain't worth trying anything. They always win. At least Mistress Blanc don't mistreat her slaves. I hear one of the fruit farms up the road a ways has an owner who's boiled people alive for just not calling him *Master.* His managers take the women to their beds and beat the men. It can be pretty bad, so you just think about how lucky you are."

Evan decided to change the subject. "Can I see my mom?"

"Dunno. Maybe in the morning if you eat breakfast real quick and make a run to the house. You'll be able to see her more in winter, when there ain't so much to do. It don't get cold, but a lot of the frogs hibernate anyway. Something about the days getting short making 'em do it."

"Do we ever go to school?"

Pup propped himself up on his shoulder and gave Evan an amused look with bright blue eyes. "School? What for? You know how to read enough to puzzle out warning signs and directions, don't you? And you can count, right?"

"Yeah."

"And we'll teach you about frogs. What else do you need to know around here?"

More than anything else, those simple sentences did it. The knowledge slammed into Evan like a brick and Evan fell back on the pallet under its weight. His situation was permanent. He would live, work, and eventually die here. He would never see his father, brother, or sister again. A hot tear slid from his eye and trickled into his ear. It was quickly followed by another.

And then Pup was sitting next to him on the pallet, holding out a pillow. Evan took it. The dried grass inside crackled.

"Use that," Pup said softly. "It hides the noise."

Evan obeyed.

THREE

The only reason a frog feels happy in the muck is that it doesn't know anything better.

—Irfan Qasad

The tomato frog's eyes goggled and glistened like peeled grapes as it peered about. A cricket, lightly dusted with vitamin powder, leaped into view. The frog's tongue snapped out. The cricket vanished, and the frog gave a satisfied croak.

A white butterfly net flashed downward. The frog tried to leap, but only managed to tangle itself. It was hoisted high into the air for a moment, then popped into a covered basket containing ten other outraged red frogs. Lizard Blanc deftly untangled the net and cast about for another tomato. Four more would fill the order, and if he caught them quickly enough, he might be able to pretend it took longer and steal a catnap among the bushes by the tree dumpies.

The thought of sleep made Lizard yawn again, and he had to force himself to concentrate on the task at hand. Overhead, the sun beat down through a thin haze of clouds that did little to blunt the heat and humidity. The water was blood warm around his ankles, and the background drone of acres of frogs was such a constant in his life that he scarcely noticed it.

Lizard caught sight of another tomato. He flicked the net down, but the frog saw it coming and leaped into the water with a *plop*. Lizard grimaced and untangled the net. He really wanted that nap. His mother said that all teenagers went through a phase of needing more sleep because they were growing, but Lizard knew that wasn't the problem. It seemed like he got almost no sleep at night these days, and it was all because of the dreams.

Another bit of red grabbed Lizard's attention, and a moment later, another tomato frog joined its croaking brethren. Not long after he had turned fifteen, Lizard's dreams had become steadily more vivid. In most of them, he was on walkabout in the Outback. It all felt so real—the bright, hot sun, the dry air, the rough rock and sandy earth beneath his feet. Usually it came as a surprise when he awoke to discover he was still on his pallet next to Pup's. When he dreamed of the Outback, it was as if the last three years on the Blanc farm had been the dream, and he always woke up feeling restless and unhappy.

"Hey, Lizard!"

Lizard straightened to his full height. He had gained several centimeters since arriving at the farm, though his build was almost painfully thin. His skin was dark as oak bark from all the hours in the sun, and his hair, kept short, had bleached from black to the same brown as his skin. He still wore the brown shirt and shorts of a mucker.

Pup stood at the edge of the tomato pool. He had also grown considerably, though not as much as Lizard, and his build was stockier. His white-blond hair shone in the sunlight, and it contrasted sharply with his heavy tan. At the moment, his blue eyes were dancing with excitement.

"Hey, Pup." Lizard turned his gaze back to the pool. "What's going on?"

"We've been summoned," Pup said eagerly. "Come on!"

Lizard's net flicked through the air and another frog went into the basket. "Summoned? Where? What are you talking about?"

"To the house! Hurry up—we have to get ready. Forget the tomato order. Nater wants us!"

That got Lizard's full attention. He had seen the headservant maybe three times since he and Mistress Blanc had brought him to the farm, and then only from a distance. "Up at the house?"

Pup nodded. "I'll explain on the way. Hurry up!"

Lizard splashed to the edge of the pond with basket and net, sending a dozen bright red frogs leaping for the water. The two young men hurried toward the processing barn so Lizard could drop off his partially filled basket.

"So what's going on?" Lizard demanded as they went.

"Mistress Blanc's giving a big party," Pup explained. "Huge! And a whole bunch of the staff is still down with yak-yak, right?"

Lizard nodded. Yak-yak was the nickname of a flu strain that brought on severe vomiting. It resisted medication and kept its victims in bed plugged to an IV to prevent dehydration. Lizard had only come down with a mild three-day bout, and that had been enough for him. Pup had somehow escaped it entirely.

"So Nater needs servers for evening. The mistress can't cancel—it's been on the calendar for months—and we've been called on."

They reached the processing barn, another log-shaped building, and went inside. Cages, crates, baskets, and terrariums full of fearful, croaking frogs were everywhere. Lizard handed over his basket to the slave in charge and explained why he hadn't finished. The slave, a brittle-looking older woman, pursed her lips but said nothing. Orders from the headservant could not be countermanded except by Mistress Blanc herself.

"Why'd he choose us?" Lizard asked when they were outside again.

"Dunno. Probably your ma had something to do with it. He wants us washed and ready right quick."

They reached the slave barn and headed for the showers. It felt strange to strip off his clothes and wash in the middle of the day. Pup and Lizard donned fresh outfits from the shelves and trotted up the familiar path to the main house. Lizard knocked at the kitchen door, and a moment later, Lizard's mother Bell motioned them inside. Her hands, face, and hair were streaked with flour. It seemed to Lizard that his mom was always dusted with the stuff. Her talent as a baker had moved her quickly up the ranks in the kitchen until only two years after she and Lizard had arrived, she was in charge of anything floury that went into an oven. Bell was quieter now than she had been in the days before the slavers, but she and Lizard stayed close, or as close as time allowed.

The kitchen was huge, with long worktables running the length of the room. A trio of enormous multi-ovened stoves loomed against one wall, and another was taken up by a belt that conveyed dishes through an industrial dishwasher. Metal doors to walk-in refrigerators and freezers gleamed, as did a stunning array of huge pots, pans, kettles, and utensils. The place was alive with noise and bustle. Men, women, and children dressed in white cut, chopped, stirred, rolled, and mixed. The air was redolent of spices, fresh-baked bread, hot oil, and meat. Lizard's mouth watered.

"Hurry," Bell said. "You have to change clothes and then Tira will show you what to do. She's the housekeeper and works right under Nater, so you watch yourself."

Bell took them through a door and bustled them up a staircase. Soft red carpeting hushed their steps and felt strange under Lizard's bare, callused feet. The walls were a soft white, and the hall itself was deliciously cool. Lizard had all but forgotten what air conditioning was like. Pup looked equally impressed, and a little nervous.

"You boys need to do well tonight," Bell instructed in her quiet, clear voice. "If you do, Nater or Tira might get you promoted from mucker to house. Understand?"

Pup's eyes lit up and Lizard's heart beat faster. A chance to get out of the ponds? That meant no more hot sun, no more slave barn, no more mosquitoes. He exchanged a look with Pup and saw he was thinking the same thing.

They reached the top of the stairs, where Bell called out to another woman who was standing in front of an open linen closet counting white tablecloths. "Tira, I've got the boys."

Tira straightened. She was a white woman with iron-gray hair, a heavy, stolid body, and steely eyes. She looked Lizard and Pup up and down. Lizard tried to look capable and competent.

"They'll need to wash off the mucker stench," she said, wrinkling her nose. "Come with me."

"But we already—" Pup began, then shut up as Lizard trod heavily on his foot.

"Yes, ma'am," Lizard said, though inwardly he bristled.

Shooting him an approving look, Bell went back downstairs. Tira, who wore silvery bands identical to Lizard and Pup's, took them up another, narrower flight of stairs to a large bathroom that resembled the one in the slave barn, except the shower area was divided into stalls with privacy curtains.

"Scrub yourselves good," she ordered. "I want no trace of mucker stink on your bodies, see you?"

Lizard bristled despite his caution to Pup moments before. Just because he worked among the mud and frogs all day didn't mean he had to shower twice to get clean. But house slaves were the elite, and muckers were at the bottom of the ladder. Bell, Lizard knew, must have called in some serious favors to get them selected and he wasn't going to let them down. If that meant being overly polite to a bitch, he would be overly polite to a bitch.

"Yes, ma'am," he said, and Pup nodded. "We'll scrub ourselves good."

"I'll put some clothes outside the door." Tira glanced down and made a sound of disgust. "You'll need shoes, too. What size? Never mind—you wouldn't know. Just go. Hurry!"

If showering in the middle of the day felt strange, it felt even stranger to do it twice, and in the privacy of a single stall. The soap carried a light perfume and there was a separate bottle of shampoo, a far cry from the harsh brown head-and-body stuff they had down in the slave barn. Even the water felt softer. And the towels were real cloth instead of something resembling bleached burlap. Lizard's earlier fatigue disappeared in all the luxury and excitement.

Pup and Lizard finished with the showers and shook out the clothes they found folded on the floor just outside the door. They each had a pair of heavy linen trousers, a white collarless shirt that was almost knee length, white socks, white leather shoes, and a heavy length of gold rope, the purpose of which baffled both of them. Pup donned the trousers and tried to tuck the shirt in, but it was too long. Lizard discovered that his shoes were rather narrow and they pinched just a bit. The pants fit, but he hadn't yet tried on the shirt.

There was a sharp knock on the door, and Tira strode in without bothering to ask if they were dressed or not. She made another disgusted sound at their state of confusion.

"The shirt stays untucked," she snapped. "The rope goes around it like a belt. Here—let me tie that. It isn't a curtain cord, you idiot."

In short order, she had them shod, shirted, and belted. The fabric was far heavier and richer than anything Lizard had worn in his life and he found he was carrying himself straighter and taller. He caught a glimpse of himself and Pup in the mirror and stared. They looked like completely different people. The heavy mucker tan made a pleasing contrast with the snow-white clothing, and Pup's eyes shone like a clear sky beneath pale hair. Lizard stared at Pup's reflection, mesmerized.

"What?" Pup said, noticing the stare.

"Nothing." Lizard cleared his throat. "We're looking good."

"You look like dressed-up frogs," Tira growled. "But you'll have to do. Come on. The guests will be arriving in less than an hour, and I still have to teach you how to serve."

What followed was a whirlwind lesson in service and servant manners. Fortunately, Tira decided to put them in charge of one of the hors d'oeuvres tables in the main ballroom for the drinks and dancing portions of the party, and that meant mostly replacing empty trays with full ones from the kitchen and giving guests directions to the bar and bathrooms. Later, during the dinner portion of the evening, their sole duty would be making sure the guests' water glasses remained full. Tira made both of them pour glass after glass from a crystal pitcher until she was satisfied with their performance.

"It's worth your hide if you spill one drop on guest or tablecloth," she warned, and bustled away. Lizard and Pup gave identical sighs of relief, then laughed. Lizard suddenly remembered his first night at the farm when he had heard Pup's laugh. He still liked the sound, though he had never said so.

A while later, the first guests began to arrive. Lizard stood behind the hors d'oeuvres table, exchanging nervous glances with Pup and trying not to fidget in his tight shoes on the hard marble floor. The unfamiliar clothes began to feel heavy and confining, and he had to force himself to concentrate on the task at hand.

Please, please please, he pleaded silently, *don't let me screw this up.*

The ballroom was two stories tall and had a pale green marble floor shot with black. A balcony ringed the upper wall with two grand staircases at either end granting access to it. The guests were all human— Lizard hadn't seen a single alien since the space station—and they wore a dazzling array of glittering jewels, bright colors, and rustling fabric. Several of the women were accompanied by an entourage of gems that orbited head and hair like tiny solar systems. Lizard managed not to stare and instead put what he hoped was a friendly, obsequious smile on his face. A tastefully small orchestra provided light music from the balcony, though no one danced—that would come after dinner. Lizard guessed there were well over a hundred people present.

A steady stream of guests began to visit the hors d'oeuvres table, and Lizard found himself very busy. He and Pup alternated bringing in food trays from the kitchen, combining half-empty serving dishes, and whisking the dirty dishes away. There was, Lizard found, a certain rhythm to it, and once he got it down, it wasn't that difficult. Once, Tira came by to inspect their work and grudgingly admitted they were doing "an adequate job." Lizard's nervousness eased and he began to wish there were something he could do about his sore, pinched feet. He had hoisted yet another tray of empty serving dishes onto his shoulder and was heading for the kitchen when an old woman dressed all in black stopped him.

"Where's the restroom, please?" she asked with more politeness than most of the guests.

Lizard nodded toward one of the staircases. "Directly through the doors under either staircase, Mistress."

"Thank you, dear." Before Lizard realized what was happening, she reached up to pat his cheek like a friendly aunt. Her bare hand touched his face, and a jolt slammed through Lizard's body. Lizard gasped, and the room twisted around him. The tray fell from his shoulder with an ear-shattering crash of breaking crystal and ringing silver. After a moment, the vertigo faded and he became aware he was on hands and knees amid shards of glass and scattered serving spoons. A ring of people had surrounded him. The orchestra had fallen silent. Tira's angry face appeared among the crowd, and a part of Lizard knew that his chances of promotion to house slave had vanished like water on a hot stove.

"Lizard?" Pup said beside him. "Are you hurt? What's wrong?"

"I don't know." He let Pup help him to his feet. "She touched me, and—"

"What's going on here?" demanded a new voice. Giselle Blanc, dressed in a pale green gown, pushed her way to the front of the crowd. She took in the scene at a glance and turned to face the crowd. "A small accident. Thank you for your concern, my friends. Please return to your conversations. Everything is under control. Orchestra?"

This last was clearly an order, and the music immediately resumed. The crowd drifted away, leaving Mistress Blanc, Pup, Lizard, and the old woman in black.

"Get this mess cleaned up," Blanc snapped. "How could you be so clumsy?"

"It wasn't his fault, Giselle," said the old woman. "The boy is Silent. Didn't you know?"

Blanc blinked. "Silent? What do you mean? How do you know he's Silent?"

"I touched him," the woman said simply. "You should have him tested, of course, but the touch is never wrong."

Blanc stood motionless for a moment. Conversation and music mingled on the ballroom floor behind her. Then she pointed at Pup. "You. Clean up this mess. You"—she pointed at Lizard—"come with me. Clara, would you mind?"

"Not at all, dear."

The two women turned and walked toward one of the exits without looking back. Bewildered, Lizard shot Pup a glance. Pup, who had knelt to gather up the debris, gestured at him to follow and gave him a thumbs-up sign.

"What's Silent mean?" Lizard hissed at him.

"Go!" Pup hissed back. "And be sure you remember your friends later."

More confused than ever, Lizard trotted away. He followed Mistress Blanc and the old woman named Clara out of the ballroom, along a corridor, and through a set of double doors into a large room paneled with blond wood. A huge silk rug covered the center of the burnished floor, and an enormous desk sat next to a stone fireplace. Shelves were crammed with bookdisks, and statues of frogs were everywhere. A wet bar occupied one corner. It was well after sunset, and the windows showed only a reflection of the room itself. Blanc motioned Clara to a leather easy chair while she opened a decanter at the bar.

"Brandy?" she asked.

"No, thank you, dear," Clara said from the depths of the chair.

Lizard wasn't sure what to do, so he stood next to the door. His heart pounded like a hyperactive hammer and he was starting to sweat. Was he in trouble for dropping the tray? Doubtful—Pup had looked happy for him. So why was he here?

Blanc splashed red-brown liquid into a glass shaped like a balloon and took up a chair behind the desk. She swirled the brandy, sipped. "You say my slave Lizard is Silent."

Clara gave a prim smile. "Of course."

"I don't understand how." Blanc set the snifter down and tapped her desk. A holographic screen winked into view and text scrolled across it. "It's as I remembered. His papers state he was found on an STL colony ship that left Earth some nine hundred years ago."

Lizard stood by the door in his tight shoes, feeling like some new species of frog that had caught Mistress Blanc's eye.

"So he wasn't born into slavery?" Clara said.

Blanc shook her head. "And I know what you're thinking. Listen, someone else would have bought him and his dam if I hadn't, and I treat my people well. He has a good home here."

"Did you rescue him from a colony ship or the dog pound?" Clara asked mildly, echoing Lizard's unspoken thoughts. A wash of long-repressed anger flashed over him and he had to struggle to stay quiet.

"At any rate," Blanc said, brushing Clara's comment aside, "he left Earth long before Irfan Qasad started creating Silent babies."

"Nevertheless," Clara said firmly, "I am Silent, and when I touched him, I *knew*."

Lizard could keep quiet no longer. "Please, Mistress," he said, and both women turned their gaze on him, "what does it mean that I'm Silent?"

"It means you're worth a hell of a lot more than five hundred freemarks," Blanc muttered.

"Silence is a form of telepathy, child," Clara said. "Once you've had proper training, you'll be able to enter the Dream and communicate with any other Silent in the universe, no matter what species they are, what language they speak, or what planet they live on." She gestured at Mistress Blanc. "Some of the frogs on this very farm produce toxins that can be refined into drugs that aid the Silent in reaching the Dream."

"How do you know that I'm Silent?" Lizard asked uncertainly. "I've never heard of it."

"I touched you," Clara told him. "The first time two Silent touch flesh to flesh in the real world, it creates a weak telepathic bond. If we were both in the Dream right now, we would be able to find each other much more easily than two Silent who have never touched. That first contact also creates a physical jolt that can be very disconcerting for those who are unprepared for it. Your Silence must be very strong, dear, for it to send you to your knees like that." She paused. "Tell me, do you have dreams that are so vivid—lifelike—that when you wake up you feel like *this* is the dream and your dream was the real thing?"

Lizard nodded in awe. "How did you know—?"

"Holy mother of god," Blanc gasped. "What if I have two of them?" She tapped something on her desk and a tone chimed. "Nater, send Bell into my office immediately."

"Yes, Mistress." The reply came out of thin air.

Lizard's head swam and he desperately wanted to sit down, but it looked like no one was going to give him permission. Dreams. The Real People told stories of the Dreamtime, the place where everything began and ended. And there were all those meditations the Real People Reconstructionists did to relearn head talk. Was it all real?

"Who's Bell?" Clara asked.

"His dam. She was on the same ship. I'm wondering if she's Silent, too."

"It does run in families," Clara agreed.

"But why wouldn't the slavers have tested them for Silence already? It seems like they would have."

"Why should they, dear? As you said, the ship was nine hundred years old, before the time of Irfan Qasad, and she was the first human Silent. Why should they spend the time and money to run a test that they thought would only come out negative?"

A knock came at the door. There was a pause. Both women looked at Lizard, and it took him a moment to figure out that they were expecting him to answer it. Fumbling with the knob, he did so, and Bell stepped self-consciously into the room. She gave Lizard a worried look that said, *What did you do?*

"Bell, come here," Blanc ordered, and Lizard's mother approached the desk. "Clara, would you . . . ?"

"Of course." Clara got to her feet, long black dress rustling. "Hold still, Bell. This won't hurt."

Lizard wanted to cry out a warning, but Clara touched his mother's cheek before he could do so. She stiffened and gave a little gasp. Clara nodded and went back to her chair.

"She is Silent as well," she said, "though not as strong in it as her son."

"All life!" Bell said, a note of fright in her voice. Lizard wanted to go to her, but didn't know if that was allowed. He stayed where he was.

"Well," Mistress Blanc said, getting to her feet. The holographic screen vanished. "Well, well, well. This is welcome news. Lizard, you need not return to the slave barn tonight. I'll tell Tira to give you a room up here. I'll decide what to do about both of you tomorrow. Clara, I have to return to the other guests. Dinner will be served soon. Coming?"

"Of course, dear." Clara rose and took Blanc's proffered arm. The two of them strolled out of the office without a backward glance.

"Son?" Bell asked. The slave bands wouldn't allow

her to call him *Evan,* but she had never used the name Blanc had assigned to him. With a small start he realized that he always thought of himself as *Lizard* now. When had that started?

"Son," Bell repeated, "what did she mean? What's happening?"

Lizard explained what little he knew. "So it looks like we're both Silent—and a lot more valuable. I don't understand it all."

"Silent." Bell looked at the leather armchair uncertainly, then apparently decided she had nothing to lose and sat in it. Lizard, greatly daring, perched on the arm. "Once in a while, I would hear the mistress or Nater mention a message that came via Silent courier. I always assumed that *Silent* meant classified or bonded or something. I never asked."

"So what do we do now?" Lizard said. "I don't think Mistress Blanc wants me back at the party, and she didn't say—"

Another knock came. Both Lizard and Bell leaped to their feet. Lizard opened the door cautiously on Pup. He slipped into the room and Lizard closed the door.

"Is it true?" he asked without preamble. "Are you Silent?"

Lizard nodded. "Mom's Silent, too."

"Wow." Pup's blue eyes were wide and round. "You both go right to the top. No more mucking for you."

"All life!" Bell sank back into the chair. "What do the Silent do?"

"You don't know?" When they both shook their heads, Pup said, "They communicate. Slipships can jump into slipspace and get to other planets and stuff—Mistress Blanc wouldn't have much business if they couldn't—but regular communication only goes as fast as light. I hear tell it'd take hundreds of years

for some messages to get where they have to go. But
the Silent can communicate with other Silent no matter how far away they are. I don't know how they do
it, but they do. Ask Old Min about it. He *says* he has
a Silent cousin, but I don't half believe him."

The door began to open, and once again Bell
jumped to her feet. Tira entered the office. Lizard's
heart lurched. He was going to be in trouble. He
was—

"Mistress Blanc told me to show you to your
rooms," Tira said deferentially. "Would you like to go
now?" While Lizard was recovering from his surprise
enough to formulate a reply, she caught sight of Pup.
Her tone and demeanor instantly changed. "What are
you doing here?"

Pup blanched. "I—"

"I summoned him," Lizard snapped. "Is that a
problem?"

"No, sir," Tira said, contrite. "I'll show you upstairs
now, if you like."

She took them up to the second floor and into a
pair of adjoining bedrooms, each with a wide, cano-
pied bed and a well-appointed private bathroom. Tira
stood in the doorway between the two rooms, hands
behind her back, eyes on the floor. Lizard was amazed
at the change. This was Silence?

"Will you require anything else?" Tira asked.

"Yes," Bell said from her room. "Supper for both
of us. Bring a wide selection."

"Yes, ma'am." Tira crooked a finger at Pup, who
was standing in the corner, trying to look inconspicu-
ous. "Come along, you."

"He'll stay," Lizard said in an imperious tone, "and
serve us our dinner."

Tira blinked, then nodded and left. Lizard waited
until both doors were shut before running into Bell's

room and throwing his arms around her. She laughed and hugged him back. Pup grinned like an idiot.

"What's this all about?" Lizard asked breathlessly. "What happens next?"

"I don't know," Bell admitted. "Look—our own rooms. They're bigger than the entire apartment back in Sydney. Why are they giving us all this?"

"You're Silent," Pup reminded her. "You outrank everybody, except maybe Nater. Even the managers have to be polite."

They spent considerable time exploring their rooms. Lizard flung himself on the bed and found the sheets were fine, heavy linen with a raw silk bedspread woven in a purple pattern. It was the first time he had lain on a real bed in three years. The bathrooms were an equal treat, each with a whirlpool bath and a multi-directional shower that fascinated Pup no end.

A while later, a knock came at the door and a slave Lizard didn't recognize wheeled a large linen-draped cart into Bell's room. The covered dishes on top rattled slightly, and delicious smells filled the air.

"Thank you, Kip," Bell told him. "You can go."

Kip left, and Lizard lifted the covers. Although he didn't recognize a lot of the food, he could see at a glance it was infinitely better than anything the muckers got, even on holidays. Bell gave it a critical kitchen eye.

"It's not the best," she said, moving the dishes to a nearby table. "But it's better than what any slave gets."

Pup stood uncertainly by the door.

"Sit down and eat," Lizard said. "That muck about you serving us was just an excuse to keep you here. There's more than enough for all three of us."

Pup's face cleared and they all three sat down. When Tira came to take away the dishes, Lizard told her that Pup would sleep at the foot of his bed in case he or Bell wanted something in the night. Tira accepted this without comment and withdrew again.

"I don't know how long we can keep it up," Lizard said, "but we may as well enjoy it now. Besides, the bed's big enough for five!"

That night, Lizard lay awake in the deliciously comfortable bed. Pup had dropped off almost the moment his head hit the pillow, but Lizard found the silence kept him awake. The windows were shut, and he couldn't hear the frogs, let alone the usual snores and sleepy mutters of the slaves in the barn loft. Soft moonlight slipped around the closed curtains, giving a dim illumination. Lizard turned on his side and watched Pup sleep. His near-white hair looked silver. The sheet had fallen away from his bare chest, revealing flat muscle and supple skin that moved with Pup's steady breathing. He was a good friend, the best Lizard had ever had. And he was damned good looking.

Lizard blinked. *Where did* that *come from?* he thought.

He watched the rise and fall of Pup's chest and was seized with the sudden impulse to reach out and touch Pup's hair, caress his forehead. Feelings churned inside Lizard, strange and unexplained. Pup was his best friend. Pup had been there for him from day one, had listened to him cry about his missing family, had conspired to avoid the managers with him. Lizard liked Pup a lot, didn't know what he'd do without him. But what did that mean?

Lizard's hand stole outward and his finger lightly touched Pup's cheek. It was warm. Pup shifted. Lizard snatched his hand back as Pup's eyes abruptly opened.

"What's wrong?" he said in a sleep-blurred voice.

Lizard's wits fled and he couldn't answer. Pup blinked and woke up fully.

"What's going on?" he said.

"I thought . . ." Lizard stammered. His heart beat fast. "I mean . . . it's nothing."

Pup gave him a long look that Lizard couldn't interpret. "Okay. Good night." He turned over and lay still.

Lizard swallowed hard. What had he been thinking? What had he been doing? There was no answer that made sense to him. Lizard turned his back to Pup and stared at the wall. So much was happening, changing so fast. He'd never get to sleep.

He fell asleep.

The wind was hot and dry, carrying the scent of dry vegetation and sun-baked rock. Overhead, a falcon screamed, a high, free sound. Under his feet, the earth was hot, sandy, and full of sharp stones, but in this place, his soles were hardened and impervious to such problems. He spread his arms to the wind, let it blow over him. This place was solid. This place was real. This place was—

Child.

He had never heard human voices in this place. These should have startled him. But he felt no fear. He turned calmly. Half a dozen people, men and women, stood beside him. They were as naked as he was, their dark hair bleached brown by the sun.

"Hello," he said.

Our time here is short, they said, and their mouths didn't move when they spoke. The words appeared in his head and in his heart. *And there are things you must know.*

"What are they?" he asked.

A collective sense of shaking heads came over him. *You must learn them on your own. We can only send you in the direction.*

"What direction is that?"

The one within you. Follow your own self. The mu-

*tants are forcing your body down a path strewn with
death and pain, but your mind remains your own.
Draw strength from us. We are the Real People, and
you are part of us. The mutants can take that from you
only if you let them.*

And they were gone. No track or broken blade of
scrubby grass showed they had ever been there. The
hot, cleansing breeze continued to blow, and the falcon called again. He turned to look up at the sky and
saw a white canopy.

Lizard awoke, muddled and confused. He was in
the wrong place. There should have been a hot wind,
sandy soil. Or a lumpy pallet and frog calls? Either
way, it was wrong. Everything was soft and white, and
the light was dim. He heard a strange bubbling noise.
Then Lizard remembered where he was and sat up.
Pup's place in the bed was empty, and the bubbling
sound was coming from the bathroom. Lizard got up
and stretched. Thin streaks of sunlight striped the floor
around the curtains, leaving the room dim. Cool air
drifted from one of the vents, and the carpet was soft
on Lizard's bare feet. He pulled on a pair of shorts,
knocked once on the bathroom door, and pushed it
open. Pup was sitting up to his neck in the whirlpool
bath, which bubbled with white water. The room was
heavy with steam.

"This is great!" Pup said. "You have to try it! Lots
of room—come on in."

"Not the shower?" Lizard asked. For the first time
in his life, he realized—truly realized—that Pup was
naked in the bath. Memories from last night stirred,
and Lizard found himself drawing back with uncertainty. Pup gave no sign that he remembered the previous night, but still . . .

"Already tried that, too." Pup grinned, and he was

beautiful. Lizard swallowed. "You coming in or what?"

"I'll wait until you're done," Lizard said, and splashed a handful of warm water at Pup's head to cover his consternation. Pup retaliated with a great gout that soaked Lizard from chin to waist. Laughing, he wiped his face on his arm. "Now I don't need a shower *or* a bath."

A few moments later, they had both finished washing up—Lizard opted for the shower—and had gotten dressed. Lizard actually had to dress twice because Pup found outside the bedroom door another set of clothes in Lizard's size. These were a long tunic and trousers in a pale yellow, with sandals similar to the type the managers wore. Pup watched him put them on in awe.

"Y'see?" he breathed. "Light yellow, and the managers wear dark yellow. You're almost at the same level they are."

"I guess," said Lizard. He held out the wrist with the metal band still encircling it. "But only almost."

"You think they'd assign you a body slave to, you know, lay out your clothes and stuff?" Pup asked tentatively. "Even someone who was a . . . a mucker?"

His eyes were so wide and his voice so hesitant, Lizard felt his throat thicken. His best friend thought it would be a privilege to wait on him? In a fit of emotion, he grabbed Pup in a rough hug. Pup didn't immediately return the gesture and Lizard felt him stiffen for a moment before hugging clumsily back. Lizard let go.

"Sorry," he mumbled.

"It's okay," Pup said in the same tone he had used last night. "Just startled me."

"It's just—I'd rather have a friend than a slave. But if they want me to have a body slave, you know I'd get you out of the muck." Lizard paused thoughtfully. "Unless you'd miss that frog girlfriend you've been seeing."

Pup snorted. "Well, your ma's waiting list is too long."

Lizard aimed a mock punch at Pup's head. Pup ducked, and everything was back to where it had been before.

"Speaking of Mom," Lizard said, and knocked on the door connecting their rooms.

Bell, it turned out, had herself finished dressing. Her new tunic and trousers were identical to Lizard's. A moment later, breakfast arrived. They wheeled the cart over to a wide window and drew aside the curtains to let in golden sunlight. They ate and talked. It was a happy meal. Lizard saw the lines on his mother's face had smoothed a bit, and she appeared much more cheerful. For a moment, it felt like a Sunday morning back in Sydney, in the days when there had been five of them around the breakfast table. The change had come because they were Silent. Lizard looked at his mother and knew the same thing was on her mind.

"Do you think . . . ?" Lizard asked.

Bell sighed and set down her coffee mug. "I don't know. We can only hope, I suppose."

"What?" Pup said. "You hope what?"

"That the rest of our family is Silent, too," Lizard said.

"Oh."

"Do you ever think about them, Mom?" Lizard said.

"Every day," she said quietly. "Every night I talk to your father, even though he can't hear me. And then I pray that your brother and sister are all right."

The door opened and Mistress Blanc walked in. All three slaves shot to their feet, but kept their eyes on the floor. Lizard caught a glimpse of green robe and thought he recognized it as the one she had been wearing the day she'd bought him and his mother from the slavers.

"I've been thinking about what to do with you," she said. "My interplanetary communication is fairly extensive, but it's not enough to justify the cost of training and maintaining my own Silent, and certainly not two of them. Therefore, I've decided to put you both up for sale."

The words slammed into Lizard like bullets. Every drop of blood drained from his face and the room swayed around him. Mistress Blanc's voice seemed to come from a long distance. Then he was sitting on the floor with his head between his knees and no idea how he'd gotten there. His hands shook and his face felt numb. The silver-colored band around his wrist gleamed in the golden sunlight. Gradually he became aware of an arm around his shoulder.

"It's okay. It's okay. It's okay. All life, everything's okay. It's okay."

The voice was his mother's. There was an edge to it, as if one wrong word might send her falling into hysteria. Lizard forced himself to breathe evenly. The room stopped spinning. Eventually he looked up. Mistress Blanc was gone. Pup and his mother were kneeling beside him. Her arm was around him. Lizard stared at the band on Bell's wrist. Bell, not Rebecca. Lizard, not Evan.

"It's okay. It's okay. It's okay," Bell repeated.

Lizard slowly got to his feet, assisted by Bell and Pup, who hadn't spoken. The three of them stood in silence. After a while, Pup cleared his throat.

"Mistress Blanc said you need to go downstairs soon so you can leave," he said. His eyes, blue as the sky, were bright with unshed tears, and Lizard knew he didn't want to shed them where people could see.

"She bought us together," Bell said, the edge still

in her voice. "She bought us together. Someone will buy us together. They'll have to. They'll have to."

Tira appeared at the door, her steely eyes hard. "Mistress Blanc is waiting downstairs." Her tone, while polite, made it clear that even Silent slaves were still slaves who needed to obey the mistress.

"We're going, aren't we?" Bell said. "All life, we're going."

She moved toward the door in a daze. Lizard's mouth was dry and his hands were still shaking. He turned and looked at Pup, and suddenly the thought of leaving him was more than he could bear. All of a sudden there was so much to say. He grabbed Pup's shoulders.

"Pup," he said, "Pup, I—"

Pup's body went stiff and a guarded look came into his eyes. "You what?" he said. His voice was wary. Something twisted inside Lizard and the words changed on his tongue.

"I'm sorry you didn't get a chance to . . . to be a body slave," Lizard said. He backed up a step and shook Pup's hand.

"Yeah. I'm sorry, too," Pup said. "Really, I am."

Lizard nodded once, then turned and followed his mother out the door.

FOUR

Freedom is the ultimate drug.
—Daniel Vik, Co-Founder of Othertown Colony

The room was exactly the same as before. Yellow pathways led between red platforms and green squares, and voices echoed off the hard walls. The only difference was that this time, Lizard had a chair to sit in.

His mother was already gone.

Lizard had gone berserk when her new owner led her away. He jumped screaming off his platform. That had been—what? Two hours ago? Three? It was hard to tell. Now he sat on the chair, dull and listless, as humans and aliens asked him questions. A small part of him wondered if his slow, stupid answers lowered his price, and he took some satisfaction in the possibility.

A jolt banged up his spine, making him gasp and rousing him from lethargy. A short, round woman with short black hair and coffee eyes removed a gentle hand from his ankle. She smiled at him as he blinked down at her.

"I just had to be sure," she said, tapping the little data pad she carried. "Don't worry—I'll be back. And you'll be free."

Lizard watched her go, not quite sure what she meant. He wasn't free. He was pretty expensive, by all accounts. All around him, almost a hundred slaves of varying species sat or squatted in their squares. Only three others had chairs to sit in. Another half dozen platforms, including the one Bell had been confined on, held empty chairs. Lizard wondered if his

mother had been placed in a different lot, which was
why her silent (Silent?) auction ended before his did.
Or maybe there was some other reason she had been
taken earlier. He really had no way to know for sure.

    . . . *you'll be free.*

The phrase echoed around Lizard's mind, but he
didn't dwell on it. He was a slave, had been for three
years and would be for the rest of his life. It didn't
matter what that woman said or did.

After a while, however, the round woman came
back, data pad still clutched in one hand. She was
smiling.

"It's all arranged." She touched Lizard's platform.
It blinked from red to green and sank to floor level.
"Let's go before they find a way to change their
minds, all right?"

"Are you my new owner?" Lizard asked uncertainly.

"Yes and no," she said. "I know that's not a very
good answer, but trust me for the moment. I don't
want to talk here. Come on. Walk behind me and
keep your eyes down. Quickly!"

"Yes, Mistress."

She pursed her lips. Lizard tried not to flinch.
"Never that," she said. "You may call me 'Mother
Ara' or just 'Mother,' all right?"

Mother? What was she, a nun? A nun who bought
slaves? "Yes, Mist— Mother Ara."

Mother Ara turned and strode away. Lizard hurried
to follow, mystified. She went around to each of the
other Silent slaves up for sale, her manner brisk yet
furtive. Lizard exchanged glances with them but didn't
speak. As the entourage grew, Lizard began to wonder
if this was an escape. It would explain why they were
hurrying and why Mother Ara didn't want to talk and
why she had said Lizard would be free. A tiny spark

of hope flared, and he let it remain. Something was going on here, and he had the distinct feeling that he and the other Silent slaves were going to benefit from it.

Mother Ara lead the group along a white corridor that looked exactly like the one Lizard and his mother had traversed when Mistress Blanc had bought them. The other slaves in the group consisted of a teenage boy and girl about Lizard's age and a young man who looked to be about twenty. All three of them were white and all three wore the standard metal slave bands on wrist and ankle.

They arrived at an airlock, and Mother Ara shooed them through into the windowless entry bay of a ship. The moment the airlock had shut and cycled, Ara gave a heavy sigh.

"Chan," she said, "open intercom to Father Adept Michel. Father, I've got them all. I'm for getting out of here!"

"Understood, and you got it," answered a deep, disembodied voice. A slight vibration immediately followed, and Lizard assumed the ship was underway. Mother Ara turned to them with a wide smile.

"Welcome," she said, "to the Children of Irfan."

She said it as if she expected them to cheer. None of them did, or even reacted, including Lizard. Mother Ara gave a small sigh. "You've never heard of us, have you?"

The others either shook their heads or mumbled, "No, Mother Ara."

"Oh well. You'll learn. Right now, though, we've come to my favorite part." She consulted her data pad for a moment. When she next spoke, her voice became deep and rich with authority. "Lizard Blanc, step forward. Hold out your hands."

Lizard's heart began to pound. What was she going

to do? Would it hurt? Humiliate? His mind flashed
back to his brother Utang and the slaver Feder. What
if she was like him? What if—?

"In the name of Irfan Qasad, founder of our order
and mother of us all, I set you free." Ara pressed her
thumb to his wristband. "Release."

For the first time in over three years, Lizard's
band sprang open. It clattered on the deck. The
ankleband followed suit of its own accord. Lizard
stared down at the stripe of flesh where his wristband had been. The skin was paler and his arm felt
oddly light.

"Do you accept this freedom and all the responsibil-
ities it entails?" Mother Ara asked formally.

"Yes," Lizard blurted out. "You mean I'm free?
Really free?"

She reached up to put her hands on his shoulders
and gave him a solemn nod. "You are free, without
reservation, exception, or limitation."

Lizard couldn't move. It didn't seem real. Ara left
him and turned to the next slave, the young man. He
was a bit taller than Lizard, with brown hair, a pug
nose, and intensely green eyes. Handsome. He was
also the owner of a small duffel bag—the only person
in the group who seemed to have any possessions.

"Jeren Drew," Mother Ara said, "in the name of
Irfan Qasad, founder of our order and mother of us
all, I set you free." His bands joined Lizard's on the
floor. Lizard's earlier flicker of hope leaped into full
bloom. It was true. All of it. He watched as she freed
the girl, whose name was Willa McRay, and the boy,
whose name was just Kite. Willa was painfully thin,
perhaps thirteen years old, with stringy dishwater
hair and a long nose. Kite was short and about fourteen. He had night-black hair and deep black eyes
that met Lizard's with wonder and awe as his bands
fell away.

"You truly mean this?" Willa said in a tiny whisper. "We're free?"

"Absolutely." Ara swept the pile of slave bands aside with her foot as if she were clearing away a pile of trash. "Come along with me and I'll explain exactly what's going on."

A light went on in Lizard's head. "Mistre—I mean, Mother—wait a minute. You buy Silent slaves?"

Ara nodded. "Among other things."

"My mom," Lizard said. "All life—my mom." The words spilled out in a babble. "She's Silent, too, but someone took her away just before you bought me and it wasn't more than an hour or two so they can't have gotten far with her and maybe she's still on the station or the ship she's on is still close by." He paused for breath, heart pounding, tension singing along his veins. Every second they spent here was one more second further away. "Please, oh please, can you find out if she's—"

Ara spun and ran out of the bay without a word. Lizard and the others stared after her. Jeren was the first to recover.

"Come on!" he said, and ran after her. Lizard and the others hurried to catch up. The corridor beyond the bay was well worn, with beige walls and a gray floor. It smelled faintly of disinfectant.

"Chan, open intercom to the bridge," Ara yelled as she ran. "Tora, get on the horn to the station. I want their general manager right now. Anna Kay, all stop. How far are we away from the station?"

Their footsteps echoed off the ceramic tiles. The group passed occasional doors, corridors, and ladders, but they didn't have time to look at them in detail. Ara didn't slow a single step and Lizard was surprised at how quickly she could move.

"Not even two thousand klicks," came Anna Kay's voice.

"Ara, what's going on?" Michel asked.

"I'm almost at the bridge, Father Adept," Ara replied. "I'll explain there."

The doors at the end of the corridor snapped open when Ara approached, and Lizard and the others followed her onto what he assumed was the bridge. It was a fair-size room, brightly lit, with several workstations and a large view screen that took up most of one wall. Currently it showed a live picture of the station, all white circles and straight lines. A readout in the corner indicated the magnification. Half a dozen humans worked the stations, and keys clattered like teeth beneath their busy fingers. Every one of them wore around his or her neck a round gold medallion the size of Lizard's palm. A rangy man with dark hair and blue eyes sat in a chair at the center of the bridge.

"I have the manager's office," said a small Asian woman in a black jumpsuit. Lizard assumed she was Tora.

Ara gestured for Lizard to come with her. "The rest of you stand by the door and stay quiet."

"Ara, what's up?" the rangy man asked. He looked to be in his fifties.

"Got a line on another Silent slave, Father, but we have to move fast," Ara said, dropping into a chair near his. Lizard realized with a start that Father Michel must be the captain. He nervously took up a position next to Ara's chair, wondering what she was up to.

"Open the link, audio only," she ordered, and a short burst of static hissed from hidden speakers. "This is Trader Araceil Rymar of Galaxic, Incorporated. Who is this, please?"

"This is Assistant Station Manager Kent," came a tenor voice. *"How may I help you?"*

"I have just received word that you sold a Silent slave named—" She gestured at Lizard.

"Bell Blanc," he murmured. His heart was pounding again.

"Bell Blanc," Ara repeated. "Earlier you told me that there were only four Silent for sale on the station. Bell, however, wasn't one of them. Was there a . . . misunderstanding?" She added a hint of menace to the last word.

"One moment, Trader Rymar. I am accessing the records." Pause. *"The slave Bell Blanc was put into a lot that went up for auction before you arrived, Trader. My sincere apologies."*

"Manager Kent, my corporation has charged me with finding every Silent slave I can get my hands on. Would you be so kind as to tell me who the buyers were and perhaps how I can contact them?"

Another pause. *"Again my apologies, but that information is confidential. We cannot under any circumstances, short of a government mandate, release that information."*

Lizard staggered, but Michel made a halting gesture.

"Manager, this is Senior Trader Michel Granger," he said, his deep voice taking on a strangely oily tone. "Is there anything we can do to persuade you? My corporation is very generous to people who aid us. We can arrange—"

"I'm sorry, Senior Trader," Kent's tone was frosted with iron, *"but that information is absolutely confidential."*

Lizard's heart dropped into his feet. Ara and Michel harangued, cajoled, and threatened, then demanded to talk to the Station Manager, whereupon they went through the same process, also to no avail. Finally, Ara met Father Adept Michel's eyes for a brief moment. He shook his head and ordered Tora to close the connection. Then he gestured at Anna Kay, who set to work at the pilot boards. Ara turned back to Lizard.

"I'm sorry, Lizard," she said softly. "Your mother's gone."

Lizard sat in the ship's lounge, staring out a porthole at the stars and feeling very strange. His eyes were red and sore, and he wore a soft brown robe and comfortable shoes. Lizard's memory of the moment after Ara told him the bad news about his mother was hazy, but he did remember tearing at his clothes. Hence the robe.

The other three slaves—Jeren, Willa, and Kite—sat clustered together, talking in low tones. Lizard didn't feel up to talking, so he ignored them. The lounge was small and dimly lit, but it was comfortably furnished with easy chairs and couches. Stars drifted steadily past the porthole. Every moment widened the distance between Lizard and the last remains of his family.

Draw strength from us.

The voice came into his head as clearly as it had in his dream, but Lizard continued to stare out the porthole. He had lost everything important to him—his family, his friend, even his name. He had been answering to the name *Lizard* as if he'd been born to it. He had no control over anything, over no aspect of his life.

We are the Real People, and you are part of us.

But they had been nothing but a dream. A simple, nighttime dream. It had felt absolutely real, but that didn't make it so.

The mutants can take that from you only if you let them.

Only if he let them. If only it were that simple.

Only if you let them.

Maybe it was.

Lizard sat up straighter. No one was going to give him control. He knew that. What if he just *took* it?

Starting with his name. Outside the porthole, the stars looked as if they were swimming below him, and if he took a step forward, he could walk on them with no effort.

Only if you let them.

Lizard firmed his jaw. So what if it had only been a dream? That didn't mean the words were any less true. He was one of the Real People, and he had been through pain and trials at the hands of mutants, just as the Real People had, and he had survived. He *would* survive. They would give him strength.

The lounge door slid open and Ara came in. She was wearing a gold medallion around her neck like the rest of the bridge crew now, and a gold ring set with a gleaming piece of green jade graced her right hand. The little group of recently freed slaves stopped talking and turned to face her. Jeren and Willa started to rise, but Ara waved at them to sit and took a chair herself.

"You aren't slaves," she said, "and you don't have to stand up whenever someone comes into the room. Anna Kay says we're well away from the station and should have slip at any moment now—" As if on cue, the stars exploded into a whirling cacophony of colors. Nausea fluttered in Lizard's stomach before the porthole darkened.

"Perfect," Ara said. "I'm sure you have a great many questions by now, and I've come down to answer them. Lizard, do you want to join us?"

"That's not my name," he said firmly.

Ara nodded, as if she'd heard those words before. "All right. What is your name?"

"Kendi," he blurted out, then blinked in surprise. It had been on the tip of his tongue to say *Evan*. Why had he said *Kendi*? Then he remembered some of the stories the Real People Reconstructionists had told around the fire on walkabout. A kendi was a magical lizard, quick and intelligent. He thought about it for a moment, then nodded to himself.

"Kendi," he repeated. "My real name is Kendi."

"Very well, Kendi," Mother Ara said. It was both odd and pleasing to hear someone else say it. "Would you like to join us? If you'd prefer to be alone—"

"No," he said. "No, I'm all right." Lizard—Kendi— drew his chair toward the little group which had formed around her. The others made room for him.

"First," Ara said, "let me explain a few things. As you may have guessed, I don't work for a corporation."

They nodded in unison. "Did you really pay for us?" Kendi asked.

"Oh yes—with good, hard currency. Once I determined each of you was truly Silent, I submitted the instant-buy bid and that was that."

"Instant-buy bid?" Jeren said, his green eyes all but glowing with intensity. An old scar framed the outside of his right eye and Kendi wondered if his owner had done that to him.

"The auction is silent, meaning no one knows what anyone else is bidding," Ara said. "But the auctioneers always set an outrageously high price that you can pay if you want to buy on the spot instead of waiting for the bidding to end. I submitted that bid for each of you, and that was that."

"Youhavethatkindofmoney?" Kite said. He spoke quickly, the words running together like drops of mercury.

"The Children of Irfan do," Ara told him. She settled herself more comfortably in the chair. "We're a monastic order. It's our duty to find Silent, especially enslaved Silent, free them, and bring them back to the monastery on Bellerophon. Before you ask, no—you are not required to join us. You are not required to do anything at all." She leveled them a clear, steady gaze. "You are free citizens. No slave bands, no owners, no owners, no obligations to anyone but your own free selves."

"Sure, sure," Jeren drawled. "You fork out that kind of cash and don't expect a thing in return? Next you're gonna ask me to pull your finger."

Willa made a shushing noise. "Don't get her angry. She could make us slaves again."

"No," Ara said emphatically. "Absolutely not. You do, however, have a choice to make. You can come with me—with us—to Bellerophon and study under the Children of Irfan. The Children will give you room, board, clothing, and a small stipend. You will receive a general education."

"Wadwedofyou?" Kite said, and Kendi had to think a moment to separate his words.

Ara seemed to do so as well. "What do you do for us? Well, if you complete your training and take your vows as a full Child, you'll work for the monastery one day for each day you spent in training. During that time, you'll receive room, board, and a larger stipend. Once your debt is paid, you can leave the Children or stay with us. It's up to you."

"We have to work for you?" Jeren said. "Sounds like slavery again."

"Yeah," Kendi chimed in, also suspicious. "What if we get there and decide we don't like it?"

Ara smiled. "You have a year to decide. After that, you're technically a contract employee. If you don't like it, you don't have to sign on." She raised a finger, forestalling Jeren's next comment. "And no, we don't leave you stranded on Bellerophon as an incentive to get you to sign. All Silent slaves we buy are given two gifts. The first is your freedom. You have that. The second is a voucher for free passage on any ship to anywhere you want to go. I'll give you that when we arrive on Bellerophon. You can use it right away, or you can save it to use for later. It's good for life. If you decide not to stay with us, you can go wherever you like."

Kendi relaxed a little. "What if we don't complete the training? I mean, you must have people drop out."

"It happens," Ara said. "If you drop the training before completing it, you still have to work for the Children one day for each day we trained you. It won't be in the Dream—you need to complete your training to do official Dream work for us—but there are plenty of other jobs around the monastery that need doing."

"WouldweloseourSilence?" Kite asked.

"Certainly not," Ara said. "We wouldn't do that, even if we could. But there is a clause that states you can't do Dream work for another company for at least three years after you leave the Children. Otherwise, we'd become a free training ground for the competition."

"You got all this in writing?" Jeren demanded.

"Every word. I'll bring you all a copy of the policies, along with your vouchers. Other questions?"

"Why did you pretend to be a trader for a corporation?" Willa asked in a tiny voice Kendi could barely hear.

"It's easier," Ara said. "There are a lot of people who don't like the Children. Corporations like the Silent Partners don't care much for us because we don't want the big profits they do and we can undercut their prices. Slavers have a grudge because we set people free, which takes them off the market and denies slave-sellers a future commission. If I had come in as Mother Ara of the Children of Irfan, for example, your instant-buy bids would have gone up even higher. They might have even refused to sell to me."

"WhendoeeriveBellephon?" Kite asked.

Ara blinked as she straightened this out. "We arrive at Bellerophon in about an hour, I think. This is one of our faster slipships. We'll get you settled in right away."

And maybe, Kendi thought suddenly, remembering what that woman had said about touching another Silent, *I can find Mom—in the Dream.*

FIVE

We need to learn to speak through Silence. Even the dead have something to say.
—Irfan Qasad, Founder of the Children of Silence

Mother Araceil Rymar do Salman Reza dropped her bags on the foyer floor with a sigh. It was a relief to be home again. The windows in the house were open, letting a pleasant summer breeze waft through the screens. Outside, the deep green leaves of the talltree that supported the house rustled, and far below came the roar of a dinosaur. The newly rescued slaves were in the capable hands of Brother Manny, who would get them settled in for the night and thereby free Ara to go home for the evening.

Then she heard it—a strange metallic clank. She frowned and stepped over her suitcases, following the noise. It came again and again in a rhythm that echoed off the hardwood floors and walls. Ara followed the sound, mystified, until she came to her son Ben's room. The noise came from behind the closed door. She knocked once.

"Ben?" she called. "I'm home."

The noise stopped for a moment, then resumed. "Come in."

Ara opened the door. Ben was lying flat on his back on a narrow bench amid a series of levers and pulleys. He was pushing a curved horizontal lever straight up. Behind him, a short stack of black metal weights rose into the air, then descended with a *clank*. Ben's freck-led face was shiny with sweat, and his flame-red hair was darkened with it. The veins stood out on his arms as he struggled to lift the bar again.

"Hey, Mom," he grunted. "Good trip?"

"Ben, what in the world?" Ara said. "What are you doing?"

"What's it look like I'm doing?" *Clank.* His voice carried a hint of annoyance.

Ara's gaze wandered about the room. As usual, the place looked like something had exploded inside a computer store. To make room for the weight machine, Ben had shoved his unmade bed to one side, crowding it against his desk. The overflowing boxes of computer parts that usually lined the walls were piled into an unsteady mountain in the corner. Ara was thankful to see that Ben had at least put rugs underneath the weight machine so it wouldn't scratch the floor. The room smelled of sweat despite the open windows.

"I meant, where did you get this from?" she said. *Clank.* "Bought it," Ben grunted. *Clank.*

Ara suppressed a sigh and felt tired. Talking to Ben lately was like trying to roll a square rock. He had always been reticent as a child, but lately things had gotten worse. Maybe it was a function of being fifteen. She was glad to see him, but a certain amount of exasperation was overtaking the feeling. Things had been so much simpler when he ran up to give her a hug whenever she picked him up from her sister and brother-in-law's house after a recruiting mission. Ara had recently decided he was old enough to stay by himself during her shorter trips—with someone checking on him from time to time—but now she questioned the wisdom of that idea.

"Who did you buy it from?" she asked. "And how did you get the money?"

"Computer work," Ben said, referring to the occasional odd jobs he did on the networks. "Found a guy on the nets"—*clank*—"who had a gravity machine and was selling this one cheap." *Clank.* Sweat rolled off him and he paused long enough to wipe his face on his shoulder.

"Well," Ara said uncertainly, "don't hurt yourself. Did you have dinner?"

Ben shook his head, straining heavily to lift the bar one more time. His arms trembled and Ara was seized with the sudden impulse to help him lift it. At last he managed to straighten his arms and hold the weight stack in place for a moment before all but dropping them with a crash. Ara was about to suggest he end the workout and take a shower when the computer chimed.

"Attention! Attention!" it said. "Incoming call for Mother Araceil Rymar."

"Put it through to my office," Ara said. She nodded at Ben and went up the hall.

Ara's office was done in the same decor as the house, with pale hardwood floors, wood paneling, and large rugs covering the floor. A leafy branch shaded one window, while the other looked out over the long drop to the forest floor below. Outside, the sun shone in a golden summer haze. Ara's desk was a moderate mess, but nothing like the sty in Ben's room. That was another change. Ben had always been tidy as a child, but in the last year he hadn't cleaned a thing unless Ara stood over him. She dreaded seeing the kitchen.

"Eliza," Ara addressed the house computer, "open call."

One wall blinked into a view screen. A silver-haired man with a kind, worried face appeared. He wore a soft brown robe. "Araceil. I'm glad you're back."

"Grandfather Melthine," Ara said warmly. "If you're looking for a report on my trip, I just got back. I can—"

"There's been another death, Araceil," Melthine interrupted. "Like the others."

She stiffened. "Oh no."

"We need you to recreate the scene, and we have to move quickly," Melthine continued. "Before the echoes die away from the Dream. How soon can you be here?" He recited a monastery address which appeared across the bottom of the screen. The place was within walking distance.

"Give me ten minutes, maybe fifteen." Ara was already reaching for a computer pad from her desk. She also snatched up one of her dermosprays and checked to make sure the drug chamber was full.

"Every moment counts," Melthine said. "I'll watch for you." The wall went blank.

Ara dashed out of her office and poked her head into Ben's room. He was sitting up, holding a free weight, elbow braced on the bench between his knees.

"Emergency investigation," she said. "Order supper if I'm not back soon, all right?"

Ben grunted and lifted the weight, bicep straining. Ara didn't know if he meant the sound as assent, or if it was a general noise, but she turned anyway and rushed toward the door.

Outside, she clattered up a set of wooden stairs to a walkway that ran above the house. Tiny flying lizards chirped and croaked in the leaves and the air was warm where the talltree shade didn't reach. The overhead sky was clear and blue, and the breeze remained pleasant. Ara, however, was covered with goose bumps. Another murder, and they had called her to investigate.

Ara hurried up the walkway which connected her neighborhood's talltree to the next talltree over. The entire monastery—and the city that surrounded it—was built into the canopy of the massive forest. Each talltree was over a hundred meters high, with thick, spreading branches that made ideal foundations for houses safely above the pods of saurians—dubbed *dinosaurs* by the original Bellerophon colonists—that stomped over the forest floor. Each tree could support half a dozen houses or more, and flexible walkways made of board and cable connected them to each other. Fine polymer netting covered the space between the cable railing and the floor of the walkway to prevent people from falling through, though the netting was hidden from view by a thick growth of ivy. Ara moved quickly from one tree to another, passing several other people with only the barest of nods until she came to the address Melthine had given her.

It was a small house, with a wide front deck and a gently sloping roof that blended neatly into the talltree. A police officer in a blue tunic stood guard at the door, and a holographic stripe of blue light ringed the house at waist level. The words DO NOT CROSS BY ORDER OF THE GUARDIANS were etched on the ring in yellow. Ara crossed the ring—it beeped at her in alarm—and held up the gold medallion that marked her a Child of Irfan.

"Grandfather Melthine called for me," she said.

The officer, a young man with pale hair and eyes, stuck his head inside the door and conferred briefly with someone Ara couldn't see. Then he motioned her inside and shut the door after her.

The sharp smell of relaxed bowel hit her. Ara swallowed, unable to see much in the dark interior after the bright outdoor sunshine.

What am I doing here? she thought. *This is a real murder with a real corpse. I'm not a detective. What if I throw up when I see the body?*

"Araceil!" boomed a voice from the gloom. Ara's eyes finally adjusted and she recognized Grandfather Melthine. "Good. The body's this way."

"Who is it?" Ara said, following him into the house.

"Sister Iris Temm."

The name meant nothing to Ara, for which she was grateful. It was bad enough to know the woman was—had been—a fellow Child. Melthine took her into the living room. The sun dropped slanted rectangles of gold light on the floor, and Ara took in her surroundings. Easy chairs, sofa, upright piano—a real one, with strings—coffee table. Shabby, but comfortable, typical for someone on a Sibling stipend. A fainting couch lay off to one side, and the body of a woman reposed quietly on it. Her arms were crossed over her stomach as if she were asleep or in the Dream. Iris Temm had been a tiny woman, almost doll-like, with curly blond hair and sallow skin. Both her eyes had been blackened and her nose looked broken. Other bruises darkened her pale skin, as if she'd been beaten before dying. Ara's eye unwillingly went to Temm's left hand. It was crusted with dried blood, and the littlest finger had a ring of cross-stitches around the base. The finger above the stitches was clearly not original to Iris Temm. As she feared, Ara's gorge tried to rise, and she swallowed hard. Grandfather Melthine had told her about this aspect of the murders, though she had never seen it. Seeing it in person was very different from hearing about it.

"The finger," she said, amazed at the steadiness in her voice. "Did it belong to—?"

"Wren Hamil." Another person, a woman of Asian ancestry, entered the room. She was Ara's height, but with a whipcord build and long hair that twisted in an intricate braid down her back. Civilian clothes, sensible shoes. She thrust a hand at Ara, who took it automatically. A jolt crackled down Ara's spine. The woman was Silent.

"Inspector Lewa Tan—Guardians," she said. Her voice was oddly harsh and raspy, as if she were about to cough. "You the consultant in Dream Theory?"

Ara nodded. The Guardians of Irfan were the legal enforcers of the Blessed and Most Beautiful Monastery of the Children of Irfan. The rank and file encompassed investigators, lawyers, judges, and other such folk, some of whom were Silent and some of whom were not. They had no jurisdiction outside the monastery, but Iris, like most Children, lived within its boundaries.

"So the finger did belong to the previous victim?" Ara asked.

"On-site DNA test says so," Tan agreed. Her tone was clipped, her words succinct, as if she wanted to get her talking done as fast as possible. "And when Wren Hamil's body was found"—she checked her computer pad—"eleven months ago, she was . . . 'wearing' the finger of a woman named Prinna Meg. Wish we could say Prinna Meg was the first victim, but we can't. She was wearing the finger of another person. Someone we haven't identified yet."

"The bruises—"

"Body's covered with them. Medical examiner will tell us more."

"Who found her?" Ara asked. She felt as if she weren't quite there, as though the world around her wasn't real.

"Boyfriend," Tan rasped. "Came over to pick her up for dinner and found her like that. My partner's questioning him. Back deck."

"Do you suspect him?"

"Not seriously. Medical examiner's on her way, but I did a prelim scan. Looks like Temm's been dead an hour, maybe two. I registered heightened levels of psytonin in her brain. Means she was probably in the Dream when she died, just like Prinna Meg and Wren Hamil. Then we called you."

What had Ara been doing two hours ago? Sitting at her desk on the ship, filling out a report on the recent buy while the four slaves that were the subject of the report slept the sleep of the exhausted. At one point Ara had looked in on them and found Willa tossing restlessly on her mattress. Jeren, in contrast, slept so soundly that Ara had to look carefully to see his breathing. Kendi and Kite snored in the bunks above him. All while a Silent sister was being murdered in the Dream.

"Where's her dermospray?" Ara asked. "I didn't see it on the couch." It sounded to Ara as though her own voice was coming from far away.

"Bagged and tagged," Tan told her. "Possible evidence."

"Time, Araceil," Melthine interrupted. "The Dream will move on."

Ara started and came to herself. "Of course, Grandfather. Is there a bedroom I can use?"

"Whole house is a crime scene," Tan said dubiously. "You just want a place to lie down, right?"

"Yes."

"Bed should be okay, then. We already checked it."

Tan escorted Ara into Iris Temm's bedroom, a small but comfortable place containing a double bed, high dresser, and two bedside tables that didn't match. The curtains were drawn in this room, making it feel gloomy. Ara lay down gingerly on the bed. It smelled faintly of bath powder.

"Need anything?" Tan asked.

"Just some quiet. I'll let you know what I find."

"I'm joining you," Tan said. "Now that I can find you in the Dream."

Of course, Ara thought. That was why Tan had made such a point of shaking Ara's hand.

"Yes, all right." Ara shut her eyes. "Just give me a few minutes to find Iris's turf. It'll be easier without another Silent mind around."

Tan took the hint, for Ara heard retreating footsteps and the sound of the bedroom door shutting.

Ara took out her dermospray, pressed it to her upper arm, and thumbed the release. With a *thump* and a hiss, it injected Ara with a tailored drug cocktail. Ara lay back on the soft pillow, then inhaled and exhaled, following a pattern perfected over many years of practice. Her heartbeat slowed. After a while, the darkness behind her eyelids shifted and slowly filled with swirling colors. They mixed and whirled until a vibrant white light became Ara's entire universe. Her body fell away and she felt light and airy. The light brightened further, growing incandescent. Then it flashed in a nova burst and vanished, leaving Ara standing on a flat, featureless plain that stretched from horizon to horizon. Soft sound filled Ara's ears, thousands of whispers that blended together like the delicate roar of a seashell.

It was the Dream.

Ara looked down. Her body felt perfectly solid and normal, as did the ground beneath her feet. This, she knew, was an illusion created by her own subconscious. Each particle of the earth she stood on, every molecule of air she breathed, was actually a sentient mind. Although every mind in the universe created the unconscious gestalt of the Dream, only the Silent could actually enter and use it. The whispers Ara heard were other Silent also in the Dream. If Ara desired, she could reach out to one or more of them, call to them.

The Silent could also sculpt the Dream into whatever environment they desired. Usually Ara chose a pleasure garden, complete with fruit trees, musical fountains, and sweet-smelling flowers. The flat plain was merely the default. This time Ara left it as it was.

Iris Temm and three other Children of Irfan had died while they were in the Dream, and the police were assuming they had been attacked and murdered there. Even the greenest student of the Children knew that injuries in the Dream were visited on the real-world body and that very few Silent had the concentration or strength to resist these psychosomatic wounds. Death by accident was not unknown in the Dream, but there was nothing accidental in this particular case. And there was the matter of the substitute fingers.

The difficulty lay in the Dream itself. Without a conscious mind to dictate reality, it reverted to the simple, featureless plain Ara now occupied. Once Iris Temm was dead and her killer left the Dream, there would be nothing to indicate either person had ever been there. No crime scene to investigate.

. Or so the murderer probably thought.

Ara closed her eyes and widened her other senses. Delicately, she probed at the ground beneath her feet and the air above her head. When Iris Temm had entered the Dream and created an environment for herself, she used the subconscious minds that were closest to her physical body—her neighbors, other Silent, even the more intelligent dinosaurs, if some of the wilder theories about them were correct. Each mind made up a piece of Iris's Dream. Since Temm had only been dead for an hour or two, most of these people should still be fairly close to her—and to Ara. This meant that Ara's Dream body now existed in the portion of the Dream created from the same minds that Temm had recently used.

And Ara could hear the echoes.

Each mind Iris Temm had touched from the Dream retained an unconscious memory of the form she had given it, a telepathic recording of what it had been. Ara stretched her own mind outward, listening, feeling, touching.

Duplicating.

Ara was an expert in Dream morphic theory, meaning she had a deep, almost instinctive knowledge of

how the Dream was put together. It also meant that
she was one of the few human Silent whose touch was
delicate enough to recreate what someone else had
done. She used that touch now.

The plain warped and changed. Forms writhed upward from the ground and crawled across the sky. A
moment later, Ara opened her eyes. An autumn forest
stood around her. Gold and scarlet leaves decorated
maple and oak trees, and the faint smell of smoke
hung on the cool air. It was a relaxing environment
with one strange feature—everything was translucent,
ghostlike. The trees looked as if Ara might be able to
push her hand through them, and the leaves looked
like colored tracing paper. This was to be expected.
The people whose subconscious minds Temm had
used to create her Dream were beginning to forget
what they had become for her. Still, it was enough to
see what was going on.

Iris Temm herself sat beneath one of the trees talking with another Silent, a lizardlike karill from the
Henkarill system. Here, Iris was vibrant and alive, her
fair skin smooth instead of bruised, her face animated
instead of still. Her movements were graceful and she
was very pretty. But Ara could see through her as if
she were a ghost.

The voice of the karill was low, and Ara couldn't
make out what it was saying. Ara wondered why Iris
called up a Terran forest instead of the talltrees on
Bellerophon. Perhaps she had been born on Earth or
had spent time there.

Temm and the karill finished their business, and the
karill vanished. Ara knew that once in the solid world
it would doubtless begin transcribing their session,
transferring letters, documents, financial accounts, dip-
lomatic communiques, and other information into
electronic or even hard copy. That was the primary
function of the Silent, keeping the lines of communica-

tion open between planets and systems separated by thousands of light-years and weeks of travel. All Children of Irfan were licensed and bonded, with oaths of secrecy not to reveal or share information that passed through their minds and hands. Temm would soon forget what she had seen, in any case. Short-term memory training was an essential part of the Children's education program, including the "forget" reflex which kept transmitted information out of long-term memory.

No, Ara thought with a small shock. *Iris will never be able to remember or forget anything again.*

The ghostly Iris Temm stretched, stood, and glanced contentedly around her forest. Ara was about to move a bit closer when she felt a ripple in the Dream, like a distortion in the air, and Ara recognized Inspector Tan's presence, though the other woman hadn't created a Dream body for herself. The presence requested permission to approach.

"It's ready, Inspector," Ara said. "Just come slowly. You'll disrupt everything if you appear too fast."

Tan faded into existence. The forest bent and rippled around her until she got her bearings and was able to insert her mind into the scene around her without forcing her own expectations on it and thereby destroying it. She looked around the forest with a sharp, practiced eye.

"Temm's over there. She just finished work," Ara said.

"I'm impressed at the level of detail," Tan said, and her voice was deep and mellow, like a fine wine.

"Thank you," Ara said, a bit mystified. Although Tan's lips moved and Ara heard the words, Ara knew that it was all illusion created by her own subconscious. In the Dream, communication consisted of concepts transferred directly from mind to mind. Ara's mind, however, expected sound and language, so it

provided them for her. Thought became reality in the
Dream. Apparently Tan's conception of her own voice
was different from reality.

At that moment the light level dropped, as if the
sun had fallen to the horizon. The leaves lost their
bright colors and fell to the ground, leaving behind
black, skeletal branches. A cold breeze stirred the pa-
pery leaves with a hiss and a rustle. Dread stole over
Ara like a cold hand. Temm had noticed the change
as well. Confused, Iris remained still, apparently concentrating in an attempt to change the landscape back.
It didn't work.

"Who's there?" Iris called in a frightened voice.
"What are you doing to my turf?"

Another gust of air whirled the leaves around in a
tiny brown tornado. From behind a tree stepped a
man. His back was to Ara and Tan, and all she could
see was that he was tall, with a broad, strong build.
He wore loose black trousers and a dark shirt. A wide-
brimmed black hat covered his hair. Like the rest of
the scene, he was translucent. Temm made a little
squeak and stepped back.

Run, girl! Ara thought, even though she knew how
it had to end. *Get out of the Dream!*

"Darling," the man said. "I'm on my way. I'm coming for you."

This didn't seem to be what Iris Temm had been
expecting him to say. "Coming for me?" she echoed,
puzzled. "What do you mean? Who are you?"

"I love you, you know. You've always known." He
took another step toward her. "We're going to make
love in the flowers. The red ones."

Tan grabbed Ara's arm. "Let's move to the other
side," she hissed. "Maybe we can see his face."

"You don't have to whisper," Ara told her. "They
can't hear us. They aren't really here." But she closed
her eyes and gathered her concentration. A Silent's

relative position in the Dream was based solely on where she expected to be. Right now Ara was *here* and she wanted to be *there*. On the count of three, *there* would be *here*. One . . . two . . . *three*.

There was a slight wrench and Ara opened her eyes. She was standing less than two meters behind Temm. Inspector Tan stood with her. Distortions rippled through the forest, Temm, and the man, as if the scene were reflected in a pool and someone had thrown a pebble in. The conversation between Temm and the man wavered and swooped unintelligibly. Ara cursed herself for not realizing this would happen.

"Hold still," she ordered Tan. "It'll clear sooner if you don't move."

After a moment, the scene settled. The man's features, however, were shrouded in the shadow of the wide-brimmed hat.

"—me alone," Temm was saying. "I don't want you near me."

The man lunged for her. Temm gave a scream and ran. Ara and Tan turned as one to follow her. Then both of them halted and stared. The bare trees came to life. They lashed downward like stiff snakes, trapping Iris Temm in a mesh of branches and bark. The wind rose and howled like a cold living thing. Temm struggled and tore at the branches, but she couldn't get free. Ara's stomach clenched in fear and she had to remind herself that this was nothing more than a recording, that the trees wouldn't—couldn't—attack her. Temm's scream wailed on the wind as the man in the wide-brimmed hat drew close to her.

"You bitch!" he screeched, and smashed her across the face. She screamed again, and Ara noticed the branches had wrapped around her shins and forearms. "I want the flowers! Pretty flowers!"

The branches stiffened and Temm screamed again. Ara realized tears were running down her face. She wanted to run, leave the Dream, or even look away, but she found she couldn't. Inspector Tan's face remained completely impassive. Iris Temm's scream went on and on, mingling with the wind and the growls of the dark man.

"I don't want to do this," he cried to the skies. "Don't make me do this!"

The cold air sliced through Ara's clothes and made the tears on her face feel like rivers of ice. Temm screamed one last time like a banshee howl. With a horrible sound that Ara knew she would never forget, the branches tore the limbs from Iris Temm's body.

The wind stopped. The branches snapped back upward with bony rattle, leaving the bloody pieces of Temm's body behind. As Ara stared in horror, the dark man knelt beside the remains.

"Why did you make me do that?" he said in a calm, chill voice. "You make me do it every time. Every goddamned time."

He reached down and came up with a small, pink object. Ara's gorge rose when she realized it was one of Temm's fingers. A bit of yellow-gray bone poked out of the torn end. Temm's sightless eyes gazed up at the black branches above them. Using the bloody end of the finger like a paintbrush, the man wrote something on Temm's forehead.

Tan leaped forward to get a look. Ara stood frozen where she was. The man flung the finger away and put his hands over his face beneath the hat. Then he vanished like a burst soap bubble. A split second later, so did the ghostly forest and the body of Iris Temm. Ara stood on the featureless plain alone with Tan. Whispers fluttered on the empty air all around them. It was as if the entire thing had never happened.

"Did . . . did you see what he wrote?" Ara asked finally. Her throat was dry and she wanted a drink with more than just water in it.

"Yes." Tan's rich voice was flat. "It's worse than I thought."

"Why? What did he write?"

Tan looked at her. "The number twelve."

Grandfather Melthine ran a hand through his silvery hair as Ara finished the story. They were in his study, a busy-looking office lined with bookdisks and comfortable chairs. Holographic models of spaceships floated just below the ceiling. Outside, the sun was setting, and purple shadows gathered among the talltree branches. The office was a bit stuffy—Melthine preferred to keep the windows shut. Ara occupied a deep armchair, and an empty glass sat on a table at her elbow. Her hands had finally stopped shaking. Inspector Tan sat rigid in another chair while her partner Linus Gray leaned against one wall. He was a tall, spare man, with ash-blond hair that was receding from a high forehead. Around his neck he wore a medallion of worked silver instead of plain gold, a symbol of his position as Inspector with the Guardians of Irfan. Tan, presumably, wore hers underneath her shirt.

"This opens up a great many questions," Melthine said at last. "We need to discuss them."

"You and Mother Ara are the experts in Dream theory," Gray said. "Whatever information you can give us will help."

"The number twelve is significant," Tan said, voice raspy again. "Obviously."

"You think Iris was his twelfth victim?" Ara asked.

Tan shrugged. "Could be. Or he might write the number twelve on all his victims. No way to know yet. If we *assume*"—her emphasis on that word made it clear what she thought of the idea—"that the number twelve means he's killed eleven other people, and if we *assume* he killed the other two finger victims, that would mean there are nine other corpses we don't know about yet. I've already checked the databases. In the entire recorded history we have of Bellerophon, there isn't a single incident in which a murder victim turned up with someone else's finger sewn on."

She sat back in her chair, as if exhausted by the long speech.

"Which means the killer came to us from another planet," Melthine said.

"No," Tan groused. "It only means we've made a lot of assumptions. He might be a native and he hid the other bodies. Or he dropped them off a balcony, fed the dinosaurs. But it looks like we need to operate on the theory that the same person killed all three women and that he's going to do it again."

"I'm not Silent," Gray said, "and I'm nowhere near an expert in Dream theory, but doesn't a Silent's landscape disappear when they leave the Dream or if they die while in it? Temm—and her forest—should have disappeared the moment she died. Why did her Dream body hang around after this hat guy killed her?"

Ara picked up the glass. She could still smell the scotch. "I imagine it did vanish. But *he* recreated her body and her turf long enough to . . . do what he did. That scares the hell out of me."

"Why?" Gray said intently.

"Because he did it without a noticeable break in the scenery. There should have been a flicker or something between the time Iris's Dream ended and he took it over. There wasn't. That means he's highly skilled in the Dream, in addition to being frighteningly powerful."

"Powerful because he could kill her, you mean?" Gray said. "There've been other Dream murders over the centuries, and in all cases the killer had to be more powerful than the victim."

"It's more than just the amount of power." Ara set the glass back down and turned her gaze to the darkening window. "First, he was able to wrench control of her own turf away from her and change it. That means his mind was stronger than Iris's. Second, he was able to disrupt her concentration enough that she couldn't leave the Dream to escape. That isn't easy to do because every Silent knows that the Dream is just that—a dream. You can wake up whenever you want. He scared Iris so much that she forgot this fact. Third, he was powerful enough to convince Iris's mind that she was being torn limb from limb. The human survival instinct is very strong, Inspector. It takes a lot of power to convince someone that they're dead. This guy is both potent and skilled, and the idea that I myself might run across him in the Dream makes me shake."

"What's the official cause of death?" Melthine asked.

"Mental trauma," Gray said. "The patterns of bruises on Temm's body are consistent with being wrapped up and partially crushed by something with an irregular surface, such as a tree branch. Her body created the bruises in psychosomatic response to what happened to her mind in the Dream. Being torn to pieces, however, is more than your average human brain can pull off, so to speak."

Tan pursed her lips. "We need to discuss the finger angle." When the others didn't respond, she continued. "Medical examiner confirmed that Temm's finger was severed and replaced postmortem. Less than an hour after Temm died, in fact. Means that the killer murdered her in the Dream, came into her house afterward, cut the finger off, sewed Wren Hamil's finger on, and left. We've interviewed the neighbors. None of them saw anyone."

"What about her boyfriend?" Melthine said. "Is he a suspect? The neighbors wouldn't think anything of him going inside."

Linus Gray shook his head. "He's not Silent. Genetic scan confirms. He couldn't kill anyone in the Dream. And he has an iron-clad alibi for the time before and after she died. He's a monorail engineer and he was driving one all day. Plenty of witnesses."

"He kills them," Tan mused aloud, "tears off a finger in the Dream, writes a number on their foreheads. Then he goes to their house, cuts a finger off, replaces it with a finger from the last victim."

"Whose finger was sewn onto the first victim— Prinna Meg?" Ara asked. "Do you know?"

"The finger's DNA isn't in any computer records," Gray said. "All we know is that the thing came from a woman and she was Silent."

"So maybe the killer *does* come from off planet," Ara postulated. "The killer brought the finger with him from somewhere else."

"That would seem to follow," Gray agreed.

"What do all the victims have in common?" Tan said. "That might give us a clue, too."

"They're all women," Gray said, ticking his fingers. "They're all Silent, and they're all Children of Irfan."

"Wren Hamil, the second victim, was a student," Melthine pointed out. "Not a full Child."

"But they're all associated with the Children in some way," Gray said. "They were all between eighteen and forty. Hair and eye color are all different. So are height and weight. None of them knew each other as far as we've been able to tell. We'll have to do a deeper comparison just to be sure, but I'm not optimistic."

"Did the forensics team find any clues at Iris's house?" Melthine asked.

"Not yet," Gray replied. "But it doesn't look good

either. No fingerprints, no blood or other body fluids except the victim's. We're looking into fibers, but since there wasn't a struggle where any would get rubbed off, we aren't hopeful."

"Why does he do it?" Ara blurted.

Tan shrugged again. "Been doing some reading, but I'm not an expert on serial killers. Maybe he hates Silent women, or just the Children. Hope we can figure it out. It'll bring us one step closer to catching him." Her face hardened. "We *will* catch him."

They discussed the case further, but brought nothing new to light. Ara walked home, jumping at every shadow and every fluttering leaf. She regretted passing up Tan and Gray's offer of an escort. The warm summer breeze only reminded her of the cold one in the Dream, and it seemed like she could hear Iris Temm's final heartrending scream in the far distance. Once, a dinosaur roared below her and she nearly leaped off the walkway in panic.

When Ara got home, the house was dark. Fear clutched at her and she ran inside. Ben's door was shut. Shakily, Ara opened it and peered inside. Ben lay face up on his bed in a puddle of silver moonlight. The sheets were tangled around him, leaving his bed as messy as the rest of the room. His skin looked like marble, and she saw with relief the gentle rise and fall of his breathing.

She almost ran into the room to gather him close to her, but stopped herself. Ben wouldn't appreciate being woken up, and the logical part of her knew the killer wouldn't come for him. He was male and not—

—not Silent.

Ara looked at her son for a long time, then gently closed the door and went to bed.

SIX

You can't buy friends. You can only shop for them.
—Yeoman Daniel Vik

Kendi Weaver woke with a small start and wondered where he was. The walls and ceiling were white plaster and they smelled of fresh paint. There were no high beams above him, and his pillow wasn't filled with—

Memory returned in a rush. Mother Ara. Bellerophon. The monastery. His room.

His room. Kendi had never had his own room, not in the tiny apartment back in Sydney and certainly not on Mistress Blanc's farm. He sat up. His window faced east, and the sky outside, barely visible between the tree branches, was just beginning to lighten. The cool morning air was scented with damp summer leaves and carried only a fraction of the breath-stopping humidity he had hated back on the farm.

Kendi stretched luxuriously, and his skin slid over smooth white sheets instead of a rough pallet cover. The room was, he supposed, fairly small by most standards, barely five meters by three. It contained only a bed, nightstand, desk, chair, and wardrobe. The white walls were bare except for a darker patch that would become a vidscreen. A set of narrow French doors next to the window led out onto a shared balcony. Birds began hesitant morning song outside.

Kendi had arrived in the room fairly late last night. The paperwork he'd had to fill out at the spaceport had lasted quite a while, and Mother Ara had left the little group in the care of a man named Brother Manny with the explanation that she wanted to get home and see her son. A hasty supper and a whirlwind monorail ride to the dormitory had followed. It had been too dark to see much of his new home, and the exhausted Kendi had fallen almost instantly asleep. A glance at the clock set into the vidscreen told him he had only slept about five hours, but three years of waking at dawn for work were hard to shake. He shoved aside the covers and stood up to stretch. His wrist and ankle felt gloriously bare. Time to get dressed.

The only thing Mistr—that is, *Giselle* Blanc had permitted him to take was the knee-length white tunic she had sold him in. Brother Manny, however, had scrounged up a spare shirt, shorts, and sandals. Kendi pulled them on and trotted up the hall to the community bathroom, which sported individual sink and shower stalls. Not as luxurious as the bathroom he had briefly shared with Pup, but a far cry above the barracklike facilities of the slave barn, especially since he didn't have to rush through his shower. It did take him a moment to figure out that the box set into the wall was a sonic cleanser that would launder his clothes. Afterward, he went back to his room. The sun had just cleared the horizon, but it was high summer and the hour was therefore still very early. Kendi stood next to the bed and realized he had no idea what to do next. His stomach rumbled.

Is someone going to come get me for breakfast? he thought. Maybe he was supposed to figure it out on his own. Would he have to pay for the food?

Then, *Where is Mom waking up?*

The thought struck down the earlier comfortable feeling. Kendi didn't even know who had bought her or where they had taken her. What was she doing right now? He imagined her scared and alone and wanted to run straight out and find her. And then, unbidden, a memory whispered in his mind.

What you cannot change, it said, *accept.*

A creed of the Real People. Kendi, the quick and magical lizard, nodded. He couldn't run out to find his mother or the rest of his family now, but that didn't mean he couldn't do it later.

Voices murmured from outside. Kendi pushed the thoughts aside and stuck his head out the French doors. He caught his breath. The view, which he hadn't been able to see last night, was spectacular. The dormitory was built into one of the tallest trees in the forest, and new-student rooms were on the highest floor. Beyond the branches framing the balcony, Kendi saw a vast carpet of white fog that stretched all the way to the horizon, where a scarlet sun was slowly edging upward. Gargantuan treetops poked up out of the mist, and small flying creatures skimmed over it like insects. It was like looking at a giant's garden.

A small group of people had gathered on the balcony, which ran the length of the floor and was shared by several rooms. With relief Kendi recognized Jeren, Kite, and Willa. Kite saw him and waved him over.

"Cantsleeptherhuh?" he said.

Kendi untangled the blur of words. "Nope. I want to explore. Is the whole monastery up in the treetops, do you think?"

Jeren spat over the side and watched it fall. "Hell of a long drop if you fell over. How long do you think it'd take before you splattered all over the ground?"

"Don't," Willa said with a shudder. "How can you even stand to look?"

Jeren grinned at her and jumped up to the waist-high balcony rail to balance on it like a cat. Willa shrieked and clapped her hands over her eyes. Kite looked concerned. Kendi swallowed.

"Jeren," Kendi said hesitantly. "Maybe you shouldn't—"

"Hey, it's easy," Jeren said. He strolled casually up

and down the rail, then paused to look down. White mist buried the ground below.

"Don'thinkyoush—"

"Whoa!" Jeren frantically windmilled his arms. Willa, who had been peeking between her fingers, screamed. Kendi lunged for Jeren, but he regained his balance with an easy grin. "Gotcha!" he laughed. Kendi scowled and suppressed an urge to punch him.

"That earns you demerits, guy," said a new voice.

They all turned to look. A young woman was striding toward them. She had curly black hair and emerald eyes set into a sharp, pixielike face. Her movements were quick and darting as a hummingbird's. A simple gold medallion hung around her neck. She looked to be in her mid-twenties.

"Hey, Sis," Jeren said. "Am I in trouble then?"

"I'm not a Sister yet, bucko," the woman replied. "I'm a second-year student and I've been assigned as your mentor. My name's Dorna Saline. Jeren, come down from there before I beat your ass."

With a flourish, Jeren jumped to the balcony floor. Willa lowered her hands.

"If you want to play with heights, Jeren, use one of those," she said, and pointed to two ropes that ended in knots big enough to sit on. The other ends were tied to branches higher up. They were clearly designed to swing out beyond the balcony, and Kendi wondered who would be brave enough—or stupid enough—to swing on such a thing. As if reading his thoughts, Dorna added, "There's a net below to catch you if you fall, Kendi. You just can't see it for the mist, yeah?"

"Howdyknowournames?" Kite asked.

"Mother Ara described you," Dorna said. "Kite, right? And you're Willa and you're Kendi. Welcome to the Children of Irfan. You probably want breakfast, yeah?"

They all assented, and Dorna took them to the end

of the balcony and down a set of stairs to a wooden walkway that led around to the front of the dormitory. Kendi looked up at it, fascinated. He hadn't been able to see much last night. The building was enormous, fully five-stories high, and it was the only building in the entire tree. The trunk ran up the middle of the building, and several branches supported it as well. Other branches framed it in fine green leaves. The dorm itself was built of warm brown wood and covered with ivy. Balconies jutted out everywhere, connected by ladders, staircases, and even sliding poles. Ropes dangled from a fair number of windows. Fresh morning dew coated every surface. The double doors in front opened onto a wide deck big enough to play rugby on. Kendi looked over the edge. An ocean of white mist obscured the forest floor below. He decided the entire place was beautiful, more homelike than any place he had ever lived. His mother would love it, and he wished with all his heart that he could show it to his entire family.

One day, he told himself firmly.

Dorna lead them through the main doors, waved to the sleepy desk clerk on duty in the high-ceilinged foyer, and herded them into a cafeteria. A food buffet took up one wall and the room was filled with long tables furnished with wooden chairs.

"You can get food at any hour, day or night," Dorna told them, "but there's a schedule for hot food. It's pretty good slop, right? We're too soon for hot breakfast, but I know that ex-slaves are always up early, so I thought I'd bring you down."

Ex-slaves, Kendi thought. *I'm an ex-slave.*

After a breakfast of cold cereal, rolls, and juice, Dorna shepherded them back outside for a tour of the monastery.

"It's kind of confusing at first," she said as they headed out, "real easy to lose your way, yeah?"

A few minutes later, Kendi indeed found himself

thoroughly lost. Because the monastery—and everything else—was constructed in the top of a giant forest, there was no way to make a regular grid of streets. Walkways and staircases made of planks and ivy-draped wire ran in many different directions on a dozen different levels. The buildings varied in size from small cottages to multistory edifices like the student dormitory, but they were all made of wood and were of similar design, making it hard to tell them apart. Some were living quarters, some were academic buildings for teaching and research, and some were business offices. Dorna pointed out the places where they'd be taking their classes, and Kendi hoped he could get his hands on a map so he could find them again.

The group walked slowly, chatting and pointing out things of interest. Dorna guided them unhurriedly along, allowing them to take in what sights they liked.

The sun, now well above the horizon, had burned off most of the mist below. Kendi quickly learned to ignore the sight of the stomach-wrenching drop that lay in wait everywhere. The air was sweet, warm, and clean, and birds mingled with small gliding lizards among the leaves, both filling the morning with song. As the morning grew old, people began to appear on the walkways and in the metal gondolas that coasted by on a system of wires and electric pulleys. Many, though not all, wore loose brown clothes and the simple gold medallions that marked them as Children of Irfan.

"Are all the Children Silent?" Willa asked at one point.

Dorna nodded, her dark curls bobbing. "Gotta be. But the monastery also employs plenty of non-Silent, both here and in the field."

"Do we have to wear brown like that?" Jeren said. "It's kind of dull, you know?"

"You can wear whatever you want, guy," Dorna replied indifferently. "Most of the Children and the students wear brown shirts or robes so everyone knows they're Silent, right? But you don't have to. You gotta wear the medallion, though."

"What are those for?" Kendi asked. "I was wondering."

Dorna went down a staircase backward like a tour guide facing her charges. "The medallion says you're under Irfan's protection and a member of the order. Only the Children and their students are allowed to wear them."

The walkways swayed under their steps. The movement didn't bother Kendi, though Willa was looking a trifle green. He glanced ahead of them and caught his breath. Coming up behind Dorna, who still walked backward, was a creature the size of a small horse. Blond fur covered a stocky body and four legs that ended in heavily clawed feet. A thick, sinuous neck rose from the shoulders between a pair of muscular arms that ended in four-fingered hands. The creature's head was flat, with wide-set, bulgy eyes and a flat mouth filled with shovellike teeth. There was a hole on the creature's forehead just above the eyes. Its forelegs were thicker and sturdier than its shorter hind legs, which gave a downward slant to the creature's back. Kendi stared in spite of himself, as did the others. Dorna noticed and turned to see what was going on.

"Father Ched-Hisak!" she said, and pressed her fingertips to her forehead in a gesture Kendi didn't recognize. "You're up early today, yeah?"

The creature made a chattering noise by rattling its lower jaw against the upper. It also made hooting sounds through the hole in its forehead.

"I'm showing around a new group of students," Dorna told him. "They just arrived last night. This is Jeren, Willa, Kite, and Kendi." Again she pressed fingertips to forehead, this time pointedly, until Kendi and the others got the hint and duplicated the gesture. Kendi couldn't help but stare. For all his bulky build, Ched-Hisak moved with a languid grace Kendi found compelling. Even Jeren seemed awed.

Father Ched-Hisak made more chattering and hooting noises. Kendi noticed he wore a gold medallion around his neck and a jade ring on one thick finger.

"He says he's glad that Irfan guided your steps to this place," Dorna translated, "and he looks forward to seeing you in his classroom one day, right?"

"He's going to teach us?" Willa blurted out.

Dorna laughed and Ched-Hisak hooted. "Sure. Lots of your teachers will be Ched-Balaar. They brought humans into the Dream when Irfan Qasad and her people arrived on Bellerophon—what?—nine hundred years ago, and they're really good at teaching."

"How will we communicate?" Kendi asked.

"You'll learn their language, just like they learned ours," Dorna said. "Humans can't make their speech sounds and they can't make ours, but you can learn to understand."

Ched-Hisak spoke again.

"Thanks, Father," Dorna said. "We'll see you around, yeah?"

He trotted away, claws clicking on the hard wood. Kendi watched him go and with a start he realized Dorna had continued on her way again and he had to trot to catch up.

"—use a translator or something?" Jeren was asking.

Dorna shrugged. "It's partly because translators can fail and partly because we've always done it that way, right? You show your respect for the culture by learning their language yourself."

"Wheredtheycomefrom?" Kite said.

"They call their home planet 'the world,'" Dorna

told him. "You'll learn more about them in history class, but the short version is that Irfan Qasad, the lady who started the Children, was the captain of a slower-than-light colony ship from Earth in the old days, back before slipships, right? When she and her people arrived at Bellerophon, they found the Ched-Balaar had already got here and claimed the place. Lucky for us humans, the Ched-Balaar were willing to share. No one knows exactly why, because most of the records from that period were lost or destroyed. A lot of people think the Ched-Balaar suspected us humans could enter the Dream and they wanted to bring us into it, right? According to legend, they told Irfan that she had to participate in some kind of ceremony. You know—to cement relations between the species? During the ceremony, the Ched-Balaar gave her a drug that allowed her to go into the Dream. She was the first human Silent, but they didn't call it that yet, yeah?"

"Why do they call us Silent?" Jeren asked.

"No one knows for sure," Dorna said. "Best guess is that it comes from the fact that human children who carry the genes for Silence don't talk 'til they're older and don't cry much as babies. Silent children, right?"

A roar thundered from below. Another roar answered it, and a second and a third. Jeren leaned over the ivy-covered railing, trying to peer down between the branches. Willa clapped her hands over her ears with a squeak. Kendi joined Jeren, but the branches beneath them were too thick to afford a view, to his disappointment.

"Whazzat?" Kite asked.

"Dinosaur." Dorna also leaned over the railing. "A big lizard. That sounds like a pod of mickey spikes. Plant-eaters as big as a truck. Harmless, unless you threaten their kids or are standing where they want to step. And they're the smaller ones."

"Is that why we're up here?" Kendi said. "Because they're down there?"

"You got it. The colonists could probably have cleared 'em out, but no one wanted to mess up Bellerophon like Earth got messed up. So they built up in the trees." She made *ook-ook* noises. "Like monkeys, right? Me, I like it up here."

"And a good thing, since we're up here to stay." Everyone turned. Ara, wearing a brown robe of her own, was approaching on the walkway. "Good morning, everyone. I see Dorna got you up and going.'

"Good morning, Mother." Dorna pressed fingertips to forehead as she had for Father Ched-Hisak. "You look tired."

Kendi, who was saluting in imitation of Dorna, saw that Ara did indeed look tired. Her eyes were heavy and her face was haggard.

"Trouble sleeping," she said. "But that's a minor matter." She turned to the little group of ex-slaves. "Did Dorna get you all fed?"

They nodded assent.

"Good." Ara smiled. "I'm a mom as well as a Mother, and I need to know you ate a good breakfast. Next, we're going shopping."

Jeren groaned. "I knew it. Fucking disaster."

"If you want to wear the same shirt every day, be my guest," Ara said. "Far be it from me to force civilization on you. But the rest of us like a little variety."

In the end, Jeren agreed to come, and Kendi was sure his grumbling was mostly for show. Ara piled them into one of the gondolas, which glided swiftly along its heavy cable. Houses, decks and walkways coasted by. The monastery was a busy place, and its byways bustled with humans and Ched-Balaar alike as the morning slipped by. A few other aliens also entered the mix. A human child scampered down a rope ladder that hung from a window and was followed by a second child. Peals of laughter faded in and out as the gondola passed.

"Does anyone ever go down to the ground?" Willa asked in her soft voice. She was sitting between Ara and Dorna, refusing to look over the side. Kendi, Jeren, and Kite occupied the bench across from them. Ara, however, didn't seem to hear Willa's question. She was staring into the distance, a distracted expression on her face. She was obviously thinking about something, though Kendi had no idea what it might be.

"Mother?" Dorna said.

With a start, Ara came to herself. "Sorry. I was woolgathering. What was the question?"

Willa repeated it.

"People visit the ground lots of times," Ara said. "The spaceport is on the ground, of course, and we also have to pump water up from the lakes and underground reservoirs. We have farming areas, too, but we try to keep that to a minimum. You can turn out a surprisingly large amount of food with some creative genetic engineering and a good greenhouse."

"Who runs everything?" Kendi asked.

"That's a little complicated, actually," Ara replied. "There's Treetown—don't laugh at the name, thank you—and there's the Blessed and Most Beautiful Monastery of the Children of Irfan, or 'the monastery,' as everyone usually calls it. Irfan Qasad founded both of them, though Treetown wasn't much of a town back then. Later she founded the monastery several kilometers away as a separate entity. In modern times, though, Treetown spread and eventually surrounded us, so we're a state-within-a-state. The Grandparent Adepts run things here, and the Co-Council runs Treetown, but the two groups are strong allies. We share the spaceport, for example, and the monastery owns a great deal of farmland just outside Treetown's borders, so everything's tangled together. There are other city-states on this continent, but Treetown and the monastery are the biggest ones."

"What's the ring for?" Jeren pointed at the emerald ring on Ara's hand.

"It indicates rank. Students like yourselves wear a ruby ring. You'll each get one soon. Topaz indicates someone who has finished studying and is now an apprentice Child. Amber is for full Siblings—Brothers and Sisters. Mothers and Fathers wear jade or emerald. The next rank is Mother or Father Adept. Their rings are blue. Grandparents have fluorite rings—indigo. And a Grandparent Adept—the highest rank— wears a ring of violet amethyst."

Willa clapped her hands. "It goes right up the rainbow!"

"Very good," Ara said. "You're an observant young woman."

Willa flushed deeply, even disproportionately, and Kendi wondered how often in Willa's life she had heard praise. He leaned over the side and watched the green growth far below for a moment, then returned his attention to the gondola. He felt comfortable in Ara's company, even relaxed. In fact, he felt more relaxed than he had in days.

The gondola coasted into a little station that, Ara explained, would send the car on a parallel wire back in the direction they had come. Several people were waiting in line for a ride, most of them dressed in brown, and six of them boarded after Kendi and the others had disembarked with the help of an attendant. The gondola coasted smoothly around a semicircle and vanished into the branches. Ara took them down a staircase and along another walkway.

"Where are we?" Kendi asked.

"Shopping district in Treetown," Ara replied. "Like I said, the city grew around the monastery and a lot of the people work for the Children or have family that do."

Kendi looked around. The buildings looked much like the monastery, except they had larger front windows with various products on display. They were obviously stores, but completely unlike the cold, sterile malls back in Sydney—malls that he had last visited over nine hundred years ago, he remembered with a strange pang. The people who had worked and shopped there were long since dust.

Ara chose the closest shop, a two-story place called "Millicent's," and held the odor open for them. "First stop," she announced, "fashion!"

Kendi paused in the doorway. "How do we pay for this?"

"Like I said back on the ship, the Children will pick up your living expenses, including clothes," Ara said. "You'll eventually have to pay it back, but we don't charge interest like the corporations do. Irfan herself made that rule, and I think it's a good one. The monetary unit on Bellerophon is the freemark. For comparison, five freemarks will get you a meal at a fast-cook restaurant. For ten freemarks, you can get a meal at a decent place, and for thirty, you get linen tablecloths and waiters with towels draped over their arms."

The interior of the store smelled like fresh leather and new cloth. It was a large place, with two sets of spiral staircases that wound upward to a balcony that ringed the main floor. Clothing of all kind hung in attractive displays and on the high walls themselves. Kendi looked around in awe. He hadn't bought anything in his three years as a slave on Giselle Blanc's farm, and before that his family had been too poor to shop in a place like this. The abundance of choice was overwhelming. The others stood near him, equally dumbfounded and uncertain.

"Go." Ara made shooing motions with her arms. "Bother the sales clerks. Try things on. Get!"

"Come on, Willa," Dorna said. "Let's see what we can find you. The boys are on their own." She towed an unprotesting Willa away.

Jeren caught sight of something and broke into a grin. "Whoa! I'm there!" He grabbed Kite's sleeves and headed toward a display of black leather.

"I guess that just leaves the two of us," Ara said to Kendi with a smile. "Let me look at you." She held him at arm's length. "Hmmmmm. You're in luck. I think brown's your color, and it's all the rage this year."

Kendi laughed. "All the well-dressed monks are wearing it?"

"You know it. Come on."

They spent a pleasant two hours picking out various articles of clothing, including socks and underwear. The sense of choice and freedom was overpowering. He could, in theory, have anything in the store, and no one seemed inclined to tell him to hurry up. The clerk brought things to him and put away what he didn't want. Kendi loved it.

Ara, meanwhile, informed Kendi that although they were now in high summer and the weather was warm, Bellerophon was overall cooler and rainier than July IV and Australia, which necessitated buying sweaters, thick trousers, rain gear, and heavy shirts. They were more expensive than the shorts and thin T-shirts that had made up the majority of his wardrobe back in Sydney, and the unexpected high prices dampened some of Kendi's enthusiasm. Despite Ara's urgings— "High quality will last longer and look better, too"— Kendi did his best to be careful. His one extravagance was a pair of fine suede boots. They were soft as butter and came up almost to his knees.

"This is the matching jacket," said the sales clerk, putting it around Kendi's shoulders.

Kendi shrugged into it and looked into the mirror. He caught his breath. The jacket looked wonderful. It molded itself to his body as if it had been tailored for him. The suede was soft and the color was a bit lighter than his skin, creating a pleasing contrast. It smelled of new leather.

"That looks perfect," Ara breathed behind him. "Kendi, that's you. Really."

"Already waterproofed for you," the clerk said. "And it has a lifetime guarantee. If you outgrow it, come back and we'll make alterations. Same for the boots."

Kendi turned this way and that, admiring the way the jacket moved with him. Ara was right—it was him. He had never owned anything like it, and he wanted it like he had wanted nothing else. "How much?" he asked.

"Four hundred freemarks," the clerk told him, and Kendi blanched.

"Too much," he said, reluctantly removing it. "I've already spent more than I should have on the boots."

"Oh, get it anyway," Ara said. "You deserve it."

"Enabling the shoppers again, Mother?" said Dorna, who came up at that moment. "I swear you'd offer champagne to a recovering drunk."

"Irfan said nothing about extravagance being evil," Ara sniffed.

"No, but the Real People did—do," Kendi put in.

"The Real People?" Ara repeated, puzzled.

He handed the jacket to the clerk, who accepted it without comment. "My . . . tribe. Balance and moderation in all things. I can justify the boots—I need good ones—but not the jacket."

"You've been a slave for three years, Kendi," Ara said quietly. "You should indulge yourself a little. And you'll be able to pay it back. Your Silence is strong, and you'll be a Brother pretty quick."

Kendi looked at the jacket in the clerk's hand one more time. He could still feel its suppleness, smell the sweet leather scent. Then he firmly shook his head, though he couldn't keep the disappointment out of his voice. "I can't. It's too much. The boots are indulgence enough."

"Your decision, then." Ara shrugged. "Let's check on the others."

Willa, Kite, and Jeren had all piled up an impressive quantity of clothing. Despite his earlier comments, Jeren hadn't stocked his entire wardrobe with black leather, though his taste in clothing ran toward daring and brash. Kite had chosen a real mishmash of styles, and Willa had selected a large number of mousy brown robes and dresses all in the same conservative cut.

"It's all she'd buy," Dorna said in mock despair. "We'll have to work on her." And Willa flushed again.

"Bill and deliver these, Mother?" asked the clerk.

"Yes, please," Ara said, and gave him the address. "Thanks for your help."

Kendi gave the suede jacket one last wistful glance as they left the store, then sighed and promised himself he'd come back and get it—or one like it—as soon as he had paid to the monastery whatever debts he incurred.

Outside, Ara declared it was time for lunch—her treat. She ushered them to an outdoor cafe where they took up a table in the shade by the railing. They had just finished ordering when a rumbling vibration shook the floor and rattled the dishes on the table.

"What the hell?" Jeren said.

Dorna looked over the railing and pointed down. "There. Take a look."

Kendi, Kite, and Jeren peered over the rail. Several

other restaurant patrons joined them. Willa hung back. Far below, well over a dozen heavy, blimpy shapes with long necks and whiplike tails moved with surprising agility. The distance and perspective made it hard for Kendi to figure out how big they were. Their heavy feet tromped the ground, making even the giant trees shake.

"They're each the size of a small house, right?" Dorna said when Kendi asked. "Lots bigger than a mickey spike. They're slow and stupid and they'll accidentally step on anything that gets in their way, so don't get too close, yeah?"

"I wonder what it'd be like to ride one," Kendi said.

Ara patted her chest in mock horror. "That kind of risk I can live without, thank you," she said. "I have enough adventure in my life without adding a dinosaur rodeo."

The group came back to the table. "ZbeingChildciting?" Kite asked.

Ara didn't answer. Once again, her gaze was fixed in the distance.

"Mother Ara?" Kendi said. "Are you all right?"

She blinked. "Woolgathering again. Sorry. Did you ask something?"

"ZbeingChildciting?" Kite repeated.

"Is being a Child exciting? It depends on what you do," Ara said. "I do field work and recruiting, so sometimes I run into . . . challenges." She laughed. "I have more fake IDs than most criminals. But I'm the exception. Most of us relay communication through the Dream or teach or do research. Once you get your degree, you can do pretty much whatever you want."

"Degree?" Willa whispered.

"Oh yes. You have to have a degree to operate in the Dream. Or you do if you want to work for us, anyway. The monastery will provide you with an extensive general education and you can choose a couple of specialties."

"Like what?" Jeren asked.

Their food arrived. The server placed high-piled plates in front of them. Kendi had ordered a ham sandwich with french fries—some foods had apparently lasted across centuries and light-years—and the salty smells that assailed his nose were delicious. The sandwich all but dripped with some sort of white sauce with a sweet, spicy tang to it. The fries were hot and crisp, and Kendi almost groaned when he ate the first one. French fries hadn't been on the menu for slaves at Giselle Blanc's frog farm and it had been years since he'd tasted them.

The server left, and Ara answered Jeren's question. "You can specialize in just about anything offered at a non-Silent university. Math, music, computers, genetics, piloting—"

Kendi all but bolted upright in his chair. "Piloting? You mean like spaceship piloting?"

"Sure. We always need good pilots in the field. You can study anything you wish. As Irfan said, 'The greater your knowledge, the lesser your risk.' "

Kendi saw himself at the helm of a starship, swooping through a field of enemy fire, dodging laser beams by the thinnest of margins. The science fiction sims had been his favorites when he was a kid, and he had always wanted to be the one in the pilot seat in every game. Not only that, as a pilot he'd have a better chance of getting out into space and finding his family.

"Kendiareyouhey!" Kite snatched back his hand, but not before the jolt slapped Kendi all the way down to his feet. He rubbed his arm where Kite had touched him.

"Careful, guy," Dorna said. "Whenever you touch someone around here for the first time, you're likely to get jolted."

"Sorrykendi," Kite said.

"It's okay." Kendi continued rubbing his arm, and something occurred to him. "My mom is Silent. How come I never felt a jolt from her?"

"I imagine you touched your mother all the time," Ara said. "You probably got jolted at some point—most Silent start that up at about age ten—but since you didn't know what it was, you may have figured it was something like a static electricity shock and forgotten about it."

Kendi looked down at his sandwich piled high with tender ham and wondered what his mother was eating. Suddenly even the fries seemed less appetizing. "I'm going to find her, and the rest of them. They're out there, and I'll find them eventually, no matter what."

"We'll help you," Ara said seriously. "The Children don't condone slavery—Irfan herself was dead set against it—and we work hard to get people out of it wherever we can."

The Children would help him? That made Kendi feel a little better. And it did make sense. After all, Ara had freed *him*. But how long would it take before he could go looking, and how long would it take to find them?

"Irfan was the first Silent human, right?" Jeren said. "Everyone talks about her like she's some kind of goddess. Do you guys pray to her or what?"

Ara smiled. "The Children don't tell you who to pray to. But Irfan Qasad was an intelligent, powerful woman, and a lot of people call on her memory for guidance. She governed Bellerophon for a long time until she resigned to start the Children, and it was because of her that Silent communication became essential to the galaxy. It was that communication that allowed the invention of slipships, in fact." Ara's voice was full of admiration.

"What happened to her?" Kendi asked.

"History is unclear," Ara said. "Most of her writings were lost or destroyed, and Irfan herself quietly vanished. Not even her own children seemed to know where she went—or they pretended they didn't. Some people say she went back to her husband, Daniel Vik." Ara spat the name as if it left a bad taste in her mouth. "But I'm not one of them. Irfan Qasad wouldn't be so stupid."

"Who was Daniel Vik?" Jeren said.

"A filthy man, one of the worst villains in history," Ara told him. "He hated all Silent and went literally insane when he discovered Silence among his own children. Why Irfan married him in the first place is a mystery. When she finally saw through Vik and demanded a divorce, he retaliated by kidnapping one of their sons and running off to the other side of the continent to what eventually became the city-state Othertown. Some people take the fact that he left as evidence that he wasn't actually the father of her children—or at least of the ones he abandoned. Vik assassinated his way to dictatorship and declared his intention to start a genocidal war on all human Silent. Irfan barely managed to stop him, though she couldn't remove him from office. She worked the rest of her life to keep him from starting that war."

"What happened to him?" Kendi asked, fascinated.

"He was assassinated himself," Ara said. "A deserved end, if you ask me. Now who's up for dessert? The ice cream here is really good."

After lunch, Ara took them back to the monastery, where in a bright, airy room they took a battery of tests on a variety of subject matters. The tests, Ara told them, would give the Children an idea of what classes each of them would need and what aptitudes each of them might have. When the results came back, Kendi found he had scored well in math and poorly in everything else. Humiliation burned in his cheeks when he saw that his scores were the lowest in the entire group. Ara, noticing his discomfort, drew him aside and put an arm around him.

"You have nothing to be ashamed of," she told him quietly. "You've been in cryo-sleep for nine hundred years and after that you were kept in ignorance on a backwoods frog farm. The principles of general mathematics haven't changed in nine hundred years, but everything else has. No one thinks you're stupid, Kendi. Certainly not me. Everything I've seen about you tells me you're frighteningly intelligent, and I think your teachers are in for a challenge if they want to keep up with you."

Kendi managed a nod. He still felt stupid.

"And look at this." Ara pointed to a section on the computer pad's holographic screen that reported his scores in dreadful red numbers. "You do have an aptitude for piloting. When you're a little older, they'll want to start you on it."

Kendi's eyes went round. Excitement made short work of the humiliation. "You think so?"

"Looks that way to me. We'll have to see." She turned to the others. "It's getting on toward supper. Your clothes should have been delivered to your rooms by now. Why don't all of you go unpack and eat? The evening is yours to do as you like. There's a sim parlor on the bottom floor of the dorm if you're into that. Explore the place or laze around—whatever you want to do."

When Kendi got back to his room, he found a large box on his bed. His clothes had arrived as Ara had predicted. Humming to himself, he opened the package and froze. With an astonished whistle he reached inside and pulled out the suede jacket. The smell of fine leather instantly surrounded him. A paper note was pinned to the lapel. *If you can't think of it as a*

*gift from me, think of it as an indulgence from Irfan.
Best, Mother Ara.*

Kendi hesitated, then pulled on the jacket with a wide, happy grin.

Ara strolled toward home, feeling truly good for the first time all day. Orienting new students was one of her favorite activities, and she particularly liked this group, Kendi especially. Maybe it was because he seemed so bright and open where her own son Ben was closed and reticent, or maybe it was because she could see Kendi had goals set for himself and firmly intended to see them through, a philosophy she admired. The impulse to buy him the jacket had been one she had decided not to resist, though it also meant dodging back to the store during the testing to buy presents for the other three as well: a black silk shirt for Jeren, a finely woven shawl for Willa, and a soft blue sweater for Kite. Ah well. She was a full Mother now and could afford the occasional impulse buy. The shopping had also taken her mind off the grisly murder.

At that, memories of the terrifying scene in the Dream slashed through her amiable mood. She felt heavy, as if the local gravity had increased. What kind of monster could do that to another human being? That he would do it again, she had no doubt. The problem was their lack of clues. The Dream left no physical evidence, and the Guardians hadn't found any at the murder site. How could they track a killer that left no traces?

Her stomach growled for supper and the walkway swayed gently under her footsteps. Ara shook her head. The investigation wasn't really her problem. She had been brought in as a consultant and she had done her job. Everything else was up to Inspector Tan and Inspector Gray.

Ara snorted. Tan and Gray. She hadn't noticed that before. Still, she couldn't get her mind off poor Iris Temm. Someone had to catch the man. Maybe she would check with the inspectors later and see if anything had turned up. Something they said might lend Ara an insight that would help them.

A shudder passed through her. Did she want more details? She firmly pushed the case into the back of her mind and brought her thoughts back to the new students. Tomorrow they would register for classes, and Ara would have to speak to Toshi about flying lessons for Kendi.

Kendi. Ara let her hand trail along the ivy-colored cable that held up the walkway. It had been almost two years since she'd taken on a private student, and she hadn't had an actual apprentice in twice that time. Ara had little patience for classroom instruction, but she greatly enjoyed small group and one-on-one teaching. Taking on students—and, later, apprentices—was also an unspoken requirement for promotion within the ranks of the Children. Ara was the youngest Silent to reach the rank of Parent and, at age forty-one, she was within spitting distance of becoming the youngest Parent Adept. Murder investigation or not, it was time to take on another student.

And who better than Kendi?

SEVEN

Would that my body could fly as do my thoughts. Unfortunately, genetic engineering can only do so much.

—Irfan Qasad

The cliff reached up to the sky. Atop it, Kendi spread his arms to the sun. Voices whispered at him, muttered in his ear, plucked at him with ghostly fingers of sound, but they didn't bother him. They were perfectly normal. The scalding sun felt good on his bare skin, and a hot breeze rushed past him, bringing the smell of dust and baking vegetation.

And then he heard his mother's voice. Kendi stiffened. He whipped his head around, trying to locate the source of the sound, but the whisper had already retreated. Had he heard it at all, or was he just imagining?

"Mom?" he said. "Are you there?"

The whispers continued to hover in the breeze around him, but none of them sounded familiar. Heated dust assailed Kendi's nostrils. He strained to listen, his heart pounding. Every fiber of his body ached for his missing family. He missed Utang's blue eyes, his mother's rich voice, his father's warm laugh, Martina's little fingers as she took his hand to cross the street. Kendi missed them like he might miss walking or breathing. In some ways it would have been better if he knew they were dead. It was somehow worse knowing that they were out there somewhere, but he couldn't talk to them, let them know that he was all right, find out if they were safe. It made him want to cry. It made him want to hit and scream and

yell and jump off the edge of the cliff. Instead he
stood and listened to the wind.

Just a word, he pleaded. *All I need is a word. Are
you there?*

The whispering mingled with the breeze, but none
of it sounded familiar. After a long moment, Kendi
went to the edge of the cliff and looked down. The
rocky ground lay some fifty meters below. Kendi wondered what would happen if he simply stepped over
the edge. Would he feel anything when he smacked
into the stones? Or were the stories true that you died
of a heart attack just before you hit? He put a foot
over the edge, then jerked it back with a little thrill
of fear once, twice, three times. Then he stared down
at the faraway ground with a hypnotized fascination.
Finally he shook his head, turned around, and slowly
lowered himself over the side. Finding hand- and foot-
holds with practiced ease, he clambered down the
sheer slope until he reached the base of the cliff.

A camel waited for him at the bottom. Kendi nodded to it. Camels weren't native to the Outback, but
centuries ago someone, probably an opal prospector,
had gotten the bright idea that they would make ideal
pack animals for the Australian desert and had a
bunch shipped in. Kendi gave a mental shake of his
head. The idea of packing a herd of foul-tempered,
biting beasts that spit and smelled onto a sailing ship
and then putting up with them for a week or more
during the voyage across the Pacific to Australia made
Kendi laugh and shudder in alternating doses.

A hold full of seasick camels, he thought. *Would
that qualify as sadism or masochism?*

Inevitably, a few camels had escaped and made their
way into the wild, where they had adapted themselves
remarkably well to the local ecology. The original
Real People ate them as necessary, and their bladders
made excellent, if overlarge, waterskins.

"Sister, may I ride?" Kendi asked.

The camel spat something brown and foul and gave Kendi a look that managed to resemble a shrug. Kendi gave a great leap and landed with the grace of a gazelle on top of the camel's single hump, even though the camel was taller than Kendi. The moment he had his balance, the camel took off at a galumphing run. Kendi clung to the dusty, furry hump with hands and thighs, whooping as the camel sped over the rough terrain. Bright wind and sunlight rushed past him while rock and sandy soil blurred into a single brown mass. They came across a billabong, a muddy water hole surrounded by scrubby trees and bushes. Birds called to each other among the leaves. The camel came to a halt. Kendi leaped down as the camel changed into a crocodile, which slid into the water and vanished. Kendi waved good-bye to her.

~ . . . *evan* . . . ~

Kendi jumped. This time he was sure he had heard it—his mother's voice. She wouldn't know his name was Kendi now, had called him by his birth name. She was here, somewhere. His heart came back into his throat and he spun around, trying to look in all directions at once. All he saw was the still billabong, the scrubby trees, and the endless Outback.

"Mom?" he called. "Mom, I can hear you! Where are you?"

He strained to listen. The endless whispering continued, but Rebecca Weaver's voice wasn't in it. Kendi closed his eyes, trying to sort through the babble of soft voices. She had to be there. She *was* there. It hadn't been a mistake or his imagination.

The breeze died around him and the whispers began to fade. Kendi kept his eyes tightly shut, staring into the darkness behind his eyelids, listening with every iota of his being. But the whispers grew softer still.

"Mom?" he said in a small voice. No answer.

He opened his eyes and stared at a blank white ceiling. Kendi blinked at it. *What the hell?* The air was a bit chilly, and he was lying down. It took him a moment to figure out he was lying in a comfortable bed in his new room at the monastery of the Children of Irfan. He sat up, a little dazed. Was the dream the Outback? Or was the dream this room?

The Outback, he decided, and lay back again with a sigh. The Outback dreams were coming with more intensity and reality of late, but they were nothing more than a symptom of Silence. The monastery was reality, as was his room and his bed. At least it was a pleasant place, one he was beginning to like. The intense longing he had felt for his family faded until it was bearable, though it didn't vanish entirely. He suspected it never would.

Outside the window, Kendi could see the sky had lightened only barely. Awake before dawn again. For a moment he lay in his warm bed, luxuriating in the fact that he didn't have to get up. He tried to drift back to sleep, but his mind was broadly awake. There was a whole alien planet out there, with a monastery and a city to explore.

And he was free.

Eventually he gave up sleep as a lost cause and pushed the covers aside. After a quick shower, he pulled on his—*his!*—new clothes, including the suede boots. He was reaching for the jacket and found himself hesitating. Should he wear it? Mother Ara's note said it was a present, but it had been a terribly expensive one and he didn't quite know how to react. No one had ever given him anything like it before. Should he write her a thank-you note? Thank her in person? Pretend it had never happened? For a brief moment, he wished she hadn't given it to him, creating this whole dilemma. Then he flashed on one of his family's interminable visits to the Outback and the words of a woman who called herself Firestarter.

A true gift doesn't put any obligation on you, she said. *Say thank you once to be polite, and then use the gift however you want.* She had then given him a set of fire-starting tools. They had been among his things on board the colony ship, though they had doubtless been ejected into space three years ago, along with anything else the slavers had decided was garbage. The thought made Kendi angry. All his possessions and those of his family—stolen or tossed aside, with no way to recover them. Irreplaceable family holograms and photographs, mementos, his favorite shirt, the journal he had kept for a year when he was in grade school—all gone forever, along with the three years of life Giselle Blanc had taken from him. She had also taken his mother. The anger grew until Kendi's hands hurt and he realized he was clutching at the suede jacket so hard his knuckles had gone pale. He made himself relax his fingers and stretch them, wincing at the pain. The anger remained. He wanted to get back at the slavers and at Giselle Blanc, find them and somehow make them understand what they had done to him, make them pay for it.

Not that he ever could. Giselle Blanc was wealthy and on a planet far away from Bellerophon. And who were the slavers? He didn't even know their names, let alone how to find them. He was stranded here on Bellerophon while his family lay scattered across thousands, perhaps millions, of light-years. The longing returned full force, mixing with the anger until Kendi's skin felt itchy and too tight.

He flung the jacket on his bed and stormed out of the room, slamming the door behind him. The doors in the deserted lobby were wide open, and the air was a bit chillier than it had been yesterday morning.

Tendrils of fog floated in the twilight among the branches beyond the wide balcony. Kendi thought about going back for his jacket, but didn't feel like turning around. Still fuming, he went down to the cafeteria, dumped a handful of rolls onto a plate without really paying attention to them, and sat down at one of the long tables. An abandoned tray sat across from him, and he shoved it aside, slopping the dark remnants in the coffee mug over the side. Kendi tore a sticky chunk off one roll and stuffed it into his mouth, chewing without really tasting.

"What happened here?"

Kendi looked up sharply. Another student, two or three years older than Kendi, was looking down at the skewed, coffee-strewn tray in confusion. He held a croissant in one hand.

"That's my tray," the student said.

"Yeah, well, it looked abandoned to me," Kendi all but snarled. "You shouldn't have . . . have . . ." Kendi trailed off. The other student had brown hair and a broad build, with large hands and impressive biceps. Wide hazel eyes looked out over a square jaw and an undeniably handsome face. Kendi swallowed and felt a flush spread from the top of his head all the way down to his toes.

"I mean . . . I mean you should've left a note or something," he finished weakly. "Sorry. I thought you were done and gone."

"No big deal," the student said in a light tenor voice. "It's not like there isn't more food. I'm Pitr Haddis." He held out the hand that wasn't holding the croissant. Kendi automatically shook it. Pitr's grip was dry and firm, but before Kendi could register anything more than that, electricity jolted his spine. Kendi almost yelped. Pitr winced at the touch, but didn't let go of Kendi's hand.

"Pretty strong Silence," Pitr commented, sitting

down and looking ruefully at his tray. The coffee had sloshed everywhere, mixing with crumbs from the remainder of Pitr's breakfast.

Kendi shrugged uncertainly. "That's what they tell me. Look, why don't I get you some more coffee? I forgot to get some for myself anyway."

"You don't have to," Pitr said amiably. "I probably shouldn't—"

"Hey, I insist." Kendi managed to flash a grin. "Be right back."

Before Pitr could say anything else, Kendi left the table and hurried back to the food bay. Several silvery urns with spigots at their bases stood in a row next to a tray of coffee mugs. They reminded Kendi of the ones he had seen as a child in the church basement back in Sydney in the days before his family had become involved with the Reconstructionists. Coffee self-service, it seemed, hadn't changed in a thousand years. Kendi drew one mug and was reaching for the second before he remembered that he hated coffee. He hesitated, then decided to go ahead with it. Otherwise he'd look the fool in front of Pitr.

Kendi put the mugs on a tray, dumped a handful of sugar packets and cream containers next to them, and headed back to the table where Pitr was munching his croissant. He accepted the mug without comment.

"What did you say your name was again?" Pitr asked as Kendi sat down across from him.

"I didn't—sorry. It's Kendi Weaver." He frowned briefly at his coffee mug, then started opening sugar packets and stirring them into his coffee. "I'm new here. Like I said, I'm sorry about your tray."

"I was pretty much done eating anyway. Just wanted one more croissant." Pitr looked at him quizzically. "You gonna drink that coffee or eat it?"

Kendi looked down. He had emptied almost a dozen packets into the mug. His face grew hot with embarrassment. "I guess I'm kind of out of it this morning," he muttered.

Pitr laughed, a bright, free sound that made Kendi smile and set his heart to pounding.

Quit it, he admonished himself. *He's just being friendly.*

But his heart pounded anyway. He pushed the mug aside as Pitr drained half of his in one long swallow. Kendi watched him covertly, trying to seem nonchalant. The silence felt heavy.

Say something, dummy. "Um, so you've been at the monastery for a while?" *Oh, good one. Maybe you should have called yourself Mr. Smooth.*

Pitr put down the mug. "I was born on Bellerophon. My sister and I are both Silent, and there was no question about us going into the Children. I'm a student now, but I'll be apprenticed pretty soon. Where are you from?"

Before Kendi could answer, two more trays landed on the table. Jeren and Dorna took up seats on either side of Kendi.

"Morning," Jeren said.

"Hey, Pitr," Dorna said. "You know Kendi?"

"We just met." Pitr drained his mug and got up. "But I was about done. I should go. Stuff to do before class."

"See you," Jeren said. Kendi watched him go.

"So what's up with you this morning, guy?" Dorna said.

"Nothing." Kendi moodily tore off another chunk of cinnamon roll and felt his temper rise again. He was just getting into a conversation with Pitr and these two had to show up and chase him off.

Why do I care? he thought. *I shouldn't. I don't. The hell I don't.*

"Something wrong?" Jeren asked.

"No."

Dorna and Jeren both gave him an odd look but said nothing. They all three ate in silence for a moment, then Dorna said, "Today you register for classes, yeah? Given any thought to what you want to take?"

"I'll end up in basics," Kendi said gloomily. "My scores were so low."

"I want to take sex ed," Jeren said with his mouth full. Dorna beaned him with a hard roll.

A while later, Willa and Kite appeared. The five of them finished breakfast and trouped back up to the lobby where Mother Ara was waiting for them. A large bag hung from her shoulder. She took them across several walkways and up two flights of stairs to another building. Kendi was completely lost again. The numbers carved into the front of the registration building read "130452," but there was no street Kendi could see.

"How do they do addresses around here?" he asked, pointing to the numbers.

"By feet above ground level," Mother Ara said. "Everyone on the lowest level has an address starting with the numbers one-zero-zero because the lowest you can build is one hundred meters above the forest floor. The next level up is one-zero-two, and so on right up to three hundred for the people way up at the top. The next two numbers indicate what section you're in—forty-five in this case—and the last number or numbers indicate what order the building went up in. So the registration office is one-hundred-thirty meters above the ground in sector forty-five and it was the second building built at that level in this sector."

"Makes perfect sense," Jeren muttered.

Mother Ara laughed. "If you need directions to someplace, ask the dorm computer to download them into your data pad."

"Don'thaveone," Kite said.

"That's why I stopped at requisitions before picking you all up." Mother Ara reached into her bag and handed each new student a data pad the size of a small book. "This belongs to you, even if you leave the Children. If you lose it, you have to buy a new one yourself or charge one against your future earnings. Upgrades are every two years or so, and those are free."

The computers gave them all something to do while they were waiting to talk with the registration counselor. Holographic screens were new to Kendi, and fun, but he wasn't sure he'd ever figure out everything his little pad could do.

"That's why you'll take a course in basic computers," said Brother Strauts when he had called up the course requirements for Kendi. They were in his tiny cubicle of an office. Strauts was a portly man with a fringe of gray hair and equally gray eyes that looked out above a quivering pile of chins. His robe was brown and the ring on his finger was yellow amber. The course list on his holographic display looked depressingly long, but Brother Strauts assured Kendi that he wasn't expected to do it all at once. "This is for the long haul, son. And one day you'll look back on this and wonder where all the time went."

Right, Kendi thought. *That's what adults always say.*

"Now this part here," Brother Strauts continued, pointing at one part of the display, "says you're supposed to start flying lessons this morning."

Kendi bolted upright. "You mean today?"

"That's what it says. Toshi will be your instructor. And it also says someone's already put in to be your one-on-one."

"One-on-one?" Kendi echoed.

Strauts nodded, setting his chins to quivering again. "Everyone gets individual tutoring on meditation and entering the Dream. It's a very intense kind of thing, and it doesn't work very well in groups."

"So who's my one-on-one?" Kendi asked curiously. The only person he'd really interacted much with here was—

"Mother Araceil Rymar."

Kendi wasn't sure how to react, so he didn't. Instead Brother Strauts finished registering him for a varied array of classes—history, language studies, beginning flight, basic science, mathematics, self-defense, and Silent ethics. When they were finished, he found Mother Ara out in the lobby, where Kite and Jeren had figured out how to link their data pads together so they could play a game. A pair of holographic monsters wrestled in mid-air between them, while Willa and Doran conversed on a nearby couch.

"You're my one-on-one teacher?" Kendi blurted out.

Mother Ara nodded. "I haven't had a student in a while, and I thought we'd be a good match." She hesitated. "If you don't think it would work—"

"No," Kendi said quickly. "I'd like it, I think. Thanks. And thanks for the jacket. It's great. I was going to wear it today, but it . . . I think it's going to be too warm."

"You're welcome," Mother Ara said. "I wanted you to have it."

That hadn't been nearly as awkward as Kendi had thought it would be. And Ara had chosen him for her student. That made him feel special for the first time in a long time.

Jeren's monster tore the head off Kite's monster. Kite made a sound of disgust. Jeren's green eyes filled with glee. "Wanna try that again?"

"I think we have other things to do," Ara said. "Dorna, would you show Kendi to the ultralight landing strip? I'll take the others."

Dorna agreed, and a fresh surge of excitement waved through Kendi. He was going to learn to fly! Already he imagined himself at the helm of a starship, dipping and weaving through an asteroid field, dodging enemy fire.

Blowing up slavers.

A grim smile slid over his face as he and Dorna headed off, their feet clumping up and down more wooden walkways. The monastery was fully awake and active now. The starship daydream faded in the full sunlight, and Kendi became slowly aware of the number of Ched-Balaar around him and Dorna. He found it hard not to stare at them.

"It's all right to look," Dorna said. Her voice was oddly soft, barely audible.

"Look?" Kendi asked, faintly embarrassed at being caught.

"At the Ched-Balaar. They don't' think staring is rude. They think humans are strange because we *don't* look at other people."

Oh. So Kendi stared. There was definite grace and power among the Ched-Balaar, and they were so dissimilar from anything Kendi had ever seen. His mind kept wanting to categorize them as horses or cows or even giant dogs, but they moved so differently and made such odd sounds that they continued to attract his eye. One of them ducked its head in greeting as they passed, and Kendi barely remembered to press his fingertips to the middle of his forehead as Dorna did.

"You'll get used to them," Dorna said, still in her soft voice. Kendi wondered if something were wrong with her. "I stared a lot when I first got here, but now seeing them and the other nonhuman Children is nothing strange at all."

"If you say so," Kendi replied. "Is that tooth-chattering and hooting really language?"

"Oh yes. I don't understand it well, but I'm learning. Buck and Lucinda know it better than I do."

"Buck and Lucinda?"

"Friends of mine. Here's the staircase. We have to go down almost to the ground for this."

The wide stairs wound downward around the talltree. As they descended, Kendi's earlier excitement returned. He was actually going to *fly*. He hadn't realized how much this appealed to him until the opportunity came up. After all, poor kids growing up on the streets of Sydney and mucker slaves working on a frog farm don't think of themselves as having the chance to become pilots. But that had all changed now.

The landing strip turned out to be a fallen talltree. The stairs came down at the middle of the trunk, which was so big it formed a nearly flat surface. The bark had been sanded off and wide platforms had been added to either side. At one end, the roots of the monstrous tree made a tangle that reached two or three stories above the trunk. A small hangar had been built there. At the other end, the branches had been cut off, leaving a long, smooth expanse of trunk that made a perfect runway for small aircraft. The fallen tree left open a stripe in the canopy, one that would easily let a small aircraft slip unhindered into the sky.

One of the side platforms was occupied by a pair of ultralight aircraft. They looked to Kendi like recumbent bicycles with a giant mutated umbrella stuck to the top. One umbrella was red, the other was green. A pair of figures was bent over the engine beneath the red one. As Kendi and Dorna approached, one of the figures straightened. He wore black, not brown, and he was several centimeters shorter than Kendi. There was a slight Asian cast to his features.

"Kendi?" he said. "I'm Toshi, your flight instructor." He held out his hand. Kendi braced himself and shook it. But there was no jolt. Toshi smiled. "I'm not Silent," he said. "I just work for the monastery."

Before Kendi could reply, a newly familiar voice said, "Hey, Kendi. Good to see you again. Did you ever finish eating that coffee?"

Kendi's heart jumped. The other person at the ultralight was Pitr Haddis. His hazel eyes were merry with suppressed mirth. Kendi's mouth dried up.

"Pitr," Kendi managed. "Hi. What are you doing here?"

"You know each other?" Toshi said.

"We met at breakfast this morning," Pitr said with a smile. "Kendi spilled my coffee and put enough sugar in his own to put three dentists' kids through college."

Kendi felt his face heat up. Dorna snorted and said, "I have stuff to do, yeah? Don't crash, guy." And she left.

"Pitr's working on his instructor's license," Toshi explained. "He needs practice teaching, so he's going to be your main instructor. I'm going to watch and step in if he flounders. That all right with you?"

Kendi swallowed. "Sure," he managed. "No problem." *I think I'm going to need lots of help with my homework.*

Pitr slapped Kendi on the back. "Then let's get started."

"Am I going to fly today?" Kendi asked.

"Yep."

Kendi blinked. "No book work first? No lectures?"

"We'll get to that," Pitr said. "But with these babies, the best way to learn to fly them is to use them. They're fitted with grav units which we can control from the ground, so if you get into trouble, the computer—or one of us—will just take over and get you down safely. You can't crash." He patted one of the struts.

"How will this teach me to pilot a starship?"

"You need to learn to walk before you learn to fly, so to speak," Pitr told him. "You have to know how to deal with atmosphere under your wings, and this is a good way to begin. After this we'll do airplanes and small shuttles. Before you know it, you'll be hitting the slipships, don't you worry. Ready to start?"

Despite Pitr's earlier promise, there *was* a fair amount of lecture on safety procedures, flight control, takeoff, landing, and engine function. Kendi hung on every word, acutely aware of Pitr's presence, how he moved, how he spoke, his gentle manner, his strong face. The time flew by until Kendi found himself sitting in the ultralight's cockpit. The cockpit and the engine were both open to the air, and Kendi felt a little exposed. His heart began to pound, and he couldn't tell if it was from excitement or from the way Pitr was bending over him to check the straps and Kendi's helmet.

"We're good to go," said Pitr, who wore a helmet of his own.

"Don't we need earplugs?" Kendi asked. "I've heard these things get pretty loud."

Pitr looked mystified. "No—they're pretty quiet, unless something's wrong with the engine."

"They used to be loud," Toshi said, speaking up for the first time since the lesson began. "But that was a long time ago."

Kendi flushed, feeling like a backwoods hick. *I'm only nine hundred years out of date,* he thought. *All life—Pitr must think I'm stupid.*

If that was the case, Pitr's face didn't show it. "I'll go up first so you can watch me take off," he said. "I'll also stay alongside you once you get airborne. Toshi will stay on the ground with the safety computer, okay?"

Kendi nodded. A few moments later, the engine on

Pitr's ultralight came to light with a gentle purr, not the rusty chainsaw sound Kendi had been expecting. Pitr gave Kendi a thumbs-up, and his vehicle wheeled out onto the runway. The pitch of the motor increased. Pitr's ultralight moved forward, picked up speed, and left the runway. It disappeared into the sky, becoming a red dot against fluffy white clouds.

"Your turn," Toshi said.

Kendi carefully guided the green ultralight forward as Pitr had taught him, then swallowed and punched up the power. The ultralight sped up, and Kendi could feel it start to lift. The wheels left the runway, dropped back onto it, then left it again. He was doing it! It was really happening!

"Pull up," came Pitr's voice over the helmet radio. *"You only have so much runway."*

Kendi obeyed. His stomach dropped and leaves rushed past him in a green blur as the ultralight sailed up into the air. Ecstasy swelled in Kendi's chest as he gained altitude, felt nothing but the bright and flowing wind around him. He glanced down and had the strange sensation of seeing emerald leaves far beneath his feet. Behind, the runway made a long rectangular scar in the forest canopy. The ultralight motor was quiet as a whisper, and suddenly he knew how a falcon must feel as it glided gently on the wind.

"Doing great," Pitr said over the radio, and the red ultralight dropped down next to Kendi's green one. Kendi flashed Pitr a thumbs-up, then clutched at his controls as the ultralight suddenly bounced and jolted.

"You're okay," Pitr said. *"Just a little downdraft. It'll clear. Okay, let's try a few basic maneuvers."*

Pitr had Kendi bank left and right, gain and lose altitude, and fly in a steady circle. Every moment was exhilarating. Kendi's movements quickly gained a deft confidence and he began to feel as if the ultralight's wings were an extension of his own body. The ultralight wasn't holding him up—he himself was flying. And it was glorious.

All too soon, Pitr said, *"Okay, it's time to go back in. You remember what I said about landing?"*

Kendi nodded, then remembered the gesture was useless over a radio. "I remember," he said aloud.

"Great. Watch me first, then I'll coach you in."

The red ultralight, easily visible against the green foliage, coasted smoothly into the long scar that made up the runway. Kendi circled the area once, then headed around to line himself up with the tree. He was only a little nervous—the ultralight responded to his slightest wish. He was just starting his descent when the ultralight jerked sideways. A strange scream hit him like a slap. Kendi yelped and tried to regain control. Frantically, he yanked hard on the control stick, trying to gain more altitude. Kendi looked around in a panic, then sucked in his breath. A big creature with leathery wings, a long beak, and wicked talons was right behind him. The beak, as thick as Kendi's arm, opened and again the strange scream tore through the sky. Kendi's stomach turned cold.

"Kendi!" came Pitr's voice. *"Are you all right?"*

"What the hell is that?" Kendi yelled.

"Dinosaur." Pitr's voice was full of forced calm. *"Shouldn't be here. The pheromones—hell, we have to get you down."*

The thing screamed again, its long wings flapping hard. Kendi gave the throttle more power and the ultralight jerked forward, though it didn't handle as well as it should have. A quick glance upward told Kendi one of the overhead wings had been torn. He swore. The creature flapped its wings, easily catching up and gaining altitude at the same time. Kendi could almost feel its beak and talons reaching down to rend and tear at the cloth wings. He yanked the control stick sideways and banked. The creature missed.

Kendi's heart was pounding so fast he was afraid it would shatter inside his chest. He wished with every fiber of his being that he were down on the safe, solid ground with Pitr and Toshi.

"Kendi," Toshi said, *"we're going to take control of the ultralight and bring you down. Release the controls."*

Another scream followed by a shudder. The creature's talons ripped through the wing and tore out a great chunk of cloth. The ultralight yawed sideways despite Kendi's desperate attempts to right it. Another scream. The beak punched through the cloth and a white pain speared Kendi's right shoulder. He looked up and saw one of the creature's glittering black eyes peering down at him. It was gripping the ultralight canopy in its talons. The beak punched downward again. Kendi braced himself for more pain, but none came as the creature hit something behind Kendi's seat instead. Sparks snapped and the dinosaur shrieked in pain, though it didn't release the ultralight.

"Dammit!" Pitr said. *"Kendi, that thing hit the remote receiver. I can't control anything from down here."*

Kendi's heart leaped into his throat. He yanked the stick sideways in a desperate attempt to get the animal to let go. The ultralight shuddered and dropped several meters. Hot blood ran down Kendi's shoulder and his back. Another shriek and the creature's beak poked down at Kendi a third time. Acting on pure instinct, Kendi twisted sideways in his seat. The beak slashed down next to him and without stopping to think, Kendi grabbed it and held fast. The creature tried to pull back up, but before it could fully react, Kendi punched it twice straight in the eye.

The creature yanked its beak out of the ultralight. With a scream of pain, it flew unsteadily away. Kendi's knuckles stung. The ultralight tilted downward, and

Kendi realized that the animal's wings had been help-ing hold the damaged ultralight aloft. He was losing altitude.

"Kendi, are you all right?" Pitr demanded. *"I'm tak-ing off right now. Hold on!"*

Kendi gritted his teeth, unable to spare the energy to answer. His shoulder was afire with white pain as he smacked the control that would activate the grav unit. Nothing happened. The ultralight was perhaps thirty meters from the treetops and closing. Kendi's mind raced. Either the entire unit was shot and he was dead, or just the controls had been shorted out. Logic said there had to be a manual activation control on the anti-grav unit itself, but where was the unit?

Behind his seat. Had to be—that was where the creature had hit when things started going wrong. The treetops were less than fifteen meters away. Kendi re-leased his restraining harness and, ignoring the screech of agony in his shoulder, twisted around in his seat. The unit was there, a small gray box clearly labeled and clearly dented. The ultralight tilted farther for-ward and the trees were rushing up to meet it. Kendi tried not to think about what would happen when his ultralight slammed into the branches. A big red button winked above a sign that said EMERGENCY. Kendi slapped it. Leaves and branches crunched the front of the ultralight. Kendi shut his eyes.

Abruptly he was jolted downward. With a yelp he managed to grab the back of his seat with his good arm. His feet found purchase on the control panel. He hung there, panting. It took him a moment to under-stand that he was no longer falling. The ultralight, tilted at a forty-five-degree angle, was hovering with its nose nestled among the uppermost leaves of a talltree.

Air brakes? Kendi thought wildly.

"Kendi, are you all right?" Pitr demanded.

Kendi started to answer, but all that came out was a squeak. He cleared his throat and tried again. "Yes and no," he said. "I managed to activate the anti-grav, but that thing stabbed my shoulder and I'm stuck here. If the control panel can't hold my weight, I'm in for a long drop."

"I'm almost there," Pitr said. *"Just hold on."*

Kendi glanced down at the branches and leaves beneath his feet. "I have a choice?"

A few minutes later, Pitr arrived and, activating his own anti-grav unit, put his ultralight into hover mode. Mindful of his shoulder and the deadly drop below, Kendi carefully climbed out of his ultralight and into Pitr's. The cockpit was tiny, built for a single occupant.

"You'll have to sit on my lap," Pitr said.

Oh, gosh, Kendi thought. *Do I have to?*

"I'll fly us back by anti-grav," Pitr said, "since these things aren't built to fly the regular way with more than one person."

The ride back was uneventful, if crowded. The close contact with Pitr seemed to dull the pain in Kendi's shoulder. They didn't speak—Pitr had to concentrate on flying. Once they landed, Kendi saw a stretcher hovering at the end of the runway. Two women in brown stood next to it. Toshi helped Kendi out of the ultralight. Blood dripped steadily down his shoulder.

"Are you all right?" he asked.

"People keep asking me that," Kendi said. "I could be better. My shoulder feels like it's on fire."

The two women turned out to be medical technicians summoned by Toshi. They got Kendi to sit onto the floating stretcher and quickly cut off his blood-soaked shirt so they could examine him. He hissed when they pulled it away from his skin. Pitr hovered nearby, worry written all over his square features.

"Looks superficial," one of the technicians said from her vantage point behind him, "but painful. I think we can treat this here, unless you really want to go to the medical center."

Kendi thought about the way Mother Ara would react if she learned he was in hospital. "No," he said. "Do it here."

One of the techs pressed a dermospray against his arm. It *thumped*, and Kendi's pain almost immediately vanished. The other technician washed the wound thoroughly and pressed the ragged edges together. Then she cracked open a plastic vial and spread the contents over Kendi's back and shoulder. It stiffened as she finished.

"This will hold the wound together and help it heal," she said. "You might have a scar, but only a faint one. I'm going to give you a dose of time-release antibiotic to keep out infection. If you get any symptoms such as nausea or diarrhea, call the medical center right away. Got it?"

"Got it," Kendi said, standing up.

The pair finished their ministrations, then piled their cases of medical equipment on a shelf beneath the stretcher and took it quickly up the stairs to the main monastery. It was only then that Kendi noticed how shaky his legs were. He started sinking to the ground. Pitr caught him before he could fall. Kendi leaned on him gratefully. Pitr's arms were strong, and Kendi liked having them support him. He wanted to lean his head on Pitr's chest, and wondered if Pitr would accept that.

Stupid thing to be thinking about, he thought. *You almost died up there.*

"It's okay," Pitr said soothingly. "Hey, it's all right. You're okay. Everything's fine."

"I'm all right," he said, still leaning. "I just . . . felt a little light-headed for a minute."

"I can understand that," Toshi said. "I've got a few dozen gray hairs myself, and I wasn't even up there."

He paused. "I suppose I'll have to talk to Mother Ara about rearranging your schedule. You won't want to be flying again after—"

Kendi stiffened and came upright. "The hell I don't!" he spluttered, and Pitr laughed.

"My god, Kendi, are you all right?" Mother Ara demanded.

"Yeah. Can I get a freemark or something every time someone asks that? I'll be able to buy my own ship in an hour or so."

"Kendi," Mother Ara said, "you scared the life out of me. My god, this isn't a good time to be flip. How do you feel?"

Kendi shrugged and winced. "Shoulder's a little stiff, but it doesn't hurt much, and they gave me some painkillers."

"I've already called the animal control board and let them have it," Mother Ara said. "The pheromone sprays are supposed to keep the dangerous dinosaurs away. I'm so sorry this happened. You must have been terrified."

"It wasn't your fault."

"I arranged the lesson," Mother Ara countered. "Pitr says you still want to fly, though."

"Hell, yes. It was great, Mother Ara." His eyes shone, the pain forgotten. "The best! I wish I could go every day instead of just once a week."

Mother Ara puffed out her cheeks. "I don't think my heart is up to that. Once a week is plenty."

They were on one of the monastery's innumerable balconies. Clouds had moved in, covering the sky in an even wave of gray. The balcony was off the beaten path, which meant they had a fair amount of privacy. There was a small bench, and a green ivy vine had twined itself around the balcony rail.

"Mother Ara," Kendi said abruptly, "if you like

someone and you don't know if they like you back, what do you do?"

Mother Ara blinked. "What? Why? Whom do you like?"

"I meant it just . . . you know . . . hypothetically and all."

"Oh. Hypothetically." Mother Ara drummed her fingers thoughtfully on her knees. "Well, *hypothetically* I think you—the hypothetical you—need to tell the person and see what happens. After all, if you don't say anything, the other person might never figure it out."

"But what if it's the sort of person who might not like me—you?" Kendi asked. "What if there could be . . . other factors."

"I'm not sure what you mean."

Kendi swallowed, suddenly wishing he hadn't said anything at all. "I mean what if the other person might not be interested?"

"I still think you should speak up. Hypothetically, that is." She smoothed her brown robe and readjusted the gold amulet that hung on a chain around her neck. "The Awakening Festival is next week. It's a traditional time to start a romance. Maybe you'll see the person there and that would be a good time to bring it up."

"Not me," Kendi said. "Just a hypothetical me."

Mother Ara got up with a smile and reached for her handbag. "Of course. Exactly what I meant. And now we have a lesson in meditation to begin."

"Meditation?"

"If you want to enter the Dream, you have to learn to meditate," Mother Ara said. "It quiets the soul and allows the mind to float free. Very, very few Silent can get into the Dream without meditating first, and it requires a lot of practice. There are practice rooms in a section of the dormitory. Ready for your first lesson? I promise it won't be anywhere near as difficult as your flying exercise. It'd be a good stress reliever, too."

"All right."

They went back to the dorm together, and Mother Ara showed Kendi to a hallway with a series of tiny, soundproofed rooms. Each room had a couch, a chair, and only a teensy amount of floor space. From her handbag, Mother Ara took a bracelet and her data pad.

"You can meditate any way you like," she said, "but most Silent like to lie down. Why don't you try the couch?"

Kendi obeyed. His shoulder twinged a bit as he lay down and he wondered if he should take another painkiller first. Nah. Best try it first without and see how it went.

Mother Ara fastened the bracelet around his wrist— it felt nothing like the shackle he had worn for three years—and activated her data pad. "The bracelet will monitor your life signs," she explained. "It also watches your brain patterns. It'll help me see what level of relaxation you get to and let me know if something is going wrong. There isn't much chance of that," she hastened to add, "because you're not trying to reach the Dream just yet and I'm not giving you any drugs. That'll come later."

"So what do I do?" Kendi asked.

"Just close your eyes and listen to my voice," she said. "Would background music or white noise help you relax? The computer can give us whatever you need."

"Drums," Kendi said. "I think I want drums."

"Baran," Mother Ara said, "play audio file 'Drums for Relaxation.'"

Immediately a soft four-four rhythm filled the room and Kendi shut his eyes. He was no stranger to meditation. The Real People Reconstructionists had been great proponents of it. As a child, Kendi had invariably found it boring and stupid, but now his view had changed. If this was the path into the Dream, the place where he might find his family, then this was the path he would follow.

He stirred a little on the couch. Lying down felt wrong for him, somehow. He couldn't get comfortable. He shifted again, trying to settle down. His shoulder twinged again.

Mother Ara, her voice soft, took him through a relaxation exercise, and he was surprised to note that it was similar to the ones the Real People had practiced. It involved relaxing each group of muscles one at a time. Mother Ara's voice droned on, telling him to empty his mind, let it go blank.

Kendi tried, but outside thoughts kept crowding in. The flying dinosaur's long beak flashing down and causing white-hot pain. Pitr's hazel eyes filled with concern. The sound of frogs peeping in the night. Rebecca being towed away, her shackles glowing blue as she reached for Kendi one last time. Lying down, he felt strangely trapped. At last he sat up and yanked the bracelet off. The recorded drums continued to play.

"Sorry," he said. "I guess I can't concentrate."

Mother Ara looked surprised. "Actually you were doing pretty well."

"Are we done?" he asked, suddenly belligerent. "I'm tired. I want to go back to my room."

"Of course," Mother Ara said. "It's been a difficult day. I probably should have skipped this lesson. Why don't you go get some rest?"

Kendi nodded once to her and left without saying anything else.

EIGHT

Pity me, for I am sick with love! Or am I sick of it?
—Captain Irfan Qasad

A few days later, the morning found Kendi lying flat on his stomach on the dew-slicked roof of a certain section of the dormitory. He peered carefully over the gutter. His heart beat funny, like it was jumping around inside his chest. Coming down the balcony below him was a pair of students, one male, one female, both dressed in brown and wearing gold medallions. The boy, of course, was Pitr Haddis. But who was the girl walking with him? Tension knotted Kendi's stomach. The girl had a thin build and wore her hair in a brown ponytail. She said something to Pitr, who laughed, and the sound sent a thrill down Kendi's back, even as jealousy began to bubble in his head.

Pitr. Pitr Haddis. Kendi spent entire evenings thinking of him, of his strong arms and handsome face, and when he lay awake on his bed that night staring into the darkness, he saw Pitr's eyes. He also spent considerable time thinking about what it all meant. To his astonishment, he wasn't upset or even surprised. Kendi supposed he had always known he was attracted to men. He just hadn't thought about it, not even after the final incident with Pup. Or perhaps *because* of the final incident with Pup. Now, however, he found himself thinking about it quite a lot.

The sun began to warm the slightly slippery wooden shingles of the slanted roof as he watched Pitr. Kendi had found some basic information about him on the computer network. He was seventeen, Silent, and his room was in the same wing of the dorm as Kendi's. Kendi had worked out the most likely route he would take to morning classes and now he was waiting on the roof for him to pass by.

This is insane, he thought as Pitr drew nearer. *I'm sitting on a roof, trying to get a look at this guy just because I like him. What if I fall?*

Naturally, the moment that idea crossed his mind, his hand slipped and he started to slide with dreadful inevitability toward the gutter. Kendi scrabbled at the shingles, but his hands were sweaty and the shingles were still slick from the morning dew. His upper body went over the edge, and with a yelp he managed to snag the gutter with one hand. The gutter wasn't strong enough to support his weight. It came away from the roof with the screech of half a dozen nails wrenched from wood. Kendi crashed to the balcony.

There was a moment of silence. Kendi lay on his back, stunned and in pain. His still-healing shoulder felt like someone had stuck a pitchfork through it. Two faces, one male and one female, poked themselves into his line of vision.

"Kendi?" Pitr said. "Are you hurt?"

Kendi wished with every aching muscle that he could sink into the planks and disappear. Humiliation burned in his face, and he wondered if Pitr would notice the difference in his complexion.

"Can you get up?" Pitr continued, holding out a hand. Kendi started to reach for it, then realized he was sill holding a piece of the gutter. He hastily dropped it and grabbed for Pitr's hand. Pitr hauled him to his feet. Kendi felt the strength behind the move and it made his legs a little watery.

At that moment, Dorna and Mother Ara came hurrying around the corner of the dorm, and Kendi gave a mental groan. Mother Ara would certainly chew him out, and right in front of Pitr. How could it get worse? He was half tempted to leap off the balcony and get it over with.

"Are you okay?" the dark-haired girl asked. "What were you doing up there?"

Kendi ran a quick inventory. Nothing seemed to be broken, though he was sure a few bruises would make themselves felt tomorrow. "I—that is—"

Mother Ara got within speaking range. "My god, Kendi," she said. "You know the rules about climbing unsafe places. What in the world were you thinking?"

Kendi was all too aware of Pitr's eyes on him. He looked at the walkway and tried to think of something to say. His mind remained blank.

"It's my fault, Mother," Dorna said.

Kendi's mouth dropped open. He shut it quickly.

"Your fault." Mother Ara crossed her arms.

Dorna chuckled low in her throat. "I'm afraid I told him about how I used to watch the sunrise from the dorm roof and I . . . I sort of . . . told him it would probably be okay. I mean, with him being Australian Aborigine and all that, he does, you know, spiritual stuff with the sun."

"Is that true, Kendi?" Mother Ara said dangerously.

Dorna shot him a heavy glance. Something about her bothered him, but he couldn't quite put his finger on it. At the moment, however, she was offering him an out and he gladly took it.

"Tribal thing," he said. "Greeting the sun. Right. I guess the roof isn't a good place to do it, huh?"

"You have the right of that," Mother Ara growled. "Good heavens, Kendi, *think* before you act, will you? You could have been seriously injured, especially with your shoulder healing the way it is."

"Sorry," Kendi mumbled, and blushed again.

"You're from Earth?" Pitr said. "You never said that before."

"Uh, yeah. Australia."

"Nebular!" Pitr said. "I've always wanted to visit Earth."

"Kendi," mused the dark-haired girl. "Is this the guy who was attacked on the ultralight a few days ago?"

"Oh, sorry," Pitr said. "Kendi, this is Trish, my twin sister. Trish, this is Kendi Weaver."

His sister! Kendi thought with a rush of relief. *She's just his sister.*

Trish stuck out her hand. "Nice to meet you, Kendi."

Kendi automatically shook it and yelped, the jolt exacerbating the pain he was already feeling.

"Whoops," Trish said. "I should have warned you that I'm Silent."

"It's okay," Kendi reassured her. "Really. Completely okay." *A sister! She's his sister!*

"Right," Pitr said. "We'd better get to class before we're late. Are you going to be at Festival tonight, Kendi?"

"Sure am," he said instantly.

"Great. We'll probably see you there. And there's your flying lesson tomorrow. Later, okay?" He flashed a quick smile that made Kendi's heart soar before Pitr headed off with his *sister*. Kendi stared after him, admiring Pitr's muscular figure from behind. A strange coppery taste tanged his mouth.

Mother Ara tapped his good shoulder, startling him. "All right, sun boy. I'm not going to add a duty shift to your week, but I think it'd be appropriate if you helped the custodian repair the gutter, all right?"

"Yes, Mother," Kendi said meekly.

"I'll see to it, Mother," Dorna put in. "Come on, Kendi. Let's go find her."

She took him by the arm and lead him firmly away.

The moment they were out of sight and earshot, she stopped and gave him a heavy-lidded stare.

"Which one is it?" she demanded.

"Which one is what?" he said, bewildered.

"Which one do you have your eye on, Casanova? Come on, be honest."

Kendi flushed one more time, and again something bothered him about Dorna. Exactly what it was still eluded him. "I—I don't know what you're—"

"Yes, you do." She leaned forward and whispered breathily in his ear. "I can tell. It's written all over you. Go ahead, you can tell me. Maybe we can figure out what to do about it."

Her breath was warm in his ear and it sent a confusing shudder through his body. "It's Pitr," he confessed without knowing why. "But you can't tell anyone!"

"Wouldn't dream of it." Dorna tucked her hand under his arm and continued walking. Kendi stumbled to stay with her. "It does make things trickier, though. I don't know if Pitr goes for the boys, even ones from Earth. I guess I could ask around."

"Don't!" Kendi said, horrified. "Everyone'll know."

"No risk, no gain, big boy. But if it's going to get you upset, I won't. Let's see." Dorna pursed her lips in thought. "Pitr is interested in Earth, and you come from the place. That seems like a logical place to start. Hmmmmm . . . Earth. What does it say to me? It says *far away*. It says *exotic*. It says *I'm available*."

"It says *hot, dry, and boring*," Kendi supplied.

"I think we'll leave that part out," Dorna said. "Now shut up and let me think." She made some *mmmmm* noises as they walked. "We could tell him you're dying of a terrible Terran genetic disorder, and you have one last request. Or maybe that your ancestors gave you a directive—to hunt down someone cute and drag him home by the hair."

"Pitr's hair is too short for dragging," Kendi pointed out.

"Don't bother me with silly details. Maybe we should just coldcock him. I've always wanted to do that to someone. It sounds so suggestive."

As they continued into the dorm and downstairs, Dorna outlined half a dozen more plans for getting Pitr's attention, each one more outrageous than the last. Kendi laughed, his embarrassment forgotten, even when they found the head custodian and told her what had happened with the gutter. The older woman sighed, muttered about empty-headed first-years, and told Kendi to meet her right after his classes were over for the day.

"Speaking of which," Dorna said, "you better fly, Casanova. Meet for supper?"

Kendi agreed and ran upstairs to get his data pad, then trotted outside into the warm sunshine. Classes. He had classes. Good. They would take his mind off Pitr. He headed down a walkway and up a set of stairs. Talltree leaves rustled in the morning breeze. Pots of flowers, both real and artificial, decorated the buildings and balconies in red and blue—reputed to be Irfan Qasad's favorite colors—for this evening's celebration, and signs and holograms proclaimed JOYOUS AWAKENING! from windows and front porches. Kendi wouldn't think about Pitr, no, he wouldn't.

The boards on the decks and walkways alternated between warm from the sun and cool from the shade. These days Kendi preferred to go barefoot, as the Real People usually did. No one in the monastery seemed to care, as long as he wore shoes to the cafeteria.

Maybe he should take Mother Ara's advice and tell Pitr at Festival. Everyone said the Awakening was a time of beginnings, changes, and new directions. Peo-

ple made resolutions for things they wanted to change
in their lives. It was also a traditional day on which
to propose marriage. It was a time of happiness, good-
will, and cheer, when it was considered bad luck to
be rude or disrespectful. An appropriate time to talk
to Pitr.

If only Kendi could work up the nerve.

The byways were busy with people, both human and
Ched-Balaar. Kendi automatically pressed fingertips to
forehead whenever he passed anyone ranked Parent
or higher. It had barely been a week since he had
arrived on Bellerophon, but he felt perfectly at home
and had already learned his way around the monastery
and memorized his schedule. Mornings and early
afternoons were spent in class. Late afternoons were
reserved for study and private lessons with Mother
Ara in using Silence. He was also required to work at
least fifteen hours a week on duty shift, doing whatever needed to be done around the monastery. Students worked jobs ranging from serving food in the
cafeteria to washing windows to gardening, depending
on knowledge, aptitude, and interest. Kendi had so far
been on outdoor cleanup, which involved going all the
way down to the ground and picking up detritus that
fell from the monastery above. He had done it twice
and so far hadn't seen a single dinosaur, to his combi-
nation relief and disappointment. All in all, though, it
was a busy schedule, and he wondered if it was designed to keep newcomers from getting homesick or
missing loved ones. Sometimes it even worked.

Kendi arrived at history class just in time. The
teacher was a brown-robed young Sister with short
blond hair, a plump build, and merry brown eyes.

"Kendi!" called Kite. "Verhere."

With a nod, Kendi took a seat at the table with
Kite, Willa, and Jeren. Although Kendi had met other

students, he liked best hanging out with the others he had been "bought" with.

"All right now," called Sister Bren, the teacher. "Let's review yesterday a little before we go on. Who remembers what this is?" In the center of the classroom appeared a hologram of a blue-green-brown planet with a single moon. Kendi instantly recognized Bellerophon. A dot of light circled the planet. The view zoomed in toward the light, and it ballooned into a meteor-pocked, gray cylinder parked in planetary orbit. It looked almost exactly like the colony ship Kendi had boarded with his family.

"The *Margery Daw*," said several students.

"And the captain was . . . ?" Sister Bren prompted.

"Irfan Qasad."

The view rotated around the planet to reveal another ship, low and round with a clear top, like a flattened bubble.

"That's the Ched-Balaar," piped up another student. "You said they don't name their ships. They got here first."

"That's absolutely right." Bren tapped at the controls on her desk and a tiny shuttle scooted away from the *Margery Daw* and docked with the Ched-Balaar vessel. "She was one of the first humans to lay eyes on an alien race. Lucky for us they were friendly." A while later, several dozen shuttles spilled out of the human ship like scattering dandelion seeds and dropped gently to the planet below. The view zoomed in again, showing humans working side by side with Ched-Balaar in the top of the talltree forest, building houses and walkways.

"Records differ on this point," Bren reminded them. "We don't know if Treetown started before or after the Ched-Balaar took the first group of humans into the Dream, but that's a minor aside. Who all did the Ched-Balaar first bring into the Dream?"

The holographic view shifted again to a nighttime campfire on a fern-covered forest floor. A group of Ched-Balaar sat near it, playing odd-looking drums and rattles.

"Irfan Qasad," Jeren called out. A sharp-faced woman with a long brown braid popped into existence near the campfire. Her expression was both thoughtful and wary. "I'd slip her space anytime."

"Jeren," Bren warned, and Kendi poked him in the ribs with an elbow.

"Daniel Vik," said someone else. A stocky, blond man who looked barely old enough to shave appeared next to Irfan.

"Yin Ping," said Willa, barely loud enough to be heard. An Asian man with silvering black hair puffed into being. The class continued calling out names until the full roster of the first human Silent was complete. Kendi didn't contribute. His mind alternated between thoughts about his family brought on by the hologram of the colony ship and thoughts of Pitr brought on by nothing in particular. A gentle breeze moved through the open window, smelling of leaves and bark.

"After it was determined that humans could indeed enter the Dream," Bren said, "Irfan Qasad consulted with a group of geneticists, both human and Ched-Balaar, and they determined that the current gene pool didn't carry enough genes for Silence—though they didn't call it that yet—to ensure the trait would continue. The *Margery Daw* carried a great many frozen human embryos, however, and they decided to alter some of them for Silence. Unfortunately, it turned out that the Silent don't develop well in artificial wombs. They just wither and die. No one knows exactly why. You'll learn more about that when you take biology."

Utang's blue eyes. Pitr's hazel ones. Slapping mosquitoes, catching frogs. Falling from the roof, grasping

Pitr's hand. Writhing in pain under snapping silver bands.

". . . do know that she married Daniel Vik and eventually had three children," Bren said. "All of them were Silent. Much of the rest of her history is up in the air. Vik did kidnap the eldest boy and disappear, probably to Othertown, since that's where he turned up later. The question is, why did he do it? Some records from the time hint that Vik suffered from depression and paranoid delusions. That he had some kind of fight with Irfan herself is almost certain, but what could possibly have . . ."

Little Martina crying in her slave square. Dad's face contorted with pain as he reached for Mom's hand. The flying dinosaur's stabbing beak. Pitr's laugh. Festival.

". . . appears that Irfan lied to him about their children. It's possible Vik knew they weren't his kids. A surviving fragment from his own writings says, 'My children don't share my genes,' which seems to be pretty clear. At any rate, he whipped the government of Othertown into a frenzy. Not all humans on Bellerophon liked the Silent, and a fair number of Ched-Balaar thought bringing humans into the Dream in the first place was a mistake. Vik was building a powder keg, and Othertown was almost ready to declare genocide against the Silent, even though Vik himself was . . ."

He would do it tonight, talk to Pitr at Festival tonight. After all, Pitr didn't seem to be the type to get angry. He had always looked gentle to Kendi, anyway. But how *would* he react?

". . . used the Dream to perform research together, even though they were on different planets and separated by light-years of empty space. As a team, they discovered slipspace and how to use it. So you could also say that Irfan had a hand in the discovery of slipspace, since she was the one to spearhead interplanetary communication through the Dream. Of course, it was slipspace and slipships that allowed Vik to get his hands on weapons powerful enough to . . ."

Pup's eyes going flat, his body going stiff. Rejection in his eyes to words Kendi hadn't quite said. What if the same thing happened with Pitr? Kendi didn't think he could face that.

". . . resigned from her post as governor in a cloud of scandal, and the question went unanswered. Did Irfan order the assassination of the governor of Othertown or did he truly commit . . ."

The room seemed suddenly close and stifling, despite the open window. Kendi abruptly found he couldn't sit still. He needed to move, to—

". . . . you think, Kendi?"

Kendi looked up, startled. Bren, Jeren, Willa, and everyone else in the room were staring at him expectantly. He scrambled to remember what Sister Bren had asked, but couldn't do it. "What?"

"Do you think Irfan ordered the assassination of the governor of Othertown?" Bren repeated patiently.

Kendi shrugged. Who cared?

"Well, it's your homework essay—all of you," Bren said. "There's half an hour left for class. Log into the system and start your research now. Work with a partner, if you want. I'm really interested in what you come up with, so turn them in tomorrow morning, all right?"

The class groaned, but got out their data pads. Holographic screens popped up all over the room. Kendi got out his own pad, and Sister Bren moved among the class, pointing out places to find both information and speculation. Several students teamed up with partners. Kendi's restlessness grew. It felt like he was back in his slave square, hemmed in on all sides.

"Wannaworktogether?" Kite blurted out.

"I have to get out of here," Kendi muttered. And when Sister Bren's back was turned, he slipped out the door.

Outside, the alternating patches of warm sunlight and cool shade felt much better than the confining classroom. Kendi heaved a sigh of relief in the bright, free air and trotted across the boards. After a moment, he sped up until he was running, all but flying over the walkways. A rope ladder caught his eye and he climbed it to a long balcony that ran the length of the building. Through the windows he saw what appeared to be a series of offices. Brown-clad humans and blond furred Ched-Balaar worked at desks or reclined on couches and pillows. Kendi assumed the latter were in the Dream.

A set of stairs at the end of the balcony led downward, and Kendi found himself on a wide platform where a life-size statue of Irfan carved in gray marble stood on a pedestal. Pots of red and blue flowers had been placed at the base. Kendi paused to examine the statue. Irfan was lifting a hand in front of her as if about to accept a gift, and her face had a determined cast to it. A scroll was carved on the pedestal. At the top were the words THE WISDOM OF IRFAN, and it was inscribed with a series of sayings:

1. A serene mind is a strong mind.
2. The Dream is no less real than what we call reality.
3. We are but caretakers of the eternal Dream.
4. You must be a person first and Silent second.
5. The greater your knowledge, the smaller your risk.
6. You may gain, but not at someone else's expense.
7. Your mind should be open, but your mouth should be closed.

8. The universe provides, we distribute.
9. Pay forward, not back.
10. The real world becomes the Dream.

Kendi read the first one aloud. "A serene mind is a strong mind." Then his mind must be weak indeed. The restlessness grew stronger. Despite Mother Ara's earlier warning, Kendi used a balcony railing to clamber up to the roof of the building and from there climb into the branches of the talltree. His bare feet found easy purchase on the rough bark. The tree flattened as it went up, and eventually Kendi was able to poke his head up out of the green foliage.

The sun shone down gold between fluffy white clouds. Small animals chirped in the leaves around him, and a hawklike bird coasted overhead. Kendi watched it pass. It felt as if he could take another step upward and fly himself. He grinned. The sky reminded him of the endless Outback, though the sun was considerably kinder. Bellerophon was a good place.

He climbed down a ways and lounged comfortably at the juncture of two thick branches. It was like being in a green cave, cool and leafy. Birds and small lizards chirruped at each other as they darted about hunting insects. A clump of dead twigs and branches had gathered where the wide branch met the talltree trunk, presumably blown or fallen there. Kendi selected a straight piece half as long as his own leg and a few centimeters in diameter. He turned it over in his hands for a moment, then produced a folding knife from his pocket and fell to whittling it. Some of the strangeness of it all washed over him. His birthplace was countless light-years away and almost a thousand years in the past, but here he was, sitting in a giant tree on a planet where humans worked with aliens to enter the Dream.

Were the Dream and the Dreamtime the same thing? Kendi tried to think, wishing he had paid more attention to the stories told by the Real People Reconstructionists. The Dreamtime was the source of everything, a place outside space and time. A part of every living creature was there, and there were those among the original tribes of Real People who had learned to walk its paths. This sounded a bit like the Dream. The original Real People had also used Head Talk—telepathy, Kendi supposed—for communication in a climate where a constantly open mouth could lead to dehydration, and the Dream as Mother Ara explained it was used for communication among mutants.

The knife continued its work, though Kendi's mind lay elsewhere. The Real People Reconstructionists had always maintained that Aboriginal culture was the pinnacle of human accomplishment, that the reason mutants could no longer enter the Dreamtime or use Head Talk was because they had left the ancient ways for a more materialistic state. The same had happened to the Real People themselves after being forcibly separated from their ancient way of life until their descendants had forgotten the Dreamtime completely. When people came to realize the foolishness of such a life, they would find it once again.

Kendi snorted. They seemed to have found it just fine without changing one bit. Of course, the Real People hadn't known about the Ched-Balaar or what could be accomplished through genetic engineering.

The problem was that Kendi couldn't seem to get the hang of it. He had gone through several meditation exercise sessions with Mother Ara, but it always felt wrong for him, somehow. The couch felt lumpy and strange, and his mind always wandered during the sessions instead of becoming calm and clear. Willa, Jeren, and Kite all said they could calm themselves right down, but Kendi couldn't seem to get the trick of it. Why?

The knife closed, seemingly of its own accord, and

Kendi looked down at the stick. It had become a short spear, complete with sharpened tip. Kendi ran his hands up and down the shaft. A few splinters here and there, but nothing a little sandpaper couldn't take care of. Why had he made it? It was as if something had guided his hands. Kendi looked at it for a long moment, then gave a little smile of recognition and of happiness.

With a grunt of annoyance, Ara shut down the data pad. Her holographic screen winked out, and she ran a tired hand over her face. The sun had moved away from her home office window and the room had cooled nicely. It was scant comfort.

Ara sighed. There were simply no other clues to be found. She had gone over every report, every image, every fact, and she couldn't find anything the Guardians might have missed. Somewhere out there was a madman who was killing Silent, and Ara was becoming more and more determined to find him. Part of her said she should leave the hunt to the Guardians, but another part of her, one with a louder voice, yammered that it was her duty to help in whatever way she could. After all, which was more urgent—saving Silent from a slaver or saving Silent from a killer? Not only that, the killer might go after someone Ara knew—her mother or her sister or her niece.

Unfortunately, Ara had the chill feeling that the only way to get further information was wait for the killer to strike again and hope for more clues.

At least Ben would be safe. She looked at the hologram of Ben, taken at age ten, that sat on her desk. His blue eyes were merry, his smile a bit mischievous. He looked nothing like her, of course. Several years ago Ara and a team of Children had been exploring what they thought was a derelict pirate vessel found in orbit around a gas giant. It hadn't been quite derelict, though the ship's only inhabitants hadn't been aware of much. They were a series of embryos frozen in a cryo-unit that had been missed or left behind for some other reason. The readout said the embryos were Silent.

Ara took them back to Bellerophon with her; indeed, held the unit on her lap for most of the trip home. Twelve viable, motherless embryos found exactly at a time when Ara's arms ached to hold a baby. Ara's doctor chose one at random for implantation. That left the others still frozen, but Ara didn't want more than one. Nine months later, Ben was born, and Ara thought she would burst with happiness. Even when he showed no awareness of the Dream by age ten, eleven, twelve, and onward, Ara still loved him. She couldn't help but feel disappointment and not a little guilt, though. Was it her fault? Had she done something wrong during her pregnancy? Or during Ben's early development? Or was it because he had spent so much time in frozen limbo? No one could give her an answer.

Now, however, it was an advantage. She wouldn't have to worry about him being killed.

The familiar sound of the front door opening came to her, followed by the equally familiar sound of Ben's footsteps. She checked the clock. School was out already? She had been working longer than she'd thought. Definitely time for a break. Ara left her office and headed for the kitchen because that was the first room Ben usually hit after school these days.

She found him staring into the open refrigerator.

"Hey, Mom," he said distractedly. "There's nothing to eat."

"Hey, yourself," she said. "Then close the door."

Ben obeyed and, with a put-upon sigh, began to rummage through the cupboards. His data pad peeked out from his back pocket, and Ara abruptly found that endearingly cute, a boyish gesture on someone who was all-too-rapidly becoming a man. When he turned around with a box of crackers, she swept him into a hug.

"Mom!" he protested. "Geez."

"Think of it as your room-and-board payment," she told him, stepping back. "How was school?"

"Fine." He crunched a handful of crackers. "You look tired. Something wrong?"

Ara hadn't told him she was consulting with the Guardians, though she was pretty sure he'd heard about the murders. Almost everyone on Bellerophon had heard, despite the Guardians' attempt to keep things quiet. She had been reluctant to mention it to him—no point in making him worry.

"I'm a little overworked," she admitted. "I need a break."

"So what are we doing for Festival tonight?" Ben asked.

"I thought the usual," she said. "Dinner here, then down to the games and the fireworks."

Ben made a face. "Does that mean you've invited *them*?"

"Attention! Attention!" said the house computer. "Incoming call for Mother Araceil Rymar."

"Put it through to the office," Ara replied as always, and left Ben to his crackers. In her office, the wall screen showed Sister Bren, one of the teachers at the monastery.

"I hate to bother you so close to Festival," Bren said, "but I wanted to talk to you about Kendi. He slipped out of class half an hour early today, and one of the other teachers saw him climbing down from a talltree a while later. I've also noticed him daydreaming a great deal during lessons. I'm afraid he's shaping up to be a difficult one. Freed slave syndrome, I expect."

Ara puffed out her cheeks in mute agreement. "He shows a lot of the signs, doesn't he? Just this morning he climbed onto the dorm roof and broke a gutter. Considering what he went through, though, I'm surprised it's not a lot worse."

"He doesn't cause disruption in class," Bren agreed. "But he won't pass history if he makes this a habit."

"He has a lesson with me in a few minutes. I'll talk to him then," Ara promised. "He's going to need counseling, I think, but you know how touchy suggesting it can be, especially at that age."

"Don't I just. Look, I won't write him up this time, but if he does it again, he'll end up with extra work detail."

Ara signed off with a grimace. Well, she should have been expecting it. Ex-slaves, especially young ones, tended to run in one of two directions—acting in or acting out. The ones who acted in stayed very quiet, tiptoeing around the monastery as if they were afraid of being noticed and sold back into servitude. Willa struck Ara as one of these. The ones who acted out went in the other direction, taking out suppressed rage and hidden fears on their teachers and fellow students. Jeren Drew was clearly one of these, and now Kendi seemed to be joining him. A precious few seemed to come through slavery relatively unscathed. Kite looked to fall into this category, but it was too early to know for sure. Maybe his strange speech was a symptom of a deeper issue.

In any case, Kendi was Ara's special problem, since she had requested him for one-on-one instruction, making her a surrogate parent in many ways. Jeren, Kite, and Willa had all been matched with other teachers. Although it was certainly possible to take on more than one student at a time, the monastery frowned on the practice, especially when it came to teaching ex-slaves. It often helped a slave's damaged self-esteem to know that the current teacher was focused on him or her alone.

A now-familiar clanking issued from behind Ben's closed door. Ara knocked, then poked her head inside. Ben was pressed into a chair, shoving at a stack of weights with his legs.

"Your aunt and uncle are coming over for dinner," she said, picking up their earlier conversation. "We'll be eating late."

"I figured," Ben grunted, face red with exertion. "Are the jerks coming, too?"

Ara put her hands on her hips. "I wish you would try to get along with your cousins. You don't have any brothers or sisters, and it would be nice if—"

"The hell it would." *Clank. Clank.*

"Watch your—oh, never mind." There were some battles not worth fighting. "Just wear something nice, and try to be polite. Clear?"

Ben shrugged, and Ara decided to take that for agreement.

"I have to go give a lesson," she continued. "I'll be back in time to start supper."

Clank. The weights stopped, and Ben wiped his face with his shirt, revealing a flash of pale, flat stomach. "You're not ordering out and telling everyone you made it? What happened—Maureen's go out of business?"

"Ha-ha. Just for that, wise guy, you can peel the shrimp for me."

Kendi Weaver made a sound of exasperation and got up from the couch. "It still doesn't work."

"Kendi, meditation and breathing exercises are very important," Mother Ara explained patiently from her chair. Their voices were deadened by the soundproofed walls of the tiny, windowless meditation cubicle. "You have to ready both mind and body. Otherwise, you'll never enter the Dream."

"I'm not saying I shouldn't meditate. I'm just saying I can't do it lying down like that. It doesn't feel right. I can't concentrate."

"Well, some Silent prefer leaning back or even—"

"I made this today." Kendi reached under his couch and pulled out the short spear. He had skipped the rest of his morning classes to sand it, and the wood was smooth and solid in his hand. After helping the custodian repair the gutter, he had wheedled some red paint and a rubber tip out of her. The rubber was to cover the spear's point.

"What is it?" Mother Ara asked.

"A meditation spear. The Real People use them to . . . commune with the Dreamtime. I'm willing to bet the Dream is really the same thing."

Mother Ara cocked her head. "Why do you—they—call themselves the Real People?"

"The Real People—Australian Aborigines—consider ourselves to be the original human race," Kendi explained. "My ancestors lived in the proper way, recognizing themselves as part of the world and universe around them, no more or less important than any other living thing. Mutants—other tribes of humans—try to separate themselves from the universe. They build houses and cars and ships. When that happens, they lose contact with each other and lose their connection with the Dreamtime. As a result, they fight and kill and enslave one another."

As Kendi spoke, he realized that he was mostly parroting a lecture he had heard Neluukatelardin give many times. Back then, he had barely listened, wanted nothing more than to get out of the hot sun and go home. But now the words took on a new meaning. Kendi had fully experienced the contrast between

Real People and mutant societies. Despite the boredom and harsh weather on walkabout, everyone in the group had watched out for everyone else and built a strong sense of community. Every single person had value; every single person counted the same as every other. A far cry from a mutant slave auction.

"What's the Dreamtime, then?" Mother Ara asked.

"It's kind of hard to describe," Kendi said. "Time and place have no meaning there. It's the beginning of everything, of all things and all traditions. This world got started there and is sort of an extension of it. Lots of powerful creatures live in it, and the Real People can walk there. Or we could until the mutants destroyed our society. After a few generations, we forgot how to do it. We forgot how to do a lot of things."

"So the Real People are Silent, then," Mother Ara mused.

Kendi shrugged and sat down again, still holding the spear. "Maybe. We were around a long time before Irfan Qasad genengineered people for it. Anyway, I can't sit when I meditate. That's not how we do it."

"There are lots of ways to meditate, Kendi," Mother Ara said. "You can use any method you want as long as it works for you."

"Then I want to try this."

Mother Ara gestured at him to continue. Kendi got up. Around his wrist he wore the medical bracelet which monitored pulse rate, respiration, brainwave activity, and blood pressure. It was slaved to Mother Ara's data pad so she could keep an eye on him with it. Kendi took a deep breath. He had spent a little time practicing his balance, but he wasn't perfect yet. He bent his left knee and fitted the short spear under it like a peg leg. The rubber tip kept the spear from skidding on the smooth floor. Then he held his hands over his groin. At first, this had made him feel uncomfortable, but he had found it easier to keep his balance when his arms and hands weren't allowed to dangle loosely. He was a bit wobbly, but steady enough, and it definitely felt better than lying down.

"Hm," Mother Ara said. "Well then—let's try it. Do you want the drumming?"

"Yeah. The rhythm helps."

He closed his eyes and a moment later, a recorded drum playback filled the room.

"Focus on your breathing," Mother Ara said in a calm, soothing voice. "Feel the air fill your lungs as you breathe in and out, in and out."

The meditation exercise continued. Once, Kendi lost his balance and had to reposition himself. All throughout, Mother Ara's quiet voice urged him to leave his body behind, ignore it. But he couldn't ignore the physical sensations—the spear under his knee, the floor beneath his feet, the clothing on his body. He suppressed a grimace, frustrated. He couldn't keep up the concentration to ignore anything. It felt like something was there but just out of reach, and the harder he tried to reach it, the further away it moved. Maybe the spear was the wrong idea after all.

Some time later, Mother Ara told him to open his eyes. The drum playback ended.

"That was pretty good," she said. "Better than before, in fact. Your heart rate dropped, and your breathing slowed considerably. Brainwave activity was a little high, but—"

"I can't do it." Kendi disentangled himself from the spear and dropped onto the couch. "It's still not working."

"Kendi, you haven't been doing this for even a week," Mother Ara reminded him. "You're doing very well. It takes months or even years of work to get to the point where you're ready to enter the Dream."

"Months," he muttered. The frog farm and its months of unchanging labor flashed before him. Had he just traded one kind of mindlessness for another? And how long would it be, then, before he got a chance to look for his family? Years? Martina would be all grown up before he saw her again, and Mom and Dad would be old and gray.

"Don't get discouraged," Mother Ara said. She shut off her data pad and put it away. "Your Silence is very strong. When other Silent touch you, they get a serious jolt. I don't think we could keep you out of the Dream if we tried. How are your dreams at night? Still vivid?"

Kendi shrugged, again feeling hemmed in by the tiny room. He glanced at his fingernail and the new chrono-display implanted on it. Lesson time was almost over.

"Practice on your own, too," Mother Ara continued. "Every moment helps."

"Okay." He gathered up the spear and checked to make sure his own data pad was in his pocket. "Are we done?"

"Not quite." Mother Ara's voice took on a more serious tone. "I got a call from your history teacher today."

Uh-oh, Kendi thought.

"She says you skipped out. You also missed language studies and philosophy. I checked."

"I had to work on this," Kendi protested, holding up the spear.

"Kendi, you can't skip class. Everything you learn there is important, especially language studies. You have to learn to understand the Ched-Balaar."

"It's boring," Kendi mumbled. "Why can't we just wear a translator or something?"

"You might not always have a translator on you. Besides, the Ched-Balaar learned our language. It would be rude not to learn theirs."

"I can't sit that long."

"Learning to concentrate in class will also help you meditate," Mother Ara pointed out. "And you can't take formal vows as a Child until you complete your education. You have to go to class, Kendi. This isn't a choice—unless you want to leave the Children entirely. Clear?"

"Yeah, okay. Can I go now?"

"Not until you swear to me that you won't skip again."

"Fine. I swear."

Mother Ara got up from her chair and sat next to him on the couch. "Kendi, I know a lot of stuff is hard for you. You went through hell, and now you're here on a world where people live in treehouses with aliens. I can understand why you'd have a hard time caring about the history of Bellerophon or deciphering Ched-Balaar teeth-clacking."

Kendi didn't say anything. He just stared at the floor and let Mother Ara's words coast past him.

"If you want to talk about any of it," Mother Ara said, "let me know, okay? A lot of times just talking makes people feel better. Or if you don't want to talk to me, you can talk to someone else. The Children of Irfan take care of their own, Kendi. Maybe we're not the Real People, but we do our best."

Kendi still didn't answer. Mother Ara sighed and patted his shoulder. Abruptly, Kendi felt like he was going to cry. He held his breath to avoid it.

"Well, all right," Mother Ara said. "You'd better get going. And I have a dinner to cook. See you at the Festival games tonight?"

"Yeah, okay." Kendi took up his spear and pad and left before Mother Ara could see the tears gathering in his eyes.

"So what's the latest on the investigation?" asked Uncle Hazid around a mouthful of curried shrimp.

Ben looked up from his plate. The question had been directed at his mother, but something in Uncle Hazid's tone got his attention.

Mom blinked. "What investigation?"

"You know," Aunt Sil put in. "The one about the Dream killer. I've heard he can change shape in the Dream. Is that true?"

"How in the world would I know?" Mom said.

"You're assisting the Guardians on the case, aren't you?" Aunt Sil said. Like Mom, she was short and round, with a heavy face and thick black hair that swooped or twisted over her head as whim and fashion decreed. She wore a corsage of red and blue flowers. It matched the centerpiece on the table. The rest of the house was decorated with more flowers and the computer played Festival music in the background. Ben liked everything about Festival except the annual family dinner. Fortunately, that part always came first, meaning he could get it out of the way and enjoy the rest of the evening.

"The case?" Mom said.

"I heard all about it from Jenine Frank at the Guardian outpost just up the walkway," Aunt Sil said. "A nice thing—you're working on a famous murder case and you don't even tell your own sister."

Ben put his fork down, unsure how to feel. "Mom? You never said anything about this."

"I—that is, I'm not supposed to discuss it," she floundered.

"Well, certainly not with someone who isn't Silent," Aunt Sil said with a friendly smile toward Ben. "They wouldn't understand. But we're your *family*."

Ben's jaw firmed until it ached, but he didn't say anything.

"Sil!" Mom said. "That's not—"

"Did you get to see the body?" interrupted Tress. She was seventeen, also short and dark haired, and

already into advanced Dream studies at the monastery.

"Yeah!" said Zayim, who was sixteen and battling
acne. "Was it all creepy? The news services said it
was all bruised."

"Kids!" Uncle Hazid admonished. "A healthy curi-
osity is one thing, but this is gruesome. It's a dangerous situation. Everyone's running scared, Ara. What
can you tell us?"

Mom's face went tight-lipped in an expression Ben
knew well. At this point, they may as well try to pry
open a clam with their fingernails. "I said I can't discuss it. Any information about the investigation that
gets out could get back to the killer and help him—
or her."

"We won't tell anyone," Tress said, opening her
eyes until they looked wide and innocent. Ben recognized that expression too, and he had long ago learned
not to trust it.

Apparently Mom had learned the same lesson.
"And how are your studies coming, Tress?" she said.

"Fine," she said. "But what about the—"

"And yours, Zayim?" Mom interrupted. "Did you
pass your first-tier qualifiers yet?"

Zayim, who was more distractible than Tress, went
on at some length about the tests he had taken in the
Dream to prove the amount of control he had. Ben
tuned it out and went back to eating. Zayim and Tress
were always talking about the Dream and what they
did there. Uncle Hazid and Aunt Sil were the same
way. Usually this meant Ben felt bored and left out
of family discussions, but this time it gave him a
chance to think. He stole a glance at Mom. She was
investigating the Dream killer? What did that mean?
Was she tracking him down in the Dream? Would she
be in danger from him?

Worry, the most familiar of all Ben's emotions, set-

tled over him like a heavy blanket. It seemed like he
was always worrying. When he was little and Mom lay
comatose on her couch doing business in the Dream,
he worried she wouldn't come out of it. When he was
older and Mom regularly left Bellerophon to hunt
down enslaved Silent, he worried she would be enslaved herself and never come back. Now he knew she
was hunting down a murderer who had, according to
the Bellerophon news services, killed at least two Silent women, and he worried that the killer could come
after her.

Don't be stupid, he scolded himself. *Mom can take
care of—*

"Attention! Attention!" chimed the computer. "Incoming call for Mother Araceil Rymar."

Mom excused herself, then came back a moment
later, her face tight with annoyance. "I'm sorry, everyone, but I have to go down to the monastery. Kendi—
my student—is in trouble. Again. Make yourselves at
home while I'm gone. I'll be back as soon as I can
and we can go down to the games."

"We'll clean up," Aunt Sil said. "But really, Ara, I
don't understand how you can work with these people.
Ex-slaves always make trouble. You'd think they'd be
more grateful—and on Festival, too."

"Not all of them make trouble," Ara said lightly.
"And it's a fine reward to see them take formal
vows."

"All that trouble and next to nothing in return." Sil
shook her head. "I couldn't stand it."

"Yes, Sil dear. That's why you're still a Sister and
I'm nearly a Mother Adept." And she swept out the
door. Ben held back a snort and Sil's face colored.
Hazid adjusted the napkin on his lap. Tress and Zayim
exchanged glances.

"She always has to throw it in my face, doesn't
she?" Sil whined the moment the front door had shut.

" 'Look at me. I'm going to be a Mother Adept.' Well, la-dee-da."

"That's just how she is," Hazid said philosophically. "She'll never change."

"Working with her little slaves all the time," Sil raged on as if Ben weren't sitting at the same table. "The woman gives time and shelter to every little bit of trash that darkens her door. Doesn't she realize how that *looks*?"

Tress nudged her brother and smirked at Ben. Ben's hands shook. He wanted to fling his plate into Sil's face, into all their faces. Instead, he got up and left the dining room. Sil and Hazid, still deep in conversation about Mom, didn't even seem to notice. In his bedroom, Ben lay back on the weight bench and, heedless of his dress clothes, started a series of reps. The room was still warm from the afternoon sun and sweat quickly soaked his good shirt, but anger pushed him onward, anger at his aunt and uncle, anger at his mother for leaving him with them so often, anger at his cousins for being so self-centered.

Anger at himself for not standing up to them.

Ben let the weight stack fall harder than he should have and set the machine for some leg work. What would it be like, he wondered, to belong to a real family? One with a father and a mother and more than one kid? Mom had tried to make Tress and Zayim into a brother and sister for him, but—

"I feel sorry for him," came Zayim's faint voice. "It's like Mom said—it isn't *his* fault he's not Silent. It's probably Aunt Ara's."

"Yeah. You think she did some kind of drug while she was pregnant and that's what screwed Ben up?" This was Tress.

Ben very carefully lowered the weight stack, letting it make only the tiniest clank as it touched down. The voices were coming in through his open window. Tress and Zayim must be on the deck that wrapped around the house.

"Maybe. You get a look at that weight machine in his room?" Zayim said. "What a waste of time. First the computers, now this. He might be able to hit the Dream if he kept working on it instead of screwing around with this other stuff. Dad says he just doesn't try hard enough."

"I read somewhere that guys who lift weights a lot do it because they think their dicks are too small and they're trying to make up for it," Tress said.

"Completely true. And the proof is that *I've* never had any interest in weights."

Tress snorted. "He always was a twerp."

Ben's jaw trembled with agitation. It was always this way with Tress and Zayim. When they were small, they had called him names like *paleface* and *shorty*. When it became clear that Ben was unaware of the Dream and would never enter it, the names had changed to *loudmouth* and *mutant*. Tress used to pinch him under the dinner table, leaving black and blue marks on his arms and legs. Zayim liked to break Ben's toys and blame it on Ben himself, which got him into trouble with Sil and Hazid. Staying with his aunt and uncle while Mom went off on her "recruiting missions," as she called them, became a form of hell. Computers and studying became at first a way to escape and later a habit. It was with great relief that Ben received permission from Mom to stay by himself while she was gone.

Tress and Zayim continued talking about him and Mom, and he became pretty sure they knew he could hear. Ben wondered what would happen if he stuck his head out the window and yelled something at his cousins. Something witty that would flatten both of them.

Something completely out of character.

Ben stared at the window. It would all be bearable if he had some decent friends, even just one. But he didn't. In the school for non-Silent relatives of the Children of Irfan, Ben had firmly established an identity as a loner. Tress and Zayim had taught him that friendly overtures could be disguises for jokes and teasing, and he had never been very good at talking to people to begin with. Being lonely was better than being a potential target.

Benjamin Rymar turned grimly back to his weights and let their clanking drown out the voices from the window.

Kendi wandered up and down the crowded evening walkways. Although the sun had long since set, everything was brightly lit. Paper lanterns hung from every eave and balcony rail, drenching the darkness with suffused golden light. Circles of drummers sat on balconies and staircases, thudding out steady rhythms and calling out encouragement to each other. Humans and Ched-Balaar alike carried a candle in one hand and a bowl in the other. The candle symbolized the campfire shared by the Ched-Balaar and the humans at the ceremony that had allied the two races. The bowl symbolized the vessel that had contained the ceremonial wine drunk by Irfan Qasad and the others—including Daniel Vik. The drugs in the wine and the drumming of the Ched-Balaar had brought a few of the original Bellerophon humans into the Dream and ultimately led to the founding of the Children of Irfan.

Irfan must have had a hell of a lot of talent, Kendi mused darkly, *getting into the Dream so easily like that.*

His mood was at distinct odds with the people around him. Everywhere people were laughing and singing and dancing to the drums. Street—walkway?— vendors sold wax candles and clay bowls and hot food and cold drink and decorative trinkets and cheap toys.

Music was everywhere, timed in rhythm with the drumming. Favored instruments seemed to be recorders and pennywhistles. Kendi wondered how they would react to a didgeridoo. He knew somewhere, on the wider platforms, Festival games were held, but he wasn't in the mood.

It shouldn't have been that big a deal. A pod of dinosaurs—those big ones with long tails and necks—had thundered slowly by right under the dormitory. They were nothing like the fast, agile creature Kendi had encountered on the ultralight. These were big and slow and stupid. What was the big deal if Kendi ran down the stairs to get a closer look? And so what if he had climbed up on the back of one of the smaller ones? The thing hadn't even noticed he was there. He had just wanted to see if he could do it, prove to himself that he wasn't afraid. But Mother Ara had thrown a fit. Now, Festival or no Festival, he had even more work detail. In fact, he had been assigned to help clean up in the morning. It was stupid and unfair.

A familiar laugh broke through the drums and laughter. Kendi twisted his head around, his heart suddenly beating fast as he caught sight of a familiar figure on a platform a ways ahead of him. Pitr. Kendi had forgotten all about Pitr, how he had promised himself he would talk to Pitr tonight. It was Festival, night of beginnings and changes. Kendi's palms sweated.

For someone who just rode a dinosaur, he told himself, *you're acting awfully scared.*

Pitr was talking in a small group of people, each of whom carried a bowl and a candle. Kendi had neither, hadn't wanted to get one until now. He remembered Dorna telling him that it would be customary to offer drinks from his bowl to other people as a way of greeting. Kendi cast about and saw a Ched-Balaar sitting doglike behind a table piled high with Festival bowls for sale. Kendi hurried over and grabbed one. He thumbed the Ched-Balaar's pad, charging the bowl to his student account. The Ched-Balaar filled the bowl with a purple liquid that smelled vaguely alcoholic to Kendi. Kendi thanked the merchant, who chattered something back to him. Kendi, who didn't understand a bit of it, merely nodded politely and turned away. He took a big gulp from the bowl—it was indeed something alcoholic—and caught up an unattended votive candle burning on a nearby rail. Forcing himself to move forward with firm steps, he approached Pitr Haddis. This was going to be it. He would find out one way or the other. As he walked, a prayer came to his mind, one he remembered from the Real People Reconstructionists.

If it be in my best interest and in the best interest of all life everywhere, he thought, *let Pitr choose me tonight.*

Mouth dry despite the weak wine, Kendi came up behind Pitr and cleared his throat. "Hey, Pitr. Want a drink?"

Pitr, who had been leaning his elbows on the platform rail with his back to Kendi, turned and smiled. So did several of the people around him. Kendi didn't recognize any of them and he briefly wondered where Trish was.

"Kendi," Pitr said brightly. "Joyous Festival. I was wondering if I was going to run into you."

"Really?" Kendi raised his bowl. "I'm here. I was wondering if I"—he had to pause to clear his throat again—"if I could talk to you for a minute."

"Sure," Pitr said, and Kendi's insides twisted at the sight of his smile. "Oh wait—I'm being rude. Kendi, this is Holda." He gestured at a petite blond girl who looked to be about Pitr's age. She had brown eyes and a round, pretty face. "Holda, this is Kendi Weaver."

Holda held out her hand. Kendi automatically set

the bowl on the rail so he could shake it. No jolt—
Holda wasn't Silent.

"You're the guy who was attacked on the ultralight?" she asked. "Pitr told me all about it. You were
pretty brave."

"Yeah, thanks," Kendi said, wondering how he
could get rid of Holda so he could talk to Pitr alone.

"Tonight's our one-month anniversary," Pitr said,
and he kissed Holda loudly on the cheek. She laughed
and pushed him away.

"Don't," she admonished lightly. "You're too cute
when you do that."

Kendi's heart froze solid in his chest. He stared first
at Pitr, then at Holda. They were holding hands. He
didn't know what to do, what to say.

"Anyway—you wanted to talk to me?" Pitr said.

Kendi continued to stare, then something broke and
his wits rushed back to him. His face began to burn.
"It can wait," he said faintly. "It was just something
about . . . about the ultralights, but it's no big deal. I
just remembered that I'm supposed . . . supposed to
meet someone at the games. I'll catch you later."

He caught up his bowl and fled before either Pitr or
Holda could say anything. He kept walking, dodging
around Festival partyers, until he found a place away
from the noise and the lantern light. His candle had
gone out. Darkness closed in around him. Insects
called and night birds sang. Two walkways met here,
and Kendi leaned on the rail to stare out into the
night. The drums were only a faint sound in the
distance.

Stupid, he thought fiercely. *I was so stupid.* It would
have been the easiest thing in the world to ask Pitr if
he had a girlfriend, a perfectly innocent question, a
question people ask all the time in idle conversation.
But for some reason it hadn't occurred to Kendi to
ask it. Stupid, stupid, stupid. He had come within mil-

limeters of making a complete fool of himself, just as
he had done with Pup. Thank all life something had
stopped him. Otherwise he'd have never been able to
look Pitr in the face again and flight lessons would
have been impossibly awkward. Sudden loneliness
welled up in him. No matter how hard he tried, it
seemed like he was always alone these days. That was
the worst part of it—being alone.

Festival night, he thought. *Beginnings, changes, and
new directions. Well here's a change for you.*

Kendi flung his clay bowl over the edge. He heard
it collide with something, probably a tree branch, and
shatter. They wanted resolutions? Here was a resolution—from now on, Kendi was going to leave well
enough alone, no matter how lonely he got.

And he wasn't going to cry about it. No, he wasn't.

The latter resolution lasted less than a minute.

NINE

*Just because I can reach the Dream doesn't mean
I want to spend my whole life there. Unlike some
people.*

—Daniel Vik

Mother Ara turned a baleful eye on Kendi and Jeren.
Kendi tried to meet it and found he couldn't. Mother
Ara had the best glare of anyone he'd ever met and,
even after repeated practice, he still couldn't stand up
to it.

"Didn't we go through this at Festival last year?"
she growled. "I truly don't know what to do with
you two."

"You could—" Kendi began.

"I didn't mean for you to give an answer," Mother
Ara snapped. "I'm tired of all this. You've been here
for—what?—a year now. An entire year. You've
signed your contracts with the Children, you have your
own teachers, you wear the ruby ring. And still you
keep breaking the rules. This may come as a surprise
to the both of you, but yes, it *is* against the rules to
hijack an ultralight and buzz a pod of mickey spikes.
You caused a stampede, for god's sake. What if someone had been standing in the way? They would have
been killed."

"I—" Jeren said.

"And don't think I know how it all works by now,"
Mother Ara continued ruthlessly. "You, Jeren, cook
up some cockeyed scheme and you egg Kendi into
joining you. Kendi, I'm especially surprised at you. I
thought you'd been making real progress. Then you

go and do this. What would the Real People say about that kind of treatment toward animals?"

Kendi ground his teeth. That line always got to him, and Mother Ara knew it. He replied with the only defense he knew. "Most of them are dead. They don't say much."

"Don't get flip," she answered. "You know I'm right. And you, Jeren . . ."

In the end, they each got an extra four hours of work detail. As they headed out the door of Mother Ara's tiny office at the monastery, Mother Ara called out, "Kendi, wait a moment."

Jeren caught Kendi's eye. "I'll catch you outside," he murmured, and shut the door.

Kendi turned back. Mother Ara was still sitting behind her desk, her hands folded on top of it. The little room was crammed with . . . stuff. Kendi couldn't think of any other way to describe it. Shelves of book-disks on the walls, a bulletin board covered with cartoons and little comics, two small statues of Irfan Qasad serving as bookends, brightly woven wall hangings with quilting and tassels, little trinkets—some tacky, some tasteful—and a dozen awards and framed certificates all crowded around a desktop littered with more disks, a data pad, and a portable telephone. Two pots of red and blue flowers had been somehow squeezed in as a concession to Festival. A head-and-shoulders hologram of a teenage boy with red hair and blue eyes occupied the ledge below the room's only window. The boy was good looking and bore no resemblance to Mother Ara whatever. Kendi wondered who he was. Nephew? Family friend? He was definitely cute, whoever he was.

Mother Ara gestured to one of two chairs opposite the desk. "Kendi, sit down again."

Kendi obeyed with all the annoyed reluctance he

could muster. She had already slammed him with more work detail. Like he had a lot of free time as it was. Now she was going to hit him with something more? He mentally reviewed the recent past, trying to remember if he had done anything else she could get him for. He had broken the dorm curfew for underage students twice last week, but no one had caught him sneaking in, he was sure. His grades weren't great right now, but official reports weren't due out for almost a month, so it couldn't be that. Unless one of his teachers had complained about him. He clenched his jaw. That was probably it. Sister Bren must have called Mother Ara again. Sister Bren had had it in for him since the first day of class, and Mother Ara would take her side. She always did.

"I've been wondering if you've given any more thought to the suggestion I made to you last week," Mother Ara said. "And the week before that. And last month."

The head of steam that had been building up inside Kendi abruptly evaporated. He knew what she was talking about, but pretended ignorance. "Suggestion?"

"Do you think about your family a lot?" Mother Ara asked.

Kendi nodded. "Yeah. So?"

"I'm not accusing you of anything, Kendi. I'm worried about you."

Kendi just looked at her without speaking.

"I said it before—you've been through a lot," Mother Ara said. "That kind of thing makes you angry, and the anger doesn't just go away because you've been freed from slavery."

Kendi remained silent.

"You're not alone, Kendi," Mother Ara continued quietly. She pushed aside a couple data disks and leaned her elbows on the desk. "The Children take care of their own, and you're one of us. Kendi, please—let's make arrangements for you to talk to someone about what you've been through."

"You mean a therapist. Someone who talks to crazy people."

"A counselor," Mother Ara said. "Someone who listens and helps you through—"

"I don't have time," Kendi interrupted. "All that work detail."

"If you'll agree to see someone, I'll cancel the work detail."

"Is that why you gave it to me?" Kendi snapped back. "To blackmail me into seeing a therapist?"

Mother Ara's face clouded and she looked ready to give a sharp retort, then stopped herself. "You know that's not the case, Kendi. I want to help you. The pain you're in is—"

"—is none of your business. Look, can I go now? I have stuff to do."

Mother Ara sighed. "All right. But at least think about what I said, all right? And don't forget your lesson this afternoon."

"Yeah, sure," Kendi said in his least convincing voice. "Can I go?"

Mother Ara nodded and Kendi quickly left the office. Who did she think she was? Who did she think *he* was? Some kind of loony? Yeah, he was angry, but he was angry at Mother Ara for giving him work detail, at Sister Bren for getting on his case all the time. If they just left him alone, he'd be fine.

Outdoors, Kendi wandered over to a railing and peered down into the green depths of the forest below. Festival flowers and decorations had sprouted on houses, balconies, and walkways everywhere. It was sunny, the first sunny day after a solid week of clouds, and the air was balmy and warm, exactly as it had been on the day he had first arrived on Bellerophon last year. A lot had happened in that time. Kendi had gained several centimeters of height and survived a year of classes without exactly failing any of them. It hadn't been easy. More than once he had been tempted to take the free one-way passage Mother Ara said he could use whenever he wanted and run off to search for his family. But each time he hadn't gone through with it. Part of it was practicality—he had no idea where to start looking. There was also the fact that he knew his mother was Silent. The most viable place to find her, it seemed to Kendi, was the Dream, with the Children to help him. That meant working hard to reach the place himself. More than once, however, he lost sight of this, and Mother Ara was always there when it happened.

"So what'd she want?" Jeren asked at his elbow. Kendi jumped.

"Don't do that," he said. "All life, you scared the shit out of me."

Jeren grinned. "Good. So what'd she want?"

"She wanted me to see a therapist. Like I'm some loony head or something. I told her I didn't have time because of all the work detail she laid on me."

"Good one," Jeren said. His green eyes darkened with anger. The white scar still framed his left eye, and he still favored dressing in black leather, even though it was summer. "My teacher's been the same way. Wants me to spill my guts to some total stranger and think that's going to make me a model citizen. Fuck that."

"Yeah." Kendi paused. "So what've you got on your plate this afternoon?"

"Besides work detail? More Dream practice, natch." His grin grew wolfish. "Yesterday I found this orgy—no lie, guy! Whole group of people rolling around on this giant mattress. I was gonna ask if they'd let me join in"—he groped his crotch—"because I'm hung like a donkey, and I know they'd want it, but my drugs were wearing off and I had to quit. You gotta get there, man."

Kendi nodded glumly. He didn't believe half of what Jeren told him about his adventures in the Dream, but even so the subject depressed him. Jeren and Kite both had reached the Dream last month. Dorna, of course, was in and out of it all the time. Willa hadn't gotten there yet, but that didn't make Kendi feel any less like he was failing. He was one of the Real People. Walking the Dreamtime should be easy for him. Why was it so hard?

Jeren gave him an odd look. "What's up with you? Old Lady Rymar didn't get you down, did she? It's not like we did anything really wrong, no matter what she fucking says."

"I just don't want to get into more trouble, Jeren," Kendi said. "You can do what you want, but I'm—"

"Hey guys," said a new voice. "What's going on?"

Kendi turned. Pitr Haddis stood behind them, one hand in his pocket. He wore brown from head to foot, and an orange topaz ring graced his finger, indicating he had finished his student training and was now an apprentice to someone ranked Parent or higher. He had earned the ring only last week. Kendi, who was now certified for light aircraft and now took lessons in heavier craft from Toshi, smiled at Pitr. He'd definitely been smart to keep his mouth shut and avoid potential embarrassment. That seemed to be the best policy for this kind of thing.

"We're bitching about Mother Ara," Jeren told him.

Kendi punched him on the arm, not hard enough to hurt, but too hard to be just friendly. "*We* aren't. You are."

"Yeah, well maybe you should—"

He never finished. Willa, in her modest brown dress, rushed up to them, face flushed with excitement. Dorna and Kite were right behind her.

"I did it!" Willa shouted. "You'll never believe it, but I did it!"

Kendi stared. Willa shouting? "Did what?"

"She got into the Dream!" Dorna crowed.

A round of congratulations and hugs, including one from Pitr, who barely knew Willa. Kendi himself would barely have recognized her. Her eyes sparkled with energy and happiness and she couldn't seem to stop smiling. She was completely unlike her normal mouselike self.

"And so close to Festival, too," Kite said. "That's supposed to be good luck."

"What was it like for you?" Kendi demanded. A finger of jealousy poked at him.

"It's magic." Willa leaned on the railing and the soft breeze stirred her fine brown hair. "You can make whatever you want there. I wanted it to be sunny, and it was sunny. I wanted green grass and I got green grass. It all felt completely real. I want to go back again."

"Not scared of the Dream killer, huh?" Jeren said with a malicious gleam in his eye.

"Jeren!" Kite said. "Leave her alone. The Dream killer's gone. No one's been attacked for months."

"Doesn't mean anything," Jeren said. "He might be lying in wait even now, looking for just the right—"

"Let's talk about something else, yeah?" Dorna interrupted firmly. "Come on, Willa. We need to celebrate, hey? What do you want to do?"

But Jeren's remarks had dampened Willa's excitement. She shrugged and toyed with the ruby student's ring on her left hand. Kendi glared at Jeren.

"I know," Dorna continued, as if nothing were

wrong. "Shopping! Time to rack up some serious debt. You boys coming?"

As one, Jeren, Kendi, and Kite backed away. Dorna's power shopping trips were legend in the student community, and they all knew from experience that they would be drafted into bearer duty. Dorna laughed and led Willa off. Kendi watched them thoughtfully.

"Something's weird about Dorna," he said. "Seriously weird."

"What do you mean?" Pitr asked.

"It's hard to put my finger on it," Kendi replied. "It's not weird in a bad way. Just weird."

"Kite's weird, too," Jeren said. "He talks funny. All the time."

Kite, who had spent considerable time with a speech therapist and no longer tore through sentences like tissue paper, punched Jeren on the shoulder like Kendi had done. A friendly scuffle broke out between the two of them. Kendi and Pitr ignored it.

"Is it something we should talk to a Parent about?" Pitr asked.

"No," Kendi said, after a moment's thought. "It may be just the way she is. Let's get some lunch."

Ara pressed the tip of the dermospray to Kendi's upper arm and pressed the release. There was a soft *thump* as it shoved the drug through his skin. Swiftly, with the ease of much practice, he slipped his red spear beneath his knee and assumed his meditation pose. Despite his careful breathing, a small knot of tension formed in his stomach.

"What if it doesn't work?" he said.

"It will work eventually," Ara told him patiently. "We haven't lost anyone yet. Ched-Hisak is the teacher on duty in the Dream right now, so if you get there, he'll be waiting to catch you. And don't worry so much, Kendi. There's no pressure. I'm not worried. You shouldn't be either."

Kendi closed his eyes. His meditation skills had increased to the point where the only thing that could wake him was a double snap of Ara's fingers or his conscious choice. He never lost his balance on the spear anymore, and at night his dreams were so vivid that he awoke confused about who and where he was. This, Ara told him, was a sign that he was moving closer to touching the Dream. Kendi had never again seen the Real People in any of his nocturnal dreaming, however.

Colors flickered behind his eyes. The dermospray was a cocktail of drugs mixed to react to his own physiology, a recipe refined over many centuries of experimentation. Very few people, Ara said, could reach the Dream without some kind of pharmaceutical aid.

Kendi concentrated as a hypnotic rainbow swirled in the darkness around him. The drugs induced a pleasant, floating feeling, but were designed not to inhibit thought processes or become physically addictive. Kendi let himself float about at random for a while, then forced himself to concentrate. His body dropped away until he was no longer aware of the spear under his knee or of his breathing or his heartbeat. Ara had said he needed to create a personal place for himself, a place where he felt safe and happy. Kendi imagined the Australian Outback with its hot breezes and dry, rocky earth. He caught a whiff of desert air, but when he turned toward it, it disappeared. A flash of sunlight caught his attention, but it too vanished when he reached for it. A falcon cried on the high wind, but the sound faded when he tried to sense which direction it came from. Voices whispered all around him, just loud enough to hear, but not loud enough to understand.

Kendi ground his teeth in frustration. It was just like every other time. He couldn't seem to—

Make a place for yourself, said the memory of Ara's voice. *A place where you feel safe and comfortable.*

And then it came to him. The Outback had never felt safe and comfortable to him while he had been in it. He had hated it. Only recently had it had any kind of allure for him. Maybe he needed to try something else. Kendi cast his thoughts back to his childhood. When he and Utang had been little, they had played at pirates and convicts, people on the run. They had used an abandoned building just up the block as a hideout, despite the fact that they had been forbidden to play there. Their imaginations had turned the basement into a cave, and Kendi had liked hiding in the cool, safe darkness. In the games he hadn't seen cracked concrete walls and a collapsing staircase. He had seen smooth stone, an arched roof, and a clean, sandy floor. A hole in the roof let in dim light and provided an egress for smoke from the campfire he and Utang would have. Ancient cave art danced on the walls instead of graffiti. It was a place to stash treasure and hide from marauding bands of British convicts, broken chains still clanking at their wrists. They would never find the entrance. It was a safe place.

Kendi brought the image of the cave firmly into his mind. He could almost feel the sandy floor beneath his feet, feel the cool air, see the bright paintings, smell the campfire smoke. Whispering voices swirled around him in a strange wind. The arched roof, the entrance tunnel, the ring of stones around the fire.

A subtle shift came over the space around his body. There was a sense of vastness, an echoing space. Kendi's eyes opened and he gasped in utter astonishment. He was standing in the cave. It was absolutely real. The cave was dim, just as he had imagined it,

with a single beam of sunlight stabbing down from the
hole in the high roof. A smoldering fire lay at the
bottom of the sunbeam, and the sharp smell of wood
smoke tanged the air. Kendi made a strangled noise,
and it echoed about the cave. His bare feet whispered
over dry sand as he staggered around the cave. It was
big enough to park a dozen cars in, and at least five
stories tall. And it felt safe.

Kendi whooped with glee and hugged himself as the
sound caroomed wildly off stone walls. He had done
it! He had entered the Dream!

Something touched him. Kendi froze for a moment,
then spun around. The touch hadn't been a physical
one. It was something else. Someone was walking
toward him, and he could feel the footsteps on the
ground as if the sand were his own skin. It frightened
him at first, but then he knew, somehow he knew, that
the touch was friendly, even familiar. A shadow
moved in the tunnel that led into the cave, and instantly Kendi knew who it was. He turned to the entrance and pressed fingertips to forehead.

"Father Ched-Hisak," he said. "I'm here."

A Ched-Balaar stepped into the cave, his head low
on his serpentine neck. His blond-brown fur gleamed
in the castoff sunlight from the center of the cave, and
his eyes were wide and happy. He opened his mouth
to speak, and Kendi braced himself for a dizzying bar-
rage of clattering teeth and strangely toned hooting.
He had been studying the Ched-Balaar language for
a year, but his understanding was severely limited.
Conversing without a translator would be difficult, but
he would manage. They would—

"I congratulate you, Kendi Weaver," Father Ched-
Hisak said in a clear voice. "You have made yourself
a fine place in the Dream."

Kendi stared, fingertips still on his forehead.

"You are surprised to understand me?" Father

Ched-Hisak said, amused. "But you know to speak in the Dream is a mere exchange of ideas. You read my thoughts, but you hear them as words."

"I forgot, Father," Kendi admitted. "So to you I'm chattering my teeth?"

"Indeed. You have a strange accent, but intelligible at every word. Come, then. I want to see the world you have created."

He took Kendi's hand. Father Ched-Hisak's palm was firm and soft as suede. That was when Kendi noticed he was naked. He looked down at himself uncertainly. Father Ched-Hisak noticed.

"You may wear anything you like," he said. "Your clothing is unimportant to such as I, but if it is important to you, then only think of what you want to be wearing and it will be so."

Instantly, Kendi was clothed in knee-length shorts and a simple shirt. This, however, felt wrong, confining. He realized that in this place he didn't want to wear clothing at all, but he couldn't quite bring himself to continue appearing naked in front of Father Ched-Hisak. His clothing wavered, shrank, expanded, and shrank again until Kendi settled on a simple loincloth.

Father Ched-Hisak ducked his head in approval. "Now. This is your safe place, the place in the Dream where no one may enter unless you allow such. The tunnel I entered led me inward from your public place, where you will eventually conduct business. Please. Here in this part of the Dream you must lead me. It is more polite."

Heart beating with exultation and excitement, Kendi lead Father Ched-Hisak up the tunnel. It was just tall enough for him to stand upright, though it was pitch black. Kendi wished he had a torch or something, and in an instant he held one in his hand. He was so startled, he almost dropped it.

"You must take care," Father Ched-Hisak warned. "Here in the Dream, thoughts become reality."

The tunnel formed a spiral that led up and out. After a few moments of walking, the spiral ended and Kendi found himself standing on a flat, rocky plain that stretched before him from horizon to horizon. Scrubby plants and ground-hugging vegetation made green-brown patches here and there. Voices whispered on the breeze, and Kendi knew they were other Silent, present but not visible to him, or he to them. Behind him rose a high cliff that seemed to touch the pure azure sky. A falcon cried overhead and dove toward the ground. A moment later, it rose again with a small animal wriggling in its talons. It was the Outback, exactly as Kendi remembered it. For the first time, it felt like home. And somewhere out there, his mother waited for him. He had but to find her.

"Come," Father Ched-Hisak said. "Show me this place."

Kendi squeezed the alien's hand and stepped with joy into his own Dream.

Ben sat on the floor in the corner of the living room and looked longingly at his bedroom door. It was shut, and he had firm orders from Mom that it was to stay that way, with Ben on this side of it. Ben shifted uncomfortably and took a sip of his drink, trying to look interested in his surroundings when he would far rather have been somewhere, anywhere, else.

The house and balcony were crowded with teenage students, teachers from the monastery, and even a few Ched-Balaar. Conversation, both murmured and loud, filled every corner. The dining room table was laden with food and drink, and the computer played bright music from every speaker in the house. Paper Festival lanterns hung from the eaves, granting cheerful yellow light to the balmy summer darkness, and the house was filled with Festival flowers, banners, and decorations. The biggest banner said, CONGRATULATIONS JEREN, KENDI, KITE, & WILLA.

Ben hated parties, especially ones like this, where he didn't know much of anyone. The guests were all Silent, and they didn't often mingle with the non-Silent. There was no rule about this—it just happened that way. Ben supposed it made sense. The Silent all had something in common, so why wouldn't they tend to stick together?

There were actually many more non-Silent on Bellerophon than Silent. However, Bellerophon's economy centered around the Children of Irfan. In the shadow of the ecological disasters that had befallen Earth, mining, farming, and talltree harvesting were all strictly regulated. Most of what the planet produced was used by its own populace. As a result, Bellerophon's economy depended on the income brought in by the Children of Irfan in order to obtain the goods and services Bellerophon couldn't produce for itself. The Children of Irfan, in turn, depended on the non-Silent for food, clothing, medicine, and other necessities. It was an equitable arrangement which, in theory, fostered an atmosphere of tolerance and respect between Silent and non-Silent alike.

It didn't, however, necessarily foster a lot of friendships. Ben lived among the Silent, attended some classes with them, but he had no friends among them. Come to that, he had no real friends, even among the non-Silent. Sure, he knew people at school, but no one well enough to invite to a party, especially a Silent party.

All four of the slaves Mom had rescued last year had managed to enter the Dream. The last one, a guy named Kendi, had done it the day before yesterday, and Mom had decided to change family tradition and throw a party on Festival to celebrate. Ben, however, suspected an ulterior motive. Mom knew very well that Ben wasn't very social, and he was sure she was hoping he'd make some friends. Festival—time of new beginnings. As a result, Ben sat stubbornly in a corner and refused to talk to anyone, except as politeness required. He knew he was being contrary, but he couldn't seem to help it.

The party did produce one bit of good—it swallowed up Aunt Sil, Uncle Hazid, and his cousins. He hadn't seen them all evening.

Ben's blue-eyed gaze drifted over the crowd, most of whom were dressed in brown. Across the room, Kendi Weaver laughed at something. Ben stared at him uncertainly. He seemed so at ease in the crowd, completely sure of himself. And he was handsome, with his dark skin, tightly curled black hair, and tall, lean build. Ben looked away quickly, but after a couple minutes found himself looking at Kendi again. He hadn't actually met Kendi, had, in fact, been actively avoiding him. Ben always avoided his mother's one-on-one students. It was awkward all around. There was also a lingering feeling of jealousy that Ben couldn't deny. Mom's students were Silent. Her son was not. Which of the two, he found himself wondering, would end up having the closer relationship?

Kendi turned and caught Ben looking at him. Ben instantly glanced away, feeling unsettled and not knowing why. He sipped fruit punch from the glass on the floor beside him. What the heck was going on? Ben had never stared at someone like that before, certainly not another—

Someone plunked down on the floor next to him. Startled, Ben turned. It was Kendi. And Ben's heart jumped into overdrive.

"Hi," Kendi said. "You're Ben, right? Your mom is my teacher?"

"Uh, yeah. I guess," Ben stammered, and silently

cursed himself. Why was he always so stupid when it came to talking with strangers? And why did this particular stranger make him blush like this?

"I'm Kendi Weaver." He held out a hand. Ben set down his glass and shook it. Kendi smiled. "Oh, that's right. Mother Ara mentioned it, but I'd forgotten. You're not Silent."

Mom talked about him to her students? Ben didn't know how to feel about that. Annoyed, maybe?

"No," he said. "I'm not."

"What a relief," Kendi said, pumping Ben's hand energetically. "All life, you have no idea what a relief it is."

Ben blinked. "Sorry?"

"Just about everyone at this party is Silent," Kendi explained, "and they've all been shaking my hand. I've been jolted so many times I feel like a lightning rod. It's nice to shake hands with someone who isn't going to zap me."

"Oh." Ben noticed his hand was still in Kendi's, though they had stopped shaking. Their eyes met for an instant. Then Ben broke away and took his hand back. He swallowed hard, floundering for something to say. Kendi leaned back against the wall.

"So what's it like growing up on Bellerophon?" he asked.

"I dunno," Ben said, and cursed himself again. But why did he care if Kendi got up and walked away?

Kendi laughed. "Yeah, stupid question. It's not like you'd know what it's like growing up anywhere else." He drained his glass. "You want some more to drink? I was going to get some."

"Uh, sure."

Kendi took their glasses and left. Ben watched him weave easily through the crowd, admiring the way he moved and realizing that he was looking forward to him coming back. What if he didn't come back?

Would that mean he didn't like Ben? Would that mean he—

"Here you go." Kendi handed Ben a full glass and joined him back on the floor. "It's a great party. Are you having fun?"

"No," Ben blurted out. "I mean—it isn't that—" He gave up. "No, not really."

"How come?"

"I don't like parties very much." He gestured at the moving sea of humans and Ched-Balaar. "Too many people, you know?"

"You want to go for a walk, then? Maybe get away from the crowd? I wouldn't mind either. It's really annoying getting zapped all the time."

Ben's instincts told him to say no. Kendi seemed loud, open, and forthright. Ben barely knew him. It would be easy enough just to refuse and things would stay the same. They would stay safe.

"Sure," he heard himself say. "Let's go."

Kendi planted his elbows on the railing and stared off into the warm night. Ben stood beside him, leaning backward and holding the top of the rail with one hand to keep his balance. The party, loud with voices and music, lay several walkways behind them and they were at a wide space, a platform with benches and several potted plants. The scent of summer flowers lingered in the air. Insects chirped and night animals occasionally called. In the distance, Festival music played.

Ben decided it was a fine night after all. The conversation between him and Kendi had died down—or rather, Kendi had stopped talking—but Ben didn't mind the silence. It was a *comfortable* silence. Usually Ben felt awkward unless the empty spaces were filled with equally empty words, but he could never think of anything to say. With Kendi, he didn't feel like he *needed* to have anything to say. Ben had never felt that before with anyone, and he liked it.

Kendi pulled himself up on the rail and perched on it. Still leaning back, Ben switched hands with a small jerk. His head ended up very close to Kendi's, and he was filled with a sudden urge to touch Kendi's arm, feel the smooth dark skin on his own. Confused, he switched hands one more time so he ended up a little farther away.

"Sitting on the rail will get you more work detail," he said.

Kendi shrugged. "If someone comes, I'll jump down." He paused. "Have you ever thought of leaving Bellerophon?"

"Sometimes, yeah. You?"

"All the time. I need to find my family."

Ben snorted. "You can have mine."

"Don't you like your mom? She's pretty cool, even if she hands out work detail sometimes."

"I like my mom. It's everyone else I can't stand."

"What do you mean?"

And Ben found himself telling Kendi about the problems he had with his extended family. It was the most talking Ben had done all evening, perhaps in his entire life. Kendi listened without interrupting.

"Sounds like our families need to trade places," Kendi said when he had finished, and Ben smiled. Kendi stared at him, still perched on the rail.

"What?" Ben asked. A strange feeling fluttered around his stomach.

"I—no, it's nothing." Kendi looked away.

"You what?" Ben persisted lightly, though he felt something heavier in the air. "What is it?"

"Uh-oh." He jumped off the rail and the moment was broken. "Someone's coming."

Ben turned. A figure was making its way toward them.

"Hey, Dorna," Kendi said when the figure got closer. "What's up?"

"Just wondering where you two have gotten off to," Dorna said. Although the night was warm, she wore a short cloak with the hood pulled over her dark hair. "The party's still going strong back there. A bunch of us are talking about going to see the fireworks."

"We're just talking," Kendi said. "How've you been?"

"A little weird, actually." Dorna sat down on a bench near a potted blueflower bush. Ben abruptly wished she would go away and leave him alone with Kendi. "I've been having trouble sleeping lately."

"How come?" Kendi asked.

Go away, Ben thought.

"Nightmares." The word came out almost dreamily. "I have nightmares about people dying in the Dream."

"The Dream stalker?" Kendi said.

Dorna shrugged. "Maybe. Do you think it's a premonition?"

"The Silent don't get premonitions," Ben put in. "That's not the way Silence works."

"I know that," Dorna said. "But don't you believe that people can have dreams that come true whether they're Silent or not?"

Ben shrugged.

"Who dies?" Kendi asked.

"I don't know. I can never see her face. I just wake up scared it's going to be me." She gave a little laugh. "Isn't that stupid? The last murder was a year ago. The Dream stalker is probably long gone."

"It's not stupid," Kendi said. "Maybe you should talk to a Parent about it."

"Maybe." Dorna gave herself a little shake. "Well, I'm going home. Maybe just telling you about the nightmares will make them go away."

And to Ben's relief, she got up and left, vanishing into the gloom. Kendi stared after her.

"What's the matter?" Ben asked.

"I've known Dorna for a year now," Kendi said pensively, "and something always bothers me about her, but I can never figure out quite what it is."

"She talks funny," Ben said.

Kendi turned. "What?"

"She talks funny," Ben repeated.

"You know, Kite said the same thing, but neither of us could describe it better than that."

Ben shrugged, not wanting to talk about Dorna. "She uses different words."

Kendi blinked at him. "Say that again?"

"She uses different words. Talks one way, then another. Different."

"That's it!" Kendi grabbed Ben's shoulders and danced him around. "Ben, that's it! Her words change. All life, but I'm dense."

"Okay, okay," Ben laughed, almost losing his balance. "It's not that big a deal."

Kendi dropped his hands. "Right. Sorry. It's just that it's been bothering me since I met her, but I couldn't figure it out. I wonder why she does it—or even if she *knows* she does it."

"Dunno. Maybe it just depends on what mood she's in." Ben scratched his nose in consternation. His shoulders tingled from the heat of Kendi's touch. "What was all that about nightmares and the Dream stalker?"

"No idea." Kendi cracked his knuckles. "I hope we never need to find out."

"We should probably get back to the party," Ben said reluctantly. "After all, you're a guest of honor."

"Yeah." Kendi paused. "Hey, you want to get together some time this week?"

Ben's heart pounded. "And do what?"

"I don't know. Hang around. You can show me your weights."

There was a note in Kendi's voice that Ben couldn't

read. Was Kendi offering friendship? Or more than that? And which one did Ben want? His heart was beating so fast, he was sure his shirt was shaking. Kendi looked at him, waiting for an answer.

"Sure," Ben said casually. "Whatever."

Far overheard, a firework burst into a bright orange flower.

Kendi looked around his cave in satisfaction. Everything was in place. The dry, sandy floor and smooth walls were exactly as he expected them to be, and the fire burned low below the smoke hole. He felt happy here, safe and secure. Father Ched-Hisak would not be visiting him this time—after several practice sessions, Kendi had received permission to enter the dream unsupervised whenever he wished. Ara, in fact, had encouraged him to do so.

"Practice," she had said, "is the only way to perfect what you learn."

Kendi made his way up the spiral to the mouth of the tunnel. The Outback, hot and dry, lay before him. The wind carried countless thousands of whispers, and each voice was a Silent operating somewhere in the Dream. Kendi closed his eyes and listened. After a moment, he was able to sort some of the voices out. He recognized several people—students and teachers both—from the Festival party three days ago. If he concentrated harder, he could narrow his focus to a single voice and follow it through the Dream to find whoever it was.

Father Ched-Hisak had been impressed with the speed at which Kendi had picked up this ability. Most Silent, he said, went through months, even years, of practice before they could sense and track particular people in the Dream.

Unfortunately, no matter how long or hard he listened, he never heard his mother.

Another familiar voice caught his ear. It sounded like Dorna. She must be practicing as well. On a whim, Kendi decided to go find out what she was up to. He concentrated, listening for the direction her voice came from, then opened his eyes and trotted off.

The Outback sun lay down a hard, heavy heat that baked Kendi's naked skin. Spiny plants tried to slash his feet, but here in the Dream, Kendi's soles were protected by a thick slab of callus and they did no harm to him. Overhead screamed a falcon, and Kendi gave it a little wave. His mind, it seemed, ran to creating animals. This was another sign of Kendi's ability. No Silent could create people in the Dream—controlling a Dream person was more than even the most potent subconscious mind could deal with—and only a few Silent could handle animals. The falcon, however, always appeared overhead without even conscious effort on Kendi's behalf.

Kendi followed the whispery sound of Dorna's voice and wondered how long it would take him to learn teleportation. Distance, Ara said, ultimately meant nothing in the Dream. Carving the Dream up into different territories was merely for the convenience— and privacy—of the individual Silent. Every Silent mind in the Dream overlapped with every other mind. Most Silents' subconsciouses, however, couldn't handle that much input all at once and they therefore created artificial barriers of illusory space to separate themselves from everyone else. Once Kendi had achieved enough mastery of the Dream, Ara told him, he would be able to overcome part of his subconscious and instantly take himself to other "parts" of the Dream without having to walk there.

Kendi clambered over a pile of rocks. One of them was a shade of brilliant red that matched the color of Ben's hair. Kendi ran a hand over his face. Ben. In the last three days, he had found himself constantly thinking of Ben. They had spent several hours together the day after the party. Ben had shown Kendi his weight machine and the computer system he had cobbled together out of spare and rebuilt parts. They had played a few sim games and then had traipsed down the stairs all the way to the bottom of the talltree forest. The cool, slightly gloomy depths with its waist-high ground cover and loamy earth made a stark contrast to the wooden walkways high in the air. They had hiked aimlessly about, keeping a sharp eye out for dinosaurs and seeing none, talking about nothing in particular.

Twice Kendi almost put his arm around Ben's shoulders, then held back. Pup and Pitr had taught him it wouldn't be a good idea. When Ben had smiled on the walkway outside the party that night—

Kendi swallowed. That smile, rare as a winter flower, had gone straight through him. He could still picture it when he closed his eyes at night, and it kept reappearing in his dreams.

All life, he thought. *You've got it bad.*

He forced himself to concentrate on Dorna as he walked. Her voice was growing louder now. As he got closer, he took several deep breaths and gradually relinquished his expectations of the landscape. He did *not* expect dry, sandy soil or a blue sky or spiny spinifex plants. He expected nothing. This was hard to do, and it slowed Kendi down. It was necessary, however. If he came into Dorna's space without releasing his own expectations of the environment, his and Dorna's minds would end up fighting for control. The stronger mind would win out, and the losing mind would feel a certain amount of discomfort, or even pain. Dream etiquette demanded that the Silent moving into the other person's turf released all expectations, just as a visitor in a solid-world home would adapt to the rules and customs of the host. For newcomers like Kendi, however, this wasn't always easy.

Kendi eased forward another step and another. The Outback melted slowly away. Kendi worked hard to keep his mind blank. Twice rocks and scrubby plants faded into view around him and Kendi took several breaths to banish them. More steps forward, and Kendi finally found himself at a wrought-iron gate set into a stone wall. Clothes faded into existence on his body until he was wearing khaki trousers and a flannel shirt. Clothing was always provided by the host Silent.

Kendi pushed the gate open and stepped into a lush, well-kept garden. He looked around curiously. So this was Dorna's turf. Flowering bushes and shrubs were everywhere, and the grass was clipped so that every blade was the same length. Flowers were laid in rows with military precision. Not one stray leaf marred the perfect lawn.

On a stone bench sat a figure with her back turned to Kendi. She wore a half-cloak with the hood drawn over her hair. Dorna. Kendi smiled and strode toward her. Abruptly, she twisted around on the bench. Kendi hissed and backed up a step.

"Who the hell are you?" she demanded.

Kendi stared. It wasn't Dorna at all. The woman on the bench was old, with wild white hair and snaggle teeth. She even had a wart on her nose like a fairy-tale witch.

"Sorry," Kendi stammered. "I was looking for someone else."

"You're intruding in my garden," the old woman screeched. "Get the fuck out of my garden!"

"Hey, it's all right," Kendi said, still backing away. "You don't have to freak. I was just leaving."

"Get out!" howled the woman. "Get him, boys!"

Kendi wondered whom she was talking to. Then a rosebush lunged for him. Thorns raked across Kendi's arm, tearing his shirt and leaving a set of white-hot scratches along his skin. Ivy twirled around his feet and ankles. Kendi turned and ran, tearing up the green vines and losing a shoe in the process. Another thorny bush scored his cheek. The grass lengthened and threatened to trip him. He dove for the gate, fear clutching his stomach.

"That's right," cackled the woman behind him. "Run from Zelda and her garden. Get out, you little shit!"

Kendi shoved the gate open and fled, bleeding and trailing bits of ivy. He ran until his legs ached and his lungs threatened to burst. When he finally stopped, he was back in the Outback. His clothes had vanished, but his arm and cheek were still bleeding.

"All life," he muttered. "What a bitch." It wasn't as if he had trespassed on purpose. He had thought she was Dorna. Obviously his tracking needed a little work, but that didn't mean the old lady—Zelda, she'd said her name was—had to shape her garden to attack him like that.

His arm and cheek hurt like hell. Kendi stared down at the scratches, willing them to disappear. His body was whole and unharmed. It was so and would be so . . . *now.*

Blood continued to flow. It dripped from his face down to his shoulder. Kendi was pretty sure that his body was bleeding as it lay on his bed in his room. Psychosomatic wounds, Ara called them. Whatever harm the Dream body encountered was usually visited on the solid one. Some Silent could overcome this, but not many. Kendi, obviously, wasn't one of them yet. Maybe he should leave the Dream and get some medical—

A wave of nausea washed over him. Kendi staggered, regained his balance. *What the hell?* he thought. Then he felt it, a . . . disturbance. He couldn't think of any other way to describe it. It was as if someone had just dropped something disgusting into a pool of water and Kendi could feel the ripples. He turned toward the feeling. A bad taste rose in his mouth and he spat. What was going on?

Curious despite the discomfort, Kendi trotted against the ripples, following them to their source. As he moved, the Outback faded again, this time with little effort on Kendi's part. That meant, he knew, that a very strong mind was at work, one that could easily shake off Kendi's puny attempt to hold on to his desert. An archway stood before him in the middle of a featureless plain. The disturbance was on the other side of the arch. Kendi stepped through.

He found himself in a giant living room. A hodge-podge of furniture—fainting couches, end tables, a variety of chairs and sofas, and low bookshelves—stood on a crazy quilt of mismatched rugs and carpets. Kendi came to an instant halt and almost cried out. On one of the sofas lay a woman. She was blond and middle-aged, with plump arms and a heavy chest. A gold medallion hung between her breasts. Chains that seemed to have sprouted from the couch itself held her down. Blood from a dozen dripping cuts and slashes covered her body, and she made faint mewling noises. Standing over her with his back to Kendi was a tall man. As Kendi watched in frozen horror, he made a swift slash with the knife. There was a snapping noise. The woman cried out, but only weakly, as one of her fingers dropped to the cushions. The man caught it up and held it like a pencil. Kendi still couldn't move. With deliberate care, the man wrote "14" in blood on the woman's forehead. The woman convulsed once, then went still.

"Shit!" Kendi gasped.

The man dropped the finger and spun. He was wearing a hat with a wide brim that was pulled low. Kendi couldn't see his face. Before Kendi could react, the man lunged.

TEN

I witnessed it once but it stayed with me forever.
                                        —Irfan Qasad

Kendi backpedaled, fear humming through his veins. The brim of the hat cast a shadow that hid most of the man's face, but Kendi could see his mouth twisted into an animal snarl. Kendi whirled and dashed for the arch. Abruptly the arch snapped shut, and Kendi slammed into a solid wall. Dazed, he felt hard hands grab his shoulders. They spun him around and a hard blow drove Kendi to his knees. Blood dripped from his nose, mingling with the blood from the cuts on his cheek. All Kendi could see was a pair of shins in front of him. One of them drew back to deliver a kick. Kendi drove himself forward, slamming into the man. Surprised, the man went over backward with a grunt. Kendi scrambled over him. He caught a blurred glimpse of the woman's bloody corpse on the sofa.

Then the room came to life. The rug he was standing on ripped itself out from under him and Kendi flew sprawling into a pile of cushions. Instantly, they molded themselves around him, piling about him and suffocating him. Kendi clawed at them ineffectually and wished for a knife, glittering and sharp. In that moment, he had one in his hand. He cut and slashed until the stuffing flew and he came free, though he was still on the floor.

The man loomed over him. Kendi lashed out with the knife. The man leaped back. A table rushed at Kendi like a battering ram. Kendi ducked, and it slid over him. While he was still underneath it, Kendi stood up and flung the table at the man. It caught him squarely in the chest. Without looking to see more, Kendi dove for one of the windows. It shattered around him. Flying glass slashed his face and forearms as he landed on hard, flat ground, but Kendi scarcely noticed. He had to get out of the Dream, get back to his body, but he needed time to concentrate. Should he take the time now or try to get away?

The man appeared at the window, face still in shadow. He was holding a needle gun. Kendi shut his eyes and yanked his thoughts together.

If it be in my best interest and in the best interest of all life everywhere, he pleaded, *let me leave the Dream.*

The gun went off with a *phut*. Kendi braced himself for pain and felt none. He opened his eyes and found himself on his own bed in his own room. Pain scored his face, arms, and most of the rest of his body. He tried to sit up, but the room spun dizzily and he fell back. Blood stained his pillow and blanket and slicked his hands. Kendi felt dazed, as if he were only half there. He should call someone for help. But who? The room darkened around him.

"Baran," Kendi croaked. "Baran, call Mother Ara. Emergency!"

The computer connected the call and a moment later Mother Ara's face appeared on Kendi's white wall. Her eyes widened when she saw the blood. "Kendi! What—?"

He passed out.

The ceiling was made of beige tile. That wasn't right. The ceiling was supposed to be white plaster. Kendi blinked, trying to figure out why it looked wrong. He put up a hand and saw it was swathed in soft bandages. Other bandages covered parts of his face and upper body. He was lying on a bed, but it wasn't his own. How had he gotten here? He tried to sit up. A gentle hand came down on his shoulder to stop him, and Kendi looked up into Mother Ara's concerned face.

"How do you feel?" she asked. "Are you in pain?"

Kendi checked. "No. Where am I?"

"Medical center. I called an ambulance. Can you talk? Can you tell me what happened?"

"Just a moment now." A man whose hair was as white as his coat bent over Kendi. His name tag proclaimed him DR. BENJAMIN YARMUL, and Kendi immediately thought of Ben. "Can you follow my finger?"

Kendi tracked Dr. Yarmul's finger, wiggled various bandaged appendages, and assured the doctor that he felt no pain anywhere. Another person was in the room, an Asian woman Mother Ara's height with a carefully woven black braid trailing down her back. She didn't speak as the doctor examined Kendi.

"The damage was superficial," Dr. Yarmul said. "All of it psychosomatic, but still damaging nonetheless. We've closed your wounds and there won't be any scars, but you'll need to keep the bandages on until tomorrow morning just to make sure, all right? We'll have to keep you here overnight for observation anyway."

Kendi and Mother Ara thanked the doctor, who then left. The Asian woman came forward and took his place next to Kendi's bed.

"This is Inspector Lewa Tan," Mother Ara said. "She's from the Guardians."

"Can you tell us what happened?" Tan asked. Her voice was gravelly, odd for a woman.

"I was attacked. In the Dream." Kendi tried to sit up again. This time the bed tilted upward with him until he was in a reclining position.

"Did you see who attacked you?" Tan asked.

Kendi shook his head. "Not really. He wore a hat that kept his face all shadowy."

"But it was definitely a man," Tan said.

"Yeah."

"Are you up to telling the entire story," Mother Ara said, "or do you want to rest?"

"I can talk." Kendi shifted position beneath the crisp white hospital sheets and explained what had happened to him. Tan held what Kendi assumed was a recording device. Mother Ara listened attentively. Kendi had thought he was fine, but by the end of it he was sweating and his heart pounded as if it had happened to him again as he told it. The bandages reminded him of the suffocating couch cushions, and he had the sudden urge to tear them off. The man was pointing a needle pistol at him, and the hospital room felt small and confining, with no place to run. He forced himself to take deep breaths and continue talking, though the sweat turned cold on his body.

"And then I called you, Mother," he finished. "That was pretty much it."

Tan leaned forward. "Kendi, you saw the killer write a number on the woman's forehead. What was the number again?"

"Fourteen."

Tan and Mother Ara exchanged glances. "You're sure it was fourteen and not thirteen?" Mother Ara asked.

"Positive," Kendi said. "Why?"

"Just making sure," Tan said.

"So how long was I out?" Kendi asked.

"About four hours," Mother Ara told him. "You scared me out of my wits. Ben's outside. You scared him, too, and he insisted on coming down."

"Ben?" Kendi's heart leaped. "Ben's outside? Can he come in?"

"In a moment." Tan leaned closer. "I need you to answer a few more questions. If you're up to it."

Kendi leaned back against the pillows. "Yeah, okay. Go ahead."

Tan went back over parts of his story, gently asking for more detail here, a simple retelling there. More details surfaced as Kendi spoke, and he reported them to Tan and Ara.

"We still don't know who the victim is," Tan said. "Though if she was wearing a gold medallion, she was probably a Child. Did you recognize her from the description, Ara?"

Mother Ara shook her head. "There are thousands of Children."

"Then I guess we'll have to do it through old-fashioned detective work," Tan said grimly.

"Any more questions?" Kendi felt tired now, and his eyelids drooped.

"Not for the moment," Tan said. "Though I'll want to go over it with you one more time a little later, when you're rested."

"You should sleep now, Kendi." Mother Ara patted his shoulder. "Inspector?"

"Wait," Kendi said. "I wanna see Ben."

"I'll bring him by in the morning," Mother Ara said.

"No." Kendi roused himself. "I want to see him now."

Mother Ara looked at the Inspector, who shrugged and opened the door. She gestured into the hallway, and Ben rushed into the room, his face even paler than usual.

"Kendi!" he said. "Are you all right? You look like shit. I mean—you didn't—you—"

"I'm okay," Kendi said. "I'm glad you came by."

"What happened to you?" he demanded. "Mom said she thought you were hurt in the Dream, but we didn't know for sure and they wouldn't let me in to see you and—"

Mother Ara put a hand on Ben's arm. "He's fine, Ben. Don't tire him out. I'll tell you about it when we get home."

Ben flushed. "Sorry. I was just—you know."

"Yeah." Kendi's head drooped. " 'S okay. I'm glad you . . . you were . . ."

"Let's leave him now," Mother Ara murmured. But Kendi was already asleep.

In the hallway outside Kendi's room, Ara gave Ben some money and asked him to go get her some juice. The moment he was out of earshot, she turned to Inspector Tan.

"Number fourteen," Ara said. "Did he skip a number?"

"Either that, or there's a corpse we haven't found yet," Tan replied. "Let me check with the ME." Tan took a small phone out of her pocket, spoke rapidly into it, paused, then sighed and hung up. "Examiner says the finger sewn to the latest victim's hand did not belong to Iris Temm. So there's definitely another corpse hiding out there somewhere."

Ara didn't know how to respond, so she said nothing.

"You should go home," Tan continued. "I've got to try and track down who and where the victim actually *is*. We'll meet here in the morning to go over Kendi's story one more time."

Ara agreed.

The next morning, she and Inspector Tan questioned Kendi again, but no new details came to light. Ara, unwilling to let Kendi stay by himself, installed him in her guest bedroom with orders to spend the remainder of the day being quiet. To Ara's surprise,

Kendi didn't protest at the confinement. Ben, meanwhile, offered to stay home and keep him company.

"Teenagers," Ara said to Tan on the front porch. "For weeks they fight doing what you tell them, and then out of nowhere they up and volunteer to do the right thing."

"Especially when it involves missing a day of school," Tan observed.

Ara, enjoying a proud maternal moment, ignored this. "Did you learn who the victim was?"

"Her name was Vera Cheel," Tan rasped.

"How did you find her?"

"Checked to see if anyone on duty in the Dream didn't turn in the transcriptions of their communications. Cheel's name popped right up. Linus is already at her house. Let's go."

Vera Cheel's house was larger than Iris Temm's, and tidier as well. The body had been taken away by the time Ara and Tan got there, for which Ara was grateful.

"What . . . condition was she in?" Ara asked as they entered Cheel's living room. It was bright and airy, with several potted plants scattered tastefully about. A vase filled with lush red roses sat on the coffee table. Half a dozen technicians were going over the different rooms with scanning equipment. Tan's partner Linus Gray was in deep discussion with one of them, and he gave them a distracted wave as they entered.

"Same as Iris Temm," Tan told her. "Pretty much bludgeoned and crushed to death while she was in the Dream."

"I suppose we should go into the Dream and get a look, then." Ara fingered the dermospray in her pocket. "It's been less than a day since Vera was killed, so the images will be stronger, I think."

"You sound hesitant," Tan said. "What's wrong?"

Ara pursed her lips, not wanting to give voice to her thoughts. But a killer was on the loose, and they couldn't afford to let a potential lead slip away. "I was wondering if I should take Kendi in with me."

"Why?"

"Kendi saw the incident," Ara explained. "His mind could strengthen the images and we might get more details, both sensory and impressionistic."

"And if Kendi's there, we might get more insights into the killer's mind," Tan said.

Ara nodded. "But he's just a student. He reached the Dream for the first time only last week. Not only did he witness the murder, he was attacked by the killer. Kendi's strong, but he's been through a lot in his life as it is, and I don't want to add to his burdens by making him watch the whole thing again."

"Irfan Qasad said that all sentient life is sacred," Tan pointed out. "Murder's the most horrible crime there is. It's our duty to use whatever methods we can to track this man down."

"I know. But I also have a duty to my student's safety and well-being."

"Well," Tan said slowly, "let's ask and let *him* decide. Now that I think about it, we need to get back to your house as soon as possible."

"What? Why?"

"I'll tell you when we get there," Tan said, "and we ask Kendi."

"The problem," Ara sighed, "is that I know what he'll say."

"Yes," Kendi said. "I can do it right now."

They were back in Ara's living room. Tan, who had put the question to him, nodded. Ben sat quietly in the corner, his blue eyes quietly taking in the entire scene. Ara still felt misgivings. Kendi was only sixteen and not the most levelheaded among the students at the monastery. On the other hand, he wouldn't be in any actual danger at a re-creation, and Ara would be right there with him.

"We should do it at Vera's house," Ara said, "so the minds around us will be as similar as possible to the ones she herself used to get into the Dream yesterday."

"What about me?" Ben said as they headed for the door.

"You stay here," Ara instructed. "We'll be back as soon as we can."

"What do you mean about the minds being the same?" Kendi asked, excited. The cuts on his face and hands had faded to fine, pinkish lines.

While Ara explained, Tan drew Ben aside and spoke to him rapidly. His face, which had been filled with disappointment, changed to a more thoughtful expression. He stayed behind without protest as Ara, Kendi, and Tan left the house.

"What did you tell him?" Ara asked.

Tan shot a glance at Kendi. "I told him it was his job to keep all this as quiet as possible and I asked him to scan the news for me. Too many people know about the attack on Kendi—the hospital personnel, for example—and I'm afraid that once the services get hold of it, Kendi's going to be in some danger."

"Danger?" Kendi asked. "What do you mean?"

"The killer knows you saw him," Tan explained. "He knows what you look like, unless—I don't suppose you're one of those Silent who looks different in the Dream than in the solid world?"

"No."

"Damn. Anyway, that means the killer may be looking for you. You're a witness. I didn't really think of it before, and that's why I wanted to come back."

Kendi shot a nervous glance around him, as if the

killer might drop out of the branches. "But I don't know what he looks like. He didn't have a face."

Ara stopped on the boardwalk. "Wait a minute. You're saying that if the killer finds out Kendi's aiding the investigation, Kendi would be in danger?"

"Possibly," Tan said.

"Then forget it. Kendi, you're going back to the house. The Inspector and I will do this alone."

"It's only a danger if someone finds out," Tan said reasonably. "News services don't even know who the victim was yet, so there won't be any reporters hanging around the house. No one will even know."

"Mother Ara," Kendi said, "let me do this. I want to help. Didn't Irfan say that all sentient life is sacred?"

"Oh no," Ara groaned. "Not you, too."

"The Real People believe the same thing," he continued. "I have to help if I can."

"This isn't an adventure, Kendi," Ara said. "It's bloody and gory and it's going to be unpleasant."

"I already saw it once," Kendi countered. "I'm still here."

In the end, Ara let herself be persuaded. They went back to Vera Cheel's house and found it empty. The technicians had completed their scans and left. Outside, dirty clouds had gathered, obscuring the sun and cooling the breeze. The red roses on the coffee table made a sharp, colorful contrast with the dreary sky. Ara wondered where Vera's body had been found, then decided she didn't want to know. Linus Gray was nowhere to be seen, and Ara assumed he was out canvassing the neighborhood. There was a certain tension in the room. Ara herself still held reservations about involving Kendi. Kendi, she was sure, was nervous, and Tan was probably anxious to get on with it.

"Let's hit the Dream," Tan said, confirming Ara's

suspicions. "I'll take the easy chair, if you don't mind."

"The couch is fine with me," Ara said tightly. "Kendi usually stands."

Kendi had brought his spear and dermospray. The dermospray was red instead of black, indicating it belonged to a student. "Does this count as a practice session?" he asked with a grin. Tan snorted and some of the tension eased.

"I suppose it does," Ara said, laughing. "Your dermospray will still transmit the fact that you used a dose of medication back to the dispensary for your practice record. The dispensary computer doesn't care why you used it. Kendi, since you're new to this, you probably can't leave the Dream unsculpted, so we'll have to meet on your turf. That'll be easier."

Tan sat, Ara lay down, and Kendi positioned himself on his spear. A triple *thump* went through the room as three dermosprays shoved the medication home. Ara let the colors swirl around the inside of her eyelids for a moment, then opened her eyes to a pleasure garden. A carpet of grass lay thick and green beneath her slippered feet, and a stone fountain tinkled musically behind her, the sound mingling with the ever-present whispering of the Dream. Orange and pear blossoms scented the soft air. Ara wore a green robe with a close-fitting hood. The garden was her own safe place, and she liked it a great deal. But there was no time for personal enjoyment. She closed her eyes and cast her perceptions into the whispers around her until she found Kendi's voice. Once she caught his whisper, she gathered her concentration. She was *here,* but she wanted to be *there,* and she would be there *now.*

Ara released her expectations of reality. There was a slight wrench and she opened her eyes in a large, dry cave. Kendi stood a few steps away. His mind, however, was everywhere, pressing against her, unconsciously ordering her not to dictate reality here. Ara obeyed, though it was difficult. To distract herself, she glanced about curiously. She had only been in Kendi's cave a couple of times and she found it a very interesting starting point.

"I do like this place," she said. "It suits you."

"Weird," he said, tugging at the white shirt he wore. "When you appeared like that, it felt like I was in a swimming pool and someone threw in a big rock."

"You're very sensitive to other people in the Dream," Ara said. "Some Silent can barely detect another person's presence." She gave him a critical look. "Father Ched-Hisak told me you usually wear a loincloth or even appear naked here. Why the shorts and shirt?"

Kendi flushed. "I—I don't—"

"You can wear whatever you like on your own turf," Ara said seriously. "Dream etiquette. And you're expected to dress the people who visit your turf in whatever you deem appropriate. This robe I'm wearing is fine for my pleasure garden, but is a little impractical for spelunking, don't you think?"

In response, Ara's robe changed into a khaki explorer's outfit. Kendi's clothing, however, remained the same. "I'll keep what I'm wearing for now," he said, a little less embarrassed.

And then Inspector Tan was there. For a moment, she appeared to be wearing an embroidered yellow robe, but it quickly changed into brown khakis similar to Ara's.

"I felt her coming," Kendi explained.

Tan gave the cave a quick glance. "Nice," she said. "Let's go."

They followed the exit tunnel up to the Outback. The desert lay before them, filling the world from horizon to horizon.

"Let's teleport to a blank space," Tan said. "It'll be faster than having our host let go of the world."

"I . . . don't know how to do that," Kendi said. "Teleport, I mean."

"Take my hand," Ara said. "I'll move you."

Kendi obeyed. Ara was *here* but she wanted to be *there,* and she would be there *now.* Another wrench, and the Outback vanished, replaced by a flat, empty plain. The Dream whispering was loud here. The moment they appeared, Kendi released Ara, dropped to hands and knees, and vomited. Alarmed, Ara knelt beside him. His Dream body flickered, semitransparent for a moment, then solidified. Kendi threw up again.

"Kendi," Ara said. "Kendi, what's wrong?"

Kendi looked up at her. "I'm sick. All life—it's like a bad flu. Oh god." He vomited yet again, a thin, clear fluid.

"The teleportation," Tan said. "He wasn't ready for it."

"The nausea will pass, Kendi," Ara said. "Just wait a moment."

Kendi spent a fair amount of time in dry heaves. Ara remained on the ground next to him while Tan waited with scarcely disguised impatience. Finally, Kendi got to his feet, face a bit green. Ara held out an empty hand. There would be a glass of cold water in it, and there would be one *now.* One appeared, and she handed it to Kendi, who accepted it gratefully. He rinsed out his mouth, spat, and took a long drink.

"We'll work on this," Ara promised. "Are you ready to go on?" He nodded. "Then let's get started. I want you to close your eyes and empty your mind, as if you were going to meditate. Then concentrate on what you remember about the murder. I'm going to be building a scene using your memories as well as

those of the solid-world minds around us. You have
to allow me to read your mind, all right?"

Kendi nodded. The sickness had left his face entirely. Ara put her hands on the sides of his head and
he closed his eyes. Ara concentrated on the whisper,
now nearly a shout, that was Kendi's mind. Images
and sensations swirled around her. *(Blood, blond hair,
chains, a number, fear, horror, pain.)* Ara widened her
senses to the greater whispering around her and gathered images from that as well. *(Shadow-faced man,
tidy house, shattered glass, bloody finger.)* Carefully,
but with swift skill, Ara arranged the images into a
picture like an archaeologist arranging a fossilized
skeleton. *(Hot anger, cold love, metallic gun.)* When it
was done, she released Kendi and opened her eyes.

The three of them were in Vera Cheel's patchwork
living room. Varieties and styles of furniture clashed
and melded. Vera sat on a sofa, chatting with a Ched-
Balaar Ara didn't recognize. A part of Ara that was
beginning to think like a detective mused that they
would have to track the alien down for an interview.
This scene was clearer, far clearer than the first one
Ara had recreated for Tan. Ara could feel Vera's con-
tentment. She was sure of herself in the Dream, con-
fident of her abilities. And she liked her strange
living room.

As Ara watched, the Ched-Balaar vanished. Vera
ran her hands through short blond hair, started to
stand, and came up short. Mystified, she raised a hand.
It clinked. Her wrist was bound with a black wristband
and chain that extruded from under the sofa cushions.
So was her other wrist and her ankles. The air turned
cold. Fear rose in Vera's chest. She hadn't created the
chains. They would be gone. They would be gone *now*.
But they remained. Ara's heart started to beat faster.

A blackness touched the room. Suppressed rage

mixed with desire and . . . love? A door opened, and
a man dressed in black entered. A wide-brimmed hat
hid his face in shadow. He strode toward Vera, who
screamed. Vera tried to gather her concentration to
leave the Dream, to escape, but the couch moved beneath her and the cushions themselves folded themselves about her body. More chains snaked out and
wound tight and cold around her body. Terror swept
over Vera and disrupted her concentration. A knife
appeared in the man's hand and he loomed over his
victim. He bent down and said something to Vera,
who only screamed again. Rage swept over Ara in
waves, and he slashed quickly. Blood flowed, and Vera
cried out. It went on and on. Ara was vaguely aware
of Inspector Tan vaulting over the furniture, trying to
get behind the couch so she could get a look at the
man's face.

And then Kendi was there—another Kendi. Ara
glanced at her student to make sure he was also still
beside her. He was, eyes wide, lips compressed. The
man cut off Vera's finger just as she died and wrote a
bloody number on her forehead. Ara felt a tiny blank
moment, a barely discernable flicker as Vera's Dream
form vanished and was replaced by the power of the
man standing over her. Dream Kendi swore, and the
man lunged for him. Ara watched them struggle, saw
the furniture erupt into movement, felt Dream Kendi's
own fear and terror. Finally Dream Kendi crashed
through the window and disappeared. The man stood
in the window for a moment, then howled once and
vanished. Vera's living room went with it, leaving Ara,
Kendi, and Tan alone on a blank plain. Tan was
breathing hard.

Ara stood stock-still. Her mouth was dry as salt and
she felt weak as a dishrag. A quick glance at Kendi
showed he felt the same. His skin was ashen.

"I didn't see his face," Tan reported. "I don't think he has one in the Dream."

"We need to get out of here," Ara croaked. "Kendi, you go and I'll make sure you get out before I follow, all right?"

Kendi only nodded. A moment later, he vanished and the dream energy around them rushed in to fill the empty space. Without another word to Tan, Ara herself let go of the Dream.

Kendi sat shakily on the couch next to Mother Ara after she sat up. Rain pattered gray tears against the windows. Kendi's hands shook and nausea oozed in his stomach. He had thought he could handle seeing it all again, but he had been wrong. This time he had felt the emotions of both people involved. Vera Cheel's fear, terror, and helplessness stayed with him, mingling with a horrible mixture of rage and love. It made him sick and scared all at once, and he felt horribly alone.

An arm came around his shoulder and drew him into a motherly embrace. Kendi buried his face in Mother Ara's shoulder and for a moment pretended she was Rebecca Weaver. Everything was going to be all right. He wasn't there. The Dream wasn't real. After a while, he became aware that Mother Ara was saying these things aloud to him, and he let them sink in. Then he broke away, eyes wet with tears he didn't remember shedding.

"Are you okay?" Mother Ara asked. Her face was drawn and concerned. "I had no idea it would be that strong, Kendi. There's no way I would have let you—"

"It's all right," he said. "I'll be okay. But all life— it was horrible."

"And we need to discuss it," Tan put in from the armchair. "Now. Before we forget any of it."

"I don't think I'll forget any of it for as long as I live," Mother Ara said. "Aren't you upset by any of this?"

"I'm upset that the killer is walking free," Tan said grimly. "Let's go over it. Talking about it may make all of us feel better, in any case."

"Kendi," Mother Ara said, "why don't you go and—"

"No," Kendi interrupted. "I want to help. He did awful things to her, and I don't want him to do it again to someone else."

"Let's at least go somewhere else," Mother Ara insisted. "Maybe get something to eat. It'll help us to concentrate on our bodies and dampen the emotions."

The three of them decided to go to a nearby restaurant. The canopy of talltree leaves kept them reasonably dry as long as they stayed under the branches, but they had to dash across the open spaces between the trees. They arrived at the restaurant, damp and breathless.

It was a little early for lunch yet, and Tan got them a booth at the back where they could talk in privacy. The restaurant was warm and dark, and the server was friendly. Mother Ara refused to let anyone discuss the case until their food had arrived. Once they had all eaten a little, Tan put her recorder on the table, and they described what had happened. Kendi was glad to discover that Mother Ara had been correct— it was easier to remain levelheaded about the entire thing with some food in him.

"My earlier suspicions were correct, then," Mother Ara said. "The killer has a very strong will, and he can attack people by forcing a new shape on the turf in Dream. That's hard to do."

"Agreed," Tan said. "Most Silent simply aren't this powerful, just like most people don't have the physical strength to kill someone with their bare hands. Good thing, too. Otherwise Dream killings would be far more common."

"He knows the victims," Kendi put in. "I think he even . . . loves them? Or thinks he does. I felt that."

"So did I." Mother Ara sipped thoughtfully at her drink. "Though he may not know them personally. He may be stalking them without actually meeting or talking to them first."

"My research tells me that most serial killers do stalk their victims," Tan said. "If this one can find his women in the Dream, it means he may have touched them in the real world. That, and the fact that he's doing his little finger trick, means he's somewhere on Bellerophon. A relief."

"A relief?" Mother Ara asked.

"Yes. It'll make him easier to catch." Tan tucked a stray strand of black hair back into her braid. "Imagine if he were on another planet. We'd never have a hope."

"What was the number fourteen?" Kendi said. "He wrote it on her forehead."

"He wrote the number twelve on the forehead of Iris Temm," Mother Ara pointed out.

"Is he numbering them—his women, I mean?" Kendi asked, startled. "If he is, there must be a number thirteen out there somewhere."

Tan gave him an appraising look. "We were thinking the same thing yesterday. Pretty smart."

Kendi felt his face grow warm at the praise and he hid behind his juice glass.

"There have only been three other Dream murders." Mother Ara put her elbows on the table. "Prinna Meg, Wren Hamil, and Iris Temm."

"Which means there are either a lot of victims we don't know about—and they aren't necessarily on Bellerophon," Tan said, "or maybe he isn't numbering his victims, but is doing something else. Maybe he's using only even numbers for some reason."

"I think there's a dead body somewhere that no one's found yet," Kendi said. He took a long drink of fruit juice. It was slightly tangy, just as he liked it, and he wondered about the strangeness of it. Less than a day ago he had watched a woman murdered and today he was drinking fruit juice. Vera Cheel would never drink fruit juice again, and that made him sad and angry, even though he had never met her. Not really.

You're being stupid, he told himself. *You don't even know if she liked fruit juice.* Still, the feelings remained. He pushed the drink aside.

Mother Ara sipped from her own glass again. "What do the women have in common? We've been over it before, but is there something we've overlooked?"

"Female, adult, Silent, associated with Children of Irfan." Tan ticked her fingers. "Ages have varied from young adult to middle age. There doesn't seem to be a pattern to where they live, either, or to the dates or times he kills them. If he was friends with all four of them, we should be comparing lists of people the victims were acquainted with."

"We need more information." Mother Ara glanced at her fingernail. "It's early yet. Maybe I should take another look at the murder scenes."

"You?" Tan raised her eyebrows. "You're a consultant, Mother Ara, not an investigator. And Kendi here is just a witness."

"I can help," Mother Ara said. "I know how the Silent mind works—"

"And I don't?" Tan said.

"Your partner isn't Silent," Mother Ara pointed out. "I'm another Silent you can bounce ideas off and who might catch something you miss. It can't hurt to have me along."

"Me, too," Kendi put in quickly.

Both women turned their gazes on him. "Kendi," Mother Ara began, "you can't think—"

"You just said that I'm an important witness," Kendi interrupted. "And you said that if the killer finds out about me, my life could be in danger, right?"

"Right," Mother Ara said warily.

"So it would be safest if I stayed in the company of the police—Guardians," Kendi said.

"I could assign someone to guard you," Tan said.

Kendi winced and tried not to show it. The idea of someone following him around all day and night—no. For one thing, it would be difficult to talk to Ben. "I can help, too. I saw things no one else did, and I felt some of the things"—a cold shudder passed through him and he tried to hide that, too—"some of the things the killer did. I might notice something the two of you miss."

They argued further, but in the end, Tan agreed that it couldn't do any harm for Kendi and Mother Ara to look around the murder scenes. Tan paid the bill and got up.

"Since you're both so eager," she said, "let's start with Iris Temm's house."

"She died a year ago," Mother Ara said as they left the restaurant. The rain had let up, though the heavy clouds remained. "Hasn't the place been sold?"

Tan shook her head. "Only living relative was a sister. Woman can't bring herself to go into the house yet or have someone dispose of the stuff inside. It's stood vacant."

The trip to Temm's house involved three slippery walkways and a gondola ride. Kendi rested his chin on the gondola rail and watched green forest coast by below. The air smelled of rain and leaves. A bit of excitement grew inside him. Ben would probably be impressed that the Guardians had taken Kendi into the houses of two murder victims in one day, and Kendi could hardly wait to tell him. Then a bit of guilt stabbed him. These women were dead, and all Kendi could think about was impressing Ben? All life, he was selfish. Still, he found himself looking forward to going back to Mother Ara's house and seeing him.

They finally arrived at Iris's tiny house. The windows were shut and the door was locked. Wet, dead leaves were scattered about the porch. Tan pressed her thumb to the doorplate and the lock clicked open. Kendi took a deep breath and followed Mother Ara inside.

It took his eyes a few moments to adjust to the gloomy interior. The air was stuffy and smelled faintly sour. After a moment, Kendi made out a living room filled with secondhand, mismatched furniture and an upright piano. A patina of dust coated everything. Kendi half expected to see a skeleton lying on the couch and chided himself for being ridiculous. Temm would have been buried long ago. Still, a vague feeling of unease crept over him. This was a dead woman's house, and it had been left just as it was on the day she had died. The Real People told ghost stories, and he shivered at the thought of encountering a pale, angry Iris Temm with a number twelve dripping scarlet down her forehead.

Tan opened a couple of windows. The fresh air helped clear away some of Kendi's unease, but didn't entirely erase it. "Look around," she said. "You can touch anything you want—the techs have been through half a dozen times."

Kendi poked about the living room, but saw nothing that caught his eye. A small foil-wrapped box sat on one of the wooden end tables and he took off the lid. A dozen chocolates, though an empty space gaped like a missing tooth. The remaining ones were covered with a white film. Kendi made a face and replaced the lid. Mother Ara, who was drumming her fingers on the piano, gave him an odd look, but didn't say anything. When Kendi moved away from the table, Mother Ara also reached down and took up the box.

Next Kendi tried the bedroom. The dust made him want to sneeze, but he held it back. It seemed disrespectful somehow to spray saliva in a dead woman's bedroom. He opened a window to let in air and the smell of rain, then looked around. The bed was normal but had been stripped of its linens. Had Iris been on it when she was . . . ? No. Mother Ara had mentioned that the body was found in the living room. Nightstand, lamp, dresser. Nothing out of the ordinary.

What were you expecting? he thought. *A big box with the word* clue *written on it?*

A bit of thunder rumbled in the distance. Kendi reached for the closet, then hesitated. The knob was cool under his hand. Various childhood fears came back to him. This was a dead woman's house, a dead woman's closet. More thunder grumbled. Ghostly images loomed in Kendi's mind, spirits reaching for his throat with hands that showed bloody stumps of missing fingers.

"This bugs me," came Mother Ara's voice from the living room, "but I can't say why."

Her words broke the spell. With a snort at his own silliness, Kendi flung the door open. He saw a perfectly ordinary closet. Dresses, robes, and blouses hung from hangers, all neatly placed. A series of shelves held sweaters. Several pairs of shoes made a perfect row on the floor, and several more were jumbled together in a heap. A bunch of scarves drooped from a set of hooks, one to a hook, all grouped by color.

Something struck Kendi as wrong. He stared into the closet trying to figure out what it was. He looked harder, then stepped back to get the full picture. Something was out of place. Something—

It was the shoes. Kendi knelt on the floor to get a closer look. Most of them were in a row, but a bunch were heaped up.

And then Kendi had it. Everything in the closet was perfectly neat and tidy, including most of the shoes. The jumbled ones were the only messy part of the whole closet, and their presence didn't make sense. He was reaching for a sandal when something made a slamming noise from the living room and Mother Ara cried out. Kendi jumped up and rushed out, heart pounding.

Mother Ara was in the living room. A handprint in the dust on the piano lid showed where she had smacked it, presumably in triumph. Tan stood by the couch, her braid over one shoulder.

"What's the matter?" Tan and Kendi asked in unison.

"The chocolates," Mother Ara said. "They were bothering me, but I couldn't say why. I didn't especially notice them before."

"Neither did I," Tan rasped. "So what?"

"There's a chocolate missing. See?" Mother Ara opened the box and held it so Tan could get a look.

"She probably ate one," Tan said. Then her expression grew interested. "You think the killer ate it? Might be able to find traces of saliva, but it's a slim—"

"No," Mother Ara interrupted. "I saw Iris's medical records. Wasn't she allergic to chocolate?"

Tan rubbed her chin. "I think she was, yeah. So why—"

"—would she have chocolates in the house at all?" Mother Ara finished with a victorious gleam in her eye. "Her boyfriend would almost certainly have known about her allergy and not given them to her.

And she herself wouldn't have eaten one. So who gave them to her and who took the missing one?"

"It's worth asking the boyfriend about," Tan said doubtfully. "Might have brought them over for himself. Or she might have bought them for *him* and he left them here."

"I may be grasping at straws here," Mother Ara said, "but Iris was the twelfth victim. There were twelve chocolates in the box and now one is missing. What if the killer 'gave' them to her and then took one himself?"

Tan still looked doubtful. "We'll check into it, I guess. Don't get your hopes up, though."

"Maybe we should count the shoes," Kendi said.

Blank looks followed. Kendi took the two women into the bedroom and explained. "Iris was too neat to leave her shoes jumbled around like that," he finished excitedly. "Maybe the killer did it or something."

"But why would he?" Tan asked.

"I don't know," Kendi admitted. "But serial killers do weird stuff, right? Maybe this is one of them." He knelt down and started sorting shoes. With the air of someone who was humoring a child, Tan joined in. Mother Ara watched from the door. In short order, they discovered there were eleven shoes in the pile. Ten of them made pairs, leaving one extra. The trio searched the closet, then looked under the bed and in the dresser. The mate was nowhere to be found.

"It's a clue," Kendi said breathlessly. "Twelve shoes, but one's missing. Twelve chocolates, but one's missing."

Tan was looking more excited now. "Twelve victims, but one finger is missing. The killer is taking souvenirs. Dammit, I can't believe we missed this."

"Fresh pairs of eyes," Mother Ara said. "Do you suppose there's anything like this in the other houses?"

Visibly restraining her enthusiasm, Tan got to her feet. "We should search through this house first. Look for anything else that comes in twelves—eggs, flowers, sets of dishes, anything. And good work. Both of you."

Kendi glowed with pride and excitedly set to work searching the rest of the house, but no other sets of twelve came up. Tan gathered up the shoes and the chocolates as evidence, though she said there was little hope of finding anything on them.

"The killer's too smart to leave his DNA on them," she explained.

"What about sweeping for trace DNA?" Mother Ara said. "If the killer came in to cut off Iris's finger and take souvenirs, he couldn't avoid leaving skin cells behind."

"The same," Tan replied, "goes for all the other people who have ever set foot in this house. It's at least thirty years old. If we sweep for trace DNA, we'll get hundreds, perhaps even thousands, of sequences. It would take years just to sort them out, let alone identify who they belonged to. Come on—I want to get another look at Vera Cheel's house."

Mother Ara turned to Kendi. "You don't need to come," she said. "Cheel's house is a recent crime scene, and there's a greater chance the news services will have found out about it and be there by now."

"I was there before," Kendi protested.

"Only because I needed you there to recreate the Dream scene," Mother Ara said firmly. "That was risky enough. I don't want you endangered, and I certainly don't want your face skating up and down the news webs. Inspector Tan and I can handle this ourselves." She put a hand on his shoulder. "You were invaluable, Kendi. None of us will forget that, all right? I promise I'll tell you all about it."

"Just don't talk to anyone else," Tan added.

"But what am I supposed to do all day?" Kendi asked, feeling only slightly mollified by Mother Ara's words.

"Do what you like, as long as you don't stay by yourself." She cleared her throat. "Kendi, I know this is a sensitive issue with you, but—well, I'd feel a lot better if you talked about this with someone. You witnessed a horrible act and you were almost killed. You really should talk about this with—"

"Not right now," Kendi said. "I'm okay. A little shaky, but okay. I don't need a therapist—or a counselor."

"Kendi, you can't—" Mother Ara halted and pressed her lips together at the expression on Kendi's face. "All right. We'll discuss it later. Like I said, do what you like for now. Go to class if you feel up to it, or stay at my house for the day."

With Ben. Kendi scratched his ear. Maybe being left out wouldn't be so bad after all.

ELEVEN

Even a gift can be poison.

—Daniel Vik

Ben was waiting when Kendi arrived at his and Ara's house. "Well?" he asked without preamble.

"I found a clue," Kendi said eagerly, and told him what had gone on. Even though Inspector Tan had told him not to talk about the investigation, he didn't think the prohibition included Ben. Ben's blue eyes went wider and wider as Kendi spoke, and he found himself embellishing on some of the details. His chest swelled and he felt like a hero, as if he had caught the murderer instead of just finding a potential clue.

They were on the living room sofa. Kendi had pulled his long legs up and he felt rather like a grasshopper. Ben sat cross-legged next to him. He wore black sweats and white socks. The weather had grown heavy and moist, and there was a faint electric charge in the air. Black-bottomed clouds were visible through the windows. Kendi was glad of an excuse to stay indoors. It wouldn't be much fun changing classes in the rain. Although water falling from the sky had been a rarity for him in Australia, it had been all too common on Giselle Blanc's frog farm, and most of the time he and the other slaves had been forced to continue working in it. Rain was no longer fun or a novelty.

"It must've been creepy," Ben said. "I wish I could have gone."

Kendi laughed. "I got creeped out a couple times,"

he admitted. "I kept expecting to find a dead body or something." He scratched his nose and gave Ben a sidelong glance. His red hair gleamed softly in the lamplight and a light scattering of freckles gave his face a boyish look. He was shorter then Kendi, and stockier. It made him come across as solid and immovable, unlike the ever-shifting, always-changing Dream.

Kendi shifted position to sit cross-legged like Ben. Their knees almost touched, and Kendi could feel Ben's body heat. A coppery taste filled his mouth. *Pup and Pitr,* he thought. *Remember Pup and Pitr.* He made himself lean casually back against the rear of the couch.

"So what have you been doing while I was gone?" Kendi asked.

"Working out." Ben pantomimed lifting weights.

"Getting some definition?"

Ben flushed slightly. "A little. See?" He rolled up his sleeve, displaying a solid arm just as a heavy sheet of rain crashed against the window. Ben dropped his arm and looked nervously at the ceiling. It sounded like someone had dropped thousands of marbles on the roof.

"Don't like storms?" Kendi said.

"No," Ben said shortly. "It's stupid, I guess, but—"

Thunder smashed through the room, as loud as a cannon. Ben jumped sideways and ended up half-tangled with Kendi. They struggled for a moment, and Kendi was intensely aware of Ben's warm body against his own. After a moment, they separated.

"Sorry," Ben said sheepishly. His eyes, bluer than deep pools of water, didn't leave Kendi's face. "Thunder always does that to me."

"Yeah." Kendi's voice was thick. "That was a big one."

Ben's eyes stayed on Kendi's, and Kendi didn't want to look away. His heart beat as fast as the raindrops.

Was he reading this right? Or was he wrong again, like he had been with Pitr and with Pup? He wanted to know, yet he didn't. Slowly, Kendi's hand crept toward Ben's.

Someone pounded on the front door. Ben jerked back and jumped to his feet. "Who the hell?"

Kendi sat up. Ben hurried to the foyer as the pounding continued. Kendi sighed. It was for the best. So far Kendi had fallen twice for someone who wasn't interested. This was probably a third time. He should put Ben out of his mind. He should—

Ben came back into the living room, leading a dripping Dorna, Jeren, Willa, and Kite. They were laughing, even Willa, and Dorna's eyes sparkled with merriment.

"You got any towels?" Jeren asked.

Ben nodded and trotted out of the room. Kendi got up. "What the hell are you guys doing here?"

Kite shook himself like a dog. His shaggy, dark hair flung water droplets in all directions. "We're looking for you. You haven't been in your room lately, and we thought you might be here."

"Why didn't you just call instead of running out in the rain?"

"It wasn't raining when we left," Dorna said. "Where have you been?"

Kendi opened his mouth to tell them about the investigation, then remembered Inspector Tan's warning. "Studying with Mother Ara," he said instead. "Tutoring. You know."

Ben came back with an armload of towels and distributed them about the room. Jeren made *brrrrrrrr* noises as he dried his hair, and it stood out in brown spikes. The scar around his left eye gleamed sharply against his skin. Willa dried herself with quiet efficiency and handed the towel back to Ben with a soft "Thank you." Dorna wrapped hers around her hair like a turban and Kite dropped his around his neck.

"We wanted to know if you wanted to play hide-and-seek," Dorna said.

Kendi shot a look at the window. Water sheeted down the pane in a solid gray mass. "Uh—"

"Not outside, dummy," Kite said. "In the Dream."

"Oh." Kendi looked at Ben. "I—"

"It'll be great!" Jeren enthused, stepping forward and blocking Ben from Kendi's view. "Dorna said it's great practice, and we all need the damn hours. Whoever's *It* gets to choose the landscape."

"And we're going to play for money," Kite said. "Whoever's *It* has to pay five freemarks to the first person to touch home base, and anyone who gets tagged has to pay *It* five freemarks."

It sounded like fun and Kendi found himself caught up in the enthusiasm. It would also take his mind off the fact that Ara and Tan were out there investigating Vera Cheel's house and he wasn't.

"Sounds great!" he said. "Let's—" Then he noticed Ben again. He was standing in the doorway to the hall, several wet towels in his hand. Ben wasn't Silent, which meant he couldn't play. Kendi hesitated. "Hey, maybe we should do something else. I mean, you know, something we can all do."

"No," Ben said in a neutral voice. "Go ahead. I should finish my workout anyway. You can use the living room."

"Hey, thanks Ben," Jeren said before Kendi could respond. He turned his back on Ben and brandished a red dermospray. "Everyone got theirs?"

Kendi produced his own from his pocket, then shot a guilty glance at the doorway. Maybe he should back out, go do something with Ben. But Ben was already gone. Kendi stood there, torn.

"Just got mine refilled before I hooked up with you guys," Dorna said. "I've been out of drugs for two days now, and I kept forgetting to go back."

"Drat it," Willa muttered. "I've only got one dose left after this one. I'll have to go to the dispensary in the morning. I hope it stops raining by then."

Jeren thumped his dermospray, then turned to Kendi. "Here, let me." He snatched Kendi's spray and pressed it against Kendi's arm before he could say anything. The familiar *thump* sounded as it shoved the drug under Kendi's skin. Willa and Kite followed suit.

"Uh, thanks," Kendi said. "I guess we better get into position."

Dorna and Kite took easy chairs. Willa sat on the floor in the lotus position and Jeren stretched out on the couch. Kendi positioned himself on his spear.

"You are one weird Aussie," Jeren said. "Aren't you afraid you'll slip and that thing'll get you in the balls?"

"No," Kendi said shortly, suddenly annoyed at Jeren. "You better be quiet. It's easier to get there without a lot of noise."

Jeren shrugged and lapsed into silence as Kendi closed his eyes.

A few moments later, the five of them were standing on the flat, featureless plain that marked neutral territory in the Dream. Kendi was the last to arrive, since he had to leave his cave and walk to the edge of the Outback before he could join the others, who had already learned to transport themselves. Whispers hissed around them.

"Who's *It*?" Willa asked. In the Dream, Kendi noticed, she seemed taller, more sure of herself.

"My mother and your mother were hanging out the clothes," Kite chanted, pointing to each person at each word. "My mother socked your mother in the nose. What color was the blood?" His finger landed on Jeren.

"Green," Jeren said. "Like snot."

"G-R-E-E-N and you are *It*." Kite's finger pointed at himself. "My turf, then. Here goes."

He spread his arms wide. The ground rumbled and the air swirled. Green shoots speared up from the ground, thickened, and widened into solid, leafy walls. New-mown grass sprouted beneath Kendi's bare feet. The air coalesced into fluffy clouds and bright sunlight. In a few moments the group was standing in the center of a garden maze. White marble statues gleamed above granite benches, and a fountain sprayed cool water high into the air.

"There are lots of entrances to the center," Kite announced, and Kendi counted eight. "It isn't a real maze—there are also lots of pathways and openings."

"Lots of places to hide, in other words," Dorna said. "Let's go."

Kite plucked a blindfold out of thin air and tied it around his eyes. Kendi marveled at the other boy's control. So far conjuring objects had proven difficult for him, though he was becoming adept at molding landscapes. Kite started counting.

"Why the fuck are we standing here?" Jeren said. "Run!"

They scattered. Kendi dodged into the twisting hedge-lined paths until he was alone. Whispers murmured sibilants all around him. He could sense other people moving about in the maze like a swimmer senses ripples in a pond, but it was hard to figure out exactly where they were. He closed his eyes and tried to sense who was where. Jeren was off that way. Willa was two pathways over. Dorna was . . . was . . . Kendi furrowed his forehead in concentration. He had a hard time fixing on her. And where was—

Kite barreled around the corner. Kendi felt him coming and his eyes popped open. With a whoop and a yell, Kite pounced. Kendi dodged and fled, trying to remember which way home base was. Kite stayed right behind him. Kendi concentrated as he ran. He needed an obstacle, something to slow Kite down. The earth rumbled, and a boulder burst out of the ground between the two of them, blocking the pathway. The smell of damp earth filled the air. Kendi continued to run down the leafy corridor. An opening to home base was just ahead of him.

"Oh no, you don't," Kite said from the other side of the rock. Tendrils of plants and vines shot inward from the two hedges, weaving themselves into a thick barrier just ahead of Kendi, who screeched to a halt. Kite started to clamber over the boulder, but it was too smooth for good purchase and he slid back to the ground. Kendi tried to push through the vegetation. It was too thick. He needed something to cut through it, or a way to go over it.

Kendi felt Kite's mind pressing on his own. The boulder started to crack. Kendi wanted the rock to exist, big and solid, while Kite wanted it to crumble into rubble. Whichever one of them could force his own perception on the other would win. They were on Kite's turf, which gave him an advantage, but Kendi's Silence was strong. Dozens of cracks raced over the boulder's surface, and Kendi could feel it weakening. Kendi narrowed his eyes. He wanted a solid boulder. He wanted the cracks to disappear. They would disappear *now*. There was a moment of resistance, then the cracks smoothed over and vanished.

"Home free!" yelled Jeren from the center of the maze.

"Dammit!" Kite said from the other side.

"Mom, Kite's swearing," Kendi yelled back in a child's singsong. "Can't catch me!"

There was a *clank,* and the final rung of a metal ladder appeared at the top of the boulder. Uh-oh. Kite's ability to conjure objects was more advanced than Kendi had thought. Kendi cast about for a way out. He could try to make the ladder disappear, but Kite had created it and they were on his turf. Kendi doubted he could overcome both those advantages at the same time. He needed to get through the hedge wall.

"Home free!" Willa shouted from the center.

Now's the time to get it right, Kendi thought. He held out his hands. He needed a machete, sleek and sharp. It would appear in his hands, and it would appear in his hands—

"Gotcha!" Kite said behind him in glee. "You're *It*! And you owe me five freemarks."

"Yeah, yeah," Kendi grumbled. "At least I get to dictate territory."

Kite grinned and the maze vanished, leaving the flat plain behind. Jeren and Willa stood next to each other, Dorna off to one side.

"Round two," Kendi said, and without further explanation he spread his arms wide and called for the Outback. Scrubby plants sprouted from nothing. Sandy soil and piles of rock sprang into being, and the sky rippled and shifted into a pure, hot blue.

"Shit," Jeren said, wiping his brow. "It's fucking hot!"

"What a mouth," Dorna observed dryly.

"Hey, Sis, you take me as I am."

"I'm not a—oh, never mind."

"Home base is this pile of rocks," Kendi said. "And watch out for drop bears."

"Drop bears?" Willa said.

"According to legend, they hide in the tops of trees," Kendi told her with an absolutely straight face. "Especially around the billabongs. When you pass underneath them, they drop on you. They aren't very big by themselves, but if ten or eleven land on you all at once, it gets pretty nasty. Smelly, too."

"You liar," Jeren said.

"Can't lie in the Dream," Kendi replied.

"Right," Dorna said. "Of course, that 'according to legend' bit sort of lets you off the hook, doesn't it?"

With an injured air, Kendi covered his eyes and started counting. Around him, he felt the ripples in the Dream as the others scattered. This time he kept a mental eye on Dorna.

"Thirty-eight, thirty-nine, forty."

Kendi felt Dorna retreat quite a ways and dodge into the brush around a small billabong. Then he lost her. Puzzled, he tried to find her again.

"Seventy-two, seventy-three, seventy-four."

Where had she gone? Kendi gnawed his lip. Maybe she had the ability to hide herself in the Dream just as Kendi had a talent for finding people. Or maybe she—

There! She was right there. Right at the edge of the Outback.

"Ninety-eight, ninety-nine, one hundred!"

Kendi made a beeline for Dorna's hiding place. He skirted a clump of scree, then flung himself around a boulder, knowing full well she was on the other side.

"Gotcha!" he shouted, and lunged.

"What the hell?" sputtered the man on the other side.

Kendi leaped back as if he'd been bitten. It was a man, blond, dressed in overalls with a tool belt. Kendi had never seen him before, hadn't sensed him either.

"Who are you?" Kendi demanded. "What are you doing on my turf?"

"Your turf?" the man said. "Kid, you better have a look."

That was when Kendi noticed he had crossed some kind of boundary. The Outback was directly behind him, but at the moment he was actually standing in some kind of workshop or garage.

The man crossed arms that bulged with muscle. "This is my territory, yeah?"

"Oops," Kendi said, backing away. "My mistake. Sorry!" he fled, face burning with embarrassment. The moment he re-entered the Outback, he felt Kite making a run for home base. Kendi raced across the hot plain, but didn't make it on time. Kite touched the rock pile and thumbed his nose at Kendi.

"ImadeitImadeit!" he said, lapsing into his old speech patterns in the excitement. "Fivemarks!"

Kendi ground his teeth and cast out his mind to track the others. Jeren was creeping closer, crawling on his belly like a snake. Willa was some ways off, and Dorna was . . . was . . . He narrowed his eyes. It felt like she was in more than one place. Abruptly, the sensation vanished and he could feel her again in only one place. Before he could try to figure out what was happening there, Jeren leaped from his hiding place behind a tree and made a break for it. Kendi spun and tackled him at the last moment.

"You're *It*." He grinned. "And you owe me five."

The game continued. Kendi did well when he was *It*, and not so well when he was hiding. The more he played, the more he became certain that Dorna was able to interfere with his talent of finding people. When he confronted her on it between rounds, however, she only smiled and called to restart the game.

After a time, Kendi began to feel the tickle that told him his drugs were about to wear off. The distraction was enough to slow him down, and Willa slapped his shoulder.

"You're *It*," she announced.

"I think I've only got time for one more round," Dorna announced, and the others concurred. "Kendi, you owe me ten freemarks. Double or nothing?"

Kendi didn't even hesitate. "Done!" He called up

the Outback one last time and counted as the others fled in all directions. Kendi kept his concentration full on Dorna as the numbers rolled automatically across his tongue. And then he felt it again. She was in two places at once. But how? Never mind—right now he had to concentrate on not losing her. Ferociously he tried to keep his mind on both her images.

"Eighty-three, eighty-four . . ."

It wasn't easy. Both Dornas were dodging, staying in continual motion. A bead of sweat trickled down Kendi's temple. Dorna ran, leaped, darted. The distance between her two images grew, making it even harder. And then there were *three* of her. Kendi gasped in amazement. It felt like he was being pulled in three different directions, but he was determined to keep his mental eye on her.

"Ninety-seven, ninety-eight . . ."

He was being pulled apart, yanked in too many directions. But he had to keep track of her. He *would* keep track of her. The Dornas moved again. There was a strange *wrench*.

When Kendi opened his eyes, he was flying.

There were thirteen roses. Ara counted them twice.

A few red petals had scattered themselves across the coffee table in Vera Cheel's bright, airy house. The windows were closed against the rain that battered the panes and Ara smelled the chemicals spread by the technicians in their search for only they knew what. She remembered the roses being on the table the first time she had visited Cheel's house so she could recreate the murder in the Dream, but she hadn't thought anything of them.

Thirteen roses. Fourteen minus one?

There was no card. Tan was examining a delivery box she had found in the kitchen wastebasket. It was white with red lettering. " 'Fran's Flowers,' " Tan read. "Let's see what they have to say."

A quick call, however, revealed that Fran's Flowers had no record of a delivery to Vera Cheel's house, nor had she bought flowers from them recently.

"Let's see what else," Tan said in her harsh voice. "Betting on the bedroom."

It took less than a minute to find the pile of underwear beneath the bed. Tan, her hands protected with close-fitting gloves, fished them out and counted them.

"Thirteen pairs of panties," she said, settling back on her heels.

"You think there were fourteen and the killer took one?" Ara said.

"Under the bed's an unlikely place to store clean underwear, so I'd say probably." Tan produced a large evidence bag and carefully placed the panties in it for lab analysis. "Have to figure out what it all means. How we can use this to catch the bastard."

Ara sat on the bed, feeling uncertain and a bit queasy. Watching Tan shove Vera Cheel's underwear into a bag felt like a gross invasion of privacy. The woman's body was already lying naked on an autopsy table at Guardian headquarters, and now two strangers were going through her most private possessions. Would a stranger sort through Ara's underwear the day after she died?

"It's a sequence," Tan muttered. She sealed the bag. "A delivery, a murder, a removal of three things. One of the delivered items, a private item of the victim, a finger. The delivery is—what? A gift? A warning? Then things are taken away."

"Including the victim's life," Ara said.

"Hmmm . . . yes." Tan crossed her legs on the floor. "Control measure? Serial killers murder their victims as a way to control them. Because they feel they have no control themselves."

A flash of insight struck Ara. "He isn't a strong person in the real world," she said. "He's weak there—or he thinks he is—which is why he kills in the Dream. Since the women die in the Dream, he needs to show some control over her solid body as well. He uses intimate objects to gain it."

"Sounds reasonable," Tan said. "So why does he cut off their fingers and sew them onto the next victim?"

Ara shuddered. "I don't know. It seems related to the addition/subtraction idea, though."

"Each victim gets a present," Tan rasped. "Then the killer takes part of that present and a piece of the corpse. He also takes an item of clothing—"

"Which the victim no longer needs," Ara pointed out.

"—and he keeps it as a souvenir." Tan brought her braid over her shoulder and toyed with it. "Serial killers usually become obsessed with their victims. I wonder if he sends them anything else. Something the woman doesn't keep?"

"Flowers and chocolates are traditional tokens of love," Ara said.

Tan straightened. "You're right! I'm stupid! He delivers a love token. When his victim—she doesn't even realize what's going on—doesn't melt into his arms, he feels spurned. Rejected. So he comes back. Kills her."

"And taking back part of the love token is only 'fair,' since she scorned him."

Tan nodded. "Need to check the rest of this house. Then the other ones."

They searched the rest of Cheel's house, but found no more sets of thirteen. By this time, the rain had slacked off to a few breezy droplets and Ara was getting hungry. The two of them retired to the restaurant they had eaten lunch in. When Tan gave her order, her voice had become so harsh, it was barely more than a whisper. After the server left, Tan reached for her water glass.

"Why does that happen?" Ara asked abruptly.

Tan peered at her over the rim of her glass. "Why does what happen?"

"Your voice," Ara explained. "It's beautiful in the Dream, but in the solid world it's . . . different."

"Euphemism for nasty," Tan said blandly.

"No, just—"

"I know what I sound like, Mother," Tan interrupted. "It isn't pretty."

"If you don't like talking about it," Ara said, getting embarrassed, "you don't have to—"

"No secret," Tan said. "My voice in the Dream is what I used to sound like in the solid world. Then that changed."

"An injury?"

Tan nodded. "Took an elbow in the throat breaking up a bar fight. Kid not much older than Kendi. Crushed my vocal cords. Took two operations to give me my voice back. I'm lucky to talk at all, though that depends on your point of view. Kid who elbowed me is a Father at the monastery these days. Teaches math or something."

"I'm sorry," Ara said.

Tan shrugged. "Nothing you did. I adjusted. Let's talk about the guy who collects fingers." She brought out her computer pad and Ara followed suit. Two screens popped into view over the table.

"We can't search the houses of the other victims," Tan rasped. "Their houses were all sold a long time ago. But we have holograms, photographs, inventories. Let's skim the reports. See if the on-site Guardians mentioned finding anything."

This work went quite a lot faster. They got through the scenes and inventories of Wren Hamil's house before the food arrived. It was an easier job for Ara to stomach. Photos, holograms, and lists of words were a lot less personal than handling clothes once worn by a woman now lying on an examination table.

They continued to work as they ate, poring over the information from Prinna Meg's house.

"There!" Tan said, stabbing at a holographic list with her fork. "That's it!"

"What?" Ara asked, leaning forward. "I don't see—"

"The book. I remember it now. Prinna Meg wasn't an antiquarian. Weren't any hardcopy books in her house, in fact, except this one. I didn't think much of it because I wasn't looking for it. See the title?"

"Ten Love Sonnets by William Shakespeare," Ara read.

"Except," Tan said, "there were only nine. The last one had been torn out."

TWELVE

If I give you wings, will you ever fly?

—Irfan Qasad

Kendi faltered. Her wings folded slightly and she was falling. She snapped them outward again and—

wings?

—righted herself. Hot, dry air rushed over her feathers. The ground was far, far below, but her eyes made out every detail. Even tiny movements grabbed her attention—

feathers?

—and the five people below her stood out in sharp detail. One of the people looked upward and staggered a bit. Dark skin, slender build, curly black hair. Falcon eyes met human eyes, and falcon Kendi dove straight down. Human Kendi raised an arm and falcon Kendi landed on it with a flurry of wings and feathers. The second falcon Kendi touched down, a moment of dizziness swept over her. She was sitting on a wiry forearm—

she?

—and at the same time standing on hot Outback sand. The dizziness passed and she clacked her beak. Human Kendi hesitantly touched falcon Kendi's feathers and falcon Kendi half closed her eyes, leaning into the comforting touch.

Other humans gathered around, staring. Falcon Kendi watched them through hooded eyes, suspicious. Then human Kendi flung his arm up and with a high, shrill cry falcon Kendi flung her wings open and clawed the air for altitude. In moments, she was high in the free, clear sky.

Kendi shaded his eyes in astonishment as the falcon dwindled into a tiny black speck against the blue. He could no longer feel her mind, but he remembered gliding on the air and dropping down to land on her brother's arm. Every memory the falcon had was also his own. A breathless excitement rushed through him like adrenaline. Ultralights and aircraft didn't even come close.

"What the hell?" Jeren said beside him.

"She's my sister," Kendi said, awed. "When we touch, I know what she's thinking. Wow! *Wow!*"

"Where did she come from?" Willa asked.

"I don't know. She was just . . . *there*." He noticed the itch behind his eyes was growing stronger. His drugs were wearing off. If he didn't leave the Dream soon, he would eventually be yanked out of it, and all his teachers said it was an unpleasant way to leave the Dream. Some Silent ended up bedridden for days from the shock. "I have to get out of here. My stuff's wearing off."

"Yeah, me too," Kite said. "Let's talk in the solid world."

Kendi shut his eyes. *If it be in my best interest and in the best interest of all life everywhere,* he thought, *let me leave the Dream.*

He opened his eyes back in Ara's living room. The rain had slowed to a few big drops that pattered against the window in irregular splashes. He disentangled himself from the red spear as the others began to open their eyes and stretch. Clanking sounds issued from behind Ben's closed bedroom door.

"Whatappen?" Kite blurted out.

"Yeah," Dorna said, perching herself cross-legged on the sofa. "What was that falcon all about?"

Kendi fidgeted. It was hard to sit still. He got up and paced the floor. "I'm not sure. I felt like I was being pulled in two directions at once, and then suddenly I was in two *places* at once. I was me, and I was also the falcon. It was . . . it was a real rush, you know?"

"Should we try it again?" Kite said, slowing down. "Go back into the Dream and see if Kendi can bring back the falcon?"

"We should call a teacher," Willa said quietly. "Mother Ara or one of the other Parents."

"Mother Ara's out with—" Kendi paused. "She's out. I don't know how to get hold of her. I want to do it again."

"Maybe Ben would know how to get hold of her," Willa said. "You should have someone with you, Kendi. Someone who knows what's going on."

Impatience seized Kendi. He wanted to get back into the Dream. He wanted to fly again, feel the air rush past his head. But he had to admit there was merit in what Willa said. He crossed quickly to Ben's door, knocked once, and opened it. Ben, face red with exertion, set down the barbell in surprise.

"What's going on?" he asked.

Kendi quickly explained. Ben got up and came into the living room. "I've never heard of anything like that," he said. "But I'm not—not Silent, so there's a lot I don't know."

"Can you get hold of your mom?" Kendi asked.

"Maybe." Ben tapped the living room wall and a section glowed into a viewscreen. "Eliza, page Mom. Tell her to call home."

"Working," said the house computer. Several moments passed and Kendi continued to fidget. The Dream was calling to him. He barely noticed that he was standing close enough to Ben to feel his body heat.

"Mother Araceil is unavailable," the computer reported.

"No surprise," Ben muttered. "She's never available."

"Try Father Ched-Hisak," Willa said. "Or Grandfather Melthine."

Ben relayed the instructions. "Father Ched-Hisak is unavailable," said the computer. "Grandfather Melthine is unavailable."

"Well, shit," Jeren said. "Come on, Kendi. It's not your fault you can't reach them. Let's go and see what you can do."

"We should wait," Dorna cautioned. "Nothing's going to change between now and when someone shows up."

"I agree," Willa said. "It could be dangerous."

"It didn't hurt me before," Kendi pointed out. "It felt great! I want to go back in now and make sure I can do it again."

Ben put a hand on Kendi's arm. "You might want to wait," he said. "It sounds to me like you're splitting up your mind, and someone with experience should watch you."

"You can watch my real body," Kendi told him. "I'll wear a medical monitor and you can keep an eye on the readout. If something starts to go wrong, you shout for help."

"I don't—" Ben began.

"Ben, I have to go in," Kendi said. "I can't hold off. Come on—help me out. Please?"

Ben gave him a look, uncertainty written all over his face. After a long moment, he nodded. "All right. I'll get the monitor."

Kendi grabbed him in a rough hug. "Thanks!"

"Okay, okay," Ben said breathlessly. "Not so rough!"

Kendi instantly let go and felt his face grow hot. It

had felt so natural to embrace Ben that he hadn't even thought. But Ben's reaction hadn't been positive. He hadn't even hugged back.

I guess, Kendi thought, *that answers my question about him. Well, we can still be friends.*

Ben, meanwhile, left the room and came back with the wristband sensor and the readout monitor. Kendi slipped the band on and went back to the others in the living room, his enthusiasm a little dampened. Ben followed. The Silent trainees were already arranging themselves on chairs and couch. Jeren handed Kendi his red spear and red dermospray.

"Let's do this bitch," he said.

"We meet," Kendi said firmly, "on my turf," and the others nodded.

Once Ben determined that the readout unit was working properly, Kendi positioned himself on his spear, injected himself, and shut his eyes.

If it be in my best interest and in the best interest of all life everywhere, he thought, *let me enter the Dream.*

A few moments later, the five students were once again standing beneath the golden sun and azure sky of Kendi's Outback. Kendi dressed them in the usual khaki explorer outfits, though he himself was shirtless, with bare feet and white shorts. Going naked or wearing a loincloth in front of a Ched-Balaar was one thing. Doing either in front of his fellow human students was quite another.

"How does it work?" Kite said. "What did you do?"

"I'm not completely sure," Kendi admitted. "It happened when I was trying to find Dorna." Something occurred to him, and he turned to face her. Her dark hair curled out from under her pith helmet. "How did you do that?"

"Do what?" she asked.

"Make it seem like you're in two places at once. Is

it like the way you can interfere with people finding you?"

She shook her head. "I don't know what you mean."

"Whenever I tried to find you in the hide-and-seek game," Kendi said, "it felt like you were in two or three different places. I meant to ask you about it, but then the falcon showed up and I forgot."

"I don't do any such thing," Dorna said. "Really. Maybe you're just misreading, or you're sensing people who have similar thoughts to mine. I mean, you've only been using the Dream for a week."

Kendi's first thought was that Dorna was lying. But here in the Dream, lies were impossible.

"Yeah, okay," he said. "Let me try it again."

He closed his eyes and tried to recall the sensation of being pulled in two directions at once. It should have been hard—they weren't playing the game anymore and Dorna was standing right beside him. But it turned out to be easy. A few seconds later, a high scream shrilled on the wind, and the small falcon circled overhead. Kendi opened his eyes.

"Is that you?" Willa looked up, shading her eyes.

"Yeah. I know she's there, but I can't tell what she's thinking. Not right now."

"She?" Kite said.

Kendi nodded. "The falcon's a female. I don't know why. She just is."

An internal voice poked at him. *Is it because you like men?* But Kendi pushed the thought away. The falcon was who she was, and that was all. He pursed his lips and whistled. The falcon instantly dove for the ground. Kendi held up an arm and she landed, making a surprisingly light, feathery bundle. The moment she touched him, he felt himself both standing on the ground and perched on his own arm. Memories of rushing air and hot sun coursed through him and he staggered a little. The falcon flapped her wings to keep her balance until the vertigo passed. Her talons were long and sharp, but they didn't do the least bit of injury to Kendi's arm.

Why should she? he thought. *She's me.*

The others moved closer to examine the falcon and made impressed-sounding noises.

"She's you?" Willa said.

"That's what it feels like," Kendi said.

"You're schizo," Jeren put in. "Shit, you've split your mind into pieces."

"I'm not crazy," Kendi said defensively. "What the hell kind of remark is that?"

Jeren shrugged. "I just call it like I see it."

Ripples washed through the Outback and Kendi spun around. The falcon flapped again. Approaching them was a man. Kendi automatically drew back. It was the dark man, the one who had killed Vera Cheel. He was coming to get—

"Hi!" the man called. "Can I approach? Is everything here okay?"

It wasn't the dark man. This man was tall and blond and he wore blue overalls. A belt of tools hung around his waist and he had large, callused hands. Kendi remembered him. It was the man whose turf Kendi had stumbled onto during the game a while earlier.

"We're okay," Kite said. "Come over. Who're you?"

"Name's Buck," he replied. "My turf's just over that way and I felt something weird, right? So I thought I'd come over and make sure everyone was okay."

"We're fine," Jeren said. There was a strange note in his voice that Kendi couldn't identify.

"Okay. Good." Buck stuck his hands in his pockets. "Nice bird."

"Thanks." Kendi stroked the falcon's feathers and she cheeped once at him. "I just got her."

"She's a part of you, hey?"

"I guess." Kendi paused. "How did you know that?"

Buck shrugged. "I can feel it. How come she takes a falcon form?"

"I don't know," Kendi admitted. "I'm new to this."

"You aren't a Child of Irfan, are you?" Jeren said evenly. It was more a statement than a question.

"Nope. I'm independent. Do some contract work when I can get it, right? Look, kid, you've got something new here, something I don't think anyone's seen in the Dream, and I'll bet there's a lot more you can do with this."

"Like what?" Kendi asked.

"Well, this is a kind of shapeshifting, for one thing." Buck scuffed at the ground with his work boot. "A part of your mind's taken another shape in the Dream, yeah? Unless you're a falcon in the solid world and the *human* I'm talking to is the little splinter."

Kite snorted.

"Right," Kendi said with a smile. "So?"

"So what if your animal friend—animal *self*—here can take on other shapes? Other animals."

Kite whistled. Willa twisted a lock of hair and sat down on a rock. Kendi blinked at Buck, suddenly remembering the dream he had had when the camel changed into a crocodile. Mother Ara had said the realistic dreams were a partial entry into the Dream itself. Had he already been doing this?

"I wouldn't even know how to start," Kendi said at last. "I mean, I just today got—"

"It'd be easy, yeah?" Buck interrupted. "You want something else—a grizzly or a tiger."

"Or a drop bear," Dorna put in.

"Uh, how about something smaller?" Willa said nervously. "Maybe a kangaroo. I saw a picture of one once. They come from Australia, don't they?"

"So you imagine it happening," Buck continued.

"Just like you imagine people wearing the clothes you want or your turf being whatever shape it takes. Which reminds me, kid—why don't you turn the sun down a little? I'm sweating my ass off, yeah?"

"That's the Outback," Kendi said. "Love it or leave it. How do you know so much about shapeshifting?"

"I have friends who do it," Buck replied. "You gonna try it or what?"

"What's your interest in this?" Jeren demanded.

Buck shrugged. "Just helping out. You don't want me around, I'll leave, right?"

"No, stay." Kendi leveled Jeren a withering glare. "He's just—just overprotective. Let me try this."

Before anyone could say another word, Kendi closed his eyes. The falcon on his arm shifted a bit and he could feel the talons gripping his arm. A tiger? No, he decided. Better something that won't attack. Koala bear? Cute, but more likely to bite than any tiger. Kangaroo then. Kendi imagined the animal— long legs, long tail, pouch. The falcon would become a kangaroo and it would become a kangaroo *now*.

A sudden heavy weight dragged his arm down and there was a heavy *thud* on the ground beside him. Kendi's eyes popped open. He found himself looking at a kangaroo sprawled on the sandy soil. She quickly scrambled to her feet and looked at him with re-proachful brown eyes.

"I did it," Kendi whispered. "All life, I did it!"

A great splash ripped through the Dream. The Out-back wavered, distorting like a bad hologram. Kendi staggered, almost knocked flat. The kangaroo made an angry whuffing noise.

"What the fuck?" Jeren yelped. Standing next to him was an old woman. With a flash of recognition, Kendi remembered her. He had stumbled into her flower garden by accident and she had animated the plants to drive him out.

"What are you little shits up to?" she demanded. Her iron-gray hair stood out like an angry dandelion. "You're sending ripples through the entire Dream. My gladiolas will never be the same."

Kendi recovered himself enough to be angry. This was *his* turf, and Ara had made it very clear to him that a Silent's turf was inviolate. Appearing in the middle of Kendi's turf uninvited and unannounced was the height of rudeness. "Who the hell do you think you are?" he snarled.

"The woman whose garden you're fucking up, that's who," the woman grumbled. And my name's Zelda. Jesus, boy—you've got to learn some control."

"And you've got to learn some manners."

"Look, boy, do you want all your neighbors mad at you or not?" Zelda said.

"I don't give a shit what you—"

"You better give a shit," Zelda snapped. "Otherwise, you're going to have a hundred Silent in all directions pretty pissed at you. That what you want?"

"No," Kendi said, then hated himself for agreeing with her. "Look, what do you—"

"Just learn to change that . . . that *thing*"—she gestured sharply at the kangaroo— "more quietly. Jesus."

"It's not a thing," Kite said. "It's part of Kendi."

"Don't tell her that," Kendi said sharply.

"You just have to make the change a little smoother," Zelda said in a quieter voice. "Here, let me show you." She picked up a stone. Kendi felt her hands touching it as if she were touching him instead. Before he could protest, she closed her hand around it. When she opened it, she was holding a bright yellow marigold. Kendi stared. He hadn't felt the change, even though she had effectively made it in his own mind.

"Wow," Dorna whistled.

"She's good," Buck said.

"How did you do that?" Kendi asked, interested despite his earlier anger.

"Practice," she said. "And a few lessons. Here, let me show you. I'll even do it for free so you'll quit rippling my garden. Close your eyes, boy, and listen to what I say."

Ben sat on the living room floor. Four bodies lay on chairs and sofa, and a fifth stood propped on a spear in the corner. All of them were still as breathing statues. Red dermosprays lay scattered across the floor. Ben hated this. The quiet bodies in the room underscored the fact that Ben himself would never enter the Dream.

He sighed and checked Kendi's readout. It was singularly unhelpful. Sure, it said that everything was fine with Kendi, but it didn't tell him what Kendi was *doing*. The familiar desire—need—to enter the Dream swept over Ben. Not for the first time he wondered what it was that prevented him. Every test showed he had the genes for Silence, but for some reason he had never expressed the ability. He had never heard strange whispers or voices. He had never woken up from a dream so vivid that he would have sworn it was real. He had never felt a jolt when touching a Silent. Not once. He knew it disappointed his mother, though she had never said so, or even hinted it. He knew his aunt, uncle, and cousins thought he was sub-human, because they *had* said so.

Since he couldn't do anything his Silent family did, Ben was therefore careful to do those activities none of *them* could do. So far, he was the family expert in computers and he was the only one who lifted weights. Indeed, he had never known his family to engage in any kind of exercise whatsoever. That was fine with Ben. If he couldn't take pride in his mind, then he would damn well take pride in his body. And the results of a year's worth of labor showed. Mom now had to buy him shirts with broader shoulders and looser sleeves. Firm muscle rippled across his abdomen, and his legs were thick and powerful.

He wondered if Kendi had noticed.

Ben got up and walked over to Kendi. The young man was several centimeters taller than Ben, and thinner. His build was more whipcord, and he was damned handsome.

Ben stared at Kendi, uncertain. Why did he feel this way? When Kendi had hugged him, it had felt good. Hell, it had felt *great*. Better than a simple, friendly hug should have made him feel. It was confusing. Did he like Kendi as more than a friend? Ben shook his head. There were lots of guys who liked—loved— other men. No big deal there. It was just that Ben had never considered himself one of them.

"God, I've had *girlfriends*," he said aloud.

But, he thought, none for more than a few weeks. Some of the other guys at school talked about nothing but girls, talked as if they thought about girls constantly, or at least daily. Ben never had. This had never worried him. He hadn't even really thought about it. Not until he had met Kendi.

Kendi remained still as a statue, hands cupped over his groin, one leg propped up on the red spear. The end was sharp and Ben knew Kendi had to replace the rubber tip every so often. Ben had once asked Kendi why he didn't simply blunt the end, and Kendi had given him a blank look.

"The Real People don't do it that way," he said.

Ben put a hand in front of Kendi's face and felt Kendi's breath warm and regular on his palm. A shiver went through him. He touched Kendi's shoulder with a hesitant hand and swallowed. He wanted to grab Kendi up in a hard, crushing embrace, hold on to him for hours, or days. After a moment, Ben put

both arms around him and leaned his head against
Kendi's chest.

Just to see, he thought, *what it feels like.*

It felt empty. Kendi wasn't hugging him back. Feeling foolish, Ben released him, careful not to knock
him over, though he doubted even that would wake
him. The more experienced Silent could be jerked out
of the Dream through physical stimuli such as a pain
or a sudden jolt, but novices usually had to concentrate so hard just to attain the necessary trance that
they completely ignored outside stimuli.

A flicker of movement caught at the corner of Ben's
eye and he spun around. Dorna was sitting up in her
chair. She cracked her knuckles. Ben's stomach
twisted sickeningly. Had he seen her hugging Kendi?

"Hey, Dorna," Ben said, keeping his voice steady.
"What's—"

"I have control," she said in a strangely deep voice.
"Well fuck me with a banana."

Ben blinked. "What?"

"About goddam time, too." Dorna got up and
looked around the room. "Well, lover-boy, you can
just tell your goody-good friends that I'm keeping control. They want to do something, they're gonna have
to go through *me.*"

"You?" Ben echoed, still confused. "I don't
understand."

Dorna laughed, a harsh, male sound. "That's because you're stupid. Now this dude"—she crossed the
room to where Kendi stood—"this dude's noticed
some stuff. Fucking prick." And she backhanded him
hard across the face.

"Hey!" Ben grabbed her wrist. "What the hell are
you doing?"

The stomach punch landed before Ben could react.
Air rushed out of his lungs and he doubled over. Not
for nothing had he been strengthening his abdominal

muscles, however, and he recovered quickly. Without thinking he launched himself forward and rammed a shoulder into Dorna. She staggered back. Ben grabbed her arm and tried to spin her around so he could shove her against the wall, but she twisted away from him. Another punch came at his jaw. Ben dodged and realized too late it was only a feint. Pain exploded in his groin and lower belly as Dorna's foot snapped up. Ben collapsed to the floor, agony written hard on his face.

"You fight like a fucking girl," Dorna said, and kicked him in the stomach. Ben cried out. And then she was gone.

Ben lay there, unable to move for some time, until the pain finally subsided enough to let him get to his feet. He checked himself, but didn't find anything sprained or broken. Jeren, Kite, Willa, and Kendi remained motionless. He staggered to the bathroom and swallowed a handful of painkillers. In the mirror his face appeared pale beneath disheveled flame-red hair. What should he do next? Call the Guardians? Maybe he should—

"Ben?" came Kendi's voice. "Ben, where are you?"

Ben made his way back to the living room. Kendi was holding his spear in one hand. The other hand he held to his cheek. The others shifted, then opened their eyes.

"My face hurts like hell," Kendi said. "What's going on?"

"Dorna slapped you," Ben said, "then she attacked me." Various cries of disbelief and astonishment caromed around the room and Ben had to wait for them to quiet down before he could explain. The pills he had taken started to kick in as he spoke, and some of the pain faded as he told the story.

"Now she's gone," he finished. "I don't know where she went."

"Dorna was still in the Dream when I left," Kendi

said. "She couldn't have been awake here. It's impossible."

"Tell that to my crotch," Ben blurted out, then flushed.

"Got you in the nuts, huh?" Jeren said. "Bitch doesn't fight fair."

"We have to call someone," Willa declared. "Ben, try your mother again. Maybe she'll answer this time."

Ben obeyed. This time, Mom's face appeared on the wall screen. For the second time, Ben explained what had happened.

"Stay right where you are," she ordered. "I'll be there in ten minutes." The screen went blank.

"You should get some ice for your stomach," Kendi said. "And for your—your—"

"My stomach, anyway," Ben said, flushing again.

He was still holding a damp towelful to his abdomen when Ara got home. Father Ched-Hisak was right behind her. Ara's face was tight with worry and she made Ben explain the entire incident over again. She wanted to examine him, but he put his foot down.

"Everyone's looking, Mom," he muttered. "And I'm not hurt that bad."

Ched-Hisak hooted and clattered his teeth. Ben, who had grown up on Bellerophon among the Ched-Balaar, understood the words better than many adult Children, though he had no more hope of reproducing the sounds than he did of sprouting wings and flying.

"I am sure we can take him to a doctor if his pain persists," Ched-Hisak was saying firmly. "We have other matters for discussion."

To Ben's intense relief, Mom nodded. "Why don't you get hold of the dorm and see if Dorna's gone back to her room? I'll talk to the others."

Ben shook off Mom's guiding hand and took a chair on his own. She pursed her lips but didn't comment as she turned to Kendi.

"You said Dorna was in the Dream when you left it," she stated. "But Ben says she attacked him *before* you woke up. That means there's an overlap. Her body was awake and moving around, even though her mind was in the Dream, is that right?"

Kendi nodded. "I guess. I thought that couldn't happen."

"It can't," Mom said shortly. "But maybe we can get a clue as to what happened. Start at the beginning, all of you, and tell me exactly what was going on. Why were you all in the Dream together? For practice?"

They all nodded in unison. Ben found himself drifting off, probably a side effect of the painkillers. He was vaguely aware of Father Ched-Hisak rejoining the group and telling them that Dorna didn't seem to be in her room or anywhere near the dormitory and that he'd ordered a search. Ben drifted again, soothed by the Ched-Balaar's gentle presence. A startled shout from Mom brought him awake again.

"You *split* yourself?" she said incredulously. "How?"

"By accident," Kendi protested. "I didn't mean to."

"A powerful thing," Ched-Hisak mused. "It will require much further study."

"Was that when Dorna woke up, then?" Mom asked.

Kendi squirmed. "Not exactly."

"Go on, then," Mom said, and Ben recognized the danger in her voice. He wanted to come to Kendi's defense, but knew from experience that such a gesture would only make her angrier, so he remained silent. So did the other students.

Kendi falteringly explained how he had decided to go back into the Dream to see if he could call up the falcon again. Mom's face got darker with every word until she finally exploded.

"What were you *thinking*?" she shouted. "Good

lord, Kendi—you haven't even been entering the Dream for a week and already you're experimenting with things no one knows anything about? Do you know how *foolish* that is? How *stupid*? What if you split your mind and couldn't bring it back together? There would have been no one there to help you."

"I'm sorry," Kendi said meekly. "It just felt so . . . *right* that it didn't occur to me that anything could go wrong with it."

"And *you*—" She rounded on Ben. "What were *you* thinking? Why didn't you call me?"

"I tried," Ben said hotly. "But you weren't available. Neither was Father Ched-Hisak or Grandfather Melthine. We couldn't get hold of anybody at all."

"Then you should have waited," Mom snapped. "You should have—"

Ched-Hisak placed a hand on her shoulder. "Mother Ara," he clattered, "we do have other things to worry about. Perhaps many beratements can come later?"

Mom looked as though she was going to say more, then apparently thought the better of it. "Right," she said.

Father Ched-Hisak turned to the students. His eyes were wise and gentle, and even though he was the size of a small horse, he somehow didn't look imposing or seem as though he was filling a fair chunk of the living room. For some reason, Ben found himself wondering what it would be like to have Father Ched-Hisak as his dad. The Ched-Balaar kept his head at human level and turned his gaze on Ben.

"Would you translate for those who understand not all my words well?" he chattered. Ben nodded, and Father Ched-Hisak continued. "Did any of you notice anything so odd about Dorna? Anything she said or did to seem strange?"

Ben translated and Jeren snorted. "This is stupid," he said. "We're all Silent. We're all weird in one way or another."

"We need to think, Jeren," Willa said.

"Look, I just want to go home before it fucking rains again, okay? Why don't you ask her teacher?"

"We will do this thing, Jeren, but now we must have you think," Father Ched-Hisak said, with Ben's translation coming a sentence behind. "An odd thing happened here and we need to find the bottom of it. To repeat: Have any of you noticed anything so odd about Dorna?"

Jeren rolled his eyes and the others thought. "Last week," Kendi said slowly, "she said she was having trouble sleeping because she had nightmares about people dying in the Dream."

"I remember that," Ben put in, glad to contribute something more than just translation. "You also said she talked funny. And there was that weird stuff she said when she woke up and hit me."

"That's right!" Kendi snapped his fingers. "Sometimes Dorna changes the way she talks. As if she were someone . . . someone . . ." He trailed off.

"Yes?" Mom said.

"Something's bugging me," Kendi said. His eyes tracked over empty air. "The way Dorna talked. It reminded me of someone, but I can't quite place—" He bolted upright on the couch. "Buck. Sometimes she talks like Buck."

Mom blinked at him, puzzled. "Who's Buck?"

"A guy we met in the Dream," Kendi said. "He gave me pointers on my falcon. And then that Zelda woman showed up." He gave further details about them.

"Kendi," Father Ched-Hisak said intently, "you said you attempted to locate Dorna, but found her in a pair of places."

"Yeah. And once I tried to tag someone I thought was her, but it turned out to be Zelda. Another time I thought I had her and it was Buck."

"I wish this to be clear. You were sure you felt Dorna, but you found someone else both times. You also felt her in pairs of places at the same time."

Kendi nodded. Father Ched-Hisak settled back on his haunches with a grumbling, muttering noise that Ben recognized as a symptom of careful thought among the Ched-Balaar, though he decided not to translate that.

"I have made studies of human psychology," Father Ched-Hisak said, half to himself. "Humans have varied and fascinating reactions to tragedy so different from members of my species. I think this is one of those reactions."

"What do you mean, Father?" Mom asked before Ben could translate.

"It is possible," Ched-Hisak clattered slowly, "that your Dorna has a psychological problem known to humans as—" But the rest of the sentence was lost, even to Ben.

"I'm sorry, Father," Ben told him. "I don't know those words."

"Dissociative identity disorder," Mom supplied. "How do you know, Father?"

"I don't," Father Ched-Hisak admitted. "I only suspect. However, it would explain many things."

"What's dishie—dissipate—" Kite said.

"Dissociative identity disorder," Mom repeated. "It means multiple personalities." When her words met with further blank looks, she continued. "Some people who suffer terrible abuse as children retreat into their own heads. The things that their parent—or parents— do to them are so horrible that the children can't believe it's truly happening, so they create other people for them to happen to. The creation is so complete that they actually become someone else, and the alternate personality takes the memory of the abuse."

"So there are other people living in Dorna's head," Willa said softly.

"Possibly. I'm not convinced," Mom said.

"It would explain a great much," Father Ched-Hisak chattered. "If Dorna has more than one self, it would make sense that she would have more than one Dream self. When we visit the Dream, after all, we become only what we believe we are. It would explain also why Kendi felt more than one Dorna—there *was* more than one Dorna, truly."

"And it would explain why her speech patterns changed," Kendi said excitedly. Then he deflated a little. "Wait. I asked her about it—why I felt more than one of her. She said she had no idea, and you can't lie in the Dream."

"That is not correct," Father Ched-Hisak said gently. "A Silent can tell an untruth in the Dream if she *believes* it to be true. I think Dorna remains unaware of the other personalities. She did not lie. She told the truth as she knew it."

"But why would she be able to get up and leave before she—or whatever personalities—left the Dream?" Mom objected.

"Human minds are powerful," Father Ched-Hisak said. "I have read of people with many personalities doing similar things. It is quite common for one personality to drink heavily, for example, and leave the other personalities unaffected completely. If many of Dorna's personalities are in the Dream, one left behind might take body control."

"She said that," Ben put in after translating Ched-Hisak's words. "She said something about being in control now and keeping it." He shuddered involuntarily. "She's insane, then?"

"This is a bad word," Father Ched-Hisak said. "If

we are correct, Dorna has many difficult problems. We shall say only that."

Mom, who had slumped into a chair, sat bolt upright. "Father, are people with multiple personalities violent?"

"Often there is a violent personality, or two, or three."

"I have a call to make, and then I'll have to leave. Ben, you and Kendi stay here. The rest of you can go or stay as you like, but *stay out of the Dream*." She got up and left the room without a backward glance. Ben watched her go with a grim expression. His mother always left without a backward glance.

Ara paced outside the door to Dorna's dormitory room, her mind moving furiously. Dorna Saline. Third-year student, average grades, student of Mother Ched-Maruk.

Serial killer?

It made dreadful sense. They had been looking for a man because serial killers were usually male and the victims in this case were women. The fact that the killer could change shape in the Dream enough to hide facial features had gone right past both Ara and Tan. If the killer could change a face, how difficult would it be to change gender?

The vast majority of Silent were stuck with their own shapes in the Dream because that was what their subconscious minds expected. *And a mind that thought of itself—or one part of itself—as male would take at least one male shape in the Dream,* Ara thought grimly.

Was this how Kendi had split himself? Kendi had largely grown up in what he called "mutant society" but was trying almost desperately to get back to his Real People roots. Had living in two worlds combined with powerful Silence to allow him multiple Dream forms?

Soft footsteps came up the hallway carpet and Inspector Lewa Tan approached, a computer pad in her hand and an intense expression on her face.

"Got the warrant," she said without preamble and pressed the computer pad to the door's electronic lock. "It was a real trick getting it. Dorna's only crime is hitting your son and there's no proof she's done anything else. Lucky I have an uncle on the bench. Baran, release lock on authority of Guardian Lewa Tan. Warranted search."

"Scanning warrant," the computer said. "Access granted."

The lock clicked open. Tan drew on a pair of gloves and hurried inside. Ara followed.

Dorna Saline's small room was perfectly tidy. Desk, computer pad, chair, bed, balcony door. No wall decorations or houseplants. After a quick glance around, Ara knelt by the bed and Tan opened the wardrobe.

"Nothing under here," Ara reported. "Not even dust. Should I strip the bed?"

"We'll get some techs to do that." Hangers scraped the roll bar as Tan leafed through hanging blouses. "We're doing an overview right now. Check the desk, will you?"

Ara moved to obey. "Where's Linus?"

"Coming. He was—shit!"

"What?" Ara spun to face her. "What is it?"

Tan wordlessly held out a pale green blouse with long sleeves. The cuff showed a small red stain.

"Blood?" Ara said.

"Maybe." Tan whipped a small scanner from her pocket and ran it over the spot. "Definitely."

"Whose?"

"This scanner doesn't have the memory to hold that kind of database. It might be hers, of course."

"Or someone else's. Do we keep looking?"

Tan eyed her. "You think just because we find one

potential clue, we stop searching? Welcome to the tedious side of Guardian work, Mother Ara. Let's get to it."

The two of them set back to work.

THIRTEEN

The smell of your deeds will follow you forever.
—Daniel Vik

"The DNA," Tan said, "doesn't belong to Dorna. Or any of the known victims."

"Is that good or bad?" Ara asked.

Tan gave her a hard look. "Bad. If it belonged to a victim, we could get an arrest warrant in five minutes. But we don't know *who* it belongs to, so we get nothing."

Ara swirled her glass around the table, making thoughtful rings of condensed water. The smell of fried onions and mushrooms hung on the air. Nicky's Restaurant, the quiet, dark place they had taken Kendi after the Dream recreation, had become a customary meeting place for Ara and Inspector Tan. Over the three days since Dorna's disappearance, Tan had begun consulting with Ara regularly—more often, it seemed to Ara, than with her partner. Linus Gray, however, was handling the non-Silent aspects of the case—coordinating technicians, interpreting their evidence, and so on, leaving Tan free to handle the Silent end.

"It's been three days," Ara said, thinking aloud. "We've checked with all her friends and they haven't seen her. She has no relatives on Bellerophon because she was brought here as a newly freed slave, so she hasn't gone to ground with anyone like that. We know she hasn't left the planet because the spaceport was put on alert for her right after she attacked Ben." A surge of anger passed through Ara, and she had to work to keep it out of her voice. "So where is she hiding?"

"My vote is still the forest," Tan said. "There are tons of places to hide, and anyone who knows basic survival skills—"

"Like the ones we teach at the monastery." Ara sighed.

"—could live out there for a long time." Tan speared a deep-fried mushroom and dipped it in spicy brown sauce. "I wonder which personality does the surviving. Dammit, we have to talk to her. Every instinct I have tells me she's connected to the murders. Too much of a coincidence that all this happened right in the middle of the investigation."

"Do you think she did it?"

"She's my prime suspect," Tan admitted. "Did you know that in almost a thousand years we've never had a serial killer case on Bellerophon? I have no precedents to work with. None. So I've been doing a lot of reading about serial killers and a lot of talking to law enforcement people on other planets. Father Ched-Hisak knows a lot about human psychology, too. They all tell me that female serial killers are rare and that women with multiple personalities tend to be more suicidal than homicidal. It's the opposite for men. In other words, the women kill themselves while the men kill other people. But there are plenty of exceptions. I'm willing to bet we have one of them. Lucky us."

"We checked the records," Ara said, still swirling her glass. "Dorna did arrive on Bellerophon just before Prinna Meg was murdered, so she's been on the planet during the killings. I just . . . I just . . ."

"What?" Tan said.

"I like Dorna," Ara said. "She struck me as a bit odd—now I know why—but she's always been nice."

"I wouldn't call the person—or personality—who attacked your son *nice*."

"You're right." Ara pushed the glass aside. "I just hate the idea that someone I know like this might be murdering people and chopping off their fingers. I keep hoping it turns out to be someone we haven't even thought of yet."

"Most of the time the murderer is the obvious suspect," Tan pointed out. "The witness you've been ignoring because he's on the outer edge never turns out to be the long-lost nephew-turned-killer. You never get to assemble all the suspects in the library to reveal this fact, either."

The waiter came to clear away their plates and ask if they wanted desert. Ara passed a hand over her round stomach as a way of getting herself to decline, but her resolve refused to solidify.

"What's today?" she asked the waiter, an older man with silver hair.

"Thursday," he told her.

"Good. I always give in to temptation on Thursday. Turtle fudge sundae, please."

"And for you, ma'am?" the waiter asked Tan.

"More tea," she rasped. "I only give in to temptation on Tuesdays."

The waiter left. Ara eyed Tan. "You might want to give in more often. Stress reliever, you know."

"Be easy to justify," Tan said. "I'm getting big pressure from higher up to solve this."

"I'll bet. Were you able to access Dorna's sale records?"

"Some. Found out she's had more than three owners. I talked to some of them. Or I talked to them through a Silent courier, anyway."

"And?"

Tan shrugged. "They never noticed any personality weirdness and don't know of any Silent who were murdered during the time they owned her. Doesn't mean much, of course. I'm still waiting to hear back from the police agencies—the killer's M.O. is pretty unique—but it's slow going. Most of the more densely populated worlds have a dozen or more governments. That means a dozen or more law enforcement agencies, and they don't always talk to each other."

"Then let's hope they talk to us."

Kendi grinned and waved as Ben came into sight. Ben nodded to him from the top of the outdoor staircase. It had become their habit to meet here after both their classes were over for the day. Kendi was still living at the Rymar house, though there had never been an indication that the killer was looking for Kendi.

"Better safe than sorry," Ara had said.

"Irfan Qasad?" Kendi had said, earning him a *why do I do this to myself?* sort of sigh from Ara.

Ben was trotting down the stairs past several students going in the opposite direction when his upper body jerked forward. His computer pad flew out of his hand and he fell. Kendi watched in shock as he tumbled down the steps. People swore in surprise and leaped out of the way. The thuds and thumps as his body hit the stairs were awful. At last, Ben came to rest at the bottom. His computer pad struck the ground some distance away and skidded over the edge of the walkway.

"Ben!" Kendi got to his side without any idea of how he had traversed the space between them. Ben's face was white, and his freckles stood out like tiny lesions. Kendi automatically reached down to pull him to his feet, but then Brother Dell's first-aid training took over and he pulled back. "Ben! Are you all right?"

Ben shifted position and groaned. "Shit."

A voice tinged with harsh laughter called down, "Loudmouth!" A pejorative, the opposite of Silent.

Kendi looked up and saw two students he didn't recognize, one male and one female. Both of them were laughing. Kendi didn't even think. He sprinted up to the top of the stairs and smashed headfirst into the male. Kendi flailed with both fists, heedless of the counterblows that rained down upon him, until a firm hand yanked him straight out of the fight. Ched-Balaar clatter ordered him to stop. Kendi swung twice more at empty air before the order registered and he obeyed. It was hard to breathe and took him a moment to realize he was dangling by his collar from Father Ched-Hisak's left hand. The Ched-Balaar's right hand held the other male student, and a human teacher Kendi didn't recognize had restrained the female. Father Ched-Hisak lowered Kendi to the deck, and Kendi found he could breathe again.

"What's going on here?" the human teacher demanded.

"They pushed Ben down the stairs," Kendi said hotly.

"That's a lie!"

An argument ensued. The two students continued to deny the charge, and Father Ched-Hisak had to restrain Kendi a second time. Finally, Father Ched-Hisak sounded a deep, rumbling noise like a foghorn that silenced everyone.

"No one can lie in the Dream," he said. "We will bring these two there to learn the truth."

Both students blanched but didn't protest when the human teacher lead them away. Father Ched-Hisak turned to Kendi. His wide brown eyes were hard.

"And you," he chattered, "you will once again find yourself on work detail."

"But they pushed—"

"That does not excuse your fighting," Father Ched-Hisak told him. "Finish this sentence: 'Serene must you walk the paths . . .'"

"'. . . and serene must you ever remain,'" Kendi said automatically. "I know, I know."

"You do not know," Ched-Hisak said. "Otherwise you would not do these things. I will register your hours. Go to your friend."

Kendi had actually forgotten about Ben. He hurried down the stairs and found him sitting on a bench next to a brown-clad Sister whose gold medallion bore a square cross, the symbol of a medic. She had his left shoe off and was examining his ankle. Ben's face was tight with pain. The crowd that had gathered was already drifting away. Kendi became aware that his own face hurt. He touched his lower lip and his finger came away red and sticky. Other parts of his body were also beginning to ache.

"It's a slight sprain and a few bruises," the Sister said. "Nothing serious." She removed a dermospray from her medical bag and it thumped against Ben's ankle. Another dermospray thumped against his upper arm. "You need to sit here for at least ten minutes for the sprain to heal. The second shot will help the pain and the bruises, all right?"

Ben nodded and the Sister turned to Kendi. She stanched his bleeding lip, gave him a shot, and declared him fine. They thanked her and she left. Kendi started to sit next to Ben, whose leg was still stretched out on the bench, but Ben pointed at the rail.

"My pad went over," he said. "Can you get it for me?"

Kendi peered over the edge and saw the pad caught in the semitransparent netting. He lay flat on his stomach and was just able to retrieve it with his fingertips. Ben accepted it with a curt "thank you."

"What's the matter?" Kendi asked.

"Nothing."

"Ben, come on. What's going on?"

Ben paused for a long time. "I don't need you to fight my cousins for me, Kendi," he said. "It's stupid."

"Those two were your cousins?" Kendi said in disbelief.

"They're creeps and they've been pulling shit like that all my life. This was nothing new."

"Ben, they tripped you down the—"

"I don't care what they did," Ben said. "I get it all the time from them. So what? They're assholes—full of shit."

"Don't tell me it doesn't make you mad," Kendi almost snapped. "They tripped you on the damn stairs!"

"It makes me mad, yeah," Ben said heatedly. "But I don't need *you* to take care of me, and I definitely don't need you telling Mom about it."

"Ben, I didn't mean—"

"Just leave me alone for a while, okay?" And Ben's face shut down. After a moment, Kendi got up and headed for the Rymar home. As a result, he was just getting in the door when Inspector Tan called to tell Mother Ara that another dead body had turned up.

The first thing Ara noticed was the smell. Mother Diane Giday's house was high up in this particular talltree, and Ara was less than halfway up the staircase that wound around the trunk when it hit her—the ripe, rancid smell of rotting meat. Ara faltered, then forced herself onward. Tan had said on the phone that Giday had been killed quite some time ago and that the body was in an advanced state of putrefaction, but Ara hadn't thought the smell of it would greet her before she even reached the front door. Now she was doubly glad she had spent considerable time convincing Kendi—ordering him, really—that he didn't need to come to the site of the murder.

The staircase ended at a wide platform. Just ahead,

Giday's little house was so high up that the roof poked up above the talltree's leaves. When Ara arrived at the address, a Guardian was just switching on the holographic generator. Around the house appeared the same ring of blue light Ara had seen at Iris Temm's home. Ara walked through it and the generator beeped an alarm, just as the other one had. Ara wondered if she was going to be crossing crime-scene barriers for the rest of her life. The Guardian recognized her and waved her on. Ara wasn't sure she wanted to go, but did anyway.

Linus Gray, his face matching his name, met her just inside the door. The stench washed over Ara and made her gag. She suddenly wished she hadn't eaten that sundae at lunch.

"Here," Gray said, pressing a dermospray to her upper arm. The drug thumped home.

"What is it?" Ara demanded.

"A neurological inhibitor," Gray explained. "It'll put the olfactory bulb in your brain to sleep for about an hour. You won't smell a thing."

He was right. The horrible stench had already faded. Ara nodded her thanks and glanced around the room. Giday's house was little more than a cottage, with three tiny rooms and a bath. Ara could see into every room from the front door. The miniature living room contained one easy chair, a short sofa, and a set of wall-mounted shelves that displayed various knick-knacks. On the couch was a lumpy bundle covered by shiny black cloth. Two Guardian technicians were just starting to tuck in the edges. Ara caught a glimpse of discolored flesh. Tan was watching, her eyes flat and angry. A small gravity sled hovered in front of the couch like a coffee table.

Gray handed Ara a set of gloves. She put them on. "Do you want to see the body?" he asked.

"No," Ara said flatly. "What about her finger?"

"Cut off and replaced," Gray said. "The DNA of the new finger matches Iris Temm's. We've already compared a sample of Giday's DNA to the samples we collected from the finger sewn to Vera Cheel's body. It's a match. Giday's DNA also matches the blood Tan found on the shirt in Dorna's room."

"So Dorna's definitely the killer, then," Ara murmured.

"Sure looks that way," Tan said.

The technicians finished tucking in the cloth. With a soft hissing sound, it sealed itself around the corpse and the couch cushions beneath it. The techs gently lifted the entire bundle onto the sled. The first tech adjusted the sled's controls until it hovered at waist level and maneuvered it out the door. The second technician nodded at Tan and followed.

"How long was she in here?" Ara asked.

"Preliminary scan suggests about two weeks," Tan said.

"Two *weeks*?" Ara gasped. "How did she go this long without being found? Who found her?"

Tan took out her data pad and consulted notes. "The down-below neighbors called in to complain about a weird smell. One of our boys came up to look around and found her. No one noticed Giday was missing because she was supposed to have left for an off-planet vacation fifteen days ago. Spaceport records show she had a ticket to DelaCruz, but she never boarded the ship. Between that, and the fact that her house is up so high it hid the smell for a while, no one even knew she had been murdered."

Ara thought about a woman named Diane Giday in the Dream taking care of last-minute business and looking forward to her vacation. Perhaps she had hummed to herself a bit or sighed with satisfaction at the completion of her last piece of work. Then a dark man appeared and turned the Dream into a nightmare, leaving her corpse to rot in her cozy little house. Ara's mouth turned down with silent fury.

"If she's been dead for two weeks," Ara said in a flat voice, "there's no way I can recreate the scene. Too many minds won't be in the same place, and most of the others will have forgotten the patterns."

Tan nodded. "I thought as much, but figured I'd ask anyway."

"Giday was probably the thirteenth victim," Gray said. "That means the killer is escalating."

Ara gave him a questioning look.

"He means the attacks are coming closer together," Tan explained. "Look, Prinna Meg was murdered almost three years ago, a few weeks after Dorna Saline was recruited into the Children, in fact. About a year later, Wren Hamil is killed. Eleven months after that, Iris Temm is murdered and we bring you in to have a look. Nine months later, this woman Giday dies, but we don't find the body until now. Two and a half weeks after that—two and a half *weeks*—the monster goes after Vera Cheel. There's going to be another victim, Ara, and soon. We have to find this guy."

"The word is out among the Children," Ara said. "Female Children aren't supposed to enter the Dream alone, and they need to be ready to leave it on an instant's notice. But you know how it goes—plenty of people disregard the advice. At last count, we have over three thousand Sisters, Mothers, and Grandmothers, and most of them figure that they're either more powerful than the stalker or the odds are against any one of them being attacked."

"Technically, they're right about the odds," Linus said. "Less than one in three thousand."

"Tell that to Mother Diane." Ara shuddered. "*I* certainly wouldn't take the risk."

"Let's do the search," Tan said. "See what clue the killer left for us this time."

Searching the cottage didn't take long. Ara found six pairs of earrings lined up on Giday's dresser and a thirteenth singleton broken in the wastebasket. "It was probably fourteen earrings and the killer broke one to make a 'set' of thirteen so he could keep one and leave twelve."

"Dorna's a she," Tan said. "Unless there's something the monastery medics don't know about."

"I don't think it's Dorna," Ara said.

Linus Gray, who was carefully stowing the earrings in an evidence bag, gave her a hard look. "Why not?"

"Call it a feeling," Ara said. "It's just—it's just—I don't know. Out of character for her."

"For Dorna, maybe," Tan pointed out. "But who knows about one of her alternates?"

"I just think we need to keep an open mind," Ara said. She started to sit on Giday's narrow bed, then stopped herself. The crime-scene technicians might want to examine it.

Tan nodded. "I agree. And you're right—it's possible Dorna didn't do any of it. But the fact that she disappeared right after one of the murders says she's got something to hide."

"Which may not be connected to this case," Ara said.

"And there are those nightmares about people dying in the Dream," Tan said. "Kendi mentioned her talking about them."

"She's not the only one," Ara countered. "I've had a few bad dreams myself."

"And I found Giday's blood on her sleeve," said Tan.

"Someone could have planted it there," Ara said. "If *I* had chopped someone's finger off and there was even the tiniest chance some of my victim's blood got on me, I'd burn my clothes. I certainly wouldn't hang them in my closet for the Guardians to find. And if I were afraid the Guardians were close to catching me, it'd be awful tempting to plant some phony evidence in the room of someone who had recently disappeared under mysterious circumstances."

"Do you think Dorna's dead somewhere?" Gray sealed the bag.

"I don't know," Ara said, worried. "I hope not. But it's a definite possibility. And what if she was murdered to keep her quiet about something?"

Tan put a gloved hand on Ara's shoulder. "Look, I don't want it to be Dorna either. But she's the obvious suspect right now and we have to talk to her, even if her disappearance and the blood are completely innocent. Come on—let's see if we can find anything else the killer left behind."

This time it was Gray who noticed it—a music disk titled *Thirteen Lucky Love Songs.* "The last song has been wiped," he reported.

"All we're doing is proving that the same killer got each one of them." Ara tried to pace the miniature living room, then gave it up. There wasn't enough room. "This doesn't give us any clues to who the killer *is.*"

"He—or she—will slip up eventually," Tan said grimly. "The nanosecond that happens, we'll nail the bastard."

Ara's gaze drifted about Giday's living room. The denuded sofa seemed to mock her, a blot in the otherwise tidy house. On the wall above the couch hung a lot of framed photographs and holograms interspersed with the occasional certificate of award.

"Has someone told her family?" Ara asked. "I'm figuring she wasn't married."

"No, she wasn't, and not yet," Tan responded.

Ara got up and went over to investigate the certificates more closely. One of them was a commendation for outstanding work in multiple message transmission in the Dream. It was signed by one Tara Linnet, Manager for Dreamers, Inc. Ara blinked, her heart suddenly pounding.

"We've been stupid!" She almost shouted. "God—completely stupid!"

Tan, who had been talking to Gray, jumped in surprise, then recovered herself. "What are you talking about?"

"There!" Ara pointed to the certificate. "Right there. We've been ignoring a potential lead."

Gray stepped forward. " 'In recognition for outstanding contribution and work in multiple message transmission,' " he read. "So?"

"Isn't it obvious?" Ara said. "Giday worked for Dreamers, Inc., before she came to the Children of Irfan. They're a corporation that offers Silent communication for a price."

"I've heard of them," Tan said. "What's the big deal?"

"You said one of the problems with tracking down information about the killings on other planets is that there are so many law enforcement agencies that don't talk to each other and compare notes," Ara said. "But what about the corporations?"

"Go on," Tan rasped.

"Dreamers, Inc., has more employees than some governments have subjects. They're not just multinational—they're multiplanetary. But for all that, they're still a single organization. It doesn't matter if one branch falls under one government and a different branch falls under another—it's still a single unit. And you can bet that if someone's been killing their employees and chopping off their fingers, they'll know about it. Why don't we ask them?"

Tan looked excited for the first time since Ara had met her. "You're right! The corps can cut straight across police boundaries."

"There's Dreamers, Inc., and the Silent Partners," Gray said, ticking off his fingers, "and Silent Acquisitions—"

"Silent Acquisitions only deals in Silent slaves," Ara said. "They don't hire out Silent to other people."

"Wonder if Dorna ever passed through them." Tan toyed with her braid. "The records that came with her were incomplete, and you can bet I checked."

"That's pretty common," Ara said. "I was the one who bought and freed her in the name of the Children, and the clearinghouse I found her in typically didn't give anything but a short medical history. Previous owners were kept in strict confidence."

"Why do they do that?" Gray wanted to know.

"Because sometimes people own slaves in places where slavery is illegal," Ara replied. "They keep the slaves ignorant of this fact. It's easier than you might think, especially if the slave doesn't speak the local language. And a lot of slaves are abused until they acquire a slave mentality. It wouldn't even occur to them to try escaping or to demand their release. It sometimes takes years of counseling to bring them out of it."

A breeze wandered through the windows, making the curtains flutter. Ara thought she caught a whiff of decaying flesh and wondered if the shot Gray had given her was beginning to wear off.

"At any rate," Tan said, "we need to start checking with the corporations. The killer's M.O. is unique, so they'll probably have no trouble remembering it if they've seen it. Then we just find out if they ever owned someone named Dorna Saline, and—"

"That might not work," Ara pointed out. "It's common for buyers to change the names of their new slaves. It reinforces that mentality—you don't even own your name—and it muddies the trail if the purchase was illegal. Dorna, *if* she's the killer, may have had a different name with every owner. For all I know, Dorna made up her current name. She was only listed as a lot number on the auction catalog."

"You didn't bother trying to check?" Gray asked.

Ara shrugged. "Why should we? Like I said, the previous owner is kept anonymous, and we give our new people as much privacy as we can, since slaves have had so little of it. It means a lot to most of them, being able to choose their own name. Some keep their slave names as is or they change the spelling or pronunciation. Some use a name from their childhood. Others make up brand new ones. Kendi did that, I'm pretty sure. I have no idea what name he was born with, and I've never asked."

Gray deflated a bit. "How will checking with these corporations help us find Dorna's hiding place?"

"It won't," Ara said. "But right now we don't have definitive proof that Dorna's involved in the murders at all. If we find another place that had these finger-chopping murders, we can cross-check names of Silent employees and slaves with the monastery records of Silent who arrived here before the murders began. We might get lucky."

"More sifting." Tan sighed.

"I believe a wise woman once told me—how did the saying go?" Ara said. " 'Welcome to the tedious side of Guardian work'?"

"Very funny."

The rotten smell grew stronger. Tan sniffed the air, apparently noticing it herself.

"We should get out of here before our suppressants wear off," she said. "I'll let the techs know we're finished so they can do the fine-tooth-comb thing. Ara, we need to contact some of these corps. Can you do it this evening, meet on your turf at, say, seven?"

"You want me to come with you?" Ara said.

"You know slavers. I don't," Tan said. "And thank god for that. I'd much rather deal with killers."

At seven o'clock Ara was in her pleasure garden. The fountain made pleasant noises and the pear and orange blossoms smelled exquisite. Usually the place felt quiet and relaxing, but now there was an undercurrent of tension and she felt an urge to keep looking over her shoulder. Twice she spun around, expecting to see a looming dark man with a hat that hid a leering face, and both times she saw nothing. When Ara felt a presence at the edge of her turf, she had to muffle a scream before she realized it was only Tan.

"Please come," Ara called.

Tan appeared, and the Dream rippled briefly around her. "You look nervous."

"Let's just get started," Ara said. "I have a contact at Dreamers, Inc. Take my arm and I'll move us."

Tan obeyed. Ara closed her eyes and cast out her senses. Dreamers, Inc., kept a permanent presence in the Dream, and the pattern of thought was familiar to Ara. She located it and focused on it. They were *here*, but she wanted them to be *there*, and they would be there *now*. The familiar *wrench* cut through her and she opened her eyes.

The brown desk and the red Oriental carpet stood in the middle of a stark, white space. There were no walls, no ceiling, no doors or windows. Just empty whiteness with a room-size square of colored silk in the middle of it. A human man, thin and spare, sat behind the desk with his hands primly folded on the blotter. An inkwell and quill pen sat to one side of a small sign that read WELCOME TO DREAMERS, INC. Everything about the space and the man said *receptionist*. Ara knew that there were actually close to a hundred receptionists on duty at any given moment to field and direct the countless mundane inquiries the company received every day, but the human mind was not geared to register hundreds of receptionists and thousands of questioners occupying the same space, and Ara's subconscious automatically filtered out what her conscious couldn't deal with. Everything she didn't need was relegated to background whispers.

"May I help you?" asked the man in a reedy voice.

"My name is Araceil Rymar," Ara said. "This is Inspector Lewa Tan. I need to talk to Marco Clark. Is he in the Dream?"

"No," the man replied promptly. "His shift begins in twenty minutes. Would you care to wait or leave a message?"

"Tell him that I need to speak with him immediately."

"To Dream Engineer Marco Clark," the man said. "Message begins: Araceil Rymar needs to speak with you immediately. Message ends. Is that correct?"

"Yes, thank you." Ara took Tan's arm and with a *wrench* they were back in Ara's pleasure garden. Birds twittered and bees buzzed among the blossoms.

"Couldn't you tell yourself if this Marco guy was in the Dream?" Tan asked. Her voice once again was full of rich, low tones.

Ara shook her head. "I've only met him in the Dream, never in person. We've never touched, and I'm not good at finding people I haven't had physical contact with. Marco can find me, though."

"So where now?"

"Let's try Silent Acquisitions. They deal exclusively in slaves, so there's a good chance Dorna passed through them at one time or another."

Another *wrench* and they were standing in another receptionist foyer. This time the rug was blue and the desk was a chrome-and-steel fortress and the person

behind it was a red cone with four flexible arms and
three eyes, but it was still clearly a receptionist foyer.
A hovering sign behind the creature read SILENT AC-
QUISITIONS, LTD.: WHERE YOUR TASTES ARE MET.

Ara again introduced herself and Tan. The cone
narrowed its eyes. "Are either or both connected with
Children of Irfan?" Its voice was like a spoon plopping in cold pudding.

Uh-oh, Ara thought. "Why do you ask?" she said
aloud.

"Please answer the question," the creature plopped.
"Are one or both of you connected with the Children
of Irfan? Please answer 'yes' or 'no.' There are no lies
in the Dream."

"Yes," Ara was forced to say. "We both are."

"I am sorry, but I am not allowed to speak with
you."

"But—"

"If you wish to leave a message for a particular
party," the creature went on, "you may hire a courier
ship with a hardcopy missive. Good day."

The reception room vanished, leaving behind the
featureless plain that was the default condition of
the Dream.

"Rude," Tan observed. "What brought that on?"

"Probably me," Ara said grimly. "The Children—
including me—have bought, stolen, swindled, and
tricked a hell of a lot of slaves out of that company
over the decades. We've probably cost them billions
in revenue by now. Silent Acquisitions seems to have
adopted a new policy of identifying Children and then
refusing to communicate with us so we can't trick any
information out of them. Bastards! Filth doesn't even
begin to describe what they do."

"I agree," Tan said, "but we need to stay focused
on the other job."

Ara let out a long breath. "Right. Sorry. I just hate slavers. Buying and selling sentient creatures is about the lowest anyone can—"

"You church, me choir," Tan said. "Can we go?"

"Right, right. Let's try the Silent Partners and see what they have to say."

The Silent Partners, it turned out, didn't know of any strange murders. Neither did DreamShapers. They were about to visit Quietude, Ltd., when Ara felt a presence brush her mind.

"Marco!" she said with delight. "He's in the Dream. Hey, Marco! My turf, all right?"

The pleasure garden appeared around them. Ara was dressed in her green robe with the close-fitting hood. She put Tan in a similar one, but blue. They both sat on the lip of the fountain, waiting. After a brief interval, a yellow sphere of light the size of a basketball whizzed over the garden wall and hovered in front of Ara. Her face showed her pleasure.

"Marco," she said. "I'm glad you could talk to me. This is Inspector Lewa Tan."

"Good morning," the sphere said in a voice reminiscent of ringing bells. "Or is it not morning on Bellerophon?"

"It's evening for us," Ara told him. "Listen, I know you're probably busy, so I'll be fast." She gave a quick explanation of the Dream murders. "Can you find out if there were any similar happenings among Dreamers, Inc.?"

"I know there were," Marco said in his bell-like voice. "It was nine or ten years ago."

Tan stood up, excited. "Can you put me in contact with the investigator in charge of the case?"

"Perhaps. I will have to go through appropriate channels. Please wait."

The ball vanished with a *pop* of inrushing Dream energy. Tan waited with ill-disguised impatience.

"Marco's good," Ara said. "He knows a lot of people."

"My drugs are going to wear off soon," Tan grumbled. "What species is Marco, anyway?"

"Human." Ara scratched her nose. "He's a practicing Zen Buddhist. When I first met him twenty-some years ago, he looked as human as you or me but now . . ." Ara shrugged. "I sometimes wonder what'll happen when he reaches Nirvana."

The ball popped back into being. Standing beneath it was a small, dark-complected man in a linen suit. He had a thin mustache, small black eyes, and equally black hair scattered with silver.

"Ara, Inspector," Marco rang out formally, "this is Ken Rashid, Chief of Security for Dreamers, Inc. Chief Rashid, this is Mother Ara and Inspector Tan, both of the Children of Irfan."

They all exchanged greetings, and Marco said, "I imagine you have little time left in the Dream with much to discuss, so I will leave you. Ara, it was good seeing you. Please visit me again when you have time."

"I will, Marco," Ara said. "And thank you."

Marco vanished with another *pop*.

"Little time left in the Dream," Rashid repeated. "I take it your drugs are wearing off?"

"In about five minutes," Ara confessed. "We'll have to be quick."

"Marco already explained to me the basics of your case." Rashid looked about the manicured lawn as if he were missing something.

"Your pardon," Ara said, and quickly produced a chair for him out of thin air. He took it.

"Almost exactly ten years ago," Rashid continued, "four women connected with Dreamers, Inc., died. Levels of psytonin in their brains indicated they were in the Dream when it happened. The first one was

missing the little finger on her left hand. The second
woman was found also missing her left little finger,
and the finger of the first woman was sewn on in its
place, and so on. This was when I was a chief investigator, before I took my current position, and the case
was assigned to me. Unfortunately, we had—still
have—no suspects."

Tan was on her feet again, eyes flashing. "Wait! The
first woman was only missing a finger? One wasn't
sewn on?"

"That's correct."

"Then she might have been the first victim!" Tan
said. "A big lead!"

"What?" Ara said. "Why?"

"A serial killer's first victim is usually someone the
killer knows," Tan explained. "If we can get a list of
people the first victim knew and compare it with a list
of Silent who have been on Bellerophon since the killings started there, we might be able to pin down a
name."

"Possibly," Rashid said. "Assuming, of course, that
the killer hasn't changed his name."

"Or hers," Tan muttered.

"Chief Rashid," Ara said, "have you ever seen this
woman?" She gestured and a hologram of Dorna Saline hovered in the air before Rashid's chair. The features were a bit blurred—recreating faces in the
Dream required tremendous concentration and more
than a little artistic skill, and while Ara had the first,
she had only a bit of the second.

Rashid studied the image thoughtfully. "I don't believe so," he said at last. "Though the likeness—my
apologies if I seem rude—isn't going to be exact. Who
is she?"

"We think she's connected to the case," Tan told
him.

Ara fidgeted on the lip of the fountain. Her drugs

were nearing the end of their course and she would have to leave the Dream soon or be yanked out of it, and right now it wouldn't be convenient to spend two or three days in bed recovering from the shock.

"Chief," Tan said, "we need to compare notes. The Dream isn't a good medium for transmitting images, and we need to spend more time talking than our drugs will allow. Can we visit you in person?"

"Of course," Rashid replied promptly. "This case has . . . nibbled at me for years, Inspector, and I would love nothing more than to solve it." Something flashed behind his eyes, but Ara couldn't place what it was.

"You are at the headquarters station for Dreamers, then?" Tan said.

"I am. I will instruct my people to look for you."

The itch grew so strong Ara couldn't remain still. "Chief, I'm sorry but I have to go. I look forward to meeting you in person."

Rashid rose from his chair and gave a little bow. "As do I, Mother."

Ara summoned her concentration and released the Dream.

FOURTEEN

The worst part about revelations is that they always feel like something you should have figured out a long time ago.

—Irfan Qasad

"But I'm *involved*," Kendi wailed. "I should *be* there."

"Absolutely not." Ara pressed the seals on her bulging suitcase. The bag shut with a hiss. "There won't be anything for you to do. Besides, you have school. You've been a big help, Kendi, and I promise to let you know everything I can, but we don't need you along on this one."

"You mean you don't need a mere student," Kendi growled.

"If it makes you feel better to pout, go right ahead," Ara said heartlessly. "I should be back in a couple of weeks. My sister and brother-in-law will come by every so often to check on you. Don't go anywhere by yourself, understand?"

Kendi gave her a sidelong look. "You don't want me to be alone because it's not safe?"

"That's right." Ara rummaged through a carryall. Toothbrush, hairbrush, comb, dermosprays, everything there. Had she packed sleeping clothes?

"Safety in numbers and all that, huh?"

"Absolutely." Carryall, suitcase, bookdisks, computer pad. Was her itinerary in the pad? Oh yes. "Safety in numbers."

"And the more numbers, the better?"

"Yes, yes." Should she take a jacket? Probably.

Dreamers, Inc., was headquartered on its own space station, and she usually found the stations a bit chilly.

"Okay. Have a nice trip, then."

Ara said good-bye to Ben—he barely paused in his workout to acknowledge her—and bundled her things outside. Kendi waved his farewell as she shut the door. Something nagged at her as she stood on the deck, something Kendi had said or something Ara herself hadn't said.

Nerves, she told herself. *Stop being such a mother hen. They'll be fine.*

She might not have been so dismissive if she had been able to see the wide grin that stretched Kendi's face.

The party was enormous. Loud music vibrated the floor and shook the rafters, and the rooms were crowded with brown-clad students. Kendi moved easily among them, dancing a bit here, trading palm slaps there. Ben watched with trepidation and not a little envy. Once again Kendi was the life of the party and Ben was relegated to the corner. He was nervous about the entire affair. Mom hadn't specifically given permission for a party, no matter what Kendi had tricked her into saying. Still, he had gone along with it because he found that lately he just couldn't say *no* to Kendi. And, he had told himself, maybe someone else would talk to him because it was his house.

So far the latter hadn't happened. Ben seemed to fade naturally into the woodwork and the partygoers ignored him after polite, dutiful greetings. Once the sun went down and the house began to fill up, Ben found himself in the same corner he had occupied at the Festival party where he had first met Kendi.

Kendi. Ben closed his eyes. He still couldn't figure it out. Things had been cool between them since the fight, and Ben knew himself well enough to realize that he had used it as an excuse to push Kendi away. And Ben found he hated it. Not even the news that Zayim and Tress had gotten twenty whole hours of extra work detail made him feel better. Ben wanted to be close to Kendi, ached to be so. And he didn't understand why he felt that way.

Music continued to throb. Ben shot a nervous glance at the computer speakers. Was it too loud? It would be all he needed to have the Guardians show up and cite him for a loud party. Maybe he should tell the computer to lower the volume, but gradually so no one would—

Ben stiffened. His mouth went dry and his stomach twisted inside him. A ghostly face had appeared at the window. Long, curly dark hair, emerald eyes, pixie features. Dorna. Her eyes met his and she gestured to him. Ben didn't know what to do. Call the Guardians? Shout for help? She had attacked him, and Ben knew the Guardians wanted to question her. Maybe they even thought she was the Dream stalker.

Dorna gestured again, pointing farther up the balcony that ran around the entire house. It was hard to see her, since the lights in the house were on and it was dark outside. Ben glanced around uncertainly. Dorna had attacked him, and that made him angry, but his mother had said she probably suffered from multiple personalities and didn't know what she was doing.

Now there's *a good reason to go outside and talk to her,* he thought.

Dorna gestured once more, then vanished from the window just as Kendi wandered by. Ben grabbed him.

"We need to go outside," he said.

"What? Why?"

"Dorna." And Ben explained.

Without a word, Kendi grabbed Ben's hand and

hauled him outdoors. The night was a bit chilly. A dinosaur called from the forest below—a high, honking sound—and a slight breeze made the leaves rustle as if they were whispering. Music continued to boom inside the house. Kendi took Ben around toward the back of the house, and Ben let him lead. He was nervous, but a small part of him liked the fact that Kendi was holding his hand. Behind the house, the wraparound balcony was more narrow, barely wide enough for two people to walk side by side.

"Where is she?" Kendi murmured. He dropped Ben's hand.

Ben said, "I'm not sure."

"Over here." A hooded shadow edged around the corner. "I'm here."

"Dorna?" Kendi asked. "Where have you—?"

"My name isn't Dorna," the figure said in a voice so quiet Ben had to strain to hear it. "It's Violet."

"Violet," Kendi repeated. He drifted a little closer. "All right. Look, half the planet is searching for you. Where have you been hiding?"

"The forest," Dorna/Violet whispered. She sounded scared. "Buck knows things. He's built a shelter for us and he finds food. But I don't like it. The dinosaurs are scary."

"They think you've been killing people," Kendi said. "In the Dream. Is that true?"

Violet's eyes went wide and she shook her head. The hood rustled against her hair. "No. Not me. And not Dorna, either. Cole is the killer, don't you see? He needs to be stopped."

Gooseflesh rose cold on Ben's arms and back. The woman was completely insane. How many people lived inside her head? Animal instinct told Ben to bolt, put as much distance between this strange creature and himself as possible.

"That's why I came," she continued. "So that you

would know what's going on. I wanted you to know
that Dorna hasn't killed anyone. Not once."

"Then why did you run away?" Kendi leaned casually against the balcony rail, as if he talked to total
lunatics every day. Ben couldn't help but admire his
calm. What if she lunged for him, tried to shove him
over the edge? "If you—Dorna, I mean—never killed
anyone, there's nothing to worry about, right?"

"People wouldn't understand," Violet whispered.
"The Guardians would cage us up, beat us. They
scare me."

"Were all those people in the Dream your . . .
friends?" Kendi asked. He edged closer again, and
Ben wanted to warn him not to. "Buck and Zelda?"

"Zelda's mean," Violet said. "Sometimes she helps
Cole. So does Rudy. He's the one who hit Ben. Dorna's talked about you to all of us. She wanted us to
meet you in the Dream because she likes you. But
Rudy isn't Silent, so he couldn't come into the Dream.
When everyone else was there, he took control and
ran away. He says he never gets enough body time,
so he took it when we weren't looking."

Ben's skin was crawling now and it was all he could
do to keep from running for help. He didn't dare leave
Kendi alone, though. He tensed, ready to attack if she
made any strange moves.

"What about you?" Kendi said. "I didn't see you
in the Dream."

"I was there," Violet whispered. "You just didn't
see me. I'm good at hiding. Listen, you have to make
sure Cole gets caught. Dorna didn't kill anyone. It's
all Cole."

Kendi lunged. The move caught both Ben and Violet off-guard. Kendi grabbed her arm and tried to twist
her around in front of him. But Violet recovered with
surprising speed. In a pair of lightning moves, she
smashed her foot down on his instep and rammed her

elbow into his solar plexus. The air burst audibly from Kendi's lungs. Violet whirled and slammed her shoulder into him. Kendi tumbled over the balcony rail.

"Kendi!" Ben shouted. He bolted toward the rail. Kendi hung by one hand, gasping in pain and fear.

"Bastard!" Violet spat. "Fucking son of a bitch!" She punched a window and glass shattered. Screams erupted from inside the house. The music played.

Ben grabbed Kendi's wrist. His back prickled and he felt vulnerable. Violet was only a few steps away, but he couldn't spare her any of his attention.

"Give me your other hand, Kendi," he said. "Hurry!"

A cold hand grabbed the back of Ben's neck and another hand put a firm grip on his groin. Ben froze but didn't let go of Kendi's wrist. Kendi swung heavily, trying to get his other arm up. Ben's hands started to sweat.

"You stupid asshole," Violet (Dorna? Rudy?) growled. "Next time I see you, you just remember that all I did was this."

She squeezed hard. Pain knotted Ben's stomach and a choking sound escaped his throat, but he kept a death grip on Kendi.

"One shove and I could have killed you, asshole," she hissed in his ear. "Remember that."

And then she was gone. The hard sound of shoes on wood faded into the night. Pain curled like a snake in Ben's lower abdomen, but he forced himself to ignore it. Kendi managed to get his other arm up and grab the balcony rail. Ben helped haul him over the edge, then both of them collapsed to the planks. Ben could do nothing but sit. He felt hot tears trickling down his face, but he didn't care.

"All life," Kendi said. "All life, she almost killed me."

"She almost killed both of us," Ben said. "We need to get help, but god—I don't know if I can stand up."

They sat there a moment until half a dozen sets of footsteps rounded the corner. Ben looked up. A group of the partygoers had come outside.

"We heard the window break," one of them said. "Are you guys okay?"

"Help me up," Ben said. "We have to call the Guardians."

Inspector Linus Gray was making Ben and Kendi repeat their story for the third time when Sil and Hazid arrived. Two Guardian officers had checked the house and a dozen others combed the walkways around it and the ground beneath the Rymar house, but they found no trace of Dorna Saline. The partyers had long since left, and the house was still a mess.

Kendi watched Ben's aunt and uncle come in. Kendi's hand, the one that had hung on to the balcony rail, was scratched and bloody, though he hadn't noticed until a few moments ago. His shoulder hurt. So did his stomach and his foot where Dorna/Violet had hit him. Or had one of her other personalities done the attacking? That seemed more likely. Violet had seemed afraid of her own shadow.

"What happened here?" Hazid demanded as he strode into the living room. Sil's gaze swept the messy room, her eyes glittering with righteous disapproval.

"Are you the owner of this house, Brother?" asked Gray, noticing Hazid's medallion and amber ring.

"I'm the owner's brother-in-law," he said. "This is my wife, Sister Sil. We keep an eye on the place when Ara goes away. Now what the hell is going on?"

Kendi bristled at the man's tone. He and Ben had almost died, and this guy sailed in here out of nowhere to yell at them?

"It's okay, Uncle Hazid," Ben said quietly. "We're—"

"You were having a party, weren't you?" Sil accused. "And the neighbors called to complain. Ben, that's just like you, to ignore what your family—"

"The party was mine," Kendi interrupted her. "Who the hell do you think you are, anyway?"

Sil's mouth fell open and Hazid drew himself up to his full height, topping Kendi by a good ten centimeters. "I am Brother Hazid Lemish and this is Sister Sil Lemish. You will show proper respect, student."

The words just fell from Kendi's mouth, as if his brain had set itself in neutral. "So Mother Ara outranks you both. Must make it hard at family gatherings."

"Listen, you—"

"I need to finish talking to these boys," Inspector Gray interrupted firmly. "You can get the full story from them in a minute."

"The Guardians questioning the ex-slave," Sil sneered. "I warned Ara that it would come to this one day."

"Yeah, you warned her that she might do something useful with her life," Kendi shot back, "instead of sniffing double doses of Dream drugs to get you through the day. Oh wait—that's what your *kids* do."

Hazid's face went purple. Sil's mouth opened and shut like a stunned fish. Ben clapped both hands over his face.

"You lying, thieving, filthy little—" Hazid began.

"That the best you can do?" Kendi said. "No wonder you haven't been promoted."

Ben was curled up on the sofa, hands still over his face. Kendi ignored him. All his anger and fear came rushing out to seek a target, and the man in front of him was a handy one.

"Listen, you piece of gutter trash," Hazid roared. "I'll see that you get put on so much work detail, you won't sleep for a week!"

"You'd rather hit me, though, wouldn't you?"

Kendi stuck out his chin. "Go ahead. Your dick will still be smaller than your wife's."

Hazid sucked in his breath and Inspector Gray stepped between them. "That's *enough*!" he roared. "You"—he pointed to Hazid—"take your wife into the kitchen and get her a glass of water. You and you"—he pointed at Kendi and Ben—"come into the bedroom so I can finish questioning you. God, now I know why I didn't go into teaching."

Hazid, face still flushed, looked as though he was going to argue. Then he gave in and guided the still-gaping Sil into the kitchen. Gray was about to march Kendi and Ben into the bedroom when a chime sounded. With a sigh, he reached into a pocket and drew out a portable phone. Almost instantly he fell into a deep conversation. Kendi, feeling a bit drained, sat on the couch next to Ben, whose face was still buried in his hands.

"All life, he's an asshole," Kendi said. "Are you okay?"

Ben nodded. A strange sound leaked out between his fingers.

"Why are you doing that?" Kendi asked. "What's wrong?"

A few unintelligible words.

"What?"

Ben got up and ran to Mother Ara's bedroom. Startled, Kendi scrambled to follow. Ben, who must have parted his fingers enough to see through them, flung himself across the bed. He was shaking. Kendi stood over him, wondering what to do. Was it a seizure? Or was Ben angry? Then Ben flung his hands away from his face and Kendi saw he was laughing. Kendi hurriedly shut the door.

"You were great!" Ben whooped. A few tears leaked out of his eyes to run down his face. "Oh my god—that was the best! I thought Uncle Hazid was going to have a stroke."

Kendi sat gingerly next to him. "Yeah. I'll keep that in mind while I'm shoveling piles of dino-dung into the next century."

"I'll help you," Ben said, sitting up. "It was completely worth it. Hey, your hand."

Kendi flexed his palm and winced. Dried blood made a red-brown crust on it, and there were still splinters stuck under the skin. "I haven't had the chance to clean it yet."

"Hold on a sec." Ben left the room and came back with a first aid kit. Gently, he wiped the blood from Kendi's hand, then teased the splinters free with a pair of tweezers. Kendi held perfectly still. The pain was negligible, and Kendi remained very aware of Ben's hands on his. Ben sprayed the wounds with a disinfectant bandage, and he seemed to be taking his time about it. Kendi swallowed. When the last part of the bandage had been applied, Ben turned Kendi's palm toward the light to inspect his handiwork.

"How's that feel?" he asked.

"It's good. Thanks."

Ben still hadn't let go of Kendi's hand, and Kendi didn't pull away. His mouth had dried up. The only sound in the room was his and Ben's breathing. Kendi's brown eyes met Ben's blue ones, trying to read what he saw there. He gave Ben's hand a tentative squeeze. Ben made no response, but he didn't let go, either. Kendi was about to make himself say something when the door opened and Inspector Gray walked in. Ben dropped Kendi's hand.

"Sorry about that," Gray said. "Long call. Let's take it from the top again, all right?"

After Gray finished taking their statements, he spoke briefly to Sil and Hazid, advising them to stay

the night so Ben and Kendi wouldn't be alone if
Dorna came back again. The Guardians would also
keep an eye on the house. Hazid was clearly outraged
to hear that Kendi was staying in the guest room.

"That insolent, mouthy piece of garbage is sharing
this roof?" he said.

Kendi thought about volunteering to stay in Ben's
room and thought the better of it, especially when Ben
shot him a look that clearly told him to keep quiet.

"You will sleep on the couch," Hazid told Kendi
after Gray had left. "And be thankful it isn't the
floor."

Kendi bit back a sharp reply. All of a sudden he
was too tired to care what Hazid said or thought. Not
only that, but something was itching at the back of his
head. He couldn't put his finger on what it was, and
it bothered him. Something someone had said or done
that was important to what was going on.

Ben avoided further contact, especially while Hazid
and Sil were watching. Hazid made a quick call to let
his offspring know that he and Sil were spending the
night at the Rymar house, while Sil checked on the
guest bedroom. Kendi's tired mind was nonetheless
alert enough to wonder if Sil was looking for slovenly
habits of the ex-slave—something else to complain
about. Kendi, however, kept few possessions beyond
his clothes. Possessions, he had decided, were something that could be taken away at any time, so there
was no point in acquiring a great many of them. It
was a bit of Real People philosophy he hadn't understood until he had lost everything he owned, including
his own body, to the slavers.

Finally, after several more glares and pointed remarks by Sil and Hazid, everyone was settled in for
the night. Kendi lay on his back and stared into the
beams above the couch. The thing, whatever it was,
still nagged at him. Oddly enough, he felt no fear that

Dorna would come back to try to finish him off. It seemed connected to the fact he was missing. The nagging itch kept him awake, despite his weariness. He thought about sneaking into Ben's room, seeing if he was awake and talking to him about it, then changed his mind. He didn't want Hazid or Sil to catch them together. Kendi curled his bandaged hand, remembering how Ben had held it. How much feeling was there? Kendi longed to come straight out and ask, but Pup and Pitr remained uppermost in his mind. What if it was all just a mistake? He couldn't risk it. Kendi crossed his arms and sighed heavily. Ben would simply have to make the next move.

It took him a long time to fall asleep.

The next morning, Sil and Hazid were still sleeping when Kendi and Ben left for classes. They rehashed the events of the previous night as they walked, though Ben made no reference to anything deeper. The sense that Kendi had missed something continued to nag at him like an itch that he couldn't locate to scratch.

The moment Kendi reached the monastery classrooms, Jeren, Willa, and Kite pounced on him, demanding more details of what had happened. Jeren seemed especially interested.

"Do they know where Dorna's been hiding?" he demanded. The scar outlining his left eye seemed to blaze against his skin. "She almost killed you."

"I don't think they know," Kendi said. "I just hope she's okay."

"Okay?" Willa almost squeaked. "Kendi, she knocked you off the balcony. It makes me shake to think that she was our student mentor and she killed all those women."

"We don't know she did that," Kendi shot back. "And even if she did—"

"—it's because she's crazy," Kite finished.

"What is this?" Jeren put in. "Some kind of Aborigine turn-the-other-cheek?"

"We don't have all the facts yet," Kendi replied lamely. "I think we should keep an open mind. Besides, who knows what Mother Ara's finding out at Dreamers, Inc.?"

Jeren's only reply was a sarcastic snort.

The day proved difficult. Thoughts of Ben mingled with thoughts of Dorna—Violet?—and he ached to talk to Ara about the whole thing. Maybe after classes were over he could drop into the Dream, see if she was there. There was a way to reach out of the Dream to contact Silent in the solid world, something Ara called *knocking*, but Kendi hadn't learned how to do that yet. Maybe he could figure out how it worked.

With a start he realized that someone had repeated his name. Sister Bren stood over his desk, her young face waiting expectantly.

"What?" he asked.

"Kendi, I do get tired of repeating questions to you," she said. "Please pay attention."

"Sorry," he muttered.

"I asked you what other gift the Ched-Balaar gave humanity. The Dream was one. What was the other?"

For once, Kendi remembered the answer. "Gravity," he said. "They gave us gravity generators."

"Absolutely correct," Bren said. "Before the Ched-Balaar, all human ships either operated in freefall, or they had to simulate gravity how?"

"By spinning," Kite said without raising his hand.

Bren nodded. "An inconvenient way to travel, to say the least. Now, I've uploaded a new program onto the student network. Take out your pads and open the file named—"

But Kendi's mind was already wandering again.

At last, classes ended for the day. He was about to

go with the others back to the dormitory when he noticed Willa splitting off in another direction.

"Where are you headed?" he asked.

Willa held up her dermospray. "I'm empty, remember? I have to go to the dispensary."

"I'll go with you," Kendi said on impulse.

They walked in silence for a while, feet tromping the swaying walkways. Almost idly, Kendi noticed that Willa wasn't quite so thin anymore. Her features weren't nearly as sharp, and her hair, formerly dull as dishwater, had taken on a distinct sheen. Her posture was straighter, and although she showed nothing of the overconfident cockiness of Jeren, she carried herself with more ease.

"You like it here, don't you?" Kendi said.

"I love it," she declared without hesitation. Her voice was much firmer than it had been a year ago. "Everything about this place is beautiful and fine."

She paused in her walking to peer over the walkway. The lush green growth below trapped the clean scent of last night's rain and was slowly releasing it, even in the late afternoon. Humans and Ched-Balaar, all wearing the medallions of Irfan, strolled up and down balconies and walkways, words mixing pleasantly with clatters and hoots. A gondola sailed past, filled with a human couple and their children. Above them and below, giant buildings and tiny houses nestled discretely among the solid talltree branches as if they had grown there. It felt more like a vacation paradise then a monastery of thousands set into a city of over half a million.

"It's beautiful," Willa continued. "I know there are dreadful things going on in the Dream and in the solid world—we saw that last night—but I still feel the serenity of the place. It's like Irfan is watching over us. I feel calm here."

"You had it hard as a slave," Kendi said.

Willa's face clouded, then cleared. "I did. I had three masters, and every one of them left a mark on me. They changed my name and they tried to change my own self. So I buried it—my own self, I mean. I buried it so deep I couldn't find it again. This place has helped me dig it back out."

"Was Willa your birth name?" Kendi said. "I never asked."

Willa shook her head. "My name was Janet. Willa was the name my last master gave me. By the time Ara bought and freed me, I had had that name longer than any other, so I decided to keep it. You changed yours again, I know."

"The Real People take names that describe them and change them whenever they need to," Kendi said. "But I think I'll be a kendi for a long time."

They continued on their way to the student dispensary. It was nothing more than a middle-size room with seven service windows along the back wall. A sign said PLEASE FORM A SINGLE LINE, and a series of ropes indicated the direction the line was to take. Because classes had ended for the day, there were several people already waiting, and all seven windows were staffed. After several minutes, Kendi and Willa reached the front and were beckoned toward a window. A male clerk sat behind it.

"Name?" he asked.

Willa gave it and handed over her dermospray. The clerk tapped several keys on his computer and the holographic screen flickered.

"You've been practicing quite a lot," he said. "No wonder you need a refill. Hold on a sec."

He popped the dermospray into a slot and tapped the computer again. A slight hissing sound whispered across the counter and a light on the dermospray winked green. The clerk pulled it free and handed it back to Willa.

"A dozen doses," he said. "Thumb here and you're all set."

Willa pressed her thumb to the plate. Kendi stared at it and something clicked inside his head. His heart jumped.

"All life!" he gasped. "All life—that's what it is!"

Willa looked at him. "What's what it is?"

"Do you have the records of all the doses that everyone uses?" Kendi asked the clerk, voice urgent.

"Well, yeah," the clerk replied, startled. "The microtransmitter alerts the dispensary whenever a student uses a dose so your teacher can keep track of how much independent—"

"Can you show me the records for another student?" Kendi asked.

The clerk looked shocked. "Certainly not. That's confidential information."

"It's a matter of life and death," Kendi said, almost jumping up and down. "Please, you have to show me."

The clerk tapped his computer and the screen vanished. "Not without authorization I don't. Listen, son, there are people behind you."

"But—"

"Next!" the clerk said pointedly.

Kendi bit his lip in frustration. Several students in the waiting area were eyeing him curiously, but he barely noticed. Abruptly, he grabbed Willa's hand.

"What's going on?" she demanded. "Where are we going?"

He said, "To find Father Ched-Hisak."

FIFTEEN

*Sometimes your worst enemy turns out to be some-
one you know.*
        —Daniel Vik, husband to Irfan Qasad

The tiny Guardian ship popped out of slipspace a re-
spectable fifty thousand kilometers from the space station headquarters of Dreamers, Inc. Alarms beeped
and Tan's fingers darted over the boards, informing
the station who they were and that they did indeed
have permission to hold their current position. Ara,
meanwhile, radioed the docking authority to double-
check their authorization. Everything was in order, as
were the reservations for their accommodations. Ara
relaxed, only then realizing that she had been worried
that some bureaucratic snafu would strand them without a place to dock or sleep.

"Docking in two hours," Tan reported from the pilot's chair.

Ara nodded and punched up an external visual on
her monitor. It was a relief to see stars and blackness
out there instead of the nauseating whirl of slipspace.
The Guardian slipship was cramped and tiny—the
bridge was barely big enough for two people—and
there was little to do on board. Fortunately the little
ship was also fast. That and good slipspace conditions
had gotten them to the station in just under eighteen hours.

Ara trained one of the cameras on the station and
beefed up the magnification, more for something to
do than anything else. The station orbited an ocean-
covered planet with a few flyspeck islands and wide

swaths of white clouds, and the thing was a real hodgepodge. Giant squares and enormous spheres were stuck together or connected by cylinders like Tinkertoys assembled by a madman. The entire station probably massed as much as a small moon. Ships of varying sizes drifted, darted, or lumbered through open spaces. Ara shook her head. She hadn't visited Dreamers, Inc., in over three years, but the station had rearranged itself in even that short time so that she barely recognized it. Dreamers had more money than even a multisystem corporation could burn, and Ara suspected the corp conducted the almost continual redecoration simply because it could.

Tan maneuvered the ship closer, and a voice came over the communication system. "You are authorized to use Dock 14–212–C. Please follow the course outlined. For safety reasons, deviation is not allowed and will result in immediate confiscation of your entire ship. Do you understand? By answering affirmatively, you agree to waive all right to liability, damages, or indemnity to your ship, cargo, crew, and passengers."

"I understand," Tan said.

A live holographic image of the station appeared over Tan's board with a bright orange line indicating the course she was to take. It dipped and swooped like a drunken piece of spaghetti, and Ara could only assume it was intended to keep them from colliding with other ships also coming in or going out.

"For a small fee," the voice continued, "you can slave your navigation computer to ours and we will guide your ship in for you."

"No thank you," Tan said. "We'll take it from here."

"As you wish. By proceeding further, you waive all right to—"

Tan shut the communicator off.

"Thank you," Ara said.

Tan grunted and turned her concentration to her flying. The station rushed up and down, swooped and turned. Other ships brushed the flight path, but never quite came close enough to hit them. Eventually, the ship nosed against a dock and Ara heard the clamps *thunk* into place. She and Tan retrieved their carryalls and, glad to be freed of the cramped ship, hurried through the airlock and into the main station. Ara asked the local computer for directions and discovered that they were quite a distance from the office of Ken Rashid, Chief of Security. The computer offered directions and a map—for a fee. Ara sighed and paid for both after agreeing that the map was for informational purposes only and she would not hold Dreamers, Inc., responsible for any damages incurred as a result of following its directions.

"I begin to see how this corporation makes its money," Tan said dryly.

After some searching, they found a transportation center and hired a cab driver to take them where they needed to go.

"First time on the Station?" asked their driver, a small, weasel-faced man complete with scraggly, whiskerlike mustache.

"No," Tan said, giving him the map. "Here's where we need to go."

And that was the end of the conversation. The driver punched buttons, muttered to his on-board computer, and the little electric car shot forward, pressing Ara into the seat.

The interior of the station was as hodgepodge as the exterior. Tunnels ranged from high, wide spaces to low, cramped rabbit warrens. Decor rambled like a patchwork quilt. Through the cab windows, Ara saw crowded streets, Greek architecture, a Chinese palace, lush parks, and stark white hallways. Some areas were clearly residences of wealthy corp officers. Other areas were so dark and crowded, Ara quietly locked her door. Humans seemed to be the dominant species, but only barely. Everywhere Ara looked she saw a new alien race. They ran, hopped, slithered, glided, stomped, and squished their way up and down the corridors and streets. Some sectors, in fact, seemed completely devoid of anything humanoid. All of them were in some way connected to Dreamers, Inc., Ara knew, though not all of the people were Silent, just as it was back on Bellerophon.

It took over an hour to arrive at the main security offices. They were a series of blocky, unimaginative-looking buildings with thick columns out front. Tan paid and dismissed the driver, then headed up the high front steps with Ara close behind her. Groups of beings, both human and non-, were scattered up and down the stairs, their voices combining in a strange cacophony of sound. The station ceiling was at least a dozen stories up, so far off it looked to Ara like a smooth, cloudy sky. The air was odorless, dry, and a little chillier than Ara liked, and she was thankful she had brought a jacket.

The foyer was a big, echoing chamber with polished marble floors. The beings hurrying through it spoke in hushed voices. Ara consulted a directory and found that Chief Rashid's offices were on the fifth floor and that the elevators were off to his left.

"He has an entire suite," Tan murmured as they moved toward them.

"I noticed," Ara said. "You know, Dreamers, Inc., is three or four times bigger than the Children. The post of Chief of Security for them would probably be something like the post of Secretary of Planetary Defense anywhere else."

"I was thinking the same thing," Tan agreed. "The

fact that we talked to him personally in the Dream says something. So does the fact that we're getting in to see him right away."

"What does it all say?"

"No idea."

The elevator took them straight to the fifth floor. An immensely tall human woman dressed in a pastel blue suit met them as they disembarked.

"Mother Araceil Rymar and Inspector Lewa Tan," she said, and it wasn't a question. "I am Denisa Ral, Chief Rashid's executive secretary. He is waiting to see you." She ushered them through a series of offices and corridors, all well lit, lushly carpeted, and decorated with holographic windows that pretended to offer scenes ranging from mountains to forests to jungles to sandy beaches. Ara wondered how Ral had known who they were and that they were on that particular elevator, then laughed at her own naïveté. Rashid had probably been keeping an eye on them since their ship slid out of slipspace.

Eventually, Denisa Ral lead them to an immense set of double doors made of polished oak. They swung wide at her touch, revealing a huge office beyond. One entire wall was a window that looked out on empty space. At the bottom corner lay a portion of the planet, a blue crescent against utter black. The room was furnished like a wealthy person's living room, with designer furniture, spotlessly shined woodwork tables, and even a fireplace. A hint of wood smoke on the air indicated that it was a real one. Ara was impressed— acquiring the wood and disposing of the smoke would be expensive undertakings, not to mention the amount of oxygen a fire sucked up.

Set against the window was an enormous desk. Ken Rashid, his silvering black hair blending in with the scene behind him, came around it as Ara and Tan entered the office. Denisa Ral closed the doors behind them. Rashid bowed slightly to each of them.

"It's nice to meet you in person," he said. "Forgive me not shaking hands, but in my current position, I can only allow certain people the ability to locate me when I am in the Dream. If you are hungry or thirsty, refreshments are over there." He gestured to a table littered with an assortment of snacks and beverages. A wet bar stood in the corner. "Perhaps we should begin?"

"Yes. And since we're being direct," Tan said, "I have to ask, Chief Rashid—why are you seeing us? Your schedule must be insanely busy. It would be easy enough to assign this to a subordinate."

Rashid's expression went rigid for a moment and Ara thought Tan had offended him. Something flashed in his eyes, and Ara remembered the same thing happening when they had spoken in the Dream. Then Rashid passed a tired hand over his face and his expression softened.

"There were four victims here on Dream Station," he said. "Polly Garvin, Minn Araq, Riann Keller, and Liss Padel. Liss Padel was my wife."

"I'm sorry," Tan said softly.

He nodded. "It was a decade ago. I usually think I'm past it; then something happens to remind me of her and I learn I'm not. Usually what I feel is anger. The bastard that killed her is walking around free. I was removed from the case, of course—conflict of interest—but it didn't matter. No more victims showed up. We never learned who did it. Ten years later, I get a message from an old friend that two monks from Bellerophon are looking for a killer who chops off fingers. I think you now understand how the Chief of Security for Dreamers, Inc., found time to see you." Rashid gave a wan smile. "But I'm being rude. Please, come and sit."

He ushered them to a group of cushioned highback chairs that huddled around the fireplace. The top of the chair was at least two heads higher than Ara's head once she sat down, and she rather felt like a child sitting in an adult seat. A round end table held a lamp and a box of chocolates. Ara thought about reaching for one, then flashed back to Iris Temm's house and the single chocolate missing from the box. Her appetite left her and she drew out her computer pad instead. Tan and Rashid took seats as well.

"Did the murders take place on Dream Station?" Ara asked.

"All four," Rashid said, and then suddenly bounded to his feet. "God, I need something. Can you excuse me for just a moment?" Without waiting for a reply, he went over to the mantel and opened an intricately carved wooden box. From it he withdrew a brown cylinder a little thinner than a finger. He waved it, and one end glowed. A curl of smoke trickled upward and Ara smelled it, harsh and acrid. Rashid put the other end to his mouth and inhaled. Ara couldn't keep from staring. She had heard about this habit, but had never seen it in action. Rashid noticed her gaze.

"An expensive vice," he said, "especially on a station. But someone in my position is allowed a few indulgences. Would you like to try one?"

"Thank you, no," Ara said.

"It's not Thursday," Tan murmured, and Ara shot her a hard look.

Rashid took his seat again and tapped the ash into a crystal receptacle. Cigarettes, Ara remembered. They were called cigarettes. "Shall I begin or should you?"

"Let's start with our end," Tan said. "Then you can tell us what you know and we can examine each other's files."

Rashid waved his cigarette in assent, leaving a trail of smoke.

"Almost three years ago," Tan began, "a Silent Sister named Prinna Meg was found dead. Levels of psytonin in her brain indicated she was in the Dream when she died. Her body was found with bruises and abrasions—indications of psychosomatic trauma. Her left little finger was cut off. Sewn to the stump was the finger of another woman, someone we still haven't identified. There were no witnesses to Meg's death in the Dream or in the solid world. A search of her house uncovered no significant clues. We took pictures and holographic images of everything anyway."

Rashid blew out a cloud of smoke. Ara found the smell dry and cloying, but didn't feel it was proper to say anything. She tried to breathe shallowly.

"About a year after that—I can give you an exact number of days, if you like—Sister Wren Hamil was also found dead. Circumstances were exactly the same. Killer cut off her left little finger postmortem and sewed Meg's finger on in its place. Eleven months later, Sister Iris Temm turned up dead in her home. Hamil's finger was sewn to her left hand. At this point, we knew what we were dealing with and we brought in Mother Ara here."

"To what end?" Rashid tapped his cigarette ash into the crystal receptacle again. "My sources—and yes, I did check up on you both—indicate that you, Mother Ara, are not an investigator."

"I was brought in as a consultant in morphic Dream theory," Ara said. "I can sometimes recreate other people's scenes in the Dream."

Rashid's dark eyes glittered and he leaned forward. "Ah! So you recreated the murder, then. Did you see the killer?"

"Yes and no," Ara said. "I saw the murderer do his work. He killed Iris by bringing her Dream landscape to life. He appeared to her as a man dressed in black with a wide-brimmed hat that left his face in shadow. I wasn't able to see his features."

"So his Dream form may be different from his solid one," Rashid mused.

"After he killed Iris," Ara continued, "he cut off her finger and used it to write the number twelve on her forehead. We're assuming he's numbering his victims. Ara's stomach began to churn. Memories of all the corpses she had seen, both Dream and solid, swirled through her mind and combined with the cigarette smoke to nauseating affect. She forced herself to go on. "We know the killer is powerful in the Dream. Not only does his mind overpower those of his victims, he also recreates their landscapes and their corpses, keeping the scene 'alive,' even after the originating Silent is dead. I didn't even notice a transitional waver between Iris's death and the killer's recreation." She stood up. "I think I need something to drink."

Rashid started to rise. "What would you like?"

"If that's the bar over there, I can get it," Ara said almost shortly. "Inspector Tan can continue."

"Things get a little more complicated after this," Tan began as Ara headed for the bar and Rashid resumed his seat. "About nine months after Iris Temm died, the killer murdered Mother Diane Giday. But we didn't find the body until after he took another victim—Vera Cheel. So we found them out of order. That confused us for a while because Cheel was wearing a finger we couldn't identify. Only two weeks had gone by between the murders of Giday and Cheel."

"So the killer is escalating," Rashid said. He ground his cigarette out.

"Looks that way," Tan agreed. "We weren't able to recreate Giday's murder in the Dream, but with Vera Cheel we got a break."

Ara sniffed the contents of three decanters before she found the brandy. She sloshed a healthy dollop into a glass and started back toward the trio of chairs. On the way, she impulsively hooked a small plate of canapes. Did Rashid always have this sort of thing just sitting out, or was it there because he knew Ara and Tan were coming?

"What sort of break?" Rashid asked.

"A witness."

Rashid bolted upright. "Someone who saw the actual murder in the Dream? Who?"

"One of my students happened on it by sheer chance." Ara settled in her chair and took a sip of brandy. It was light and dry, and it burned pleasantly all the way down until it outlined her stomach in warmth. She let it settle a moment before describing what Kendi had experienced. During the retelling, she had to pause for two more sips of brandy.

"Unfortunately," she concluded, "none of this gave us a clue to the killer's true identity."

"At first," Tan put in, and Ara thankfully let her take over the narrative again. She settled back into her chair and popped a salmon-cream-cheese puff into her mouth. It was delicately and perfectly seasoned.

"After Mother Ara had a chance to investigate the solid-world murder scenes," Tan continued, "she noticed something. Each of the victims had received a gift before she died. We assume it came from the killer. The gifts were always some sort of love token that came in a set that matched the victim's number. Iris Temm, the twelfth victim, received a box of twelve chocolates. Vera Cheel, victim number thirteen, received thirteen roses, and so on. After the killer did his work, he took a single token back, so Temm's chocolate box had one missing, for example."

"Strange," Rashid murmured. Ara tried to read his expression and found she couldn't.

"But that's not all he took," Tan said. "He also took some sort of intimate object—a pair of panties, an earring, a shoe."

"And a finger," Rashid said grimly.

"Until recently we also had no suspects, but then things changed." Tan remained still and upright in her chair, reciting the story as if she were a recording. "A student at the monastery recently exhibited strange behavior—irrationality, wide behavioral changes, alterations in word use—and then she attacked another student."

"My son," Ara put in.

"After the attack, she disappeared," Tan said. "When we searched her room, we found a shirt with Diane Giday's blood on the sleeve. Unfortunately, we haven't been able to locate this student."

"She," Rashid said. Ara had expected him to get excited that they had a suspect, but he seemed perfectly calm. "You think the killer is a woman? The one you showed me in the Dream?"

"We aren't sure," Tan admitted. "Her disappearance is highly suspect, of course. So is the blood on her shirt cuff. But as Mother Ara once pointed out, a smart killer—as this one seems to be—wouldn't keep a shirt that might have picked up the victim's blood. She may have disappeared because she was murdered by our real killer, who's trying to throw us off the trail. In any case, we're still trying to find her so we can have a chat."

"I see," Rashid said. "I think it's obvious we're both looking for the same person, in any case. I notice that your victims are all Silent women connected to your organization. Since some carried the title 'Mother' and others the title 'Sister,' I assume their ages varied. This fits the profile of our victims as well—females of various ages connected with our organization. Did your victims have any connections with each other? Common friends or people they knew on the job?"

Tan shook her head, making her long braid whisk back and forth like a broom. "We checked extensively. Nothing came up. What about yours?"

"Only one," Rashid said. "Polly Garvin, the first victim, was an acquaintance of Riann Keller, the third victim. But we weren't able to draw any other connections. Perhaps we should trade files and see what we find."

Computer pads came out and the transfers were made. Ara nibbled on more salmon-cream-cheese canapes and glanced about the luxurious office before opening anything.

What a place this would be to work, she thought. *A view of the universe and people to make you little dainties.* Then she remembered the dark, narrow warrens that probably made up the majority of the residences and workplaces on Dream Station. Slavery was legal here, and Dreamers, Inc., owned many thousands of them, some Silent, some not. It might be fine here for the people on top, but the ones holding up the bottom had a hard time of it.

With a sigh, Ara opened the file on Riann Keller's death. Tan and Rashid were already reading silently, pictures and text mixing on their holographic screens. Tan pointed to one part of a picture and it magnified. Ara caught a glimpse of a pair of dead, filmy eyes staring at nothing. She shuddered. Someone— Dorna?—had left a trail of death and sorrow across an entire galaxy.

A pile of text appeared on Ara's screen and she found she couldn't bring herself to read closely. Too much pain, too much sorrow, too much death. How did Tan deal with this? Although the Dream stalker was Bellerophon's first recorded serial killer, Treetown and the other city-states had their share of violent crime. Otherwise, the Guardians wouldn't exist.

Ara's eye wandered across the text, not lighting long enough to read more than a word here or a phrase there.

. . . psytonin levels indicate . . .

. . . complete loss of . . .
. . . suspect must have attacked the victim . . .
. . . named Dorna, and a son . . .
. . . found approximately two hours after . . .

Ara gasped and scrolled frantically backward. Had she seen—yes, there it was. *The victim had two children, a daughter named Dorna, and a son named Cole.*

It suddenly occurred to Ara that she and Tan had never mentioned Dorna's name to Rashid. There was so much information to trade, it was easy to leave things out, even obvious facts. Ara called for Tan and Rashid's attention and quickly explained.

"I remember the daughter," Rashid said excitedly. "Is there an image of her in your files? The image you showed me in the Dream was too wavery for a good identification."

Tan called it up for him. Dorna's head and shoulders appeared, her identification holo for the monastery. Rashid studied it a moment, then addressed the computer. "Reverse aging on this holograph ten years."

Dorna's face changed. Her cheeks became rounder, her features larger, until she looked to be fifteen or sixteen. Rashid's eyes glittered. "That's her! That's Riann Keller's daughter."

"So she *is* the killer," Ara murmured. She should have been glad, even excited, at the confirmation, but all she felt was a lingering disappointment.

"Who was the father?" Tan asked.

"None on record," Rashid said. "We do know, however, that Riann Keller was known for having many . . . casual male acquaintances."

"Let's draw a scenario, then." Tan cracked her knuckles, the first time Ara had seen her do such a thing. "According to my sources, serial murderers and people with multiple personalities are always abused—even tortured—as children. That's why some of them kill, displacing anger from their parents to innocent bystanders. Dorna Keller was one of these, abused by her mother. As she grew older, she took Polly Garvin—a friend of her mother's—as her first victim because Garvin was available, easy to get to. Then she stalked and killed Minn Araq before getting up the courage to kill her mother, Riann Keller. But naturally that didn't satisfy her. It never does. So she killed Liss Padel. But then what happened to her?"

Rashid was holding himself rigid in his chair, clearly controlling both pain and anger. Ara wanted to say something to him, but something made her hold back. She suspected Rashid no longer wanted sympathy. He was seeking justice—or revenge.

"It's in the file," Rashid said. "Riann Keller had a gambling problem and a history of petty theft and larceny. We were about to fire her, even though she was Silent. She signed a contract with Silent Acquisitions."

"Slavers?" Ara said incredulously. "What for?"

"Her children," Rashid said in a flat voice. "Dorna and her brother Cole were both Silent. It's legal here to sell yourself or your underage children into slavery, and it appears that Riann Keller needed to clear a few debts with some . . . unsavory moneylenders."

Ara's blood chilled. Her mind wouldn't quite accept the idea. Selling your children to cover your own mistakes? She tried to imagine fastening a shackle on Ben's wrist and ankle before handing him over to a total stranger. The picture wouldn't come.

"Riann was killed two days after signing the contract," Rashid concluded. "At first we thought her death might be connected to the local underworld, but the missing and reappearing finger belayed that."

"Why didn't she try to sell them to Dreamers, Inc.?" Tan asked.

"I'm not sure," Rashid said. "There's no record of her making an offer. It may be that their continued presence on Dream Station would remind her of what she had done, or perhaps she thought she would get more from Silent Acquisitions."

"So if we add this to our working scenario," Tan said, "it may explain how Dorna got up the courage to kill her mother—she was spurred by the news of her sale. Chief Rashid, when did your wife die in relation to Riann Keller?"

Rashid's face looked carved from stone. "Five days. We wondered about that. Several months passed between the other murders, but Liss was killed less than a week after Riann."

"More rage," Ara murmured. "She killed her mother, but was still too angry to hold off killing again. She slowed down after that, you'll notice. Liss was the fourth victim, and Prinna Meg was the tenth, if the numbering is accurate. That means that in the last ten years, she 'only' killed five other people."

Tan toyed with her braid. "This doesn't help us find Dorna. And none of it—except maybe the blood—is hard proof. Any decent defense lawyer would serve our heads to the judge. Chief Rashid, are there any files on Dorna? School records and such things? We might get an idea from them."

Rashid was tapping at his pad when Ara felt something brush her mind.

~Ara,~ came a familiar voice. *~Ara, can you hear me?~*

Startled, Ara sat upright. *~Ched-Hisak? What's going on?~*

~Your student Kendi wants to see you in the Dream. He asked me to contact you because he has not yet learned to do so. According to him, the matter is urgent, and I agree. Can you come?~

Ara glanced at Rashid. Tan was peering over his shoulder at the data on his pad. Her first instinct was to dismiss Kendi, but another, more reasonable, voice told her she should listen.

~Give me a few moments.~ she said. Ched-Hisak's presence left her mind and Ara got up.

"I need to go into the Dream," she said. "My student—the one who witnessed the murder—wants to talk to me. May I use that couch over there?"

"Please," Rashid said absently, eyes glued to the display.

"What's going on?" Tan asked.

"I'll tell you as soon as I find out," Ara replied. She crossed to the sofa, lay down, and drew out her dermospray. After a moment, colors swirled behind her eyelids. Tan and Rashid's conversation dwindled into the distance. The last thing she heard was Tan's puzzled voice.

"Look here," she said. "Cole Keller got into trouble twice for setting the school restroom on fire. That's also a symptom of . . ."

The fountain sprayed high into the air, which was delicately scented with orange blossoms. Ara perched on the lip of her fountain and a moment later she felt another knock, this one infused with a question.

"Of course," she said aloud. "Please come."

Ched-Hisak and Kendi appeared before her in a rush of Dream energy. Kendi instantly fell retching to hands and knees. Ara knelt beside him. She had forgotten that he hadn't yet learned to adjust to instant transport within the Dream.

"It's all right," she soothed in her best motherly voice. "Just try to breathe."

Eventually, the heaving subsided and Kendi let Ara help him to his feet. Ched-Hisak waited patiently as Ara conjured up a glass of water for Kendi. He accepted it gratefully, face pale.

"We still have to work on that," she said. "Now—what's so important?"

Excited color returned to Kendi's face and he tossed the glass over his shoulder. It vanished before it hit the grass. "It's Dorna," he said. "She didn't do it. I have proof?"

Ara thought about what she and Tan had learned in Rashid's office. "Kendi, I'm sorry, but I just don't have time for this. I'm sitting in the office of the station's Security Chief, and his time is—"

"Just listen, will you?" Kendi pleaded. "I have evidence."

"He is correct," Ched-Hisak put in. "I would listen."

That checked Ara. "All right," she said. "Go."

"Okay, the drug that gets us each into the Dream," Kendi said. "It's tailored, right? Each person has their own mixture, and no one else can use it. One Child's drug won't work for another."

"I know this, Kendi," Ara said. "What does it—"

"I'm just setting the stage," Kendi insisted. "Okay, we don't have to pay for the drug, but the Children do keep track of how much you use, and for students they do more than that. A student dermospray has a microtransmitter that alerts the dispensary whenever we use a dose so our teachers can keep track of how often we practice in the Dream."

"Right, right," Ara said, barely concealing her impatience.

"Just before Vera Cheel was killed," Kendi said triumphantly, *"Dorna didn't use her dermospray."*

Ara blinked, but didn't answer.

"I know this," Kendi went on, "because she was between fill ups. I remember she mentioned it when she and the others came over to play hide-and-seek. She said she'd been out for two days, but kept forgetting to go down to the dispensary for more, and it was during those two days that Vera was killed. When I remembered this, I asked the clerk at the dispensary to look up Dorna's record, but he wouldn't do it until Father Ched-Hisak and Inspector Gray got permission. That took a whole day. Otherwise I would have tried to talk to you earlier."

"And the records confirmed that Dorna hadn't used her dermospray?"

Kendi shook his head. "She hadn't. And she hadn't used it anytime before Iris and Prinna were killed, either. We checked. And there's no way she could enter the Dream without using her drugs."

"She could have gotten them from somewhere else," Ara said doubtfully, "or used a different dermospray."

"This is unlikely," put in Ched-Hisak with a bob of his head. "Her dermospray would have registered the transaction if she had moved her drug, and there is nowhere on Bellerophon that could mix her exact drug cocktail, unless they had her medical records. A black market for Dream drugs does not exist—they have no effect on those for whom they are not designed."

"True," Ara admitted, and she let a tiny blossom of hope bloom in her chest. "But that leaves an awful lot unexplained. We found the blood of one of the victims on a shirt in Dorna's room."

"You did?" Kendi said, surprised. "Well, maybe the killer planted it there. But still . . ."

"What?" Ara asked.

"There's something else," Kendi said. "It happened right after you left. Ben and I—that is, *I*—invited a few people over that evening, and—"

"You had a party?" Ara growled. "I don't recall giving you permission to have—"

"You said the more people who were around me and Ben, the better," Kendi said loftily. "I was just doing what you said."

"I didn't say that—never mind. We'll discuss that later. What happened?"

"Dorna showed up," Kendi said. "She blamed the killings on someone named Cole. We figure he's one of her alternate personalities, but if Dorna didn't use her dermospray before any of the killings, she—or he—couldn't have—"

Ara stiffened. "What was the person's name? The one Dorna said killed people?"

"Actually it wasn't Dorna talking," Kendi said. "It was a personality named Violet. She seemed nice until I grabbed her, and then I think she switched to another—"

"Kendi," Ched-Hisak interrupted. "Mother Ara asked of you a question."

"Oh. Sorry," Kendi said. "What was it?"

"What was the name of the person Dorna said was killing people?" Ara repeated.

"Cole," Kendi said. "She blamed the killings on someone named Cole."

Ara blinked. "That's the name of Dorna's brother."

"She has a brother?" Kendi said. "Where is he?"

"Let me see if I can find out," Ara said. "Give me a moment." She closed her eyes and felt around the Dream. After a moment, she found Lewa Tan's solid-world mind nearby. Ara reached for it and gently knocked.

~Yes?~ came Tan's mental voice.

Ara quickly explained what Kendi had told her. ~Do you know where Cole is now?~

Excitement rippled across Tan's mind like the smell of cinnamon. ~There's information on him in the file. Listen to this—his school record says he set the bathroom on fire. Twice. Another time he was cited for *setting a cat on fire. Arson and cruelty to animals are both hallmarks of a serial killer. Dorna isn't our killer. Cole is.~*

~But what's Dorna's connection, then?~ Ara said. But even as she spoke, it fell into place. *~They're a team. Cole kills them in the Dream and Dorna cuts off fingers in the solid world.~*

~Which would explain the spot of blood on Dorna's sleeve and how the victims died, even though Dorna hadn't entered the Dream.~ Tan said. *~Okay, okay. Let me talk this out.~* Brief pause. *~Dorna and Cole. Both abused as kids. Dorna develops multiple personality disorder, Cole becomes a sociopath. Cole is a coward, but also a dominator who needs to control. It's why he kills—he's trying to control his victims and he kills them when they don't fall in line. He also dominates his sister, Dorna. They're both Silent, so when dear old Mom sells them off as slaves and they're split up, they can keep in contact. Cole stays aloof and remote, ruling and killing from the Dream because it's safe there. He bullies his sister—or one of her personalities—into doing the dirty, bloody work in the solid world.~*

Ara nodded, though Tan couldn't see her. *~This complicates everything. Back when we thought Dorna was the killer, we at least knew what planet she was on. But Cole could be anywhere in the galaxy. How are we going to track him down?~*

~Sales records are the best bet.~ Tan said. *~Once we explain why we want him, even the anonymous sales people will probably open their records to us. All we have to do is threaten to spread word through the Dream that they bought and sold a serial killer. They'll cave in or watch their business dry up.~*

~You're evil.~ Ara observed. *~I like that.~*

~Cole is younger than Dorna by about two years.~ Tan said. *~So he'd be about twenty-four. Want me to come in there and start looking?~*

~I can handle this end.~ Ara told her, secretly glad to be out of Rashid's office and away from files full of pain and death. *~You keep trading notes with Rashid and see if anything else comes up. I'll get started with Silent Acquisitions right now and let you know what turns up.~*

They parted company and Ara opened her eyes. Kendi sat on the grass of the pleasure garden, drumming his fingers impatiently on his thighs. On Ara's turf he was dressed in a long linen shirt, loose scarlet pants, and a matching scarlet fez hat. Ara thought he looked rather dashing. Ched-Hisak was nowhere to be seen.

"He said he had stuff to do," Kendi said in answer to her unspoken question. "So what did Inspector Tan say?"

Ara recited the conversation word for word. Kendi listened raptly, his face a picture of awe.

"How did you do that?" he demanded. "You even imitated her voice."

"Training, O my apprentice," Ara said. "You'll learn to do the same thing. Come on—we have some slavers to bully."

"Can we walk, please?" Kendi asked. "I don't want to barf my guts out on someone else's turf."

"We do have to work on that." Ara sighed. "It's not normal. But yes, we can walk. This way."

A few moments later, they were standing before the same chrome desk on the same blue carpet Ara had seen before. The Silent Acquisitions sign indicated the company was willing to meet Ara's needs, though she had her doubts on that score. The same red cone-shaped alien—or perhaps another member of the same species—greeted Ara and Kendi with the same cold pudding voice Ara had heard before.

"Are either or both of you connected with the Children of Irfan?"

"We are investigating a series of Silent murders,"

Ara told the creature, "and we have evidence that the
killer came through your slave warehouses. I need to
speak with someone immediately."

The creature's expression, if it had one, didn't
change. Instead, it said, "One moment," and vanished,
taking the reception area with it and leaving Ara and
Kendi standing on an empty plain. Whether the creature had left the Dream entirely, or simply gone to
another part of it, Ara didn't know.

A few moments later, another office appeared. This
one had red carpet, scarlet wallpaper, and red plush
furniture. Even the woodwork and the tables were
red. Standing in front of the cherry-wood desk was a
rather pudgy man wearing a kimono of embroidered
red silk. Kendi rubbed his eyes.

"Fashion pain," he muttered, and Ara nudged him.

"I am Sales Manager Leethe," the pudgy man said.
His tone made it clear that, although he hadn't made
up his mind about Ara and Kendi, he was inclined
toward hostility. "How may I help you?"

"My name is Mother Araceil Rymar of the Children
of Irfan," Ara said. "This is my student Kendi
Weaver. I am investigating a series of murders on the
planet Bellerophon. So far over a dozen Silent women
have been murdered in the Dream, and we have uncovered evidence that indicates the killer was sold
through your company. I would like to see the sales
records."

"Quite impossible," Leethe said. "Our sales records
are confidential."

Ara's temper started to boil. Women were being
murdered—another could go at any time, in fact—and
this little man was citing confidentiality? Images of Iris
Temm and Vera Cheel, torn and bloody, swam before
her and mixed with Diane Giday's rotting corpse. She
drew breath to snap out a reply, then carefully let it
out. Kendi's eyes were on her.

Serene must you ever remain, she told herself. *Serene, serene, serene.*

"I'm not sure you fully understand the situation, Manager Leethe," Ara said. "This person has tortured and murdered fourteen Silent women in the Dream. Five of them were monks at our monastery."

"The problems of the Children of Irfan are of no concern to this company," Leethe said, smoothing his scarlet kimono. For a moment, Ara expected the red color to come off on his hands like blood. "You and your kind cost us millions in revenue every year with your lying, thieving ways. If Emperor Bolivar and Empress Kalii hadn't granted you protection, we would have—"

Ara raised her hand. A bolt of lightning cracked from her fist and smashed a hole in the ceiling. Kendi gasped and leaped back. Leethe went pale.

"How—how *dare* you attack my turf," he sputtered. "Empress or not, you'll hear about—"

"Shut up," Ara snapped. There was a time for serenity and a time for anger. "Let's get a few things clear, Manager. First, the fact that I could crack your ceiling proves that I'm stronger in the Dream than you are, and that means you're going to listen. Second, if you don't cooperate with me, I will see to it that every corner of the universe hears about how Silent Acquisitions withheld information in order to protect a killer of Silent. Of *Silent,* Manager. How many customers will you lose and how many Silent will refuse to cooperate with your company when word of this gets around? Third, there is something you are going to see, whether you want to or not."

Before Leethe could say a word, Ara reached into the Dream around them and *twisted.* A blindfold appeared over Kendi's eyes and earplugs stopped his ears. He tried to pull them off. Ara could feel his resistance, but although he was strong—perhaps even stronger than she—he didn't have her decades of experience. Leethe's Dream office resisted Ara's touch, but his power was nowhere near Ara's, and his office melted and reformed under her anger. She snapped her fingers. Abruptly they were standing in a dead, black forest. A ghostly Temm ran screaming, and the branches tore her to pieces. Ara gestured, and the Dream changed again. Vera Cheel, transparent and wavery, sat wrapped in heavy chains on her sofa, scarlet blood pouring from a hundred wounds. A shadowy man in black chopped her finger off and wrote a number in blood on her forehead. Leethe made a low, animal sound in his throat and slapped his hands over his eyes. Ara mercilessly yanked them back down. The Dream changed one more time. Diane Giday's corpse lay stinking and slippery on her living room couch.

"Stop it!" Leethe cried. "You're making this up. It's not real!"

"It's real enough to prevent you from concentrating enough to leave the Dream or teleport away," Ara growled. The smell from Giday's corpse burned the very air. "Even a slaver must have some conscience— or a sense of self-preservation. The monster that did this passed through your hands, Manager. Tell me what I need to know so I can find him."

Leethe had clapped his hands over his eyes again, but that wouldn't block out the smell. "Just end it, woman, and I'll tell you."

Ara snapped her fingers. The scene vanished, replaced by Ara's pleasure garden. The soft tinkling of the fountain and pleasant birdsong contrasted almost ghoulishly with the horrible images that had been there only moments before. Kendi's blindfold and earplugs evaporated. He blinked reproachfully at Ara and started to speak, then silenced himself under her heavy glare.

"The records, Manager Leethe," she said levelly.

"And don't even think about leaving the Dream and not returning. I'm very good at whispering, and I have your scent."

Leethe lowered his hands. His pudgy face was pale above the scarlet kimono. "I told you I'd find them for you, and I will."

Ara conjured a chair for him and he dropped heavily into it. Kendi perched on the lip of the fountain next to Ara. Ara wondered if he noticed how the dynamics of her relationship with Leethe had changed. They were on Ara's turf now, and Leethe was sitting with his head lower than hers on a chair she had created. All of these were signs that Ara was in charge. She made a mental note to point this out to Kendi later as an example of Dream protocol.

Leethe closed his eyes, reaching out of the Dream to someone else—a records person, Ara assumed.

"I'll need dates," Leethe said. "And names."

Ara gave him Cole and Dorna's names and the date of their sale. Leethe opened his eyes.

"I thought you were looking for one person," he said. His tone was petulant.

"He has an accomplice," Ara told him. "Hurry it up."

Leethe shut his eyes again. A few moments later, he drew a deep breath and stood up. "Cole and Dorna Keller were both sold to one Mr. Barry Yaree, a human on the planet Trafalgar. He's a legal coordinator there, and his Silent slaves provide communication among circuit judges because Trafalgar is a low-tech world that doesn't allow artificial long-distance communication."

"And where can I find Mr. Barry Yaree?" Ara said.

"He usually creates a tropical beach for his turf," Leethe explained. He described it further, and as he spoke, a pattern began to form in Ara's mind. Eventually, she received enough of Leethe's thoughts to find Yaree in the Dream.

"Thank you, Manager," she said when he was done.

Leethe vanished from his chair without further comment, leaving overlarge ripples and tears in his wake as a parting shot. Ara let the garden resettle before turning to Kendi.

"What was with the blindfold?" he demanded.

"There was no need for you to see it all again," Ara said.

"You don't have the right," Kendi said levelly. "You're not my mother."

"That's correct. I'm your teacher. And it's a teacher's duty to prevent harm to her students, both in the Dream and out of it."

"You don't blindfold me in the Dream and you don't stop up my ears," Kendi said. The anger in his voice was clear. "I'm not a slave, and I have the right to make my own choices about what I see and hear. If you don't think I should see something, then I'll leave. Horses and slaves are blindfolded. People are not."

Ara opened her mouth to refute this, then snapped it shut. "Point," she conceded. "I'll remember that next time."

Kendi looked surprised that she had given in. He nodded. "So what's next?"

"We're going to talk to Barry Yaree."

Barry Yaree happened to be in the Dream. He was a tall man, well over two meters, with an unruly shock of red-blond hair. Ara barely came up to the waist of his bathing suit. Behind them, a tranquil tropical sea lapped at a perfect white beach beneath a warm, benevolent sun.

"I remember those two," Yaree told them. His voice was oddly high and flutelike. "The girl was pliant enough, but her brother—what a lying little sack of trash. Lazy, mouthy. No matter how carefully we trained him, he couldn't seem to get into the Dream. And he was always giving us headaches. Broke stuff, stole, kept trying to get the female slaves into bed. Finally, one day he actually grabbed my wife's rear end. I had the little shit beaten and then I sold him. He didn't seem to care. I kept the sister around for another year or so, then got a good offer and sold her, too."

"He never got into the Dream?" Ara said. She was already developing a crick in her neck from looking so far up.

Yaree shook his shaggy head. "Not once. Went through a truckload of drugs and cost me a pretty set of credits, too."

That was strange, Ara mused. Cole must have gotten in later, then. Or had he been faking the fact that he couldn't get in? "Did you change their names?" she asked.

Yaree nodded. "To Jack and Jill. I thought it fit."

"Who did you sell them to?"

"A private slave dealer on Traveler III," the woman said. She had improbably blond hair, dark eyebrows, and a body that was slowly going to seed. Her turf looked like the grand ballroom of a fairy-tale castle. "I was actually a little sad to see him go."

"Despite what he did to the cat," Ara said.

"Well, nobody's perfect." The woman shifted position on the throne she occupied. Her long blue dress, slit high up the side, revealed a fair amount of leg. "The little devil was insatiable, too."

"Sorry?" Ara said. Beside her, Kendi shifted uncomfortably.

"He wanted it morning, noon, and night," the woman said in a wistful voice. "Couldn't even bend over to adjust my stockings without him popping up behind me, the cutie. Hung like a donkey, too. God, what a time I had with him.''

"And still you sold him," Ara said, unsure whether to laugh or be sick. Kendi stared.

"Well, you can only take so much," she said. "I mean, the cat was one thing, but the third time he set the greenhouse on fire—well, enough was enough. If you see him again, tell him I said hello."

"Of course," Ara said faintly. "What did you change his name to, by the way?"

"Little Tadpole." The humanoid lizard stuck out a long tongue and licked its own eyes. "But I call all my new slaves that, and he may not remember it. I only had the little creep a couple weeks."

"Why is that?" Ara asked.

"He kept yanking off my daughter's tail," the lizard said. "Thought it was the most hilarious thing. I punished him, but he didn't seem to give a shit. And his discipline was null. Couldn't even get the bastard to meditate for ten minutes. No wonder he was such a bargain. He ain't trainable, you ask me."

"Who did you sell him to?"

Ara sighed as she and Kendi crossed the border into his Outback. They should leave the Dream long enough to take food and bathroom breaks, but Ara didn't want to stop just yet, not when they had some good momentum going.

"He must have been lying," Kendi said as they walked over sand and stone. The walking was a concession to Kendi's teleportation nausea. "All of his owners said Cole couldn't reach the Dream, but he obviously did."

Ara nodded. "Cole couldn't do what he's been doing without a lot of practice. Sheer power can ac-

complish a lot, but it can only take you so far, and
he's shown a hell of a lot of skill. I'm willing to bet
he lied about not being able to reach the Dream, then
started hoarding the drugs from all the 'extra practice'
his owners made him do so he'd have a handy supply
for when he *really* went in."

The Outback sun lay hot and heavy on her back
and Ara began to wonder how long this trail would
go on. This set of drugs, her second, was starting to
wear off, and she didn't want to get a third hit—it
would make her headachy and out of sorts when she
finally left the Dream. Her solid body was getting hungry, and the feeling was manifesting in her Dream
body as well. Kendi was also looking tired and uncomfortable. It was growing difficult remaining civil to
people who bought and sold Silent like cows or sheep.
Still, she didn't want to give up. Every moment it took
to find the killer was another moment closer to the
time when he would murder someone else.

The next person on the list of Cole's owners was
Betta Drew, a small, dark woman about as tall as Ara,
though she was bone-thin and much older. Her hair
was white and her teeth protruded. Her turf was a
stark white room with three hard-backed chairs. The
ladderback pressed uncomfortably against Ara's spine,
adding to her current discomfort. She was going to
have to leave the Dream soon and give it up for the
night. A glance at Kendi told her that he was remaining at her side by sheer will alone. She was
tempted to tell him to leave, then decided not to. As
he had pointed out, she was not his mother, and if his
drugs wore off completely and he were yanked out of
the Dream—well, being left flat on his back for a day
or two would be a lesson he wouldn't forget in a hurry
and it would keep him out of trouble.

"That one!" Betta spat. "I'm sorry I ever laid eyes
on him. Backtalker, mouthy, lazy. And a destructive

streak. My dog disappeared a week after he arrived, and I'm sure he was responsible, though I can't prove it. Worthless, too—couldn't get into the Dream no matter how many drugs I gave him."

"Did you change his name when you bought him?" Ara asked. "I'll need to know so I can keep tracking him."

"I always change their names," Betta said irritably. "Easier to keep them docile. Good psychology. All my slaves take my last name."

"And his first name?" Ara prompted. The headache was growing and her stomach growled. She would have to leave within the next few moments. Kendi shifted uncomfortably on his chair.

"I named him after the very first slave I ever owned," Betta said. "Now *there* was a hard worker."

"The name?" Ara said, barely civil.

"Drew, of course," Betta said. "Jeren Drew."

SIXTEEN

We can't all be Silent, nor should we want to be.
—Daniel Vik

Kendi swallowed. It took all his concentration to hold on to the Dream. His drug dose had to be almost completely gone by now, but he didn't want to leave. He felt lightheaded and flimsy, as if he might vanish at any moment.

"Jeren is Cole?" he said incredulously. "He's Dorna's brother?"

"He must have lied about his age," Mother Ara said. "Jeren said he was barely twenty, but Cole Keller is twenty-four. My god."

They were in Mother Ara's pleasure garden again, and Kendi was glad of it. Betta Drew's sitting room was a nasty place, and Betta herself had made Kendi's skin crawl.

"All life—I just remembered," he said. "Jeren sometimes calls Dorna 'Sis.' We all thought he was joking with her by pretending to call her 'Sister Dorna' when she wasn't actually a Sister yet."

And that one woman said Jeren was hung like a donkey, he thought, *just like Jeren told me he was. I thought he was kidding.*

"It was a joke, all right," Mother Ara muttered, and for a moment Kendi thought she was replying to his unspoken words. "He's been playing with us from the beginning—pretending to learn meditation, then pretending that he had only just made it into the Dream. I—" Mother Ara paled and put a hand to her mouth.

"What's the matter, Mother?" Kendi asked.

"Oh my god," Mother Ara said in a voice so choked Kendi could barely understand her. "The night after I freed the lot of you, I peeked in on you while you were sleeping to see how you were doing. Jeren was sleeping so soundly that I actually checked his breathing. Later I found out this was when Iris Temm was . . . being killed. He was killing her right in front of me, and I didn't do a thing."

"You didn't know," Kendi pointed out.

"I should have known," Mother Ara said softly. "I'm a Mother, almost a Mother Adept. I should have spotted the fact that he wasn't asleep. I didn't even look through his possessions. He must have had a dermospray on him. I should have known."

"You wanted to give us privacy," Kendi told her, shaken by her agitation. "You had no reason to think it was . . . one of us."

Mother Ara didn't look convinced, but she said, "We have to move. Kendi, you leave the Dream and call Inspector Gray. I'm going to backtrack along Jeren's owners and see if—oh, hell. This means I'm going to have to leave and come back, and it'll be my third dose today. Well, there's nothing for it."

Kendi found his hands were shaking and he was getting dizzy. "Look, I'll get out and call the Guardians, then come back in and help you. We need to talk about this."

"You don't have to—" Mother Ara paused. "Well, all right. Another person might make this easier, and you already know what's going on. I'll meet you back here in half an hour." And she vanished. Kendi shut his eyes. Another wave of dizziness washed over him, making it hard to concentrate. His body drifted like a feather on the wind.

If it be in my best interest, he thought, *and in the best interest of all life everywhere, let me leave the Dream.*

He opened his eyes on Mother Ara's guest room, a small space with a simple bed and nightstand. It was dark outside. The meditation spear was firmly under his knee, and he carefully came down off it as another wave of dizziness hit him. Mother Ara had warned him that letting his drugs wear off and yanking him out of the Dream would leave him debilitated, possibly for days, but the dizziness was his only symptom. He must have just made it.

Ben poked his head into the room. "I thought I heard someone moving around in here. How did everything go?"

"I have to go back in again." Kendi reached for the dermospray that sat on the nightstand with shaking hands. "Listen Ben—you need to call Inspector Gray, and quick. He needs to find Jeren."

"Jeren?" Ben said, surprised. He leaned against the doorjamb. "Why?"

Kendi sat on the bed and quickly explained. Ben's expression went from puzzled to skeptical to amazed. Kendi abruptly wished that he could draw Ben down beside him, have Ben put an arm around his shoulders. Ben looked comforting and solid after the slippery, shifting Dream, and Kendi wanted something to hold on to. Ben was also sensible and reliable, someone who could be counted on to do the right thing instead of taking stupid risks like Kendi.

"I never did like Jeren," Ben muttered. He was still leaning against the jamb. "I guess I'll get the Guardians."

"Thanks, Ben. You're great" Kendi pressed the dermospray against his arm, thumbed the release, and reached for his spear.

Ben watched Kendi slip back into his trance and hated it. Once again he was waiting on the sidelines while someone else acted. Ben was always waiting,

waiting for his Silence, waiting for his mother, and now waiting for his—waiting for Kendi. Sure, once in a while he got to do something interesting like call the Guardians, but it was always minor. Even when Dorna had shown up at the party, Ben had hung back while Kendi acted. He hated it. Maybe it was time to make some kind of change, take a risk, *do* something.

Like call the Guardians, he prompted himself.

Ben tapped the section of wall that became a vid-screen. "Eliza, call Inspector Linus Gray from the Guardians."

"Apology," said the computer. "The connection cannot be made."

Ben raised red eyebrows. "What? Eliza, try again."

"Apology. The connection cannot be made."

"Eliza, why not?"

"Unknown."

Puzzled, Ben left the guest room and trotted into Mom's study. She had a separate phone account through the screen there. A square sheet of wood sat in place of one of the windows, the one Dorna—Violet, whoever—had broken two nights ago. Ben had cleared out the glass and boarded up the window himself. He tapped the wall and ordered it to call Inspector Gray.

"Apology," it said. "The connection cannot be made."

A bit of nervousness crept over Ben's skin like mouse claws. Something was obviously wrong. Maybe it was just a local glitch and he should run to the neighbors. Except a cold feeling told him the glitch wasn't a stuttering chip in the system. He was turning to leave the room when a glitter of metal on the floor near Mom's desk caught his eye. Ben crossed the room to scoop it up.

It was a silver charm bracelet. Ben stared at it in the light of the overhead fixture. He had never seen it before. Granted, he didn't make a habit of rooting through his mother's belongings, but he was sure he'd remember something like this. Mom didn't go for ostentation, and there was nothing unassuming about the bracelet. It clanked and jingled in his hand. The silver charms included a heart, a tiny rose, six little plaques that spelled out I-L-O-V-E-U, and a kitten, among others. A terrible feeling descended on Ben, magnifying his earlier nervousness. With shaky fingers he counted the charms.

Fifteen.

And Ben knew.

Dorna/Violet hadn't come to the house to warn Kendi and Ben about Cole. She had come to plant the bracelet, must have thrown it into the room when she broke the window. Kendi had said Diane Giday was the fourteenth victim. Mom was to be number fifteen.

Icy fear splashed down Ben's back, followed by a small surge of relief—Mom was light-years away at Dream Station. She was safe. Then he remembered that Cole or Jeren or whatever his name was killed people in the Dream.

Where Mom and Kendi were right now.

Ben rushed back to the guest room and slapped Kendi hard in the face. He had to bring Kendi out of the Dream, tell him so he could warn Mom. But Kendi didn't move. Ben slapped him again, then pinched him, then got a glass of cold water from the bathroom and splashed him with it. No reaction. Ben cursed. An experienced Silent would have noticed the sensations, even in the Dream, and come out to find out what was wrong. But Kendi was new to the Dream, and could reach it only by teaching himself to ignore his body completely.

Ben sprinted for the front door, intending to dash

over to the neighbors to use their phone. He stopped just short of the foyer. His heart lurched.

"Just leave it, Ben, okay?" Dorna said in the doorway. "Don't make it worse."

"What are you doing here?" Ben demanded. His voice shook. "Did you jam up the phone?"

Dorna nodded, and now that Ben was looking for it, he could see a resemblance to Jeren. They had the same cat-green eyes, the same sharp facial features.

"I visit here a lot," she said. "Mother Ara trusts me and didn't always guard her passwords. The right access, and the phones go down. Please, Ben—just forget it, okay?"

"Forget what?" Ben stalled.

"Forget trying to call the Guardians. That's what you're trying to do, isn't it? Cole's going to kill Mother Ara, and I'm sorry—in more ways than you know."

More fear clotted in Ben's throat and he fought to remain calm. "Where is he? Where's Cole?"

"His body is in his room, but his mind is in the Dream," Dorna said. "And that means he's everywhere."

"Why my mom?"

"Because he loves her," Dorna replied simply. "But he knows she doesn't love him back. The proof is that she hasn't worn the bracelet Jeren had me deliver."

"She doesn't even know who it came from," Ben blurted out. Why was he arguing with her? He had to warn Mom somehow, get help for her.

"There's the proof. If she loved him, she would know." Dorna spread her hands in supplication. "Please, Ben. Just leave it. If your mom's not already dead, she will be in a few minutes. I know it's going to be miserable for you, but we can't change that. If you call the Guardians and tell them about my brother, that would make *me* miserable. Why should we both suffer?"

The woman was diseased. Every instinct Ben had told him she was poison, that he had to get away from her. He tensed to lunge past her when she spoke again.

"Aren't you forgetting something?" she said. Ben froze. Her voice was different—lower, older, and cracked like an old coffee cup. Dorna's posture had changed, too. She stood more stiffly, as if her joints hurt. "If you leave the house, you're leaving your little sweetie all by himself. Who knows what might happen to him?"

"You won't hurt him," Ben said with more conviction than he felt. "He's your friend."

"Not *my* friend." With surprising speed she dodged past him and ran toward the guest room. Ben spun to follow, heart pounding, stomach tight. He charged into the guest room to find Dorna a few meters away from Kendi, who was still standing in deep meditation, spear propped under one knee. He looked peaceful, vulnerable.

"Dear, dear, dear," Dorna said in her old woman's voice. "What a little pisser. Cute, though, in a gawky, spring chicken sort of way. And you were right, Benny-boy. I wouldn't kill him. But Rudy might. Do you want to take that chance?"

Ben stood in the doorway, torn. Cole was probably attacking his mother this very moment, bringing the Dream to horrible life around her and tearing her to pieces. But if he left to get help, Kendi would be left alone with a lunatic bent on some kind of revenge. If he could find a way to remove Dorna from the picture, everything would be all right. But Dorna had proven twice that she was a better fighter than he was, despite the weights he lifted. He needed a weapon and glanced desperately around the room without seeing anything.

"That's right Ben," old-voice Dorna taunted. "What are you going to do? Hit me? Try to kill me? Actually make a decision? Poor Benny-boy can't make up his mind to save his life. Does he love Kendi or not? Should he save his mother or his boyfriend? Should he attack the old lady or run for help? Poor Benny-boy, always waiting, never acting. Poor, poor Benny-boy."

Ben lunged for her. Laughing, she danced out of the way. Ben threw a punch, but she blocked it and landed a fist in his stomach. Ben backed away, gasping. Dorna's hand went to her belt and came up with a large knife. The blade vibrated with a sound like a dog growling. Dorna swung it, and it sheered through a bedpost like paper.

"Who the hell do you think you are, boy?" she snarled in a deep, masculine voice. "You think you can get the best of me? I'll kick the shit out of you." She lunged and the knife roared. Ben leaped backward, almost knocking Kendi over. "Poetic, isn't it? Dorna's brother is killing your mother in the Dream and I'm killing you here in the solid world. Mother and son dying at the same time. Let's end it here."

She drew back the snarling knife. Ben reached back and snatched the spear from under Kendi's knee. Kendi collapsed to the floor. Ben yanked the rubber tip off the spear and flung it with all his strength at Dorna. It stuck with a meaty *thunk* and she screamed. The knife clattered to the floor.

Blessing every weight he had lifted, Ben grabbed up Kendi in a firefighter's carry and ran out of the room without looking back. He made it out the front door and into the darkness beyond. The walkways were deserted at this time of night. Kendi was a limp, heavy weight across his shoulders. Ben hesitated.

Dorna had said that Cole was at this moment in the Dream with Mom. By the time he got to a phone, called the Guardians, explained the situation, and got them to act, Mom—and possibly Kendi—would be long dead.

Ben hurried across the walkway to the next talltree over and found a staircase that led downward. Kendi bounced and flopped on his back like a warm rag doll, but Ben could feel him breathing. The steps clattered under his heavy feet, and the darkness amid the talltree leaves and branches was all enveloping. Ben could hardly see where he was going, but he didn't need to. This was his neighborhood, and he knew every stair, every plank, every leaf and branch. After a moment he came to an alcove where the staircase made a turn to follow the trunk of the talltree. Ben eased Kendi off his shoulders and set him carefully on the boards. Working quickly, he pushed Kendi's inert body against the talltree trunk where the shadows were the thickest.

His body is in his room, but his mind is in the Dream.

"You'll be safe here until you wake up," Ben whispered to him. "Please be safe."

Then he took off for the monastery at a dead run.

This time it was the Outback. Ara agreed it was easier for her and Kendi to meet and talk there since Kendi had to use his private desert as a transition from one Silent's turf to the next unless he wanted to suffer nausea and vomiting. Ara had promised to start working with him on more instantaneous movement, but that would have to come later.

"All right," Ara said. "Two of Jeren's previous owners confirmed strange murders and finger mutilations going on while they owned him. More nails in his legal coffin once the Guardians catch him. Are you sure Ben called them?"

"No, Mother," Kendi said testily. "But he said he would. It's just the same as the last four times you asked."

"Sorry." Ara sighed, sinking down onto a boulder. "I'm a mom, I worry."

The Outback sky was clear and perfectly blue. Rock and scrubby plant life stretched in all directions, bringing the smell of vegetation baking in hot, dry air. Ara was uncomfortably warm, but she had to admit that Kendi had created a unique and realistic turf. Overhead circled a falcon. She screamed once and Kendi smiled up at her.

"What is that like?" Ara asked. "I've been lax in my teacher duties by not talking to you about it, but so much has been happening."

"I'm not really aware of it until she touches me," Kendi said. "Then it's like our memories merge and there's two of me, but still only one." He paused. "Mother Ara, when can I start looking for my mom?"

Ara started. Kendi hadn't mentioned his family in a long time and she had supposed he had stopped wondering if he would be able to find them.

"Once you reach Brother," Ara said, "you'll be able to do fieldwork in the solid world, if that's what you want. You can start doing what I do—seek out Silent slaves and buy them for the Children—and see if you can track your family that way. But that won't be for some years yet."

Kendi looked unblinkingly up into the sun. "Why can't I look for her in the Dream? She's Silent, and I've touched her a lot. I should be able to find her."

"You can certainly look," Mother Ara said, trying to think how best to let him down. "But Kendi—not all Silent are able to reach the Dream. Ben, for one. Your mother may or may not be able to enter here. And even if she does, there are millions of Silent all throughout the galaxy. Sure, touching her in the solid world makes it easier to look for her, but you don't have any idea where or how to look."

"I'm good at tracking people," Kendi pointed out. His face was a mask of intensity, but his voice was hoarse. "And I'm good at sensing things in the Dream. Why can't I sense *her*?"

"For all those reasons I just mentioned, Kendi," Ara said gently. "It isn't your fault, you know."

"Yes, it is," Kendi said. "I should have begged Mistress Blanc to buy Dad and Martina and Utang. I should have tried to find some way to escape and find them. I should have found a way to stop them from getting on the colony ship in the first place. I could have done a lot of things."

Ara kept her voice low, though her heart ached in sympathy for him. "None of those things would have helped. I think you know that, but you feel guilty that you're free when your family isn't."

"I'm going to find her—and the rest of them," Kendi insisted. "If that means I have to make Brother and then Father younger than anyone else ever did, I will. We were all supposed to be on Pelagosa, building a new colony together. I didn't want to go, but now I'd give everything to be there."

"Kendi, you can't—"

The Dream rippled. Ara felt the splash move against her. Kendi jumped as if he'd stepped on a snake.

"What was that?" he asked.

"I'm not sure," Ara said. "What would—"

"Ara."

Fear stabbed through Ara's chest. She and Kendi spun around and saw him. He stood only a few steps away, dressed all in black. A wide-brimmed hat hid his face. Ara felt the blood slip from her face. Her breath came short and fast. Kendi's eyes were wide.

"Ara, my love," the man said. "Did you like the bracelet?"

It took every scrap of courage she had, but Ara did it. She stepped in front of her student. "Kendi, get out of here," she said. "He wants me, not you."

"I'm not going to leave you alone with him," Kendi insisted.

"The skinny Silent who saw me with my last girl-friend," the man said. "Kendi, is it? You heard her. Leave. You aren't involved."

Kendi stepped around Ara to stand beside her. Ara mentally screamed at him to stay put, to do as he was told for once. She almost tried to shove him back, but was afraid a sudden move might send the dark man over the edge.

"Kendi, I'm ordering you to leave," she said through gritted teeth. *Because I can't leave until I know you're safe.*

"You can't get us both, Jeren," Kendi said. "Give it up."

The black man backed up a step. "Who's Jeren?"

Shut up, Kendi! Ara thought. *Shut up, shut up, shut up!*

"We know, Jeren." Kendi took a step toward him. "We know about you, we know about Dorna. We know about it all. So why don't you just give yourself up? We don't want to—to—" Kendi fell silent. Ara suspected he was going to say *We don't want to hurt you,* but he couldn't lie in the Dream.

"You don't know anything," the dark man said hoarsely. "You can't prove it's—"

Movement flashed down from the sky. A brown blur whipped past the black man's head and ripped off the man's hat, revealing Jeren's face. The scar around his left eye—

Did his mother do that to him?

—shone white against his skin.

Jeren made a choking sound and clapped his hands over his face. For a moment, Ara thought he was going to drop to his knees and start crying. She allowed herself a small sigh of relief. Once unmasked, Jeren's power was gone. All Ara had to do now was get him to tell her where his body was so she could—

The world exploded. With a cracking *boom* the ground came to life. Giant stone fingers jabbed upward, trying to trap Ara in their grip. Kendi shouted and leaped sideways. Fear stabbed through Ara, but she didn't even think. A sledgehammer appeared in her hands, and she swept it in an arc around her. Stone shattered in a dozen directions and Ara scrambled free. She glanced at Kendi, dreading what she might see. He was crouching a little ways away.

"Get out, Kendi!" she yelled at him, but he seemed too dazed to understand her.

"You bitch!" Jeren screamed. "I watched you in the Dream and fell in love with you. Now I have to kill you."

Ara didn't bother responding. She raised her fist and a bolt of lightning flashed down from the clear blue sky. It smashed the ground only a few steps away from Jeren. The thunderclap made Ara's ears ring and knocked Jeren backward. He somersaulted to his feet in an inhumanly smooth motion.

"You missed," he snarled. "You wanna fight, huh? Fine by me."

A howling wind tore across the Outback and slammed into Ara and Kendi, bowling both of them over. The air whooshed out of Ara's lungs and she felt herself tumbling end over end. Then she slammed into something hard. Pain ran down her back and ribs. Dirt and sand stung her eyes, making it hard to see. For a moment she panicked. Then the hard-won control took over. This was the Dream, where she could dictate reality. Ara concentrated for a split second, and a stone wall rumbled up out of the ground before her. The wind cut off. Ara cleared the grit from her eyes. Kendi lay next to her, looking dazed.

"Kendi, get out," she hissed. "Kendi!"

But he didn't respond. Ara grimaced. She and Jeren both had been tearing at his turf, ripping it apart and reshaping it. This all tore at Kendi's very mind, and he didn't have the experience to cope with it. It was the same effect that Jeren's manipulation had had on his female victims. It didn't bother Ara because this wasn't her turf, but she couldn't leave Kendi behind to face Jeren alone.

The earth shuddered and boomed. With a thunderous *crack* the stone wall broke and crumbled into rubble. Jeren stood on the other side, less than two meters away. Ara's hand snapped out and a neuropistol appeared in her grip. She fired. The beam struck Jeren square in the chest.

He laughed. "You're a woman," he snickered. "You can't hurt me."

Ara swallowed. A battle in the Dream was a struggle between two minds fighting to control reality, and the stronger one would usually win. Jeren was obviously more powerful than Ara had thought—his mental image of an unhurt self was stronger than her image of the blast from a deadly weapon. But there were other ways to fight.

"A woman like your mother?" she said.

Jeren actually blanched. Ara gestured and the rubble vanished. Kendi slowly got to his feet. Trying to keep Jeren's attention on her, she locked eyes with him and stepped forward.

"Your mother hurt you a lot," she said, and wished desperately she had had time to read some specifics from the file on Riann Keller. Best to stick with the basics. "She beat you and made fun of you, didn't she? You and Dorna both. You hated her, but you also loved her, didn't you, Jeren? That's the way you feel toward all Silent women, isn't that right?"

Jeren retreated a step. Ara didn't even blink.

"You thought if you could make someone love you, everything would be all right. You wanted to give your mother's friend Polly Garvin presents, but you were afraid, so you made your sister do it for you. And when Polly spurned you, you killed her. The same went for Minn Araq, didn't it?

"Shut up," Jeren said.

"Dorna wanted a souvenir," Ara continued. "Something to prove she'd been brave enough to do her brother's bidding. So she took things—a finger, a bit of clothing, a piece of one of your presents. How does that make you feel, Jeren?"

"I said, shut up!"

"That was when you tried it on your own mother. She didn't love you either, even after the presents. So you killed her, too. But then came the cruelest blow of all. Your mother had sold you and Dorna into slavery, and the slaver was already on his way. How did it feel to watch your sister carted away in electric shackles, Jeren?"

She had been hoping to break him down, but instead Jeren responded with pure invisible force. Ara flew backward several meters and plowed into the ground. She felt something snap, and it was suddenly hard to breathe. She tried to roll to her feet, but a wave of pain stopped her. Before she could react further, thick green vines sprouted from the ground and whipped around her body like snakes. A little ways away, Kendi lay similarly entangled. Jeren strode toward her, green eyes blazing.

"You're going to die now," he said. "I'm going to crush you and listen while you scream."

"It won't help," gasped Kendi, and Jeren spun to look at him. "Ben knows who you are. He's already

called the Guardians. They're on their way to pick
you up right now."

Jeren stared. Ara tried to summon up the concentration to leave the Dream, Kendi or no Kendi, but
the pain that wracked her chest and back was too
great. The vines continued to twist and writhe, sliding
over her skin and making her cry out despite herself.

"Then," Jeren said, "I'll have to kill you both fast
so I can get the hell away."

He snapped his fingers and one of the vines tore
Ara's arm off. Ara screamed, and blood spurted from
her shoulder. Another scream, a different one, pierced
the air. A brown-and-blue thunderbolt smashed straight
into Jeren's back between his shoulder blades. He
dropped flat, and Kendi's falcon clawed for altitude
with yet another cry. Kendi, who was obviously recovering from his daze, let out a whoop of glee—

—until Jeren leaped back to his feet with inhuman
ease. In his hands he held a shotgun.

"No!" Ara cried.

The gun went off. The falcon tumbled to the ground
in a mass of bloody feathers.

Ben plowed through the lobby of the dormitory,
past the startled night clerk, and up the hallway
toward Jeren's room. It was two doors down from
Kendi's. His chest burned and his legs ached from the
exertion of running so far at top speed, but he ignored
the feeling. When he reached Jeren's door, he twisted
the knob and wasn't at all surprised to find it locked.
Ben shoved against the door, but it didn't budge. He
backed up and slammed into it as hard as he could.
Pain throbbed in Ben's shoulder. The door, made of
thick talltree wood, didn't budge. Heedless of further
pain, Ben smashed into it again. Nothing. Panic
sprouted and spread. Jeren was at this moment attacking his mother and Kendi. He had to get inside.

A door popped open farther up the hall, and Willa poked her head into the hallway. She looked sleepy. "What's going on?" she yawned.

Without stopping to explain, Ben shoved past her and into her room. She squeaked in protest as he bolted past her bed toward the door that led out onto her balcony. Adrenaline singing in his veins, he yanked it open and shot out onto the shared balcony. He ran down to Jeren's room. The lights were on, and through the clear panel of the door he could see Jeren lying on his bed. His hands were folded over his stomach and a slight smile twisted his lips. Ben tried the door, but it was also locked. With chilly fingers, he pulled his shirt over his head and wrapped it around one arm. Then he rammed into the door.

More pain pulsed at his shoulder. The door didn't break, or even budge. He tried twice more with no effect. Jeren continued to smile.

Jeren raised the shotgun and pointed it straight at Kendi. Kendi swallowed and strained against the vines, but they were tough as steel. Ara's face was gray, but she was somehow still conscious. Her torn arm lay a little ways away. Jeren's finger tightened on the trigger, and Kendi wondered if it would hurt.

"Cole!"

Jeren jerked his head sideways. Kendi followed his gaze. Dorna stood a few meters away. Her face was pale and waxen beneath dark curls. The vines tightened around Kendi's body and his ribs creaked.

"You can't do it, Cole," she said. "It isn't fair."

"Shut up," Jeren—Cole—snarled. "You do what I tell you."

"If you kill Ara now, I won't be able to get her finger. She isn't on Bellerophon, remember?" Dorna said. "I have an unbroken line all the way back to Mom and past her to Mrs. Garvin. You can't kill her."

Her voice dropped in pitch, became more intense. Kendi stared. "You can't kill her, Cole. I won't let you."

"I told you to shut the fuck up!" He swung the shotgun around and pointed it at her.

"If you try to kill her here, we won't help you anymore," Dorna said flatly. "And we'll stop you."

Cole laughed. "Who?"

The Dream rippled and a wave of nausea washed over Kendi. A moment later, a group of people stood behind Dorna. Kendi recognized the old woman Zelda and Buck in his blue coveralls. A short blond girl with downcast eyes and violets in her hair stood just behind the latter. A dozen others were there as well, both male and female. All of them were staring at Cole.

"We will," they said in one voice.

Ben looked frantically around the balcony. Willa stood in the doorway to her room, looking frightened. "Ben," she said. "What's going on?"

Ben's eyes fell on one of the rope swings dangling from the branch above. He snatched it up and jumped onto the balcony rail. Clinging to it like a monkey, he kicked backward and sailed out over dark and empty space. A moment later he swung forward, heels pointed straight toward Jeren's door. He hit the panel hard, but it still didn't break.

Cole laughed. "Look at you," he sneered. "Just can't keep it together, can you, Sis?" He pointed the shotgun back at Kendi. "He'll be first. Then I junk Ara."

With an animal howl that chilled Kendi straight through, the multitude lunged forward. Cole spun, surprised, but only for an instant. The shotgun in his hands changed shape. Cole pointed the machine gun at the advancing horde and fired. The gun made a hoarse coughing sound, and blood poured from a thousand wounds. People fell like mown grass, their bodies vanishing the moment they touched the ground. Zelda dropped and vanished, as did Buck and Violet. In the end, only Dorna was left standing. Her cheek bled scarlet from a near miss and she looked dazed. Cole raised the gun.

Ben hit the door again. The shock traveled all the way up his body and seemed to fuse his spine. A thin crack appeared. He kicked back, swung over empty space and, ignoring the pain in heels and knees, hit the door yet again and again and again.

"You won't," Dorna whispered.

"I will," Cole said, and fired. Dorna staggered backward, blood gushing from her chest and stomach. She made a low choking noise and dropped to her knees. Then she disappeared.

"You shit!" Kendi said, struggling against the vines. Ara didn't move, but she must still be conscious if she was in the Dream. Or had she already died and was Cole keeping her image here?

"You're dead, Kendi," Cole said with a too-wide grin. "Sorry. It was nice knowing you." He pointed the machine gun.

The door shattered. Falling shards made ribbons of Ben's trousers and sliced his legs, but he scarcely noticed. He landed on his back, slid partway across the floor, and fetched up against Jeren's bed. Heedless of the sharp polymer pieces all around him, Ben scrambled to his feet. Without thinking, he snatched up a paperweight from the desk and brought it down hard on Jeren Drew's head.

Cole stiffened. He made a small sound in the back of his throat. Then he vanished. Kendi's vines instantly

disappeared, as did the ones binding Mother Ara. She
lay ashen faced on the ground, her arm lying a step
away like a grotesque stick of firewood. Blood was
pouring from her shoulder again. Kendi knelt beside
her and patted her face.

"Mother Ara," he said. "Mother Ara. You have to
leave the Dream. Can you do it?"

She opened her eyes, but they didn't focus. Her
mouth moved, but no sound emerged. She was dying,
that was plain. The fact that she was still alive mystified Kendi. She had lost far more blood than any
human could survive. Of course, this was the Dream,
and if Mother Ara had decided she wasn't dead yet,
she wouldn't be. But Cole's attack had hurt her, badly.
Instinct told Kendi that she needed something to hold
on to, something that would help her heal the damage.
Kendi looked at the severed arm for only a split second before catching it up. It was heavier than he had
expected, and bits of flesh hung from the tattered end.
Kendi held the arm to its rightful place at Mother
Ara's shoulder.

"You can't do it," Mother Ara croaked.

"I can," Kendi said to her. "My people are re-
nowned for their healing."

Mother Ara made a choking sound that Kendi realized was a sort of laugh. "Tell Ben I love him."

Kendi looked down at her, uncertain what to do. If
Mother Ara didn't believe he could heal her, he
wouldn't be able to do it. He wasn't skilled enough in
the Dream yet to force his will upon her. He had to
prove that he could heal her so that she would believe
it and heal herself.

Except the only way to do that would be to heal her,
Kendi thought. Tears sprang to his eyes. He had to
find a way to make her believe. He had to—

A tiny *meeping* sound made him turn. The sound
came from the falcon. He had forgotten about her.

Kendi dashed over and picked her up. Her pain washed over him, merged with him. It staggered him for a moment, but then his health merged with her wounds and overcame them. She was *wounded,* but he wanted her to be *healthy.* She would be healthy *now.* Kendi spun and held her out so Mother Ara could see.

"All life!" he cried, and flung the falcon skyward. She faltered a moment, then flapped strong, wide wings and ascended to the sky.

Mother Ara closed her eyes. Her body flickered like a hologram with a virus. Kendi dropped beside her again and held the arm in place. Tears ran down his face, but he forced his voice to remain steady.

"I call upon the blood of my ancestors," he said. "Heal this woman who is my teacher and restore her to health!" Mother Ara was *wounded,* but he wanted her to be *healed.* She would be healed *now.*

Nothing happened. Mother Ara's body flickered again, stabilized, faltered. A tear fell from Kendi's eye and dropped through her to land on the sandy Outback soil. Then she vanished.

A low sound escaped Kendi's throat, but before he could react further, the earth rippled and Mother Ara reappeared with a splash of Dream energy. Her face was pale, but her arm was firmly back in place. She sat up and looked down at herself as if surprised. Kendi stared.

"It worked," he said. "All life, it worked." With a wild whoop he flung his arms around her. Mother Ara winced.

"Careful," she said. "The arm, the arm."

Kendi released her. "Sorry. You're all right then?"

"A little sore, but otherwise fine." Mother Ara flexed her arm in wonder. "Thank you, Kendi."

"You're welcome, Mother," he said.

No further words were needed. Both gathered their concentration and vanished from the Dream.

Kendi opened his eyes onto darkness. Night insects chirped and a cool breeze washed over him. He wasn't standing up—he was lying crumpled in a heap on a hard surface. Cautiously, he sat up. What the hell? Where was his spear? How had he—?

Frantic footsteps barreled around the corner. Startled, Kendi leaped to his feet, then staggered dizzily under a sudden headache. Too many Dream drugs in one day. A strong, solid arm went around his shoulders and steadied him.

"Are you okay?" Ben asked. "Is Mom okay?"

"She's all right," Kendi said muzzily. "Where the hell am I?"

"Let's get home," Ben said. His arm still lay warm across Kendi's shoulder, and Kendi found it comforting. "I'll explain, and then you can tell your side. Are you sure you're all right?" His voice thickened. "I was . . . I was worried."

Kendi looked at him. His eyes had adjusted well enough to see Ben's face, but he couldn't read his expression. "I'm fine, Ben. I'm fine with everything. I really, really am."

And then Ben was kissing him.

EPILOGUE

Sometimes you need to talk about what happened with someone who's been there, too.

—Irfan Qasad

Kendi and Ben waited at the edge of the landing field as Mother Ara and Inspector Tan disembarked from the ship. Ben's hand lay tentatively in Kendi's, as if he might snatch it away at any moment. Kendi didn't push the matter, letting Ben set the pace, though he did give Ben's hand a reassuring squeeze. Ben flashed a brief smile at him, and Kendi was sure his heart would dissolve into a helpless mess and puddle up somewhere around his feet.

The landing field of the spaceport was surrounded by an almost invisible fence of wire polymer to keep the dinosaurs out. Talltrees loomed beyond it, high as skyscrapers. It felt strange to look at them from this low vantage point. Humans, Ched-Balaar, and other aliens moved about the airfield and the port buildings, creating a strange mixture of voices, clattering teeth, and other noises. Mother Ara's left arm was in a sling, and Kendi caught the metallic gleam of a heal splint beneath the cloth. It surprised him how glad he was to see her again. The final confrontation with Cole/Jeren had only taken place three days ago, but it felt like a month had passed. Ara looked a little pale, but her step was firm. Inspector Tan came beside her, crisp and pressed as always. As they drew closer, Ben's hand quivered slightly in Kendi's, but he didn't let go. It occurred to Kendi that in some ways facing a mur-

derer in the Dream was easier. At least you knew
what the killer was going to do.

Mother Ara caught sight of them and her step
quickened with a smile. When she was only a few
steps away, she noticed that her student was holding
hands with her son. She halted, looking confused.
Kendi's heart skipped, and Ben's fair complexion went
a shade paler. Then she burst out laughing and, stepping between them, put an arm around Ben's
shoulder.

"That explains a few things," she said, and kissed
him on the cheek. Tan watched impassively.

"Mom," Ben protested. "We're in public."

"You can hold his hand, but you can't kiss your
mother," Mother Ara observed with a shake of her
head. "What did I do to deserve a teenage boy?"
Then she sighed. "I want to get home. We'll have
a home-cooked meal from Maureen's and exchange
stories. Inspector Tan is paying."

"Oh?" Tan raised an eyebrow.

"The Guardians owe me that much," Mother Ara
said firmly.

"She's been saying that all the way here," Tan
groused to Kendi. " 'Get me something to drink, the
Guardians owe me that much.' 'I get the bigger sleeping room, the Guardians owe me that much.' "

"And don't forget my exorbitant consulting fee,"
Mother Ara added as they walked into the spaceport
building and headed for customs. "I'm thinking it's
time for some serious house redecoration."

Some time later, they were all sitting around the
dining room table. Tan had begged off after paying
for the food, claiming she wanted to get a head start
on writing reports. Mother Ara, meanwhile, refused
to let anyone talk about Jeren/Cole or Dorna during
the meal, citing a desire to eat, not throw up. Eventu-

ally, the table held nothing but dirty plates and empty take-out packets.

"Excellent." Mother Ara sighed, brushing a stray crumb from her sling. "Just like Mom used to buy."

Kendi looked at her, chin in his hand. "You're certainly in a good mood."

"It's something to do between nightmares," Mother Ara said frankly.

"Kendi told me what Jeren did to your arm and all the . . . all the rest of it," Ben said. "Scary, huh?"

Mother Ara nodded. "I haven't gone into the Dream since then. Not even once. It'll take me a while, I think, but I'll manage eventually."

"Ben's a hero, did you know that?" Kendi said, clapping him on the shoulder. "I didn't even know until I got out of the Dream. He was pretty amazing."

Ben blushed and stared down at the table.

"Oh? What happened?" Mother Ara demanded.

Kendi explained, exaggerating only a little. Ben's flush deepened until his face matched his hair. Mother Ara looked at him.

"So you saved my life, did you?" She leaned over and kissed him on the cheek. Impulsively, Kendi did the same thing. Ben jumped, then looked as though he wanted nothing more than to slide under the table and disappear.

"No fair," he muttered. "Caught between my mom and my . . . my . . ."

"Boyfriend," Kendi said. "The word you're looking for is *boyfriend*." He shot Mother Ara a look. "So you're okay with this? With Ben and me, I mean?"

"I'm glad Ben's found someone," she said, "and I'm not going to ask the various questions that spring to mind, since I don't think I want to hear the answers. But I'm warning you, Kendi—you hurt my son and I'll remove your lungs with a pair of chopsticks."

"Mom." Ben protested, and Kendi laughed.

"Deal," he said.

"All right, then." Mother Ara pushed herself back from the table and fixed Kendi with a look he couldn't read. "Kendi, I wanted to ask how you've been lately."

"How do you mean?" he asked.

"Have you been sleeping all right?"

Ben opened his mouth to answer, but Kendi kicked him under the table and he clamped his mouth shut, though concern flashed in his blue eyes.

"I've been having a few nightmares of my own," Kendi admitted. "It's been . . . rough. I know what you're going to say," he hastened to add before she could speak. "You want me to talk to someone."

"Kendi, you can't expect to—"

"I was going to say I think you're right," Kendi interrupted. "It's too much shit to deal with on my own. Too much. And I don't . . . I don't . . ." He trailed off. Ben's hand stole into his, and Kendi squeezed it.

"You don't what?" Mother Ara asked quietly.

"I don't want to end up like Jeren," he whispered.

"I don't think you would, Kendi," Mother Ara said. "No matter what happened to you. But for now—I know just the person for you to talk to. His name is Brother Kwan, and I think you'll like him. How about I give him a call first thing in the morning?"

As Kendi nodded, a knock came at the door. Mother Ara rose and admitted Inspector Tan. She carried a computer pad. After greetings and an offer of dessert—refused—Tan sat at the table with them and opened up a holographic screen display.

"Thought you might want a report on Jeren or Cole or whatever the hell his name is," she rasped. "He's still in the hospital. You clocked him a good one, Ben. He's lucky to be alive."

"I didn't want to kill him," Ben said. He paused. "Well, maybe a little."

"He was a monster," Tan said. "Whether he was made that way or born into it, I don't know and don't care. In any case, he'll be spending the rest of his life in the high-security psych unit at the med center. To tell you the truth, though, I don't think he's much danger to anyone."

"How so?" Mother Ara asked.

"He's not Silent," Tan replied. "At least, not anymore."

All three of them stared at her. Finally Kendi said, "What?"

"Absolutely true," Tan said. "He's awake and aware of his surroundings. He's articulate and intelligent. His head wound has healed nicely, thank you. But he claims he can't feel the Dream at all. Not even catch a whisper."

"Like he's never lied before," Kendi said.

"When I touched him, no jolt," Tan said. "Not even a tingle. We had a whole bunch of Silent come in to touch him—human, Ched-Balaar, other aliens. No one felt a thing. We don't know if he's lost his Silence because Ben scrambled his brains or if it's because he's doing it to himself—won't let himself enter the Dream because of what happened there. Genetically, he's Silent, but in practice, he isn't."

"How's he taking it?" Mother Ara asked.

Tan gave a wolfish grin. "Not well. He screams a lot. They had to put him in a soundproof room so he won't disturb the other patients."

Kendi shifted uncomfortably. He didn't know how to react to this news. Jeren had killed a lot of people, had tried to kill Mother Ara—not to mention Kendi himself. But after walking the Dream, Kendi couldn't think of a worse punishment than no longer being able to visit it again, and he had only found the Dream a few weeks ago. Jeren had been actively Silent for years and years. Kendi shuddered. If Jeren hadn't died, this was certainly the next closest thing. He decided to change the subject.

"There were tons of people at Dorna's funeral," he said. "Word got around pretty quick who she was and what she'd been doing. It was gross. A lot of them just wanted to get a look at her. We didn't stay long."

"I don't know how to feel about her," Ben said. "I mean, the stuff she must have gone through to become what she was—I can't imagine it. But she helped Jeren kill all those women. Anytime she wanted, she could have told someone and saved a whole bunch of lives."

"Jeren had her on a pretty short leash," Tan said. "A Guardian team did find her hiding place in the forest. She had a miniature cryo-chamber, one just big enough to preserve a human finger. It had Vera Cheel's pinky in it."

"She saved us at the end," Kendi said. "She came in and stopped Jeren from killing us long enough for Ben to get to him."

"But the only reason she did it was because I was out of her reach," Mother Ara reminded him. "If I had been on Bellerophon, she would never have done a thing."

"She did warn us at the party," Kendi said. "Or Violet did, though I suppose it's all pretty much the same thing."

"Oh yes," Mother Ara said, putting her good elbow on the table and leaning forward with a glint in her eye. "I almost forgot. Do tell me about this party."

And Kendi reached for Ben's hand again.

See what's coming in November...

THE DEVIL AND DEEP SPACE
by Susan R. Matthews

Set in the critically-acclaimed "Judiciary" universe, *The Devil and Deep Space* features reader favorite hero Andrej Koscuisko caught up in a conspiracy between political backstabbing and military corruption.

45901-6

THE FATHOMLESS CAVES
BOOK SIX OF THE WITCHES OF EILEANAN
by Kate Forsynth

In Eileanan, the sea-dwelling Fairgain have refused to sign the Pact of Peace. Driven by ancient hatreds, they have devoted themselves to destroying all who dwell upon the land. To help bring peace, Iseult's flame-haired twin Isabeau must face her most difficult challenge yet.

45902-4

To order call: 1-800-788-6262

DREAMER

A Novel of the Silent Empire

Steven R. Harper

0-451-45843-5

THE DREAM...
...is a plateau of mental existence where people are able to communicate by the power of their thoughts alone.

THE SILENT...
These people—known as the Silent—find that the Dream is threatened by a powerful Silent capable of seizing control of other people's bodies against their will...and may be causing tremors within the Dream itself.

THE RISK...
And if the "normals" learn of this, they will do anything to capture the Silent for use as a weapon—and the Dream itself may be shattered forever...

S572